## Also by Phaedra Patrick

*The Curious Charms of Arthur Pepper*

*Rise and Shine, Benedict Stone*

*The Library of Lost and Found*

*The Secrets of Love Story Bridge*

*The Messy Lives of Book People*

*The Little Italian Hotel*

# The Year of
# What If

## Phaedra Patrick

PARK ROW
BOOKS

PARK
ROW
BOOKS™

Recycling programs
for this product may
not exist in your area.

ISBN-13: 978-0-7783-1089-1

The Year of What If

Park Row Books
22 Adelaide St. West, 41st Floor
Toronto, Ontario M5H 4E3, Canada
ParkRowBooks.com

Printed in U.S.A.

For all my family and friends

# Carla Carter's Diary

*Twenty-one years ago*

Dear Diary,

Happy birthday to me! So, this is it. I'm twenty-one today and I'm feeling excited and sort of mature and, to be honest, also a bit scared. My birthday's fallen on Friday the thirteenth this year, something Gran has surely noticed. She's going to be on edge all day, expecting the house to be struck by lightning or for my candles to set fire to her curtains. I seriously doubt she'll be expecting the big news I'm going to share with her after my birthday tea, the decision I've been deliberating over for months.

My birthday presents felt extra lucky this morning. Gran gave me a tiny glass eye on a silver necklace, telling me, "If someone or something is jealous or wants to harm you, the eye will reflect or distract them." It sounds useful, if highly unlikely. The pendant belonged to my mum, and I saw tears in Gran's eyes when she fastened it around my neck. It's really tough for her with Mum and Granddad gone, and hard for my little sis, too, which makes what I'm about to tell them both even more difficult.

Jess has been teasing me about getting old. I suppose an eight-year gap between sisters seems pretty wide when you're only thirteen. She bought me the cutest little brass paperweight in the shape of a four-leaf clover, and I already know my aunts Mimi and Evelyn will insist on reading my tea leaves.

Gran and Jess are putting the finishing touches on my cake in the kitchen. It's my favorite, sponge filled with jam and buttercream, and the house smells of vanilla and strawberry. I don't believe in premonitions but I already know what Gran will say when I go back downstairs. "If you blow out all twenty-one candles at once, you'll be married within the year. Miss any and the number left is the number of years until your wedding day."

I'll try not to roll my eyes. The older Gran gets, the more she believes in this kind of stuff. Mimi and Evelyn are the same, forever reminding me and Jess about an old curse that claims women in our family are destined to be unlucky in love. When I blow out my candles, I'll try to emit the tiniest puff of air, to leave them all alight. That way I won't walk down the aisle until I'm forty-two!

Why would I even think about marriage at my age anyway? Life is short, and losing Mum is proof of that. She was the only one in my family who didn't care if she opened an umbrella indoors. "Act now, think later," she used to tell me.

I can't believe she's been gone for eleven years, and the longer she isn't here, the more I miss her. The more I want to be like her.

So, I've made up my mind to do just that.

Dear Diary, I've decided to drop out of university to go traveling for a year.

There, I've put it in writing now, so have got to do it.

Yes, I've completed two years of my business studies degree. Yes, I'm scoring A's and have made some great friends. Yes, I know I'm usually Miss Cautious and that Jess really misses me when I'm away at university, but she isn't a kid any longer and there will never be a perfect time for me to go traveling. I just feel like there's something or someone out there, beckoning me. Call it intuition or a sixth sense, but I have to explore what it is and throw caution to the wind for once. I think it's what Mum would have wanted.

And who knows? Maybe there is a special person waiting for me so I can prove our family curse wrong, once and for all.

Wish me luck!

# One

Fortune

THERE WAS ALWAYS A FOOT-HIGH PILE OF STATISTICS reports on Carla Carter's desk and dozens of thank-you cards and wedding invitations pinned to her office walls. All the bouquets sent to her by happy clients made her office look and smell like a flower shop, and she loved to nurture the blooms, trimming the stems and changing their water each day. It was a great feeling when she opened cards from couples that said, "We're such a great match, thanks to you."

The old saying goes that you can't choose your family, but Carla thought that actually you could. If you were looking to meet someone special, hoping a relationship might lead to marriage, weren't you technically auditioning that person to be part of your family or perhaps wanting to start a new one? Therefore, wasn't it foolish to select a partner based on their blue eyes making your heart skip a beat, or because you both loved watching old movies on rainy Sunday afternoons? Surely, there had to be more substance and certainty to such matters.

People made plans and decisions each day of their lives— where to go on holiday, what college course to take, even whether to have ketchup or mustard on a hot dog. However, love was something often left to chance. Was it really likely you'd meet your ideal match while reaching for a can of soup in the supermarket or when ordering a glass of Merlot in a busy bar?

Someone who made you sing like a Disney princess while hanging out your washing was all very well, but you could spend weeks, months and even years getting to know someone, only to discover they were still hung up on an ex, believed in UFOs or were related to a serial killer.

When Carla had married her first husband, Aaron, love (or was it lust?) had skewed her sensibilities, making her jump into marriage feetfirst. And then look what had happened. Her subsequent, devastating divorce appeared to validate her family curse even more. From then on, Carla had made it her mission in life to help prevent others from going through a similar energy-sapping, emotion-wrenching, soul-sucking, crushing experience.

And that was why she'd set up her matchmaking agency, Logical Love.

Her business ethos was framed and displayed on her office wall.

*Logical Love*
*Meet your match, scientifically*

*We're a different kind of matchmaking agency, helping you to find your perfect partner in a logical way. We don't believe in swiping a screen to dismiss someone within seconds. Instead, we employ a much more in-depth approach. You're likely to be pragmatic, maybe even a little jaded, and your head probably rules your heart.*

*Don't worry, we're exactly the same!*

*Through our comprehensive range of questions and unique al-gorithms, we help to take away the uncertainty of finding your soulmate, making it more practical to meet your right match. Love can become a decision rather than a chemical reaction.*

*Join us—you're in safe hands.*

Carla was living proof that her business model worked. She and her fiancé, Tom, had met through the agency, scoring an overall suitability factor of eighty-four percent. It was one of the highest figures ever recorded at Logical Love and she was delighted (and somewhat relieved) that her search for Mr. Right was over. In one month's time, she'd become Mrs. Carla Taylor, finally putting an end to her family's jinx/spell/hex (or whatever it was her gran, sister and aunties believed in) forever.

She smiled as she sat down in her office chair, perusing a list of that week's love matches, when her sister barged into her office.

"You've got mail," Jess sang, tossing two pink envelopes in front of her.

Carla liked her desk to be neat at all times, and she never opened her post until after she'd dealt with her emails. "You should learn to knock," she said, promptly moving the two envelopes to her in tray.

Jess shrugged. "It's not like you're in a meeting or anything."

"We're at work. We should try to keep things professional."

Jess performed an eye roll. "Come on, we're sisters. Lighten up."

Since she'd founded the agency ten years ago, Logical Love had flourished and Carla now employed a team of sixteen people, including Jess as her customer data manager, and her gran, Lucinda, in a part-time accounts position. She treated them exactly the same as her other employees, and their hard work and support meant she couldn't be accused of nepotism.

Jess nudged the in tray with her backside as she sat down on the corner of Carla's desk. She picked up the two envelopes again and waved them in the air. "They look like invitations, if you ask me."

Carla pursed her lips, really wanting to check her clients' matches. They made her feel like a mother hen proudly surveying her chicks, but to satisfy her sister's curiosity she opened one of the envelopes.

A thank-you card said *Love is the greatest science in the universe* and had chemical symbols on the front. A photo inside showed a man and woman in their late thirties, both wearing space helmets at Cape Canaveral. They'd met through the agency and had attended a rocket launch while on their honeymoon.

"Aw, cute," Jess said, peering over her shoulder. "Another success story, though I'd prefer a nice beach break."

Carla nodded in agreement and pinned the card to her corkboard. She and Tom had agreed to defer their own honeymoon until they both had more space in their busy schedules. Today was the first of May and she'd already attended eight of her clients' weddings or engagement parties this year, so far. She always took the same gift to each, a red heart-shaped casserole dish with a lid to encourage couples to cook and eat together.

"Open your other card." Jess bounced on her heels.

Carla reached up to touch her eye-pendant necklace, something she did when she felt anxious. She eased out a card and admired the horseshoe graphic and the word *Lucky* in shiny pink lettering.

"It's from me and Gran," Jess blurted.

Carla frowned at her sister, wondering why she'd present her with a card when they worked in the same office together. Their apartments were only a couple of miles apart and they both dined with their gran a couple of evenings a week.

She flipped open the card and read the message.

*Invitation*
*Dear Carla*
*Friday, May 1st, 5:30–11:00 p.m.*
*Be ready!*

Carla glanced at the date on her watch. "That's today…" she said, her stomach beginning a churn of worry. "Be ready for what, exactly?"

"For a family get-together before your wedding." The excitement in Jess's voice shone through. "Your bachelorette party, one of your last nights of freedom…"

Carla swallowed uncomfortably. As soon as she and Tom had become engaged, her relatives started to swamp her with well-meaning advice, such as popping a coin in her shoe when she walked down the aisle, for good luck and prosperity, and not to wear pearls on her wedding day because they represented tears.

She'd suspected they'd plan *something* to celebrate her marriage and had caught them whispering together a few times. When her gran pursed her lips and whistled in a mock-innocent fashion, it had made Carla wince.

Sharing superstitions was like a currency among her relatives, and the narrative often changed as the stories were passed along the family grapevine. She and Tom had planned their small, sophisticated wedding in fine detail, and their invitations even featured a list of FAQs, so her relatives would be clear about what would happen on the day and when. Her aunt Mimi once showed up to a cousin's wedding dressed as Catwoman because she'd heard the reception was fancy dress, and Carla didn't want to risk a repeat performance.

"Please tell me what you've planned," she pleaded with Jess. "You know I don't like surprises." To be truthful, they made her feel a little motion sick and she definitely didn't share her sister's fear of missing out on anything.

"It's a secret," Jess said. "We're taking you somewhere exciting and, um, insightful. Don't you want to have some fun before you get married?"

Carla tried not to worry about the words *we're taking you*. It was easy to picture Jess, Gran, Mimi and Evelyn joining hands together around a huge cauldron, plotting her fate. Was there anything more annoying than people with a secret who told you they had one then refused to share it? Especially if they were your own family.

"How about going to an escape room or a murder-mystery evening?" she said, offering up something she'd actually enjoy. "I love things that involve skill and teamwork. Doing something this evening isn't ideal for me..."

Jess pulled a face at her. "Are you sure you're really my sister?" she asked. "The one who dropped out of uni to go traveling when she was twenty-one? What happened to your sense of adventure?"

Although Carla knew she was joking, Jess's words still stung. Certainty in her life was like a safety blanket she didn't like to cast off. "Adventure doesn't pay the bills," she murmured. *And it led me into a failed marriage*, she thought to herself.

The two sisters glanced at each other warily, as if sensing a widening chasm between them. Carla often thought if she applied the Logical Love algorithms to her own family members, her match statistics wouldn't be very high, especially with Jess. "I have some fresh data to analyze," she said, picking up her report again.

"We'll see you outside at five thirty." Jess coolly turned on her heel.

Carla wasn't sure what her sister muttered when she slammed the office door shut, but it sounded like, "You're too bloody particular." The cards on the corkboard fluttered and then stilled in the momentary draft.

"*Particular* can mean anything from *distinct* to *specific* to *extra-special*," Carla called after her. "All three are positive."

She perused the report and tried not to worry about her family's plans for that evening, telling herself they only wanted the best for her. They were excited about her and Tom's wedding, and this was their way of showing it.

Now all she had to do was turn up and get it over with. She tried not to overthink the words *exciting* and *insightful*.

# Two

## Magpies

AFTER CARLA FINISHED WORK, SHE HEADED DOWN-
stairs to meet Gran and Jess at the front of the building. She
was one of those people who'd prefer to be twenty minutes
early rather than five minutes late. There was a sickly taste of
pear drops on her tongue, even though she hadn't eaten any,
and her nerves about the evening weren't helped by her gran
parking haphazardly on the pavement. Carla didn't even know
if they were going out for food or not, so she'd nibbled half a
sandwich just in case.

Lucinda wound down her car window. "I know, I know,
honey," she called out. "I swerved to avoid a black cat on the road.
I didn't want it to cross our path. We want only good luck today."

On the rare occasions she drove, Lucinda added a paisley
silk headscarf and huge sunglasses to her usual outfit of flared
jeans and embroidered moccasins. Her seat belt squished her
ample curves, making her body look like it had been freshly
upholstered.

Carla ducked her head to speak through the car window. "Where are we going? Can you give me a clue? Am I dressed appropriately?" She wore a crisp white shirt and tailored black trousers to work each day and ran a hand over her curly copper hair that she'd scraped into a bun. Her aquiline nose made her look more suited to wearing an Elizabethan neck ruff than jeans, and she liked to think her polished appearance showed clients she took their matchmaking seriously.

She tried to embrace her distinctive looks and imperfections and encouraged her clients to do the same for themselves, therefore the Logical Love entry process didn't feature any questions about appearance. Moles, birthmarks, too much hair (or too little of it) and crooked teeth gave a person character, and if anyone wanted to date only gods and goddesses, Carla told them to try a different agency.

"You look supersmart, always do." Lucinda blew her a kiss. "Jess has planned your evening and I don't want to spoil her surprise."

Carla jangled the keys in her hand, waiting to lock the agency's front door. Above it was a large pink plastic Logical Love sign, designed by her sister. The two *o*'s in the logo were red and shaped like hearts. "She told me to be here at five thirty," she muttered, pacing up and down on the pavement.

After a few more minutes, Jess finally appeared. She wore an ethereal orange maxi dress that complemented her long, russet hair. Her several thousand followers on Instagram often mentioned her Pre-Raphaelite looks when they "liked" her photos of tarot readings, crystals and runes.

"Sorreee," Jess said. "Got tied up." She took something black and silky out her pocket and dangled it from her finger.

Carla recoiled. "Is that lingerie? Where the hell are you taking me?"

Jess laughed. "It's a blindfold."

"What on earth for?"

"It's a thing on TikTok. Blindfolding people, taking them to places and filming their reactions. It's hilarious."

"It sounds sinister," Carla said, her temples throbbing. She was forty-two, too old for this stuff. "I need to lock up first," she said, touching her pendant for comfort.

"Chill, it's going to be fun."

"You're blindfolding me and bundling me into a car. I'd call it kidnapping."

The fabric strip covering Carla's eyes was tight, letting in only a slit of light at the top. She gripped the back seat of the car as her gran swerved around a corner, jolting her from side to side. She wasn't sure how long they traveled for, maybe twenty or thirty minutes, and her gran's sweet honeysuckle perfume made her feel queasy in the confines of the car. As they drove over a bump in the road, she dug her fingers into the leather upholstery. "I'm supposed to be meeting Tom this evening. He'll wonder where I am…"

"Don't worry, I called him. He's staying home to play with his origami or something," Jess said.

"It's kirigami," Carla corrected. Tom worked in product development for a packaging company, though his big ambition was to design and produce his own board games. "Origami just involves folding paper. Kirigami is the art of folding *and* cutting. He's working on some pop-up paper games for our guests to play at our wedding reception. They're intricate and very clever."

"Oh," Jess replied flatly. "Nice."

Carla noticed her dry tone. Could Jess possibly be jealous of Tom? Her sister had recently endured a string of dating disasters. Romanticizing the idea of meeting someone through chance or fate alone wasn't paying off.

"Maybe you can share photos of Tom's games on Instagram, alongside the ones of you burning sage and playing with runes,"

Carla said. It was supposed to make her sister laugh, but the only sound that followed was the hum of tires on the road.

As the journey progressed, Carla tried to tune into other noises as a clue to her surroundings. She heard distant screams and a seagull cawing overhead. Something smelled like caramel and freshly made doughnuts, and her stomach lurched when she realized her family had brought her to the seaside town of Silverpool.

It was where she and Jess used to holiday as kids, with Gran and their grandad, Ted. Their trip had always included a visit to Vadim, an automated genie on the seafront who "told" your fortune for fifty pence. Vadim's crystal ball lit up with a mystical green light as he jerkily waved a hand and spoke in a strong Eastern European accent: "This is Vadim speaking. I can read your future…" A ticket appeared from a slot and Lucinda used to read all their fortunes aloud with glee. Throughout her childhood, Carla really did believe the bearded mannequin could tell her fortune, something she found unnerving rather than exciting. How *could* he know such stuff about her?

When the car came to a halt, she heard the hand brake wrench on. The driver's door slammed, and the side door opened, causing a rush of air to wind around Carla's ankles. A hand circled her elbow and helped to guide her onto the pavement. "Watch your step," her gran said.

As the three of them moved forward with Carla in the middle, she felt like she was being frog-marched toward a guillotine.

After a while, the hard surface beneath her feet changed to something more uneven, like planks of wood. The swish of waves came into earshot and grew louder.

They carried on walking until Jess shouted out, "*Stop. We're here.*"

Carla's hands shook as she reached up to remove her blindfold. She screwed her eyes shut against the evening light and slowly peeped through her lashes. Vaguely aware Jess was still filming her, she felt her mouth dry as she surveyed the seaside pier and the gray North Sea shifting and growling in front of her. There was a Ferris wheel, bumper cars and, directly in front of her, a ramshackle purple wooden hut painted with silver moons and golden stars. The peeling sign read:

Mystic Myrtle
Clairvoyant. Tarot. Crystal Ball.

"Oh *no*," Carla said, her stomach plunging to the depth of her body.

"It's good to find out what the future holds, before you get married," her gran said sagely.

"This place looks cool." Jess lowered her phone.

Carla dug a hand into her hair. "How many times have I told you both that Tom is my perfect partner? Why do I have to visit a stranger, who will make up a story about my future, to prove it to you?"

"Myrtle's not a stranger," Lucinda said. "She's your second-cousin, twice removed."

Carla sighed. It was easy to lose track of her long list of relatives. The majority of them were female and highly superstitious, and she wondered how they were breeding without many men in the picture. There must have been some point in their family history where their beliefs had become habit and then culture, until they'd been assumed as facts and part of everyday life.

Her gran and granddad had been happily married for fifty years before Ted died, *proving* the family curse was a fairy story. "Our family jinx is a figment of everyone's imagination," she protested. "It's your belief in it that keeps it alive."

Jess yanked Carla close and hissed in her ear, "Gran's not getting any younger and she *really* wants to make sure Tom's the right man for you. Especially after your marriage to Aaron. Do this for her, and try to bloody enjoy yourself for once…"

Carla had noticed her gran's shrinking stature and how her hands trembled when she baked or worked on the agency's accounts. Lucinda insisted it was just old age and refused to answer Carla's gentle questioning about her health.

She nodded and touched her pendant again, looking around for some kind of escape. A magpie strutted along the pier, bringing to mind one of her mum's sayings. *"One for sorrow…"* Carla said aloud, looking around for a second bird. *"Two for joy,"* she said with relief, when she spotted its companion. Then she shook her head. She'd tried to abandon these silly superstitions a long time ago and hated it when they crept back. Mimi had once put her off gummy bears for life by telling her eating something with a face meant its counterpart died somewhere else in the world.

"Myrtle has a real gift," Lucinda said firmly. "We're lucky she's going to share it with us."

Carla was about to object again, but she saw a hint of worry and longing in her gran's olive-hued eyes. She only had to have her palm read, or tea leaves examined, or whatever other tools Myrtle employed to aid her so-called talent, and then all this would be over. She, Gran and Jess could go somewhere else, perhaps for coffee, cake and a nice walk along the seafront. It looked like visiting an escape room was out of the question. She glanced through the door of Myrtle's hut and thought she saw the glint of a crystal ball.

*If I can't trust my own family, who can I trust?*

# Three

Tarot

CARLA'S PALMS WERE CLAMMY AS SHE SURVEYED the worn navy velvet chairs crammed into the waiting area of Myrtle's shack. She shouldn't have been surprised to find Mimi and Evelyn, two of her gran's younger sisters, waiting there already. Although Mimi and Evelyn were actually Carla's great-aunts, she referred to them as her aunts or aunties. The two women looked very similar facially, with rounded cheeks and ski-jump noses, but they had wildly different temperaments and senses of fashion.

Actress Mimi had recently married for the fifth time, and Carla suspected her previous failed relationships weren't due to any family curse but because her aunt expected to be treated like a star at all times. Mimi didn't walk, she *swept*, as if she was in a Broadway theater production. She looked like she'd raided the backstage wardrobe for feathers, turbans and huge costume jewels.

Retired teacher Evelyn was meeker and slightly older than

Mimi. She wore a turtleneck sweater with a string of pearls, giving her the air of a wartime librarian. She'd never tied the knot and only really socialized with her relatives (if Mimi ever let her get a word in edgewise).

"Here's Carla, our very own leading lady," Mimi announced, standing up to fling open her arms. "Come here, my darling. Let's discover what the future holds for you and your beau. *So exciting.*"

Carla found herself engulfed in Mimi's black velvet cape, coughing on her musky perfume.

Evelyn remained seated with her handbag on her knees, as if waiting to be called into a doctor's appointment. "It's lovely to see you, Carla," she whispered, tapping Mimi on her elbow. She pointed to the sign on the internal door that read *Quiet, Reading in Progress.*

Mimi theatrically held a finger to her lips. She ushered Lucinda into an empty chair, and Jess slid into the remaining one, leaving Carla standing up.

As Carla waited, perspiration trickled down her spine. She cricked her jaw from side to side to relieve its tension.

"This is a good thing for you," Mimi said, with the point of a scarlet-nailed finger. "Our family jinx is a terrible thing. I trust you two girls know the *full* story of what happened?"

*"Ahem."* Lucinda cleared her throat and shot Mimi a coded stare. "They've heard it umpteen times already. It's not the best time to—"

"Of course it is," Jess interrupted with a mischievous grin. "I love hearing about our family legend."

For Mimi, this was akin to someone calling out *Action.* She patted both corners of her lips and rearranged her cape. "In the 1920s our family was much like any other. We've always had predominantly more women than men, and our ladies fell in love, got married and all was fabulous. Our ancestral line undoubtedly shows a history of long marriages, right up until one century ago, when your great-great-grandaunt Agatha became a victim of ill will.

"Against her parents' wishes, Agatha announced her intention to marry a scoundrel. It transpired that her intended husband was already betrothed to someone else, who was actually a real-life witch. When this witch found out about her love rival, Agatha, she cursed her and decreed that she and all her female relatives henceforth would never find marital bliss.

"Now, Agatha was a headstrong woman, a family trait." Mimi looked at Carla, Jess, Lucinda and Evelyn in turn as if telling them a campfire story. "She and her beau decided to elope, but as they stood at the altar together waiting to say their vows, the groom clutched his hands to his chest. He suffered a fatal heart attack and dropped dead on the spot." Lucinda mimed the scene, acting out both parts, of the hapless groom and then Agatha's mouth dropping open with horror. "Afterward, Agatha lived a long and miserable life full of grief and regret and, for one hundred years, our ladies' relationships have been doomed."

"I can vouch for that," Jess said with a comedic tut.

Carla blew into her cheeks and huffed. "Gran was happily married to Grandad for half a century. She's living proof this story is nonsense."

"Lucinda is an anomaly," Mimi said mysteriously.

"It's vitally important Myrtle gives us *all* some good advice," Evelyn added. "Especially about relationships."

They all jumped when Myrtle's door swung open with a bang. The hunched figure of a stranger hurried out clasping a tissue to her face. She let out a sob as she rushed out of the hut.

A stocky woman wearing a black velour tracksuit with a silver fringed scarf around her shoulders and matching glittery running shoes appeared in the room. Her thick winged black eyeliner matched her jet-black hair, emphasizing the pale scalp and complexion that suggested she didn't see much daylight. She was probably in her mid to late sixties and she surveyed the group with a raised fine eyebrow and shrewd eyes. "Why do I only see you lot at funerals, weddings or when you want to know the future?" she asked. At first her face was stern, then her lips twisted into a small smile. "Who's first?"

Jess jumped to her feet. "Me."

"Jess, this is Carla's—" Lucinda started to protest.

"It's okay, let her go," Carla said. The small space seemed to be shrinking around her and she really wanted to get out of here.

The remaining women chatted while Jess had her reading. "Is Tom superstitious at all?" Evelyn asked, her voice still hushed.

Carla shook her head. "He's interested in the history of superstitions and how they originated, without actually believing in them. After all, how can a horseshoe possibly bring anyone good luck?"

She was met with a sea of fierce stares.

"It's scientifically impossible," she said under her breath. She felt sorry for her past relative Agatha, who was known for the death of her fiancé rather than anything else she might have achieved in her lifetime.

"It's lovely you've met someone special," Evelyn whispered. "I've actually met a very nice person, too."

"You *have*?" Mimi immediately sat up straight. "Since when? Why do I not know about this?"

"We've been taking time getting to know each other," Evelyn said, a smile skirting her lips. "His name's Bertrand and I'd like you all to meet him soon. I'm hoping Myrtle will have some joyous things to tell me."

Jess suddenly burst out of the room with her phone clasped in her hand. "Ohmygod," she rasped, pausing to upload a photo of a tarot card layout to Instagram. "Myrtle is *amazing*."

"What did she tell you, honey?" Lucinda asked.

"Lots of things." Jess began to count on her fingers. "One, I'm going to be working near water very soon…"

"That's doubtful." Carla rolled her eyes. "Unless I install a fish tank in the office."

"Ha ha, funny. Well, *I* believe her," Jess said, her eyes shining. "Two, I'm going to get engaged within the next twelve months and, three, Myrtle can see me holding a baby."

Carla's urge to shout *Rubbish* was overwhelming. She'd added Jess's details to the Logical Love database a couple of years ago, but her sister hadn't scored any matches above forty-nine percent. It was highly improbable she was going to get a new job, meet someone special, receive a marriage proposal *and* become pregnant within a year.

Myrtle's crooked finger appeared around the door, beckoning the next person into her lair. A hand pressed against Carla's back, pushing her up out of her seat, and her armpits prickled when she entered the tiny space. Small colored glass windows cast a patchwork of light across the room, and there was an aroma of patchouli and cigarettes. Black-and-white photos on the wall featured fortune tellers from times past and Myrtle standing beside bygone celebrities like Liza Minelli, Elizabeth Taylor and Cary Grant. Carla wondered if they were fake compositions.

"There used to be a magnificent theater in Silverpool," Myrtle recollected, as if reading her thoughts. "The stars used to flock to me for readings and I still host the occasional TV, film or pop star. Keanu Reeves was my favorite. He has an intriguing aura."

Carla sat down and knitted her fingers together as a shield. "I should tell you that I appreciate your profession but don't believe in fortune-telling."

Myrtle's lips curved into a small smile. "You *used* to believe…"

"I don't think so."

"We met once, when you were a small girl. Do you remember? You came with your mother to see me. I predicted you were going to be a successful businesswoman, something to do with numbers and people. I see you're wearing Suzette's necklace."

A sharp pain stabbed Carla, as it always did when she thought about losing her mum. Her fingers crept to her pendant and she held it tightly. Myrtle's description could apply to most jobs. "I don't believe in luck. I think things happen randomly or because you set certain processes in motion."

Myrtle's deep violet eyes intensified. "You're much more insightful than you think."

A tingle ran down Carla's spine. She *sensed* it was a bad idea to be here.

"You should follow your feelings more, deep in here." Myrtle rubbed her own belly. "Like you used to do."

"I don't..." Carla started, then clamped her mouth shut. She supposed she did used to follow her gut more, especially when she'd gone traveling or gotten married the first time around. After her divorce, she'd started to question things much more, and facts, figures and things that could be proved had become her friends. "If you and I really have a gift, we could have predicted what would happen to Mum," she said in a prickly tone.

Myrtle's expression was unreadable as she gathered her cards together. "You may wish to record this reading on your phone," she said. "Do you have anything on your person that belongs to Tom? Jess told me you're getting married soon."

Carla took a key ring out of her pocket that incorporated a screwdriver, bottle opener, scissors and tiny tweezers. "He gave this to me. It's incredibly useful." Not wanting to offend Myrtle, she set her phone to Record.

Myrtle cupped the key ring in her hands. "Shuffle the cards and think of a question."

*How can I kill my family and get away with it?* was the first one that popped into Carla's head. Her second, more involuntary thought was *Please tell me that everything will be okay with Tom.*

Taking the tarot cards back, Myrtle placed six of them on the table in a symmetrical layout. She handed the key ring back to Carla. "Who likes cats?" she asked.

"Half the population?" Carla gritted her teeth. She didn't really listen as Myrtle reeled off a vague list of observations, questions and predictions, that she should be wary of The Knight of Wands and that The Magician had something to do with positivity and confidence.

It was only when the fortune teller said "You met Tom a long time ago, didn't you?" that Carla's attention snapped back into focus.

She shifted warily in her chair. "We went to the same school but he's two years older than me, so we didn't really know each other back then." She'd always thought it was a strange coincidence that they'd subsequently matched through Logical Love, though she didn't tell Myrtle this.

Myrtle raised her eyes as if communicating with someone on the roof of her hut, then she let out a loud *"Ouch."*

Carla inched back. "What is it?"

Myrtle winced and rubbed her own elbow. "You had an accident while you were traveling, a couple of decades ago. I can *see* you lying on the ground with people looking down at you. You hurt your arm."

A hazy picture began to form for Carla, of staring up at the blue sky, unable to move because of pain searing through her body. She'd fallen from a horse and broken her arm while riding in Spain.

But how could Myrtle possibly know about this?

"You met a man of great importance to you, during that time," Myrtle continued. "You're destined to be reunited and he holds the key to your true happiness."

Carla wrinkled her nose in disbelief. During her gap year from university, she'd visited several places, including Amsterdam, Barcelona, Sardinia, Majorca, Portugal and Paris, and had enjoyed a few fleeting romances along the way. None of the men she'd dated had been particularly important to her. "I met my fiancé *before* then," she corrected.

Myrtle shook her head, her tasseled earrings swinging. "You met someone very special to you while traveling, a once-in-a-lifetime connection." She paused for effect. "It's *not* Tom."

Carla's pulse rocketed and she swept a hand under the table, trying to grab hold of her handbag. "Thanks for your...insight. I think my gran's next to see you."

"There's more," Myrtle said. "I can see more things..."

But Carla stood up abruptly, almost knocking her chair over. More images were filtering back to her from her accident and she headed blindly toward the door.

"You met a man you'll love forever during your gap year. You didn't return to finish university." Myrtle's voice followed her. "He's still overseas, waiting for you. He'll help to end your family curse..."

Carla stumbled into the waiting area, trying to feign composure as her gran, sister and aunts looked up at her expectantly. She fumbled to stop her phone from recording.

"Told you she was amazing," Jess said. "What did she tell you?"

Lucinda craned her neck. "Um, are you okay, honey? You look a little washy."

Carla took a deep breath and held the air in her lungs. She counted to ten to compose herself and brushed an imaginary speck of fluff off her trousers. There was no way she was going to give credence to anything Myrtle had told her, especially because Jess, Lucinda, Mimi and Evelyn would hang on to every word. They might pass the story along a chain of relations, where it could twist and take on a new narrative.

"Nothing very exciting." Carla plastered on a smile, trying not to think of the various old flames she'd met while traveling. "Myrtle just told me what I already know. Tom's my soulmate, we're getting married soon, and we're going to spend the rest of our lives together."

# Four

## Predictions

FOR THE REST OF HER EVENING IN SILVERPOOL, CARLA felt like her pendant chain was fastened too tightly around her neck, making it hard for her to breathe. She couldn't focus on mixing cocktails—the next activity Jess had planned for the evening. The guy serving them had a shaved head and sleeve tattoos that made his arms look embroidered. He referred to himself as a mixologist.

"I've studied and practiced skills for mixing and creating drinks," he said as he poured spirits and fruit juices into a silver container and shook it with great flourish. He explained how cocktails are made up of three elements: the core base spirit, the balance of sugar and then bitters used for seasoning.

Carla would usually have loved learning about the chemical element of the activity. She liked knowing how things were constructed, and as a child had been known to dismantle radios to see how they worked. Now her thoughts couldn't settle. One moment they were back in Myrtle's hut, with the fortune teller's violet eyes piercing into her soul. The next, she desperately wanted to see Tom, so he could reassure her the predictions were utterly nonsensical. Of course Carla hadn't met her perfect match while traveling during her gap year. It was a ridiculous, laughable claim, and their Logical Love statistics proved it.

Carla pictured Tom at home with his scalpel, sheets of paper and card, carefully cutting out and assembling his board games, and she chanted their percentage match in her head, *Eighty-four, eighty-four.* Myrtle *must* have gathered information about her prior to the reading and invented the rest. It made her feel like a little girl again, standing in front of the eerie Vadim.

The rest of her family were enjoying themselves. Evelyn had treated herself to a raspberry mojito, which gave her cheeks a bubblegum-pink flush, and Jess flirted with the mixologist, offering to read his palm. Mimi mixed exotic spirits, adding sprigs of rosemary and slices of pineapple, and Lucinda took command of the cocktail shaker. Her wedding ring winked as she poured herself a nonalcoholic margarita.

When Ted had passed away six years ago, Lucinda's house had been flooded with her friends and family. They huddled together like penguins in harsh weather conditions, bringing her lasagna and herbal tea. They gave Lucinda manicures, ran her bath and combed her hair to help her through the dark days, just as they'd done when Suzette died. They looked through photo albums with her and brought cotton handkerchiefs to mop her tears.

Ted had been a solid presence in all their lives, an amiable, quiet man with ruddy cheeks and a shock of white hair. He kept colored pencils in his jacket pocket and showed Carla how to draw cars and rabbits. He always smiled at Lucinda as if he'd won the top prize at bingo.

Even as a girl, Carla knew she wanted a relationship just like her gran and granddad's, a caring, warm mutual love that would last for a lifetime.

Her subsequent marriage to Aaron must have been a moment of foolishness, a rush of hormones, or even a bout of rebellion against the superstitions and worries her family had instilled in her. After her divorce, Carla's skin had felt sore and pitted, like she had deep acne scars that were impossible to get rid of.

Sometime later, she'd watched a TV dating show where a woman had compiled a long list of things she looked for in a partner, and the host had ripped it up, saying it wasn't realistic. Yet, it had planted an idea in Carla's head. What if *both* parties had a list of questions? What if their answers formed a solid ground for dating? A lightbulb had flicked on in her head, and the idea for Logical Love was born. Working on questions, research, probability and branding, then locating premises and more had taken her mind off her failed marriage.

Did Carla herself have an ideal type? She'd say it was someone who was calm, stable, kind, friendly and not Aaron.

Carla gulped down one cocktail after another, not bothering to listen to their names or to identify the flavors. She hoped the alcohol would get rid of Myrtle's words in her head, but it only made them more vivid.

"I think that's enough for you, honey," Lucinda said, taking a glass from her hand. "Try one of my alcohol-free cocktails instead. You don't want a fuzzy head in the morning. Are you thinking about Myrtle's reading?"

Carla's brain was cannonball-heavy in her skull. "No." She glugged one of her gran's concoctions instead, not wanting to share that the fortune teller had pretty much condemned her upcoming marriage. "Nothing to declare."

During the drive back home, her relatives chatted and laughed around her about their own predictions. Carla smiled and tried to seem interested but she'd heard enough about fortunes to last a lifetime. She leaned against Mimi's shoulder, and her eyelids started to flutter.

The next thing she knew, someone was prodding her knee.

Carla hazily opened one eye and found herself alone in the car with her gran, parked on the drive of her bungalow. "Where's Jess?" she asked with a yawn.

"I dropped her off, along with your aunties. You've been having a good old snore."

"Oops, sorry."

"You'd better sleep at my place, so I can keep an eye on you."

Carla agreed this was a good idea. It was already past midnight, too late to call Tom, who was usually in bed before eleven o'clock. He was an early bird rather than a night owl.

He hadn't messaged her, and she wondered if he was curious about where Jess and Gran had taken her for the evening. He viewed her family with a mix of warmth and amusement, coupled with bewilderment and slight fear.

In comparison, Tom's folks were rather ordinary. He was an only child from a tiny family and Carla had only spoken to his parents via video calls because they lived in France, where they ran a small hotel. She'd get to meet them in person for the first time just before the wedding.

To Carla, her gran's bungalow was the coziest place on the planet, with plants on every surface and lots of brightly colored rugs and knitted cushions. Good-luck trinkets and ornaments could be found everywhere. A model of Lord Ganesha, the elephant-headed Hindu god of beginnings, sat on the mantelpiece, and a lucky maneki-neko gold cat waved its paw on the windowsill of the living room. Lucinda claimed the acorns in a bowl on her coffee table represented the might of the oak tree and its ability to withstand lightning.

As a child, Carla had played hopscotch in her gran's backyard, trying not to step on the gaps between the paving stones in case a bogeyman came to get her. If she grazed a pavement crack with her toe, she lay in bed at night with her covers pulled up to her eyes, half-expecting a strange figure to emerge from the shadows.

"Go on, off to bed with you," Lucinda said, opening her front door. "You can sleep off the Singapore slings in your old room. Make sure you drink lots of water and I'll bring you some toast and jam."

Carla shook her head. "I really can't eat anything, thanks." She padded groggily along the hallway and into her old room, pleased there were still some of her old clothes and belongings in the wardrobe. Lucinda found it comforting to keep them around her home.

Carla switched on the bedside lamp and picked up a photo of her mum off the bedside table.

Suzette Carter wore a straw hat and had freckles on her nose. She'd been captured on film while spinning around in a raspberry-red dress, so the fabric was a blur. It was the kind of wholesome image used to advertise breakfast cereal.

She touched her mum's face, hating that she could hardly remember her voice. She did have pockets of memories of her, like the sun shining through her strawberry blonde hair so it looked like a halo, and how they used to sit at the dining table together threading glass beads onto strips of leather. At least she still had these pictures in her head, unlike Jess, who was only two when their mother died.

Carla placed the photograph back and wondered if Myrtle might have seen it, or other ones Lucinda had on display. What information might she have gleaned? She yawned, too tired to contemplate this stuff.

She found one of her old T-shirts to wear in bed and crouched down to feel around for a pair of socks in the bottom of the wardrobe. When her fingers hit something hard and rectangular, she pulled it out and realized it was the travel journal she'd kept during her gap year. There was a photo of her on the cover, younger, laughing and carefree. "I look like Mum," she whispered to herself, not that aware of the resemblance before. She shivered and sat down on the bed, then pulled the covers around herself.

Carla's travels had taken place before the iPhone was invented, prior to YouTube, Twitter and Facebook. When you escaped, you *really* could escape. Each place she'd visited had been awarded a few pages in her journal, and she opened it up.

She'd added diary entries and pasted in concert tickets, menus, hand-drawn maps and a diving certificate. She'd recorded her travels on a pocket camera, developing her photos along the way. There were names and phone numbers written on beer coasters and scraps of paper. Some people she could remember and others she couldn't.

She'd kept in touch with Gran and Jess via postcards and calls from pay phones on roadsides or in cafés, living in the moment without today's expectation of sharing all your activity online. Friendships and relationships had been formed en route through chance meetings rather than via a database and algorithms. Carla had attempted to speak different languages, got lost in foreign towns, kissed strangers and ate food she'd never heard of. Things she'd never do now.

Flicking through the journal allowed smells and sounds to come alive in her memory, taking her back in time. She could almost taste olive oil on her tongue and hear the call of hawkers who sold fake designer handbags on street corners. She'd worn an ankle bracelet with tiny bells that tinkled when she walked and ate giant slices of watermelon for breakfast.

One photo showed her posing on the back of a motorbike, her arms wrapped around a charismatic English musician she'd met after his gig in Lisbon. "Adam Angelino," she said aloud. He had been so cool.

She found a card for a hair salon in Barcelona, and saw she'd scrawled the name *Pedro (Mr. Passionate)* on the back. He'd insisted she go dancing with him, after he'd cut her hair.

As she turned the pages, other recollections filtered back,

of Fidele, a warmhearted diving instructor in Sardinia who'd introduced her to a tiny purple octopus that lived in the shallows. She smiled ruefully as she pictured clinking beer bottles with him at sunset, thinking if it had been a different time, a different place, they could have been perfect together.

Then there had been Ruben, an intelligent teacher who'd showed her the sights of Amsterdam, taking her to many museums, writing poems for her and discussing Vincent van Gogh's mental health until the early hours.

Daniel had been a penniless eco-warrior in Majorca who'd lived in a deserted farmhouse with fellow travelers, an abundance of chickens and no electricity. After a few weeks, Carla could no longer survive without running water and had decamped to a nearby hostel.

Her travels had allowed her to cast aside all her responsibilities at home for twelve months of freedom and possibility.

Carla rubbed the back of her neck, feeling guilty about revisiting romantic encounters from her past, if only in her thoughts. None of her exes from two decades ago compared to the wonderful relationship she had now with Tom.

Her eyes settled upon a photo of her standing next to a tan-colored horse in Spain. Its front legs were crossed and she adopted a similar pose. As she recalled Myrtle's words about an accident, she sucked in a sharp breath.

More memories filtered back, of how she'd missed her footing while dismounting. She'd thudded down onto the sand, where she'd yowled in pain and clutched her elbow. Vacationers had gathered around her in the afternoon heat, peering down and asking if she was okay, where was she staying and was she with anyone? Someone had taken her to the hospital, where the nurses exchanged exasperated looks over the top of Carla's head at having to deal with yet another tourist injured from a horse ride. A kindly doctor had taken pity on her and drove her back to her hotel afterward.

A few days later, Carla revisited the horse and had her photo taken alongside it to prove there were no hard feelings. It had been all her fault, after all.

She flipped through the rest of the journal and discovered several blank pages at the back where she'd added her own title, *Adventures—to be continued...*

Carla yawned and closed the book, letting it slip from her fingers to the floor, and she settled down into a woozy sleep. All the relationships and experiences she'd just revisited belonged firmly in her past. Tom was her Mr. Right, whatever Myrtle might say.

So, why couldn't she stop wondering about the mysterious, important man she'd supposedly met twenty-one years ago? And how could he possibly be part of her future?

# Five

Games

CARLA WOKE THE NEXT MORNING AND HEARD HER gran singing in the kitchen, a homey sound she could listen to for hours. Her pillow was marshmallow-soft, and golden daylight flooded the room. She'd love to stay around for breakfast, but it was already past ten and Tom made brunch for her each Saturday. He'd probably be wondering where she'd ended up last night, so Carla forced herself out of bed. On her way out of the room, she stepped on the journal that lay splayed face down on the carpet.

Lucinda stood in the kitchen surrounded by various dishes, measuring spoons and glass jugs. She had a smudge of flour on her nose and was immersed in reading a letter. As soon as she heard Carla, she lowered it, placed it down on her countertop and promptly covered it with a place mat.

Carla spotted the hospital logo on the top before it disappeared. "Everything okay?" she asked cautiously.

Lucinda's eyes lingered on the place mat for a second too

long. "Absolutely fine, just a routine appointment." She snatched up a spoon. "I'm making pancakes. Want one? Or are you feeling a little delicate?"

Carla closed one eye and winced. "I think there's a rugby match going on in my head."

"Tsk. Why not get back into bed and I'll bring you coffee and a headache tablet instead? You haven't said much about your reading. I want to know what—"

Carla's nose tickled and she wrinkled it, not managing to stave off a sneeze. A further two loud ones followed and she was glad they'd interrupted her gran's questioning.

Sneezing three times in a row was supposedly bad luck and Lucinda eyed her warily. She passed Carla a tissue and said, "Bless you."

The saying originated from some cultures' belief that your soul could escape your body through a sneeze, and Carla dismissed this silly thought as she washed and got dressed. In a rush to leave the bungalow, she stuffed the travel journal into her bag rather than put it back in the wardrobe.

A little later on, she wilted at the smell of cooked sausages outside Tom's place.

He lived on the outskirts of Manchester in a compact one-bedroom terraced house. Apart from his much-loved compendium of board games, he was a minimalistic kind of guy, happy for his apartment to be all gray, white and chrome until he'd met Carla. As a bit of fun, and trying to inject some color into his house by stealth, she'd started to leave behind items whenever she stayed over, like a yellow glass vase, a pink plastic photo frame, or a fringed velvet cushion or two. She was pleased when Tom left them in place, proving she was welcome in his world.

They were going to rent a tiny new two-bedroom house after they married, a stopgap while they saved up and looked around for their forever home. Carla wasn't sure where Tom would fit all his games, and there wasn't enough space to invite friends over for drinks on the strip of paving stones that was supposed to be a garden.

Although they often spent Sunday mornings exploring flea markets, buying vintage framed prints to display on the walls of their new place, Carla couldn't help feeling apprehensive about living with someone else again. After splitting with Aaron, she'd found it liberating not having to wipe shaving-foam smears from the bathroom taps, or moving forks out of the knife section of the cutlery drawer. She loved wearing her favorite ugly slippers with a hole in the sole that weren't fit to be seen by anyone else.

"Hi," Carla called out as she let herself inside Tom's house. She just wanted to sink into his arms and forget last night ever happened.

"Hey there," Tom said, moving around the kitchen wearing a Clue apron she'd bought him for Christmas. It featured a large graphic of Colonel Mustard.

The frying pan in Tom's hand prevented her from giving him a hug. He slid sausages, bacon, hash browns and mushrooms onto two plates and added a spoonful of baked beans. "I thought you might be hungry after last night, so I've cooked you a full English breakfast. How was your prewedding surprise? Jess told me she had a secret plan for you."

Carla sat on a stool, and the smell of the cooked food made her feel rocky. "Gran, Jess and two of my aunts basically kidnapped me. They dragged me to see a fortune teller."

Tom set the plates down and smiled sympathetically. "Poor thing, though you don't need to be a psychic to predict they'd do *that*." He wriggled his fingers in the air as if casting a spell. "So, what did Mystic Meg say?"

"Her name was Myrtle and it's no laughing matter..." Carla cut into her bacon.

"Did she predict a lottery win? Are we going to be millionaires soon?"

"Damn it, she left out that part." Carla bit her lip, wondering how much she should actually tell him, about Myrtle's claim he wasn't the man for her and that someone else was waiting for her overseas. Tom already thought her family was weird without making things worse. "She claimed she could see Jess with a baby," she finally said.

"Yeah? I bet she'll make a cool mum."

Carla nodded, trying to ignore a fleeting rush of sadness. Occasionally, when she saw kids skipping home from school carrying Mother's Day cards they'd made in class, or chattering excitedly at the ice cream truck, she wished she had a small, sticky hand to hold, too.

Acting as a part-time surrogate mother to Jess had stolen away her urge to do it all again with a child of her own, so it was strange how her heart twanged with a mix of longing, relief and regret. She struggled to swallow a piece of hash brown.

Tom detected she'd gone quiet and sought out her eyes with a smile. "Lucky for us we're both over forty and love being a family of two."

She nodded and forced down a piece of egg.

After they'd eaten, Tom's state-of-the-art dishwasher wasn't working, so he rinsed the pots in the sink and Carla dried them. They spent Saturday afternoons playing board games and she hoped the gentle rattle of counters in a box would help soothe her headache. His living room had the sparse serenity of an exclusive spa where music tinkled, his candles smelled of amber and Carla felt relaxed and cocooned, an experience she didn't get anywhere else. Instead of being Carla Carter CEO, she could kick off her shoes, sink into Tom's arms and just be herself.

She glanced at her fiancé intermittently, thinking how his studious expression added to his handsomeness. Carla sometimes caught him looking at her, too, as if he couldn't believe his luck.

He had the jawline of a cartoon superhero and his broken

nose, from a childhood fall, gave his face intrigue and character. She liked how sprigs of dark chest hair escaped from the neck of his shirt, tickling her nose whenever she leaned against him. Tom never displayed any awareness of his good looks, and this modesty made him even more appealing.

What did she love about him the most? She supposed it was the way he could see the good in everyone and that there wasn't a problem in the world they couldn't fix together. So, the thought of perusing other men in her travel journal made the hairs on Carla's arms stand guiltily on end.

Tom and Carla sat on the sofa and played a game of Trivial Pursuit, answering the questions and complimenting each other. "Oh, well done" and "Great answer," they said. She loved how her diamond solitaire engagement ring sparkled as she moved pieces around the board.

Afterward, Tom took a sketchbook out from under a cushion and cradled it to his chest. "I've got something to show you," he said. "It's my idea for a new board game, Destination Next."

Carla sat forward on the sofa. "Oh, great, let me see it."

He flipped over the pages so she could look at his drawings. "Each element will be made out of recycled cardboard, and the board pops up so you can transport it around easily. Each player gets a counter—a suitcase, sunhat, sunglasses, etcetera, plus a paper passport. You have to solve clues and move around the board, collecting passport stamps as you go. I'm thinking the game could include a rubber stamp with ink. It'll be lots of fun."

"I love it," Carla said. "But what happens when your passport is full?"

"It means you've won the game."

"Does that mean you can only play it once? An inkpad and stamp aren't recyclable, so what about using peel-off stickers instead? That way you can reuse the passport, too."

Tom stared at her with admiration in his eyes. "Fantastic idea. Thank goodness you're so practical."

Carla felt inexplicably wounded by his compliment, prefer-
ring the words *resourceful* or *imaginative*. "You're practical, too."

"And that's why we're so great together." Tom planted a kiss
on her nose. "I'll add your idea to my presentation. I've been
up all night working on it."

"Presentation?" she questioned.

He beamed and nodded. "I've been waiting to tell you some
incredible news. I found out yesterday that I've been invited to
Game Player Con."

"That's fantastic!" She hesitated. "Um, what is it?"

"Only the biggest boardgame convention in the world, taking place in Denver next week," Tom gushed. "Some guys saw
me talking about my games online and reached out to me. They
love my ideas and want to meet face-to-face. My manager says
I can take the time off work because it's job-related."

"So…you want to fly to America? *Next* week?"

"Yes." He took her hands in his. "I've always wanted to run
my own business, and this is my *big* chance to show off my
work and make some great connections. It could really turn
my luck around and I'd love to earn more money for our new
life together."

Carla cricked her neck, feeling like someone had tugged
the doormat she'd been standing on. When they'd previously
discussed booking a honeymoon, Tom had struggled to find
space in his schedule. Late spring was also Carla's busiest time,
with users of Logical Love trying to find a romantic partner
for the summer. They'd both agreed to postpone their honeymoon until later in the year. "What about our wedding arrangements?" she said.

"Everything is good to go. We've booked the church for our
ceremony, and the community hall for our reception. All our
invitations have been sent out and we've confirmed the catering order. My parents have arranged their flights from France
and can't wait to meet you. We know who's going to be sitting

next to who at dinner, so we can kick back and relax before our big day. The convention should be fascinating—hundreds of game designers and players under one roof—and we'll be able to add more games to our collection. I'll get so much inspiration." He brushed a lock of hair away from Carla's cheek. "Perhaps you could join me. We could tack a few days onto the end of the convention and call it an early honeymoon."

Carla liked playing games but didn't want to celebrate her nuptials with thousands of fanatics. Flying to Denver sounded expensive and grueling before their wedding day.

She'd hoped to spend the run-up to their wedding in a cozy bubble, hanging out with Tom in coffee shops to discuss the minutiae of their big day over hot chocolate (avoiding the cream and chocolate flakes on top, of course, because she wanted to fit into the off-white column dress she'd bought from a vintage shop). It was impossible to foretell what the weather would be like at the beginning of June, and she wanted his help choosing versatile blankets, for guests to sit on outside if the evening was warm, or to wrap around their shoulders if it was cold. Yes, these were all things she could do by herself, but they'd be much more fun together.

More than anything, Carla was determined their wedding day would be the opposite of her and Aaron's extravaganza. Her ex loved being the center of attention and had played a forty-five-minute set on his guitar, engaging their guests in a sing-along. Life with Aaron had been like riding a Jet Ski on choppy waves, exciting if unpredictable, whereas time with Tom was like a peaceful sail on a pretty lake.

"It's sweet of you to invite me…" she started, still trying to make the timing work in her head. "But it's very short notice."

"I won't go if you don't want me to," Tom instantly replied, with a concerned frown. "I can turn the opportunity down."

"Oh no, don't do that," she jumped in. "How long are you planning to be away for?"

"Maybe a couple of weeks, perhaps a little longer. It's a long way and I want to make the most of things."

"Wow. That long?" Carla's headache intensified and she squinted an eye. Myrtle's words about Tom not being her perfect match ramped up in her brain. Would a loving fiancé really jump on a plane just before his wedding? "I'm not sure I can—"

Tom squeezed her hand. "Look, see if you can fit it in your calendar. It'd be great if you can make it, but two weeks isn't that long apart when we have a lifetime together ahead of us." He stood up to select a different board game from his shelves. "Now, do you fancy a game of Connect Four or Monopoly?"

# Six

Lucky Pixie

THE LOGICAL LOVE OFFICE WASN'T OFFICIALLY OPEN for business on Sunday, but Carla liked to catch up on her admin work over the weekend.

After seeing Myrtle and spending Saturday with Tom, thoughts about her gap year and her fiancé's upcoming trip to Denver were still spiraling around in her thoughts. She hoped being alone in the office for a while would help to calm her ever-busy brain. Work was her sanctuary, a place where she could control everything, like how the conductor of an orchestra makes sure all the musicians are in sync.

Carla changed the water in her vases of flowers and breathed in the quietness of the building. There were no splashes of coffee on the kitchen countertop and she didn't have to make small talk about the weather around the water cooler. While she browsed her online calendar to see if there was any possibility of accompanying Tom to Colorado, she ate a sandwich she'd made at home. During her gap year, she'd developed a taste for the preformed plasticky squares of orange cheese that usually garnished cheap burgers and had never shaken the craving.

Two weeks was a long time for her to leave the agency, even though she knew Jess and Gran would keep an expert eye on things. It still rankled Carla that Tom had magicked up time to travel that he hadn't been able to find for their honeymoon.

She sighed deeply when she couldn't find more than three or four consecutive free days in her calendar. She had a few meetings with potential clients lined up, including one with a minor member of the Danish royal family. Hopefully, she and Tom would be able to take a proper honeymoon later in the year.

A quick online search showed the Denver exhibition hall was situated miles away from any art galleries, museums and shops, and the flights and hotels were extortionately priced, making her feel a little better about not going.

Carla was about to bite into an apple when she thought she heard the agency front door opening downstairs. Perhaps she hadn't locked it properly? She cocked her head, listening for more signs of movement. When footsteps sounded on the stairs, her heart pattered wildly and she raised her apple like a grenade. Tiptoeing across her office, she peeped around her door and came face-to-face with her sister. "Oh gosh, it's you," she gasped, pressing the fruit to her chest.

"Oh, you're here." Jess huffed. "I noticed the front door was ajar."

"I'm catching up on some work. Have you forgotten something?"

Jess's eyes darted back toward the stairs. "Um, yes. I…" Her words trailed away and color rose in her cheeks. "Look, I'll just fess up. I've snuck in to run my details through the database."

"What? To find a match?"

Jess replied with a short nod.

"I thought you believed in meeting someone through fate and luck, and the wind blowing in the right direction—"

"I do. But if I'm going to meet someone, get engaged and have a baby pretty soonish, I need a helping hand."

Carla allowed herself an imaginary fist pump. Destiny sometimes needed a shove in the right direction. "I can help you, if you like?"

Jess nodded once. "Yep, if you don't mind. Sorry for dragging you to see Myrtle. I could tell you hated every moment."

"It was interesting and I appreciate your efforts. The cocktails tasted great, from the little I can remember."

Carla wheeled a spare chair across her office, and the two sisters sat side by side in front of the computer. Carla located Jess's profile and opened it. "Your details are still in the system but you need to answer a few additional questions. Hundreds of new clients have joined since we last ran your data."

"Let's hope I have more luck this time around." Jess crossed her fingers in the air. She took a silver pixie ornament out of her pocket and set it down on the desk. "My new lucky charm."

Carla slid the keyboard across to her. "I doubt that thing is going to help," she said. "He has an evil smile."

While Jess updated her information, Carla made coffee until her sister called out her name. Carla sat back down, tapped the submit button and watched as an arrow began to rotate. The two sisters looked at each other hopefully.

After a couple of minutes, a chime sounded and three matches appeared on the screen, the best one highlighted in red.

"I may be looking at the future father of my child," Jess joked, leaning forward to examine the names and brief profiles. "Hmm, that's weird."

"What is?"

Her sister performed a one-shouldered shrug. "I *think* my top match is the same as last time. He has an unusual name. I'm pretty sure our match was forty-nine percent back then. Now we're supposed to be sixty-two-percent suited…"

"Are you sure?" Carla leaned closer toward the screen. "Did you make lots of changes to your data?"

"Hardly any, and there weren't that many new questions."

Carla checked the man's profile in more detail. "He's very picky so has been in the system for a long time. Your match score shouldn't have changed *that* much. Something doesn't seem right."

"Could the algorithms be wrong?"

Carla shot her sister a stare. "They're constant, mathematical equations that I devised personally. Client data is the only variable."

"Right." Jess shrugged. "It's probably nothing."

Carla couldn't leave anything to chance. This situation baffled her, and she could think of only one way to quickly test the system. "I'll run my details against Tom's again, to make sure everything's working correctly."

She answered the additional questions then pressed the submit button with a confident smile. Again, the two sisters waited until Carla and Tom's suitability score flashed up on the screen.

60%

"*What?*" Carla shouted and stared at the figure. Something felt stuck in her throat and she began to cough. "That's not right. In fact, it's impossible." She coughed some more.

Jess thumped her on her back. "What's wrong?"

Carla jabbed a finger at the screen. "There must be a glitch in the system because we're eighty-four percent suited, not sixty. We need to get in touch with Data Daze immediately. They designed the data interface and app." She snatched up her phone and located their number, clicking her tongue when she reached an automated message. "Damn it, there's no one there." She noticed on her phone screen that Tom had called her a couple of times, but *this* was more important.

"It *is* Sunday," Jess reasoned, taking a moment to think. "There's someone I could reach out to…" She paused. "I, um, had a fling with one of the data guys."

Carla's jaw hung open. "You *did*? While Data Daze was working for us?"

"Hey, it happens. He's called Arnie and he still messages me."

"That is totally unprofessional," Carla scolded. She then side-eyed her sister. "Can you reach him today?"

"Possibly. He really likes me. Get some fresh air while I try to contact him."

"I have to stay here…"

"You can't control everything in life, and sorting this out can be my apology for taking you to Silverpool. Why don't you call Gran or something? She's been quizzing me about your reading. She thinks there's something you're keeping from her."

Carla felt her neck mottling and she shifted her gaze.

"There *is*, isn't there?" Jess prompted, her voice rising. "What did Myrtle tell you?"

"Nothing." Carla ran her tongue over her teeth. "I'll go for a walk," she said, grabbing her coat.

Jess picked up the silver pixie and handed it to her. "Take this guy and don't worry. Give me an hour to sort this out."

Carla marched around the village center, where couples and families huddled outside coffee shops. She stood in front of a travel agency, gazing at the photos of blue skies and beaches in the window, wishing she could feel the sun on her own skin. Spring hadn't fully kicked in yet and she was fed up with the unpredictability of the English weather. One week there was a snowstorm, the next there was hazy sunshine, followed by a week of heavy downpour.

After precisely one hour, she headed back upstairs. She took off her coat and placed the silver pixie on the desk. "So?"

Jess picked up the ornament and toyed with it, not meeting her sister's eyes. "Heyyy."

And in that one word, Carla knew something was terribly wrong. "What is it? What did Arnie say?"

Jess set the pixie down again with a thud. "Data Daze updated their system a couple of years ago, meaning they changed our interface, too."

"Changed it?" Carla squinted.

"Yeah, a standard business procedure we didn't need to know about. Unfortunately, in the process, it appears some of our questions and their corresponding answers got switched around. It's probably why my percentage match with the client changed so much."

Carla sat down heavily on the edge of her desk, shoving her in tray to the side. "So, you're saying that, two years ago, there was a period of time our system was faulty?"

"Yeah."

"And how long did this go on for?"

Jess's lips moved without any sound coming out for a while. "Like, a year," she finally said.

Carla gripped the desk to keep upright. "Twelve months?" she spluttered.

"Technically, yes, but Data Daze sorted it out as soon as they spotted the issue."

"We matched clients incorrectly for a year." Carla heard blood whooshing in her ears. "Surely we'd have seen an increase in client complaints during that time…"

Jess fell quiet, redness spreading across her face. "Well, yeah, there was a report that showed a spike."

"Why the hell didn't you bring it to my attention?"

"I spoke to the team." Jess's voice grew smaller. "We assumed the increase in client dissatisfaction was due to the pandemic. People were meeting online rather than in person, so didn't feel as connected. I didn't want to worry you, so we presented you with the positive matches only."

Carla glared at her sister. "What happened to the report?"

Jess gave an audible swallow. "I buried it."

Carla laced her fingers across the top of her head and pressed down, wishing she hadn't just heard *that*. "You all met without me? This is *my* business, *my* algorithms and *my* reputation, and you *hid* this data from me? You're my sister."

"At work, I'm the customer data manager and I thought it was the right thing to do. Arnie says everything should have functioned normally since the problem was resolved." Jess gnawed her lip. "And we're really only *half* sisters."

It was a comment she flung at Carla whenever she wanted to wound her, and it always worked. Their fathers' names on their birth certificates were both blank, something that connected them and that could also divide them.

Floating spots in her eyes made it difficult for Carla to see properly. "*Should have functioned normally* isn't good enough," she said. "We need a full and proper audit."

"They made a mistake, which has been corrected. Arnie said a full check could take weeks to run. This stuff happened two years ago, and our clients don't need to know anything about it. We've gotten away with it, so don't act like we're screwed."

Carla's eyes flashed and she clamped her lips together, not wanting to blast words at Jess she might regret. She pressed her palms against her fiery cheeks and tried to think.

Logical Love had potentially paired hundreds of clients over a twelve-month period who weren't supposed to be together, and she and Tom had also matched during that time. Had their eighty-four percent compatibility score been incorrect, a mistake thrown out by a problem in the system? Was their true score really much lower?

The sixty percent was still a decent enough match but one Carla wouldn't have considered, especially after Aaron. It meant she and Tom were actually forty percent *mismatched*. And didn't his decision to visit a game convention in Denver before their wedding prove that?

She tried to wrench the possibility from her mind.

Carla wiped her face with the cuff of her blouse, scratching her face on a button. She stared at all her cards and flowers, and they made her feel like a fraud. Her clients had relied on her, trusted her with their hopes, dreams and futures, and she worried she'd let them down badly. How many couples had she set on the wrong path with the wrong partner? How many would end up like her and Aaron, torn apart and miserable?

Jess tried to take hold of her arm. "You okay?"

"Oh yes, I'm absolutely marvelous, thanks. Never better." Carla jerked her body away. Failing hundreds of couples was terrible, and a doubt was also spreading in her mind like algae on the surface of a stagnant pond. It was something Myrtle had warned her about and which Carla had vehemently denied.

Tom was no longer her ideal match.

Was she about to walk down the aisle with the wrong man, all over again?

# Seven

## Red Dress

CARLA SHOVED HER ARMS INTO HER COAT SLEEVES and rushed out of the building, ignoring Jess's shouts for her to return. Her sister's deceit was too painful to contemplate and she couldn't face spending another second in the same vicinity as her. She couldn't believe her own team had hidden things from her, even if they thought it was the right thing to do at the time.

She hurried through the streets with tears streaming down her cheeks. A corner of the park provided a brief respite and she sat on a bench facing the trees, gulping deep breaths of air and trying to force herself to get a grip.

Carla had always been good at math, able to see patterns and formulas that others couldn't. She liked things that could be explained, things that had reason and were tangible. As a child, fairy tales had thrown up too many questions for her pragmatic mind, such as why didn't Cinderella leave her stepsisters and get a job with employers who appreciated her skill set more?

And why did princesses pin their hopes on marrying for money rather than setting up their own businesses?

She and Jess used to have heated debates about such matters.

"If stories have endured through time there must be some truth in them, or else people wouldn't pass them on," Jess said.

"You can't prove these things actually happened," Carla argued. "Think about it, Jess, no one ever wore glass slippers."

"You can't prove that. Perhaps they did."

The sisters usually reached a stalemate, resulting in Jess flouncing to their shared bedroom to look at her angel cards and Carla scribbling notes on why she was right.

She tried to apply her realistic thought process to her current situation. Telling herself Tom was *still* her perfect partner meant overriding her faith in the matchmaking system she'd created.

Carla loved Tom and she tried to ignore the worries that were muddying her emotions. She desperately wanted to see him so they could talk things through logically.

She waited until her emotions settled down a little, tied her hair into a tighter bun and briskly walked over to his apartment. Her hand shook as she opened the door, and even more so when she saw Tom standing in the middle of his hallway, a suitcase parked at his side.

"Hey, you," he said, moving forward for a hug. "I've been trying to get ahold of you. Didn't you see my missed calls?"

"I've been at work, trying to sort something out." She tucked her head under his chin, relishing the beat of his heart against her cheek.

"Are you okay?" He pulled back to look at her. "You look upset. Is it your family again?"

"No...well, yes." Carla's eyes settled on the passport sitting on top of his suitcase and she chose to ignore it. "I *need* to talk to you."

He looked at his watch. "I don't have long. A guy from the convention has been in touch. A client canceled, meaning there was a spare flight ticket available. It will save me a lot of money and I get to fly business class, too."

The excitement in his voice made Carla feel even more wretched and her throat ached when she spoke. "When are you leaving?"

"Now. My Uber is going to be here in four minutes." He glanced at his watch. "Um, three…"

"Oh." Carla dropped her arms to her sides. How could she tell Tom about the issue at work, their mismatch and Jess's deceit in such a minuscule amount of time?

"Sorry. I did try to reach you," he reiterated. "What did you want to talk about?"

She swallowed her words away. "It's fine, probably nothing."

"Are you sure? I can cancel the cab…"

"Yes." The word sounded strangled when it came out of her mouth and every part of her wanted to yell *no* instead. *She* needed him more than some crappy boardgame convention, but she didn't want to spoil his opportunity. "It's a surprise you're going so soon, that's all."

Tom kissed the top of her head and smoothed a lock of hair off her forehead. "You look a bit tired, probably overworking as usual. Why don't you take a break somewhere, too? See if Jess wants to go somewhere nice for a few days? Maybe a girls' weekend away to relax?"

"I really don't want to—"

Tom's phone pinged to say his Uber had arrived. He tugged his suitcase onto the path outside and Carla followed him. "I've left something for you on the coffee table," he said, pressing his lips against hers. "You can play it while I'm away."

"Thanks." Her voice sounded blank.

"I'll call you when I get there, probably tomorrow because it's a long flight. Please don't forget to lock up for me."

She waved to him from the front step, then wrapped her arms across her body as his taxi disappeared around the corner.

Inside the house, Tom had finished a prototype of his board

game and had left it on the coffee table. There was a tiny paper sunhat and a passport with her name written on the front. The game was beautifully crafted, a fine display of his talent.

He'd also left her a note.

*Darling Carla,*
*You can play this game and pretend you're on holiday! The stickers haven't arrived yet, so I look forward to playing it with you properly—on our wedding night. I can't wait until we're man and wife.*
*Love you lots,*
*Tom x*

Carla pressed the note to her chest. It should make her feel better, assuring her that everything was still fantastic between them. She wanted to picture them lying on a four-poster bed together, with white silk curtains billowing as they played his new game. But all she could do was cry.

She left Tom's place, locked his front door and caught a taxi back to her own apartment. As she took a shower, she let the steaming-hot water run off her body until her skin was tight and numb. Her insides were tangled in a huge knot, and her concerns about her and Tom's suitability grew bigger and stronger until she felt like retching.

Carla wanted to discuss things with him in person, a conversation not hampered by their work schedules or different time zones. If she waited until he returned, there'd only be a week or so until they married, to see if they really *were* still suited for each other. And then there was Myrtle's insistence that a man she'd met two decades ago was actually *the one* and still waiting for her overseas.

What the hell was she going to do?

Carla called into work to say she was sick, something she'd never done before because she liked to appear invincible. With her stomach cramping, and unable to face Jess, she paced around her apartment, fretting about the couples she might have set on the path to destruction.

She called Arnie at Data Daze and ordered him to take the Logical Love entry form offline immediately and to run a full audit. She requested a list of the questions that had been mixed up during the system update and emailed her team with details on the issue.

Carla messaged Jess and instructed her to personally contact every couple who'd matched (or in fact mismatched) during the twelve-month problem period. Her sister was to say it was a courtesy call, to ascertain if clients were still together and if they were happy. Only then could Carla assess the full magnitude of the situation and decide on a way forward.

Jess replied, Okay.

Carla glared at her sister's response, having expected an apology, assurances or a promise to keep her updated. *Okay* did little to stamp out Carla's fears, about her business, her fiancé and her sister.

The couple of phone conversations she managed to have with Tom, after he'd arrived in America, were hampered by delays on the line and a crackling noise that sounded like cellophane. He gushed about the games he'd discovered, the people he'd met and the initial interest in his work. Whenever he asked Carla how she was, she didn't have the heart to tell him the truth.

Her travel journal offered a welcome distraction, and she focused on the pages, pasting down corners of photos that had peeled away, looking up restaurants, bars and shops online to see if they still existed. She browsed photos of men she'd previously dated, trying to assess if any of the relationships might have been more significant than she'd originally thought before deciding that they hadn't been.

She looked up a few of their names on Facebook, too, and it was strange seeing people who'd been a brief part of her life, and how they'd changed over time. Carla felt like a stalker, prying into their personal information, even if they'd displayed it for the world to see. A couple of them no longer lived overseas, so wouldn't even count in Myrtle's prediction.

More memories trickled back to her, of eating paella on a beach in Barcelona and admiring Salvador Dalí's melting-clock paintings. She thought about the men she'd met and also about her previous self, the young woman who'd lost her mother and left England to travel for a year without much of a plan, except to escape her family superstitions for a while. It was like getting back in touch with a long-lost twin.

When Carla had finished her maintenance work on the journal, she tidied her apartment and found a box stashed away in her spare room that contained some of her mum's belongings. There was a red dress, a straw hat and a worn brown leather luggage tag. They were musty and there were still grains of sand at the bottom of the box.

Carla washed the dress and watched it flap on the clothing line outside. When it was dry, she tried it on, and somehow the color made her feel braver, made her eyes brighter. And when she looked in the mirror, it was like Suzette Carter was staring right back at her, urging her to follow her own instincts.

# Eight

## Journal

ON THE THIRD DAY OF HER SELF-IMPOSED SOLITARY confinement, Carla sported pink semicircles under her eyes, a dead giveaway of anxiety and lack of sleep. When her doorbell rang, she sat up from her slump on the sofa, hoping Jess had finally shown up to apologize. A glimpse of her gran's ample shape through the patterned glass told her otherwise.

"Bacon hot pot," Lucinda called out as a greeting, offering Carla a casserole dish. "I heard you two girls had a disagreement. Are you really sick, or are you hiding?"

Carla let out a sigh and opened the door farther. "Both."

They headed to the kitchen, where Lucinda set the dish down on the countertop. "Jess said Myrtle's reading has made you all nitpicky."

"It's not *just* about the reading," Carla snapped then regretted it. "Sorry, Gran. There are other things, too." She threw herself into a chair.

Lucinda surveyed her. "I'll pop this in the oven, and you can tell me all about it."

Carla's stomach rumbled. She hadn't eaten properly and she loved her gran's cooking. There was nothing better than thin layers of potato, onion and bacon, cooked until crispy.

"Now, honey, care to share what's been going on?" Lucinda asked, eyeing the travel journal that lay open on the dining table.

Myrtle's predictions had continued to balloon in Carla's head, on the verge of bursting. She glanced at her phone, knowing a recording of the fortune teller's words remained there. She really hoped they were hogwash, but was increasingly unsure. "I hoped you wouldn't ask me..."

Lucinda rolled her eyes. "Fat chance of that."

Carla reluctantly picked up her phone and cradled it in her hands. She found the voice recording and pressed the play button. "Okay, you wanted to hear this..."

The two women leaned forward and Lucinda cocked her head.

Carla listened to Myrtle's descriptions of the six tarot cards more intently this time, with the color draining from her cheeks. Each supposedly related to a man from her past.

"Good heavens," Lucinda said when the recording ended. "That's some proclamation. I don't think Myrtle's trying to irk you, though. She's been helping people for many years."

"*Help* isn't the word I'd use. Look, I know Mimi loves spinning a yarn about our family curse, but you and Granddad were so perfect together. I thought Tom and I were, too, but now everything feels...foggy. Your marriage proves the jinx is nonsense, so why can't our family draw a line under it and move on? Jess wants to meet someone special and needs to be sure of her choices, too. I don't want her living in the shadow of some weird family legend."

Lucinda smiled tightly. She raised her cup to her lips but

didn't drink. "Ted and I *were* happy," she agreed. "But our marriage wasn't exactly the one I wanted, the one people thought it was..." She let her words drift away.

Carla frowned. "I don't understand."

"Your granddad and I were a great team. Heck, I even became pregnant on our honeymoon. But after your mum came along, our relationship changed. A lot."

Carla's insides tightened, like a corset lacing together. "Granddad idolized you. I remember his eyes shining when he looked at you. You held hands wherever you went."

"Yes, I loved that about him." Lucinda smiled and her eyes grew misty. "And I was proud of him, too. We were close in many ways, but not in *others*. We probably weren't the right, um, *romantic* fit."

"Oh." Carla felt her cheeks growing hot. "Are you saying that—"

"Ted was my best friend and we were devoted to each other," Lucinda cut in firmly. "We loved each other in most senses of the word, if not others. We had a long and successful marriage and, in our day, you just got on with things. Would I say I was unlucky in love, like our family curse states?" She took a long while to consider this. "In terms of passion, I'd say that I *was*."

Carla felt a great weight settle upon her at the realization that a marriage she'd idolized her entire life may not have been so perfect after all. Above all, she hated that her gran had compromised her own desires. "*Oh*, Gran..."

Lucinda waved her words away. "Nothing for you to get all sorrowful about," she said, standing up from her seat. "I'll get that hot pot out of the oven. We don't want to eat burnt potatoes, do we? It was Ted's favorite meal and I miss making it for the old fella."

Carla stared after her, her mouth downturned. She knew she'd struggle to eat when the casserole dish arrived on the table and she suddenly, urgently, wanted to know her gran had been loved in a way she'd truly wanted. "Was there ever anyone else, before Granddad?" she asked tentatively.

A flush rose up Lucinda's neck, reaching her chin. "Oh, my." A smile gave her face a brief girlish appearance and she set down her fork. "Only once before."

"Who was he?"

Lucinda shook her head, but then her lips parted, unable to hold on to a secret. "When I was nineteen, I spent four weeks in Spain with a friend of mine. We used to go to a tapas restaurant and order the cheapest things off the menu, just so we could sneak a peek at the gorgeous waiters, brothers Juan and Carlos. After they'd finished work, we shared sangria and Manzanillo olives with them. We walked and talked on the beach until the sun rose the next morning." She let out a dreamy sigh.

"When Juan kissed me, I felt like I'd touched an electric eel. Zap. My whole body went all tingly." Lucinda shimmied her shoulders. "Ah, but we were young and lived in different countries. I told myself it was a holiday romance, nothing more. Though, sometimes, when I was with Ted, feeling all *plain*, I couldn't help but wonder if Juan would have been a better fit for me. It made me feel ever so silly and guilty, thinking that way."

"It's not silly at all." Carla sat back in her chair, dismayed she no longer knew of *any* marriages in her family she could aspire to. The weight of expectation for hers and Tom's to be the first to work out was growing even greater.

"Do things feel electric when you're with Tom?" Lucinda's eyes flickered, embarrassed yet hopeful.

"Yes, of course," Carla replied quickly, though she had to admit her feelings for him were more like the gentle hum of a cat's purr rather than a bolt of lightning. Regardless, she was sure she'd have been attracted to Tom if she'd met him through sheer chance.

"Well, there's your answer, no matter what any database or

Myrtle says." Lucinda paused and nodded to herself. She ran
her tongue across her lips. "Unless…"

"Unless what?"

"Unless you want to make *absolutely* sure."

Carla swallowed at the use of that word. *Absolutely* meant *un-
equivocally* and *unquestionably*. Even with algorithms, there were
no complete certainties. "I can't go rushing off overseas to trace
men from my past, if that's what you're…" She paused, astonished she'd predicted what her gran had been about to suggest.

An understanding look passed between the two women.

Lucinda raised her eyebrow. "You went traveling before,
for a full year."

"That was ages ago, when I was single." Carla tossed her hair
and wished that she'd washed it.

Lucinda pulled the journal toward her and looked at Carla's
photos of Barcelona. "I know someone who lives not far from
there. Babs always sends me Christmas cards and invites me to
visit. I'm sure you'd be welcome, too."

"I can't just run off and leave the business…"

"You've got me and Jess to help."

Carla dug her fingernails into her palm. "I've got *you*," she
corrected. Her jaw clenched when she thought about the issues
with her sister. The idea of traveling was like a puzzle in her
head with the pieces not fitting together. "It's not that easy."

"It's as easy as you make it, honey. You once embraced
adventure—"

"Until I met Aaron…"

"You can't blame him for all the ills in the world."

She lowered her eyes. "No, just the majority of them." Her
love for her ex-husband had been like a stories-high waterfall,
a bass drum booming, a New Year's firework display. She had
never since experienced the same extreme highs and lows, before or after him.

Lucinda set down her fork. "You have to follow your gut instinct. What is it telling you?"

Carla again fought against Myrtle's insistence of her perceptive qualities. "Meeting men from my past would feel... adulterous."

"Heck, not if you look but don't touch. All you're doing is talking to them, and this is for Tom as well as for you. He'll want to be damn sure he's marrying the right person, too. And *I'm* invested in all this. My wedding hat cost a fortune."

Carla couldn't help laughing. "Where would I even start?" she asked, shaking her head.

"Looks like you've been studying the task already." Lucinda nodded toward the journal. "You could follow in your own footsteps. Didn't you go to places that Suzette once visited?"

Carla touched her pendant and didn't know if her heart was pattering from excitement, nerves or sheer terror. "Time moves on. People move on."

"Myrtle said this man is overseas. You've got phone numbers, cards and addresses. Taking a little break before your wedding will give you space and time to reflect..."

Carla toyed with her fork. "I love Tom," she protested. Would she just be running away from one mess and into a different one? There was little she could do at Logical Love until investigations had been carried out.

Lucinda patted the back of her hand. "I know you love him, honey, and my greatest wish is to see you smash our family curse to smithereens. Spending some time away, catching up with a few folks from your past, will stop you worrying if Tom's your ideal match or not. Or else you might end up wondering for the rest of your life...like I did."

Carla eventually agreed that her gran's words made sense. She could take a couple of weeks to revisit her gap year, while the Logical Love system was under review. Two weeks to be *absolutely* sure about Tom, while he was in America. She could argue that it wasn't very long to meet her exes. However, she'd known within days of meeting Aaron that she'd marry him.

Maybe the intuition Myrtle had mentioned was buried deep inside her after all. Carla certainly felt a leap of excitement, a pull, an urge telling her to jump on a plane, that overruled the anxiety nagging in her mind. "I could meet them and ask a list of Logical Love questions…" she suggested.

Lucinda sighed and shook her head. "You need to see how you *feel* about them, not issue a questionnaire. Ask them one important question max and don't encase your emotions in kryptonite. Do you remember one of your mum's favorite sayings? *Act now—*"

"*Think later,*" Carla completed it. She reached out to touch a small, ripped map of Barcelona in the travel journal and re-read her own words at the back. It was like she'd written them in the past as a calling to her future self.

*Adventures…to be continued.*

# Nine

## Gifts

LUCINDA PROMPTLY GOT IN TOUCH WITH BABS, WHO offered Carla a place to stay on the Costa Brava. Before she could change her mind, Carla booked a flight to Barcelona, departing the day after next. With such limited time to find a supposedly significant ex from her past, she'd *have* to rely on her gut instinct. She wanted to disprove Myrtle's predictions as soon as possible so she could walk down the aisle with Tom and *know* he was the man she was supposed to spend the rest of her life with, all while easing her gran's concerns.

When Carla landed in Spain, the sky was powder blue, and the heat felt like the blast of a powerful hairdryer on her skin. She disembarked the plane, took the shuttle bus to the terminal building, picked up her luggage and swiftly exited through security before her worries made her turn back.

On the concrete concourse outside, taxis beeped their horns and long, sleek buses swept past with sunlight bouncing off their windshields. Palm trees swayed in the arid air and tourists wearing bright colors scurried around her like exotic beetles. There was a smell of sunscreen mixed with diesel and coffee.

Lucinda had given Carla three gifts for her journey. A huge yin-yang luggage tag was attached to her suitcase, and a medallion-sized Saint Christopher necklace swung across her collarbone like a pendulum, a supplement to her eye pendant. The third present was from Myrtle, passed on via Lucinda. It felt like a block of soap wrapped in a silk scarf printed with stars and Carla hadn't opened it yet.

Mimi and Evelyn had also issued her with a list of instructions, such as, don't put a mirror in your suitcase in case it cracks and brings you seven years of bad luck, and always sleep with your head in the direction of the door. Against her gran's advice, Carla had also brought a list of Logical Love questions.

She examined a map on her phone, a blue dot moving as she crossed the road to the café where she was supposed to meet Babs. A group of men sat outside, drinking cups of coffee and playing cards and dominos. They sucked on hand-rolled cigarettes, squinting against the smoke that spun into the air. None of them paid Carla any attention, the opposite to her gap year when she'd received several offers to help with her luggage. At the time, she'd been quite offended. Did they really think she couldn't carry her own backpack? But now she felt rather invisible and inconsequential.

She'd thought there might still be an intrepid traveler locked deep inside her, who'd spring to life when she reached foreign climes. But the bravado of Carla's youth had gone AWOL, replaced with a thousand reasons why she should have stayed at home instead. She could be getting her eyebrows freshly waxed and her nails painted peach with white half-moons on the tips. More importantly, she could be untangling the issues with Logical Love's database. Instead, she was outside of Barcelona–El Prat Airport, feeling like someone was beating their fists on her chest.

Carla paced back and forth in the heat, glancing at her watch every few seconds. Her ride from the airport was late—very late—and she wondered if Babs had forgotten about her.

As she paused to roll up her black trousers to her shins, she questioned why she'd worn such a formal outfit to travel in. Her feet had swelled in her laced-up shoes, and her cotton blouse stuck to her back with sweat.

Her phone buzzed as a message arrived from Tom.

Safe travels. Have fun x

She'd called him last night, to tell him she was taking a break in Spain.

"Brilliant. With Jess? Are you sightseeing, shopping or chilling out?" he'd asked.

His encouragement had made her feel even more guilty and Carla was relieved when crackling on the line had broken up their conversation. "Sorry, Tom, I can't hear you." She'd half heartedly stuffed a finger in her ear. "I'll call you when I get there…"

A scarlet open-top car screeched up beside her, making her jump back. A Spanish pop song blared out and a man hung his arm across the passenger seat as if around the shoulder of an invisible girlfriend. He was in his early-to-mid-thirties, wore Ray-Bans and had the slicked-back hairstyle of a fifties crooner. At first glance the car looked expensive, but Carla noticed rust around the wheel arches and how the leather upholstery was taped together in places.

"Carla, yeah?" he shouted while drumming a beat on the steering wheel.

She lifted a hand to shield her eyes from the sun. "Um, yes…"

"I'm not supposed to park here," he barked. "Babs sent me. Jump in."

Carla lugged her suitcase onto the back seat, next to a straw hat and a pair of headphones. She sat on the passenger side, wondering if the man was Babs's son, or even her grandson.

The moment she fastened her seat belt, he roared off, taking the corner like he was in a race. "I'm Fran," he said in a Cockney accent, skimming an eye over her clothes. "Your first time here?"

Carla supposed she did look more like a bank manager than a tourist. "Second." She raised her voice above the music. "Is it that obvious?"

"Nah." He winked. "By tomorrow you'll look like a local."

As they took the highway out of the city, the wind whipped Carla's hair into a bird's nest and she swept it out of her eyes. She craned her neck to see the billboards at the side of the road, advertising tavernas and car hire companies. A good-looking man with folded arms and a megawatt smile advertised newly built apartments. *Find Your Happy Place*, the board said.

During her gap year, Carla had attempted to translate signage in her head, to ease herself into different languages. It was amazing how much you could pick up from them. "Do you live here?" she asked Fran.

"Yeah. I only meant to stay for a few weeks but this place has a way of seducing you, and I've now been here for two years. Babs told me you're here looking for someone..."

Carla put on her sunglasses, which allowed her to open up a little. "I'm trying to trace a few people from my past."

"If anyone can help you, Babs can. She knows every man and his dog. How do you know her?"

"I don't. Not really. She's a friend of the family."

"At least there's some connection. Not like some of the waifs and strays she picks up."

Carla furrowed her brow in confusion but didn't ask questions.

After another half hour on the road, she caught sight of a turreted castle tower and biscuit-hued walls in the distance.

A road sign said Blanca del Mar. A lush green headland rose above the periwinkle sea, and white boats bobbed on the gentle waves. The sun winked and glittered like silver candy wrappers on the surface of the water. Carla was so used to the English drizzle, she'd forgotten the sky could be so blue. The warm air swept over her face, and she could already feel the tip of her nose glowing from the sunshine.

They headed inland, traversing a few winding side streets. Cats slinked along the pathways and lay on walls, catching the sunrays.

Fran's car rattled over cobblestones and they passed a multitude of arched stone doorways. Supermarkets on street corners displayed fruit and vegetables in colorful crates outside and Carla looked up at electrical wires crisscrossing overhead. A pair of running shoes hung from one of the cables. The scenery was so vivid it made her think of the word *clairvoyance*. It had supernatural connotations but translated as *see clearly*. It was like a veil had been lifted from her face.

"Beautiful, ain't it? Worth escaping to," Fran said.

Carla nodded readily.

He eventually pulled up outside a small bar called Babs's Place. It had wooden picnic tables outside and a multitude of blackboards on the walls. *Live Karaoke Most Nights! Your Home Away from Home! Eat, Sleep, Drink and Sing Your Heart Out.*

Carla pursed her lips. This wasn't the quaint little seaside apartment she'd hoped for. In fact, it looked rather dingy.

Fran got out and heaved her suitcase off the back seat. "Come on," he urged. He opened the shiny black front door to the bar and Carla narrowed her eyes as she entered the dimly lit space. There was a smell of beer and a whiff of sweat. As her eyes adjusted to the darkness, she saw even more signs. *Be Quiet When Leaving the Premises* and *No Smoking.*

"Babs!" Fran hollered up the stairs. "Your guest is here."

The woman who descended wore fluffy pink slippers, a cotton nightdress and curlers in her platinum hair, as if she'd just gotten out of bed. She switched on a light and Carla could see how the sun had turned her skin acorn brown. Her cleavage looked like it had been finely pleated.

"Well, just look at you," Babs said, eyeing Carla from head to foot. Her voice had a raspy quality. "Spitting image of your mum, aren't you?"

Carla took a moment to digest this information. She'd assumed Babs was a friend of her gran's, but now that she looked closer, she was younger, most likely in her early sixties. "Did you know Suzette?" she asked.

"'Course I did, petal. Me and Suze were great pals, back in the day. Come on upstairs, let's get you settled in." She nodded at the suitcase, and then jerked her head at Fran, indicating he should carry it.

"What did your last servant die of?" He sighed as he grabbed the handle.

"You don't want to know." Babs cackled. When they reached the top of the stairs, she playfully squeezed his bicep.

"Do you require my services for anything else, milady?" Fran flourished a bow.

"That'll do for now, kind sir." Babs watched him as he disappeared downstairs. "Solid gold," she said and let out a dreamy sigh.

Carla widened her eyes.

"Hey, don't look at me like that. I'm allowed a bit of fun at my age. Not hurting anyone." Babs laughed again. "Some people think he's my son."

Carla blushed.

Babs showed her to a tiny bedroom. "No en suite, I'm afraid. There's a bathroom across the hallway, and the bed's nice and comfy. Come and find me in the front room when you've freshened up."

There were only a few hangers in the wardrobe and no drawers, so Carla left half of her things in her suitcase. She took in the single bed with the tartan sheets and the wonky bedside table. Everything looked clean, but she hadn't stayed anywhere this simple since her gap year. Back then, she'd lodged in the cheapest places possible, sharing a bedroom with other travelers, or, sometimes, even the neighborhood cats. If she and Tom ever spent a weekend away, they chose country houses that sported manicured lawns and served smoked salmon for breakfast.

She cleaned her teeth and unzipped the front pocket of her suitcase to retrieve Myrtle's present. Carla stared at it for a while with a growing sense of dread before unfastening the silk. Inside was a pack of tarot cards with The Magician brandishing a wand on the front. Carla blew out her cheeks and shoved them under her pillow.

Babs's front room looked typically working-class British and parked in the eighties. There was a fringed lamp, patterned rug and lots of teak furniture, making it difficult for Carla to believe she was actually in a Spanish seaside town. Photos everywhere showed Babs grinning with different people while holding a microphone. She noted there weren't any of Fran, or any children, either.

The biggest photo was on the mantelpiece, enlarged, so the image was fuzzy, featuring Babs, Suzette and a handsome guy wearing a white fedora on top of his dark curls. Babs looked much younger in the shot, all long blond hair, cobalt eyes and an orange bikini top the same color as her tan.

Carla picked up the photo and smiled at her mum. She didn't hear Babs entering the room.

"I still miss Suzette." The landlady appeared alongside her. "Suzy Soo, I used to call her. We used to have a good old laugh, always getting up to mischief. We traveled together, lived together, almost like sisters. I bet you really miss her, eh?"

Carla nodded. "All the time." She peered more closely at the picture. "Who's the man in the middle?"

"Handsome, isn't he?" Babs beamed, taking the frame from her. "That's my ex, Diego. Bless him. We split up a few years ago after ages together. He's a doctor and lives not too far from here. A wonderful man. Me and Suzy met him on our travels. When she returned to the UK, I stayed in Spain, and Diego and I fell in love."

Carla could hear the warmth in Babs's voice when she talked about him. "You sound like you're still in love with…" she said, then frowned. The statement had arrived out of nowhere, from deep inside her.

"There's no doubt about it." Babs shrugged a shoulder. "But me and Diego are better off apart than we were together, or that's what we've agreed. And we haven't got any kids, in case you're wondering. Would've been fantastic but I've had plenty of other blessings to keep me busy. I always envied your mum for having that great big family of hers." A wistful expression fell across her face for a moment. "Last thing I knew, you were getting married. Lucinda told me about it in a Christmas card. Must be ten years ago, I reckon."

"It was sixteen years ago, and we split up after four, just after I'd turned thirty."

"Ha. That's ironic. I thought you ran some kind of match-making agency."

Carla felt herself tense up. "I do. My divorce inspired me to set it up."

"I don't believe in those agencies, myself," Babs said, setting the photograph back down. "I wouldn't have met Fran that way."

Carla swallowed. "So, you two are…?"

Babs nodded. "No point sitting around moping after me and Diego split up. I do my thing and I don't want to know what he gets up to, in case I don't like it. While I'm looking for my Mr. Right, I may as well audition a few Mr. Wrongs. And I reckon animal magnetism is all down to pheromones, not filling in some questionnaire. Anyway, that's enough about me. Your gran said you're searching for some fella? Anything I can help you with?"

Carla looked down at her hands. "It's complicated. I'm getting married in three weeks' time, but…" She didn't finish her sentence, noticing she was on the verge of oversharing to a stranger. "I want to catch up with a few people first."

"I *see*. Other men?" Babs smirked with a knowing nod. "Kind of like a *shopping list*?"

"More of a *window*-shopping list, and I'm definitely not going to buy anything."

"Sounds like fun. Count me in." Babs glanced at her watch. "Ooh, is that the time? You'll have to tell me everything later on. I've got to get glammed up for my show."

"Show?" Carla cocked her head.

"Sure. People don't come to my bar to see plain old Babs Smith. They come to see superstar Babs-Lee Johnson. I host a karaoke evening a few times a week. It's how I met Fran. He belts out a mean Frank Sinatra. Are you going to join us this evening?"

In truth, Carla couldn't think of anything worse. She already regretted traveling here, and a night of karaoke might tempt her to pack up her case again. "It sounds great, but I'm tired after traveling."

"No problem. Feel free to make yourself a cheese sandwich. If you're lucky, you might find an onion in the cupboard, too."

Later that evening, Carla smiled when she found the kind-of-shiny orange cheese she loved in the fridge. She changed into a casual black sleeveless dress and sat down on her bed to eat it. A badly sung version of "Sweet Caroline" blasted out from downstairs so loudly her windowpane rattled. There was lots of raucous laughter and shouting and she imagined Babs and Fran singing cheek to cheek.

Carla lay on her front, sucking the end of her pen as she looked through her travel journal once more. She had just two weeks overseas to find the man who was *allegedly* supposed to hold the key to her happiness, which meant she'd only get to spend a few days in each place.

She scanned all the mementos she'd pasted in her journal, and a business card hung at an angle, as if asking to be seen. Although she didn't believe in such omens, Carla reluctantly peeled it away from the page anyway, examining the faded writing.

"Okay, then, you first," she said aloud.

Tomorrow she'd try to find Pedro the hairdresser. Aka Mr. Passionate.

# Ten

## Spider

CARLA FELL ASLEEP TO THE SOUND OF A WOMAN downstairs murdering an Adele song. When she woke the next morning, it was nine thirty and her bedroom seemed suspiciously quiet.

She stared up at a stain on the ceiling. It felt lonely waking up in a single bed without Tom, and she began to wish she'd gone to America instead. The quicker she could trace, meet and discount the men from her past, the sooner she could return home to choose blankets for her wedding reception.

She hoped Tom's hotel wasn't very glamorous, either. A beige hotel bedroom with brown carpets and a hairdryer bolted to the bathroom wall might make him regret leaving her behind. She hadn't yet told him all her reasons for coming to Spain and wasn't sure how much to disclose.

Carla heard the toilet flushing and heavy footsteps on the landing. While she was waiting for the building to fall quiet again, she took the tarot cards out from under her pillow and opened the box. Six of them had yellow sticky notes attached and she separated them out—The King of Cups, The Magician, The Knight of Wands, The Hierophant, Death and The Lovers. If she remembered correctly, they were the ones Myrtle had used in her reading.

Carla liked the illustration of The Knight of Wands the most. A handsome man rode a horse while brandishing a stick. Trying to recall the fortune teller's words, she thought the card might represent someone bold, passionate and charismatic. Could it possibly relate to Pedro? She shook her head at her own gullibility and tossed the cards back onto her bedside table.

Traveling had left her feeling tired and her skin dehydrated, so Carla cleaned her teeth, showered quickly and smeared moisturizer with a high SPF over her face. When she exited the bathroom, she almost collided with Fran on the landing. He wore a very small towel around his waist and nothing else, not leaving much to the imagination. She tried not to stare at the large wolf tattoo spanning his torso.

"Oops, apologies." He grinned, not looking sorry at all. "If you're looking for Babs, she doesn't get up until noon."

Carla shifted her eyes and mumbled "Thanks" as she hurried toward the kitchen.

Babs had left a note propped against the toaster. *Help yourself to anything in the cupboard. There might be some tea bags if you're lucky.* Next to it was a timetable for buses to Barcelona.

Carla folded it up and pushed it into her pocket. She placed the list of Logical Love questions in her handbag and, not wanting to risk seeing Fran half-naked again, she decided to grab some food in the city.

There was a bus stop at the bottom of a hill, a few hundred yards away from Babs's Place, and Carla stood there waiting, watching as Blanca del Mar sprang to life. Waiters bustled around the cafés, sporting black shorts and white shirts as they served up coffee and pastries. Crockery clinked and chatter hummed. The air was already hot and hazy, and she sported her sleeveless black dress again, her toes feeling naked in her sandals.

The bus took her directly into Barcelona and arrived in the late morning. The sight of La Sagrada Familia, with its four main towers fluted like the pipes of a church organ, turned her head. Standing one hundred meters tall, the towers were topped with mosaics that glistened in the sunshine. The unfinished church appeared to be constructed out of stalactites and stalagmites, or even melted candle wax. On closer inspection, Carla could identify thousands of intricate carvings made of sandstone, concrete and granite. There were religious figures, flowers and even a turtle holding up one of the entrance pillars. Building work was ongoing and the church was surrounded by cranes that looked like strange mechanical appendages to the structure.

After getting off the bus at a large square, Plaça de Catalunya, she decided to explore the city on foot. She wanted to do some sightseeing but was also procrastinating before trying to find the first of her old flames.

It was eighty degrees in the city, and the hot air caught the back of her throat. Carla bought a bottle of water and a sandwich from a street vendor on La Rambla, nibbling and drinking as she walked. Groups of tourists gathered on street corners, their necks straining as they gazed up at the glorious Gothic Spanish architecture all around them. Businesspeople rushed to work, while tattooed locals carried or rode their skateboards. She paused to watch a street artist whose hand flew across his paper as he sketched a caricature of a couple who dissolved into giggles at the result. Cafés showed off oversaturated photos of their paella dishes, making the vegetables look Day-Glo fluorescent and the king prawns overly red. Birds sang, cars tooted and Carla overheard many different languages all around her.

Her phone battery was running low—mustn't have charged properly overnight—and she bought a street map to help her negotiate the maze of narrow streets in the Gothic Quarter. She hummed tunelessly to herself, to try to stop questions from whizzing around her head. Would Pedro still be working in the hair salon? Would he remember her? Would she feel a buzz of excitement when she saw him? Her innards became a tight knot and she threw half of her sandwich into a bin.

She soon lost track of her orientation, her route taking her along narrow side streets, past vintage shops selling clothes by the kilo and walls covered in graffiti. The air was cooler here, her surroundings cast in shadow, and goosebumps popped up along her forearms.

Eventually, she arrived at the address on Pedro's business card and looked all around her with a growing sense of unease, not recognizing this place at all.

The hair salons she frequented these days had sleek signage, fresh flowers and marble floor tiles. This one looked grungy with a handwritten price list taped to the window.

Carla smoothed down her dress and paused in the passageway. Her fight-or-flight mechanism kicked in and a voice in her head urged her to run. *Leave now, while you have the chance. You know in your heart that Tom is the man you're supposed to marry.*

A man appeared in the doorway and called out to her. "*Bon dia.* You are looking for a haircut?"

Carla froze on the spot. With only seconds to decide whether to stay or leave, the options flickered in her mind. She gave him a strained smile and eyed him from behind the anonymity of her sunglasses. He wore tight black jeans, a faded T-shirt and a belt with a silver eagle buckle. His hair was streaked black and gray, and silver stubble covered his chin and upper lip. He looked like lots of other men she'd seen around the city and, with no photos of Pedro in her travel journal, she wasn't sure if it was him or not.

"Lady?" he prompted.

It was then Carla spotted something she recognized, a small

spider tattoo on the side of his neck. An image flashed in her head of her brushing her lips across it, and heat rose in her cheeks. Oh god, it *was* him. "Yes, *sí*," she whispered, and her words hung in the air.

"Okay. Good." Pedro's expression didn't change. He swept an arm to indicate she should follow him inside.

Carla's legs were like liquid as she entered the salon. A radio played in the background, Euro disco and two men speaking excitedly in Spanish. Pedro gestured for her to sit down and he draped a towel around her shoulders. When his fingers touched the nape of her neck, a tingle ran down her backbone.

She looked at herself in the mirror and saw the vivacious young girl who'd traveled across Europe had been replaced by a rather tired-looking woman. Why did it always come as a shock to spot gray hairs among the copper, and laugh lines around her mouth?

*Where has your sense of adventure gone?* Jess's voice nagged in her head.

*Well, I'm here now, aren't I?* Carla silently answered it. She mimed snipping a little off the ends of her hair to Pedro.

He washed her hair, his strong fingers expertly massaging her scalp. "Are you on holiday?" he asked in a silky, strong Catalan accent.

"Yes, I'm staying with a friend in Blanca del Mar for a few days." Her jaw hurt from thinking of what else to say. "I think you cut my hair once before. A long time ago…"

"Ah? It is good you came back." Pedro gently towel dried her hair and led her back to her seat.

Carla didn't usually find having a haircut to be a sensuous experience, but there was something about the way he moved around her, his body gently brushing against hers, that made her nerve endings feel alive. "You and I actually went out together a few times," she nervously added. "You knew all the best places to go in the city."

Pedro stopped cutting with his scissors held midair. He looked at her reflection in the mirror, his eyes sweeping over her. "Ah, yes? I think I remember this."

His creased brow told Carla otherwise.

"Your name is…um, it is…" He floundered.

To save them both the embarrassment, she said, "It's Carla."

"*Sí*, of course." Pedro grinned, flashing a ruby set in his molar. "It is very good to see you again." He cut her hair swiftly and the blast of the hairdryer made it difficult to spark up further conversation.

After the haircut, Carla saw Pedro had trimmed her bangs too short, so they only just skimmed her eyebrows, but she smiled and took out forty euros anyway.

He paused as she handed the notes to him, his fingers lingering close to hers. "The haircut is half price if I can take you out this evening," he offered. "We could catch up."

Carla pricked up her ears, a sense of déjà vu washing over her. Had he used this line on her before? It certainly sounded familiar, and the words *take you out* sounded a bit too much like a date. Pedro had never been a big love in her life, so how could he possibly be significant to her future? She wished there could be a neon arrow flashing above his head, so she could know for sure. Her only way to find out was to spend more time with him. "I'd prefer to pay you in full and have the choice."

*Oh no. Did that sound too flirty?*

Pedro threw his head back and laughed. "This is a good deal. We can meet here at six thirty?"

Carla gulped, hesitated and then nodded.

It was easy to occupy a few hours in the city, even when her head was spinning. She made her way to the majestic statue of Christopher Columbus pointing out to sea, flanked by lions and winged women at the base of his plinth, and then toured the surrounding streets.

As the time ticked by, her heart rate gathered pace until she thought it might crack her rib cage. Her stomach felt hollow as she retraced her steps to Pedro's salon.

The hairdresser stood waiting for her, one leg crooked against the wall while he scrolled on his phone. She eyed him for a while, doubting she was his usual type and wondering if he made a habit of inviting his clients out.

Pedro took her to see the geese that lived in the Gothic Quarter cathedral and pointed out Casa Batlló, a building with skull-shaped balconies and a roof with iridescent tiles that reminded Carla of a dragon's scales. They took a taxi to Parc Güell, a pretty park at the top of the city. It featured a giant lizard covered in a patchwork of mosaics, a petal-pink house and spiky black wrought-iron gates, fairy-tale architecture in an urban setting. Benches covered in multicolored tiles curled like snakes, giving a bird's-eye view of the city rooftops and the sea beyond.

They made small talk and meandered along narrow pathways together, until Carla was acutely aware that the chatter and laughter of tourists had fallen away. They entered a shaded walkway where the walls slanted at an angle, giving it an off-kilter feel. Pedro's pace slowed and he moved closer to her as she admired the mosaic discs that decorated the ceiling. She sensed his eyes were upon her rather than the architecture and felt the atmosphere between them shifting.

"This place is stunning," she said, avoiding eye contact with him.

"*Sí*, so are you."

Carla's throat tightened and she stepped away. The area suddenly felt too secluded. "I'm thirsty and I need something to eat."

"Of course. I will take you to a bar that sells the best paella in the city."

When Pedro smiled, Carla saw a glimpse of the young man she'd once been attracted to. She tentatively nodded in response.

Barcelona was vast and Carla didn't know its layout well, plus she *was* dehydrated and ravenously hungry. She strolled with Pedro to a nearby small bar with rickety tables dotted across the pavement. Now that they were out in the open, she found his attention less intense. A family was playing in a nearby park and there were plenty of diners around them.

Pedro drank beer from the bottle while she sipped a glass of Tempranillo. He asked all about her gap-year travels, not giving any hint of remembering the time they'd spent together.

Carla's memories were hazy, too. She'd been on maybe three or four dates with Pedro and they definitely hadn't slept together. Even though she'd found him exotic and worldly-wise, the opposite of boys she'd dated at school, falling into bed with people she hardly knew wasn't her thing.

She showed Pedro a photo of Tom on her phone and told him about their wedding, noticing he was looking at her like a lion circling a wounded antelope. Again.

When he traced his finger across the back of her hand, Carla snatched it to her chest. "I paid in full for my haircut, remember." She laughed uncomfortably, trying to lighten the mood.

"You are here and I am here," he said with a suggestive curl to his lips. "We are attracted to each other."

"I'm engaged."

Pedro shrugged. "We only get one lifetime."

Carla shivered and glanced at her watch. Perhaps she'd nicknamed him Mr. Passionate because of his pushy nature? Surely, he couldn't be the man Myrtle had mentioned. "I should go," she said, starting to stand up from her seat.

"So soon?" Pedro moved his chair closer and she could smell something sweet and smoky on his breath, very different from Tom's citrusy scent. "The night is early. We could go dancing, or back to my place to listen to music. I can show you how to salsa."

Carla felt foolish for coming here, especially without Babs

knowing exactly where she was. She was a long way away from home and longed for the comfort of Tom's sofa. "Sorry, no," she said, more firmly this time.

There was a flare of annoyance in Pedro's eyes and he gripped his beer bottle. "This is why you came to find me, no? You liked me in the past, and now...?"

Carla picked up her handbag and thrust her hand inside it, rummaging around for her purse. Instead, she located her list of Logical Love questions and a pen and pulled them out. She cleared her throat as she glanced over them, feeling Pedro's eyes still boring into her.

"What is the most important thing to you in a relationship?" She read from her piece of paper, meeting Pedro's gaze head-on as she waited for his response.

"Huh?" he said, one of his eyebrows shooting upward. *"What?"*

His confused expression made Carla feel more in control and she ignored her gran's suggestion of asking one question max. Straightening her back, she asked him another. "What do you look for in a partner?"

The hunger in Pedro's eyes fell away, replaced by a touch of fear. "Partner?" he muttered and swigged his beer. "We are only just friends."

"Do you put your own happiness first or your partner's?" Carla continued with her pen poised. "Do you like to please someone through gifts, a show of affection or by doing thoughtful things for them?"

Pedro quickly looked over his shoulder and motioned to the waiter for the bill.

"On a scale of one to ten, how important is trust to you?"

Taking out his wallet, Pedro threw money onto the plate. "Um, you said you wanted to leave."

"I'll need a taxi to take me to the bus station." Carla raised a finger. "I do have another few questions, though..."

Pedro stood up, knocking his leg against the table. "I am feeling tired now," he said, faking a yawn. "It has been a nice night but I want to go home." As they left the bar, he shared a strained look with the waiter.

They crossed the road and he waved for a taxi, directing the driver where to go. After opening the door for Carla, he ushered her inside.

She wound down the window, doubting she'd ever see him again, something she was more than fine with. There was no way he was the man she was seeking. "*Gràcies i adéu*, Pedro."

"*Sí, adéu*, um…" His eyes went blank.

"Carla," she said, winding the window back up. "My name is Carla Carter, soon to be Mrs. Carla Taylor."

The taxi dropped her off at the bus station and she looked all around, trying to find one to take her back to Blanca del Mar. A man wearing a green uniform asked Carla if he could help and pointed her in the right direction. "Your bus is leaving now. You will have to hurry… *Quick*," he added.

Carla sprinted across the concourse, her feet slapping against concrete. She felt her phone jiggling in her pocket and then heard it clatter to the ground. After stumbling in her haste to scoop it up, she just managed to squeeze through the doors of the bus as they swished shut. "*Gracias*," she panted.

The driver mopped his brow, indicating she was lucky to have made it on board.

She nodded, showed him her ticket and slumped down into a seat.

It was dark outside, making the window next to her look like a mirror. The humidity had caused her bangs to retract, so they appeared blunter and shorter—even more outdated, if that was possible. Carla burst into laughter at the absurdity of her situation, because if she didn't laugh, she'd cry. She was a happily engaged woman with a wonderful fiancé and had come here to meet a lothario who'd been a minuscule part of her past, and who'd now given her a terrible haircut. She cursed herself for going to see him again, for coming to Spain at all. What had she ever seen in someone so arrogant and selfish? And he didn't even remember her. Carla took Pedro's business card from her bag and scrunched it in her fist.

Looking down at her phone, she saw its screen had cracked, splitting her reflection in two. "Damn it," she groaned aloud.

She desperately wanted to hear Tom's voice, to convince herself she didn't have to trace any more men from her past, but her spirits fell further when she could only reach his voicemail. "Hey, just checking in with you," she said, a tremble in her voice. "Call me when you get this message."

She opened Tom's Instagram page and saw he'd already posted several photos from his trip. Her fiancé grinned in front of a huge event prop, a two-stories-high game of Monopoly, where the pewter dog and top hat were almost as tall as him. In the other couple of shots, he smiled among a group of people in a bar. One was an attractive blonde woman, all teeth and glossy hair, holding up another prototype of Destination Next.

Carla chewed the inside of her cheek, feeling wounded that her version of the game wasn't the only copy, and she rammed the phone back into her bag.

*You have no right to feel jealous*, she told herself as the bus pulled onto the highway and sped back toward Blanca del Mar. *No right whatsoever.*

# Eleven

## Eyeliner

CARLA COULDN'T HAVE BEEN MORE RELIEVED TO hear noisy chatter and "I Got You Babe" blasting out at midnight from Babs's Place. She stood in the doorway of the bar, looking into the dark crowded scene. Bodies were silhouetted against the sparkles of silver and gold reflected from the revolving mirror ball, and Babs stood onstage beside Fran and a karaoke machine. She wore a black leather corset and tight jeans, and had back-combed her hair into a messy beehive. She and Fran gazed into each other's eyes as if they were actually Sonny and Cher in the sixties. They'd never have matched through Logical Love, but their chemistry crackled.

Their duet was met with whoops and applause and, as a finale, Fran swept Babs back in his arms and nestled his face into her neck.

*Maybe, just maybe*, Carla thought as she clapped, *it suits some people to meet through chance alone.*

Unable to summon the energy to push through the crowd

to reach Babs, Carla trudged upstairs instead. Pedro had left her feeling like she needed a shower when really it was all her own doing.

She splashed her face in the sink and peeled off her clothes, leaving them in a heap on the floor in her room. After climbing into bed, she pulled a pillow over her head and clamped it to her ears while "Bat Out of Hell" made her floorboards jump.

The next day at noon, Carla and Babs sat on high stools at the bar, facing each other with rounded tired shoulders. The area was dark, devoid of the life and lights of last night, and smelled of whisky and air freshener. Fran had gone out to buy strong coffees and pastries to boost their energy levels.

"I overdid the sangria," Babs groaned, rubbing her forehead. "The fruit makes it seem more innocent than it actually is. How did the search for your first fella go?"

Carla echoed her grunt. "I'd score our match twenty-five percent, and subtract five for the hideous haircut he gave me." She pointed to her bangs.

"You do look a bit like Joan of Arc," Babs said. "Never mind. Plenty more turtles in the ocean. Hopefully you'll have more luck with the next guy on your list."

"There isn't going to be a next one." Carla let out the deepest sigh. "Meeting Pedro was a disaster and I've had enough."

Fran arrived back and placed brown paper bags and huge cardboard cups on the bar. "You ladies look like you need sustenance. I know I do."

They nodded at him wearily but gratefully.

He crossed the room and used a screwdriver to lever the front panel off a speaker, displaying more tattoos across his back.

Babs's eyes fixed on him. "I hope you know what you're doing..." she said.

"Don't worry about it. I'm an expert."

Babs rolled her eyes to Carla. Fran's biceps rippled and Babs looked down at her own hands, tracing a finger over her raised blue veins. There was a touch of regret in her eyes, and she suddenly looked all of her sixty-plus years. She tore the corner off a pastry and batted the flakes off the bar with her hand. "I cleaned your room earlier and spotted the tarot cards on your bedside table. Are you interested in those things?" she asked Carla.

"Not really." Carla's coffee was so hot it made her tongue feel fuzzy. "A fortune teller gave them to me. They're supposed to relate to the men I'm going to meet."

"Me and Suzy Soo used to drink cider, look at the tarot and tell each other's fortunes. It was probably a load of rubbish, but a lot of fun," Babs said. She thought for a moment. "You know, she used to tell me that your family believed in some kind of relationship curse..."

Carla nodded and sighed. "Unfortunately, that's true."

"Can I take a look at your cards?" Babs asked. "Someone in the bar told my fortune a few weeks ago, so I might remember some of them."

Carla went to her bedroom to retrieve the pack. She handed them to Babs, who lingered over the ones with the sticky notes attached.

"I'm a bit rusty, so I'm looking at the images to jog my memory. I know that kings are supposed to take charge and that they enjoy the finer things in life. Obviously, The Lovers is all about romance, connection and also temptation." She winked and tapped a different card, The Knight of Wands. "You have to watch out for this hothead. He's fiery with a temper."

"That sounds just like Pedro, the man I met yesterday," Carla said glumly.

"Tsk, don't let one maggot ruin the apple cart." Babs picked up The Magician. "This guy is more positive. He's got lots of energy and drive to make things happen. The Magician casts a spell on people and is a real showman."

Her description was similar to Myrtle's and Carla peered more closely at the illustration of the man wearing a black cloak with his arm raised triumphantly in the air. She knew exactly who it reminded her of.

Adam Angelino had been fun and glamorous. Over the few weeks they'd spent together in Portugal, Carla had gotten hooked on the excitement of dating a minor rock star, the VIP areas at local music festivals, the gorgeous people he knew and the jealous glances she received from other women. She remembered boarding a flight with tears streaming down her face when their relationship had ended.

Picking up her phone, she found his website and showed Babs a few photos of him. Adam was still performing in a band, gigging in hotels along the Algarve. He looked just like she remembered him, all spiky black hair and eyeliner, and the twinkle in his eyes gave her a floaty feeling, like she'd drunk half a bottle of rosé wine on a sunny day. "He must have met thousands of women over the years," she mused aloud. "Pedro's proof that I'm not that memorable."

Babs tutted at her. "Rubbish. You'll never be any younger or more fabulous than you are today. Remember that." She took a closer look at Carla's phone. "This fella looks all starry and bright. A singer, eh? Portugal's only a two-hour flight from here. You could message him now," she urged with mischief in her eyes.

Carla tugged her earlobe with unease. "I don't think so. I haven't managed to speak to Tom properly yet, so he doesn't know the full story of why I'm here. It's probably best to leave things alone, especially after Pedro."

Babs picked up the deck of cards again. "You're only one card down and still have five to go."

Carla looked at the shots of Adam again. She remembered dancing with disco lights bouncing off their dark glasses, and him cartwheeling in the sea with his trousers rolled to his knees.

When she thought about the sweet, special couple of months they'd spent together, a flutter started up in her stomach. Did it make her a bad person for feeling this way, especially while her fiancé was in America? "It's not advisable or wise to meet him again," she said.

"Can you really go home and forget this important man exists? You could message Adam now."

Carla toyed with her pendant and browsed the list of gigs on Adam's website. He was performing in Carvoeiro, a small Portuguese coastal town she'd once visited, the night after next, and Babs's words took root in her head. Could she really abandon her search and forget any of this had happened?

"It's up to you, petal," Babs said.

Carla eventually nodded and she sent Adam a brief message. "There? Happy now?" she asked Babs, setting her phone back down on the bar with a thud.

"I will be if he replies."

They were finishing their coffees when a ping from Carla's phone echoed around the room.

Babs's eyes twinkled. "Is that him? What did he say?"

Carla held up her phone so they could both read the message together.

Hey you. Of course, I remember you. Fun times. When/where would you like to meet (I'm in Portugal)?

Carla held her breath. How about after your gig in Carvoeiro? she replied.

Sounds great to me. See you there. Looking forward to it!

Babs punched the air. "I'd jump on a plane to join you if I didn't have a couple of karaoke evenings lined up." She ran a critical eye over Carla's black dress. "Do you have anything more exciting to wear when you meet him?"

"Not really."

"Well, let's do something about that. You'll want to stand out, not blend in." Babs smiled at her. "I've got a good feeling about this one."

And the problem was, Carla had a good feeling about Adam, too.

After they'd tidied their coffee cups and paper bags away, Babs followed Carla to her bedroom. She bent down and sighed as she rummaged through Carla's suitcase. "Your stuff is smart but has zero pizzazz. I'll fetch some of my outfits, to see if there's anything you like."

A few minutes later, an array of floaty dresses with embroidery and tassels, silk tops with bell sleeves and paisley ankle-skimming skirts covered Carla's bed. "You can keep anything you can fit in your luggage. I used to wear these things onstage and have got loads of them. We should give your makeup a trial run, too, before you meet Adam."

Carla sat in the living room on a chair while Babs brandished a brush and hairspray, trying to make her bangs look less severe. She added flicks of black kohl to Carla's eyes and dabbed red lipstick on her lips. "You'll look like Joan Jett by the time I've finished with you," she said.

"Who's that?" Carla asked from the corner of her mouth. "Please go easy on the eyeliner."

"Sorry, no." Babs laughed.

The TV was playing in the background and Babs occasionally glanced at a property program while she performed Carla's makeover. "I love this show, *Find Your Happy Place*," she said. "Gorgeous people selling gorgeous houses and apartments. Me and Diego used to watch it together and never liked the same ones."

Carla didn't look at the screen, instead staring into space as she wondered why Babs and Diego hadn't worked out as a couple when Babs obviously still adored him. "Have you been separated for a long time?"

"Three years and four months, though we were never married. I didn't see the point in a piece of paper proving we loved each other, but it was a major bone of contention for Diego." Babs brandished a blush brush with intent. "He comes from a big family who all expected us to walk down the aisle and have kids. When I didn't get pregnant, I felt under scrutiny, judged, like I wasn't a proper woman. Diego never made me feel that way, but it was how niggles started in our relationship.

"They got bigger and I kept pushing him away, testing his love for me, I guess. Diego kept assuring me, until one day I pushed him too far." She applied color to Carla's cheeks too vigorously, tears welling in her eyes. "If I've ever felt second best, I did it to myself. He was my only family, and now there's just me."

Carla's heart tugged for her new friend. She moistened her lips, wondering if she was inadvertently pushing Tom away, too. Searching for her exes was like another test or entry requirement for him to join her family, and the longer they were apart, the deeper her search was becoming. The secrecy was like cotton candy on a stick, growing bigger and getting stickier. "Perhaps it's not too late for you both," she said.

Babs gave her a rueful smile. "I've told myself the same thing a thousand times over. Yet, here I am, running my little bar, and Diego's out there saving people's lives. Perhaps we were never a good match after all." She took a moment to gather her thoughts. "Anyway, speaking of family, while I was digging out some clothes for you, I found something that belonged to your mum." She took a folded piece of paper from her pocket and handed it to Carla.

It was yellowing and looked ancient, the writing faded to pale gray. There was a column of dates and names and one of them was underlined a couple of times.

*Agatha.*

Carla said it out loud with surprise in her voice. "Our family curse supposedly originated with someone called Agatha. Maybe mum was researching our ancestry."

"Ooh, spooky. Perhaps I should have left it in my wardrobe," Babs said, chuckling. "Keep it if you like."

Carlie studied it again. "Thanks. It looks like Agatha's fiancé was called Lars and the date next to their names says 1923. There's no surname for either of them." She rubbed her jaw, thinking. "I wonder why Mum was looking into the past..."

"Well, why not?"

"Whenever I asked her anything about her travels, she told me to look forward and not back. She said I should never look to anyone else for my happiness or I'd end up disappointed."

"That sounds like Suzy Soo." Babs smiled. "She always knew where she was going and what she was doing. Not like me. Now please stop rubbing. You'll smudge your makeup."

"Sorreee," Carla said, unaware she'd lifted the saying from Jess. She placed the family tree into her bag.

As she closed her eyes and allowed Babs to apply more shadow, she couldn't help but wonder why her mum had been looking into their family tree and what she'd hoped to uncover. Perhaps Suzette had been hoping to end their family curse, too.

# Twelve

## Roses

"THERE'LL ALWAYS BE A BED FOR YOU HERE, A BASE for your travels," Babs said when she and Carla said goodbye to each other early the next morning. The landlady's eyes were bleary, her lashes still loaded with last night's mascara. "Suzy would want it that way."

Carla hugged her tightly, not really wanting to leave, yet somehow knowing she'd see her new friend again. An idea popped into her mind. "Come to my wedding. Gran would love to hear your stories about my mum. Ask Diego, too."

"Aw, thanks, petal. I wouldn't miss it for the world. I suppose it gives me an excuse to reach out to my ex-fella."

"Just like you're encouraging me to get in touch with mine."

Babs laughed and batted Carla's arm. "Now, don't blame me for any of this."

Fran appeared and put her suitcase in his car. He sat in the driver's seat, turning his music up loud and drumming the steering wheel while Babs and Carla shared their final hug.

The two women waved to each other until they were both out of sight, and Carla rested her head back against her seat. There was a lump in her throat, and anticipation squeezed her chest. She wanted to stay with Babs, to discover more photos and stories, but her time overseas was short.

The sea appeared motionless and was the color of brushed steel. A multitude of blue shades merged with lemon and peach in the sky, the start of a beautiful day. Carla had left home only three days ago but it seemed like much longer. It had already allowed her to jettison one ex from her hit list and to discover her mum had been conducting some kind of family quest. She kicked off her orange wedged sandals and rearranged the leopard-print dress Babs had given her.

"Told you that you'd look like a local in no time." Fran nodded at her. "So, where's your next port of call?"

"Portugal," she said. "I've booked a hotel there for three nights. What's next for you?"

Fran stared straight ahead at the road. "I haven't thought about it much. I'm still having fun with Babs." He cast Carla a brief look. "Unless you want to take me with you to Portugal?"

Carla wasn't sure if he was joking or not. The words *still having fun* sounded temporary and transient, a reminder Fran was passing through Blanca del Mar without putting down any roots. She considered how Babs was busy pursuing the wrong men when the one she really loved, Diego, was there all along. The irony wasn't lost on her.

When they pulled up at the airport, Carla thanked Fran for all his help and swerved his clumsy attempt at a kiss.

She could never understand how a two-hour flight could result in a journey that took more than double that length of time, from all the waiting around, and she touched down at Faro Airport after noon. Reaching Carvoeiro took a further hour by bus and when Carla arrived at her hotel, she found it was spacious and bright compared to Babs's Place.

Tiny halogen lights bounced off the cream marble flooring in the lobby, and tourists strolled past her carrying various inflatables—flamingos, sharks and loungers.

She dumped her suitcase in her room, not bothering to unpack before she headed back outside. She wanted to make the most of her time here and to enjoy her new surroundings.

Carvoeiro was a small fishing village, less deluged by tourists than some of its larger neighbors. An elevated boardwalk took her to Algar Seco, a spectacular set of rock formations the color of pale copper. They'd become pitted through centuries of seawater and winds, giving them the look of a Martian landscape. She remembered the intriguing world of caves, gnarly towers, tunnels and shallow blue pools that she and Adam had explored, two decades earlier. They'd swum in the bay surrounded by large holes in the rocks that acted as windows onto the seascape and horizon. Afterward they'd *ouched* as they'd walked barefoot over the hot, sharp stones and let their skin dry in the sunshine.

Next, Carla made her way into the town, where a cluster of whitewashed Mediterranean buildings perched above a horseshoe-shaped bay of golden sand. Holiday villas sprawled along the hillside, and a galleon swept across the shimmering sea, causing toddlers to point excitedly at the "pirate ship." She could smell coconut and vanilla as couples lovingly rubbed sunscreen onto each other's bodies or lounged around reading the latest bestseller.

Although her surroundings were beautiful, a touch of homesickness made Carla feel listless and alone. She had no one to tell about a kitten she'd spotted asleep on the seat of a moped or to point out mother-of-pearl earrings she loved in a shop window.

She was hungry and thirsty after her flight and took a seat at a beachfront café.

Eating outside in the sunshine could make any food taste like a gourmet meal, and she ordered Diet Coke and an omelet. Feeling conspicuous among all the couples and families around her, Carla messaged Babs to say she'd arrived safely on the Algarve.

Her phone rang while she was still holding it, and her spirits leaped when she saw Tom's name appear on the screen. "Hi there," she said cheerily, running a hand through her hair.

"I can't believe we've got a clear line for once," Tom replied. "Sorry the signal's been terrible out here. Between that, work and the time difference, it's been tricky to keep in touch. It's *so* good to hear your voice."

Carla moved her face to feel the warmth of the sun on her cheeks. "I'm really missing you," she said with a sigh.

"Me, too." Tom voice also sounded rueful. "I'm guessing it's after lunchtime where you are? I'm just waiting for my eggs and bacon to arrive in my room."

"I thought it was all pancakes and black coffee out there. It's midafternoon here," Carla said, smiling at the waiter when he brought her drink. "How's everything going?"

"Absolutely great, I'm having the best time. Though I wish you were here," he added. "Everyone seems to love my work, saying it's *awesome*." He affected an American accent.

"That's because your games *are* brilliant."

"Don't." He laughed. "I'll get all bigheaded and then my top hat won't fit for our wedding. Anyway, what have you been up to? Did you say you're in Barcelona with Jess?"

Carla bit her lip, not quite able to remember the last thing she'd told him. "I actually came here on my own. I've been in Barcelona shopping, sightseeing and staying with Babs, one of my mum's old friends. She owns a little karaoke bar on the Costa Brava."

"*Oh,*" Tom said. "That doesn't sound very cultural or relaxing."

"No, but it's been nice talking to her about Mum. They went traveling around Europe together in their twenties and it's been fun seeing some old photos. Babs gave me a family tree that Mum had been working on."

"Did all your relatives fit onto one piece of paper?" Tom laughed. "Mine would fit on a postage stamp."

"There's a few gaps and question marks, and the tree ends in the 1920s." Carla stirred the ice cubes in her glass with her straw for a few moments. When an image of Pedro and his ruby-capped tooth appeared in her mind, she squirmed in her chair. "I've actually moved on to Portugal now."

"Right." Tom fell quiet as he absorbed this fact. "That was quick. What was wrong with Spain?"

"Nothing at all. I found out someone I know is performing here tomorrow night and I want to check out his gig." She followed her words with a pause, gathering the courage to tell him more about her mission. "He's actually someone I met ages ago, during my gap year..."

"Oh, great, that's a coincidence," Tom interrupted. "The same thing has happened to me, too."

Carla placed down her glass with a thud. "It has?"

"I bumped into someone I went to university with, Sara. We both studied engineering and then worked for the same business for a while. It's been nice to have some company out here."

Questions queued up in Carla's head, such as, was Sara the smiling blonde in his Instagram shots, and *how* close had she and Tom once been? She pictured them laughing over after-work cocktails and tried not to affect a cool tone. "Is she also working at the convention?" she asked, trying to feign indifference.

"Yeah, she's a designer, too, though more on the electronic side of things. I really love her work and she's been singing my praises to all her contacts."

"Fabulous," Carla said, using a word not usually in her vocabulary. Her guilt and jealousy battled for supremacy, and she reminded herself that Tom and Sara had met by accident, whereas she was meeting her exes intentionally. "I need to be honest with you about something," she told him. "That musician I'm going to see, well, we once had a bit of a thing together."

Tom was silent again for a few seconds. "What's his name? Have you told me about him before?"

"It's Adam. We only dated for a couple of months and it wasn't a major love affair or anything." She shook her head, trying to convince herself, too.

"Good, or else I might feel jealous."

A question itched on Carla's tongue and she decided to let it out. "Did you ever date Sara?"

"Ah…" Tom started, followed by a short cough. "Only for a year or so and nothing came of it. We were both too dedicated to our work."

Carla had expected him to say *no*. A cloud drifted in front of the sun, darkening the sky, and she took off her sunglasses. *One whole year?* She'd thought her fiancé was in Denver with a lot of games fanatics, not an ex-girlfriend. "I don't think you've mentioned her before," she said, forcing a smile when the waiter brought her omelet.

"I didn't think it mattered. Do you really want to know about my exes? I've never asked about yours." He didn't give her a chance to answer. "There's nothing to worry about. Sara and I are just good friends."

As Carla assembled her thoughts, readying herself to tell Tom more about Myrtle's prediction and the tarot cards, a woman's muffled voice appeared on the other end of the line.

"Tom, Tom. You've got to come and see this… Oh, whoops, sorry, didn't see you on the phone." Giggling followed.

"Five minutes…" Tom whispered to this other person.

Carla bit the end of her straw, chomping it flat. "Is that Sara? I thought you were waiting for eggs and bacon…"

"I've ordered room service," Tom said. "Sara's shower isn't working properly and I said she could use mine. We're grabbing a quick bite to eat before a meeting this morning. It's an important one for both of us."

Carla's eyes narrowed. "Can't she call the hotel maintenance people?"

"She did, last night, and they're fixing the problem this morning. It made sense for her to use my bathroom and order brunch and, oh…" Tom trailed off, as if only just realizing how things might appear. "You don't think that…? Honestly, Sara's only been here for ten minutes. I've been looking out my window, talking to you."

Carla cut a piece of omelet with her fork and pushed it around her plate.

"You can trust me, one hundred percent," Tom said. "Just like I trust you."

"I know that, but—" Carla's words were interrupted by a knocking noise sounding on the line and Sara's voice again.

"Tom, hun, our food has arrived."

"Sorry, I've got to dash," he told Carla. "Wish me good luck for this morning. Love you."

"Love you, too. I need to tell—"

The phone clicked before she could finish her sentence.

Carla ground her teeth and glared at her phone screen. She quickly checked out Tom's social media again and saw he'd added several photos of him in a bar with colleagues. In a couple of them he stood next to the pretty blonde woman again and had tagged her as Sara Jenkins. The photographer had caught them midconversation, gazing at each other and laughing.

Carla shoveled a piece of omelet into her mouth, hardly bothering to chew it before swallowing.

She should be pleased Tom was doing well in the States, but all she could picture in her mind was Sara in the shower, crooking her finger and asking Tom to pass her the soap. She tried to drink through her flattened straw and made a slurping noise so loud a woman at the adjacent table threw her a stare.

Carla returned it and felt even more lost and confused, as if her parachute had failed and she'd dropped onto a desert island with no sign of habitation.

More people gathered at the tables around her, ordering cocktails, laughing together and talking until the noise seemed to crescendo around her. She stood up and threw too much money on the table to cover her bill.

Leaving her food and drink half-finished, Carla set off back walking to her hotel, feeling very much alone.

# Thirteen

Rocks

CARLA SPENT THE NEXT MORNING TRAIPSING AROUND Carvoeiro town, dropping into boutiques to browse gemstone rings and white linen dresses edged with *broderie anglaise*, with no intention of buying anything. Her conversation with Tom had taken the veneer off her holiday and she ate an ice cream with two chocolate flakes stuck in it without really tasting it or thinking about the fit of her wedding dress. Fortunately, Babs's leopard-skin-print dress she was wearing was comfortably spacious.

In the afternoon, Carla lay around her hotel pool, trying to read a romance novel she'd picked up from the hotel library. Her thoughts were still with Tom rather than the lovelorn couple in the book and she had to keep rereading the pages.

As her day progressed, her worry about her circumstances gave way to irritation. If her fiancé was hanging out in his hotel room with an ex, why should she feel guilty about going to see Adam perform? She hadn't been to a gig in ages and she decided to throw herself into the opportunity.

After quickly eating a pizza around the hotel pool, Carla retreated to her room, where she applied smoky eye makeup and coral lipstick. She wore her hair long and curly and put on one of Babs's flouncy black lace dresses and matching flat pumps, a look Carla might have sported back in her early twenties. She made sure she took her list of Logical Love questions along with her.

Adam was performing at the Conquistador hotel, farther inland. It was a seventies concrete cube of a building, the kind of place that served fries with every meal, including breakfast. A big poster in the lobby featured Adam with a purple-and-green aura, as if he'd been snapped in front of the Northern Lights. He pointed a finger, and his eyes followed Carla around the lobby like the gaze of the *Mona Lisa*. His majestic hair looked exactly the same as it had twenty-one years ago and Carla nervously ran a hand over her own.

There was a hum of excitement as other tourists waited to be admitted to the entertainment lounge. Sundresses showed off peeling pink shoulders and rose tattoos, and when the doors opened, there was a rush for the bar and the best seats. The stage at the far end of the room was already set up for Adam's act, with a microphone and a piano strewn with red silk roses on top of it. Carla's heart thrummed at the thought of seeing her ex again and she bought a glass of sangria packed with ice and pressed it against her hot cheeks.

She took a seat at a round table on her own, but was joined instantly by a group of women on a bachelorette party. The bride-to-be wore a white veil, a very short wedding dress and a plastic ball and chain around her ankle. "Adam, Adam," the group chanted.

When the lights dimmed, whistles rang out and Carla sat bolt upright. Music struck up and then, there he was, holding both arms in the air, the coolest man she'd ever met in her life, Adam Angelino.

A delicious flush enveloped her body and Carla couldn't help smiling to herself, knowing he was going to be meeting *her* afterward.

A couple of hundred women in the audience cheered and sang along as Adam belted out hits by Coldplay, Bruno Mars and Robbie Williams, without delivering any of his own tracks. He still had the same commanding stage presence and rich baritone voice that she remembered. Nothing much else had changed except he was a little thicker around the waist. In fact, Carla thought, his moves, patter and good looks appeared frozen in time.

Adam performed a series of big rock numbers until the lights dimmed and he sashayed to the front of the stage. "*Obrigado.* Thank you, my friends, you're very kind." He wiped his brow with a red satin handkerchief. "This next song is for a long-lost friend of mine, who's joined us this evening. We once shared some very special moments together."

It slowly dawned on Carla that he was talking about her, and a smile stiffened on her lips. Was he really calling her out in public? Her body became so rigid she could only move her eyes.

The first bars of "Purple Rain" rang out, and dry ice billowed onto the stage, instantly transporting Carla back to the first time she'd met the singer.

A few fellow travelers had invited her along to a local music festival where Adam had been performing. He'd asked for an audience member to join him onstage, and Carla and her friends had jumped up and down on the spot with their hands raised. Adam had pointed to Carla and held out his hand, helping to pull her through the crowd and up onstage beside him. Her friends had whistled and catcalled her.

Dry ice had puffed all around them, stinging Carla's eyes and catching in her throat. She'd coughed until tears streamed down her face. Adam had knelt down to serenade her, and all she could do was stuff a fist to her mouth. She'd wished a trapdoor would appear so she could drop down into it and disappear.

He'd stopped his performance midballad and mouthed to her *Are you okay?*

Carla had shaken her head, and when Adam escorted her offstage, his band had played on. She'd felt stares of pity and disgust from the audience piercing into her, and now Carla wanted to flee the room all over again.

When Adam finished singing "Purple Rain," he plucked a handful of roses from the top of the piano and stepped down off the stage. Women waved at him frantically. "Me, choose me," they hollered.

He handed out the flowers, fixing his eyes on various audience members, until he stood in front of her holding out a rose. "Hey, Carla," he said with a warm grin. "Meet you outside at ten thirty."

"See you later," she managed to croak, astonished he'd recognized her after all these years—and underneath so much makeup.

Adam was deluged by a rush for selfies after his show. One woman begged him to autograph her thigh. "I'm going to get his signature tattooed on," she cried out.

Carla kept an eye on her watch, her nerves cantering as their rendezvous time grew closer. She stepped out of the room, sped through the lobby, and paced up and down in front of the hotel. The warm evening, the sangria and the rose made this feel more like a date, something that left her throat feeling tight. *This is a fact-finding mission only*, she reminded herself.

"Carla?" Her name rang out from behind her.

She spun around to see Adam walking toward her, wearing a wide smile. He'd changed into a gray suit and a white T-shirt, with a leather satchel across his body. Now that he'd removed his eyeliner, she could see his face was tanned with friendly crinkles around his eyes. Offstage, his spiky black hair looked too dark and heavy, as if he was wearing a hat made of raven feathers. She recalled he had a badly etched bat tattoo on his shoulder that she'd once thought was the epitome of "cool."

And, oh god, she still found him attractive.

"Hi," she said, tentatively raising a hand in a wave. As Adam grew closer, he looked even more handsome and she swallowed awkwardly.

"Shall we head down toward the beach?" he asked.

"Sure."

They started walking in step.

"Mind if I take this off? I forgot I was wearing it." Adam reached up and pulled his hair so it came away in his hand, revealing his bald head underneath. He stuffed the wig into his satchel. "I sometimes think it's part of me."

"*Oh.*" Carla stopped dead and tried not to stare. "I didn't know..." She narrowed her eyes. "Did you wear that thing while we were dating?"

"I didn't need it then." He laughed.

"You don't need it now."

Adam ran his hand over his head. "My audience might disagree."

"Do you give them the choice?"

"Fair point."

It was like Adam had stripped away a layer to reveal the real person underneath, which made their rapport feel easier and more natural. Adam the fantasy figure was disappearing, replaced by a living, breathing middle-aged guy.

"How did you find me in the audience?" Carla asked.

"I dug out a couple of old photos of us and looked you up online. You run some kind of dating agency in the UK?"

She nodded. "Yes, Logical Love."

"Great name, though surely the two words don't fit together."

"A bit like you and the wig."

They laughed and the years retreated further away.

"You only performed a couple of your own songs onstage," she observed.

Adam let out a sigh. "A major record label signed me, a few months after we split up. I was supposed to be their next big thing, but I didn't score a hit and they dropped me pronto. I felt like a has-been in my midtwenties and didn't have a backup plan. I lost my confidence and didn't perform for a couple of years, until I met someone who helped me back on my feet. We got married, had a daughter and I found an office job selling car insurance."

"That seems like a waste of your talent."

"Thanks. I really appreciate you saying that. Music still called out to me. Everywhere I went, everything I did, there was always a soundtrack playing in my head as if I was in a movie," Adam said. "I played a few gigs in hotels to pay my bills, and I'm still doing it. People on holiday want to hear old favorites, rather than anything I've written. I try to slip in a couple of my own tunes toward the end of the night. By then, they've had so much sangria they'll sing along to anything."

"I could tell which songs were yours. They were packed with emotion and stood out," Carla said truthfully.

Adam patted a hand to his chest. "That means a lot to me. I wrote them for my daughter, Romy. She's sixteen now and is probably a bit embarrassed to see her old dad wearing eyeliner."

"I bet she's proud, really."

He flashed Carla a grateful grin. "Maybe. She's been writing her own music since she was little, so I like to take a bit of credit for that."

Piano music tinkled and candles flickered in the outdoor restaurants along the seafront. There was a smell of grilled fish, and the indigo sky was streaked with violet. Lights in the white houses on the hill made their walls shine ochre, accentuating their rows of tiny windows. Adam waved to several other performers they passed by, and Carla remembered all the fist bumps, high fives, kisses on both cheeks, hugs and phone numbers pushed into his pockets.

"It looks like you're enjoying your life now," she said.

"It took me a long time to find my happy place. My wife left me a few years ago and it's been especially tough on Romy. I had to rely on babysitters and friends to look after her so I could perform. Things are getting easier now that she's older.

"I still live by twilight, working while others enjoy themselves, and I sleep when they're waking up. It's not an ideal career for maintaining relationships, unless you're with someone else in the business. Are you single or married?" he asked.

"I'm divorced and about to marry again, in less than three weeks' time."

"Oh, congrats. Good luck with that. I hope things work out. It's a shame I didn't have a crystal ball before I walked down the aisle. I wonder if I'd do things the same way again."

Carla smiled to herself at his turn of phrase. "Well, actually, I did have one." She began telling him about her visit to Myrtle and how she was tracing her past exes.

"So, you have the chance to make sure your future's going to be rosy?" Adam remarked. "That's amazing. I wish I'd had that. Tell me more about your business, too."

She liked his positive spin on things and they chatted more as they walked. They sat down on a bench together, splaying their hands so their fingers almost touched. It was difficult to deny her growing sense of connection with him, her old emotions creeping back.

More pieces of the past slotted in place for Carla, like riding on the back of Adam's motorcycle along the coastline at midnight, gazing up at the stars and kissing on the beach to the sound of the ocean waves.

"I loved your spontaneity," Adam said, smiling at her with a twinkle in his eyes. "You used to meet me after my gigs and we'd make out in hotel corridors. Do you remember we first met because you jumped up onstage and grabbed my mic, demanding we duet together? You choked on the dry ice."

Carla's mouth flattened and she frowned at him. "It didn't happen like that. You picked me out of the audience and invited me to join you."

Adam shook his head. "No. I'd spotted you, we made eye contact, and your friends egged you on to climb up onstage. I worried you might trip over the wires. You had a coughing fit and I had to carry on singing, hoping you were okay. Security guards escorted you off the stage."

"You led me off. You were really kind." Carla stared at Adam, wondering which one of them was right. She wished they had a video recording, to replay the moment. How could two people remember something so differently?

"I wanted you to meet my family and you refused," Adam remembered, breaking eye contact.

"Me?" Carla exclaimed. "I'd have loved that."

"You found every excuse under the sun not to go. I had to constantly assure you that I loved you and wanted to take things further…"

"Our relationship was never that serious. We had lots of fun." She crumpled her brow, her own memories confusing her. "I also remember crying on the plane when I left Portugal."

"I was in tears, too." Adam's frown lines grew deeper. "You know what? I can't actually remember why we split up."

Carla twisted her lips. "Me, neither." She wondered what other things from her past she might have rewritten or forgotten. Perhaps one of the men she'd previously dated *had* been more significant than she'd initially thought. "Whatever happened, I'm sorry. I really liked you."

"Me, too." He placed his hand on top of hers in a friendly, haphazard way. "I think we had something good together. Call it a premonition, but I knew we'd see each other again one day. I always wondered, what if?"

Carla let out a laugh. "You'd feel right at home with my family. They believe in things like that, too." She paused, flicking a glance at Adam, finding it impossible to rule him in or out as "the one" from her gap year who was waiting for her.

Adam glanced down at her engagement ring. "Your fiancé must be a good guy if he supports you being here."

Carla coughed, though she didn't need to. "Tom doesn't really know the full reason…"

"Ah, that's not so great."

She worked her tongue around her teeth. "Yeah, I know."

Adam insisted on walking her back to her hotel, where they stood beneath a tree. The heat of the night made Carla feel a little breathless.

"Shall we grab a drink together?" Adam suggested. "We can carry on catching up."

Carla closed her eyes for a moment. She'd love to talk to him into the early hours like she used to. It would be so easy to sit in a dimly lit bar with him, the glow of candles lighting their faces. "Maybe another time?" she said, fighting the temptation.

"Do you mean in a different time, and a different place?"

She nodded slightly, still not able to accept Myrtle's predictions as being possibly true. "I think so."

"I understand. Tom's a lucky guy." Adam laughed in spite of himself. "The spontaneous old me wouldn't have cared about that and asked to kiss you."

"The spontaneous old me might have let you."

"It's probably good we're both older and wiser."

With some reluctance, Carla nodded.

Before she left, she thought of one Logical Love question to ask him. "If you could relive one moment in time, what would it be?"

Adam didn't hesitate. "When Romy was born. I wanted to look after her forever. I knew I'd give up my life for her and nothing has ever compared to that," he said. "What would you choose?"

Carla ran through numerous occasions in her head. She hadn't experienced anything as monumental as the birth of a child, and she didn't want to think about her first wedding. When she recalled any big events in her life, her mum's funeral came to mind. "There are so many options," she said with a small shrug.

"That's a good thing. I'm glad we had the chance to meet up, and I hope you find what you're looking for." Adam paused. "I'm free tomorrow afternoon, if you'd like to meet for coffee, no strings attached. Just two friends enjoying each other's company again." He pressed his fingers to his lips and blew a kiss from his fingertips.

It was a little cheesy and something he used to do at the end of his stage act when they were dating. Carla would catch the kiss and hold it in her hands. This time she didn't.

"Please think about it." Adam walked backward, holding her gaze, and they smiled a little goofily at each other until he gave her a final wave and vanished around a corner.

Carla stood for a while with her arms wrapped around her body in a hug. She and Adam still had a spark, but their meeting had been more about gaining some kind of closure for the past rather than reigniting something for the future.

So, surely, she could discount him from her search for her significant ex.

Couldn't she?

# Fourteen

Wool

CARLA SWAM LAP AFTER LAP IN HER HOTEL POOL THE next morning, all her senses tingling. The water was cold and sharp against her skin, and the smell of the chlorine was tangy. Seeing Adam again had left her feeling more alive, more special. For the first time in ages, she didn't just feel like someone's organized boss, or annoying sister, or reliable fiancée.

However, there was no way she was going to cancel her wedding for the sake of a couple of hours spent with an ex. Adam was right that she should be more honest with Tom about the extent of Myrtle's prediction. But the longer Carla was away from her fiancé, the more she was beginning to believe there might be some truth to Myrtle's words. She kept thinking about her mum and why she'd been delving into their family history.

Carla climbed out of the water and pulled on her beach dress, not caring if her hair would dry and frizz in the sunshine. The freckles that had appeared on her shoulders looked like scattered sand. She gathered all her things together and took a seat at the poolside café, where she ordered a coffee and egg on toast. A few late-night revelers lay sprawled on sun loungers around her, and many vacationers hadn't yet made it out of bed. Her phone pinged and she read a message from Adam.

Morning! It was great seeing you last night. Want to meet for coffee at 2?

Carla knitted a hand into her hair, not sure what to do. She had only one day and night left in Portugal and did she really want to tempt fate by seeing Adam again?

She was still considering her response when her phone vibrated with an incoming Facetime call. She smiled when she saw Gran's name on the screen, looking forward to giving her an update on her travels. Instead, she found Lucinda was accompanied by Jess, Mimi and Evelyn. They sat in a line, making Carla feel like she was auditioning for a talent show.

She carried her phone and belongings up to her room, making small talk as she went.

Mimi looked resplendent in a bouffant gray wig topped with pearls and feathers, and her cobalt satin dress pushed up her bosom as she fluttered a face fan. Carla observed that she'd adhered several beauty spots to her face and cleavage. "*Bonjour,* Carla," she said.

Carla peered more closely at her phone screen. "Are you going to a fancy-dress party, Aunt Mimi?"

"*Non, ma cherie.* I've scooped the lead role in a new theater production, playing Marie Antoinette. The director says I'm a complete natural and can hardly believe I'm not a French royal. I've been living and breathing everything *française.*"

In comparison to Mimi, Jess looked like she was attending a business meeting, dressed in a white blouse with her russet curls tied back so tightly it pulled her eyebrows up her forehead. Her lips were thin and tight, as if she'd been forced onto the call, and Carla sensed there was still a fault line running between her and her sister. She didn't know how to thaw the ice.

She opened her mouth, about to tell her gran, aunts and sister about the family tree Babs had given her, when a small man with a horseshoe of wiry black hair appeared beside them on the screen.

He wore a woolen sweater with red poppies and sheep on the front and held a plate piled high with slices of Victoria sponge. He handed out the cake and napkins to the others and took a seat next to Evelyn.

"Carla, this is Bertrand," Evelyn said, peeping through her eyelashes at him.

Bertrand pretended to tug the peak of an invisible hat. "It's a pleasure to meet you, Carla. I promise I'm taking very good care of your aunt. She's very special to me."

Evelyn's face flushed to her hairline, and a smile lit up her face.

Carla had never seen her aunt look so happy. "I'm really pleased to hear it," she said. "How did you two meet?"

"We both reached for the same knitting pattern book in the library and Evelyn insisted that I should read it first." Bertrand chuckled. "My friends had been teasing me about my newfound hobby, but Evelyn agrees there's something about the clack of knitting needles that's ever so soothing. I invited her for coffee and scones and we've been sharing knitting patterns ever since."

They exchanged a coy, lingering look.

Mimi pressed her hands together into a prayer. "Love is truly in the air." She paused for dramatic effect. "Because Jess has also found someone special."

"*Mimi.*" Jess shot a look of horror at her aunt. "I've been on a couple of dates, that's all."

Carla angled her head in surprise. It hadn't been long since they'd run Jess's details through the Logical Love database, so her sister must have moved quickly. "You have?" she asked, speaking directly to Jess. "Did you match with someone through work?"

Jess bristled and she rearranged her ponytail. "I've been for a few drinks with Mr. Forty-Nine Percent."

"I thought he was now sixty-two percent?"

"It doesn't have the same ring and it's not like we're serious or anything."

"Some things need space to flourish," Evelyn said, giving Bertrand's arm a squeeze. "I'd advise you to carve your initials into a pink candle. Add a little rose oil before burning it at midnight while chanting the name of the person you desire. It really worked for me."

Bertrand's face flooded with color and Jess broke into an embarrassed cough.

Mimi gave Jess's knee a nudge, obviously relishing her self-appointed role as the family oracle. "You simply must share your other news with us, too."

*"No way,"* Jess said under her breath.

"Don't hide your light under a bushel. You should *own* your successes, like I do. You can't expect anyone else to congratulate you, if you don't do it yourself."

Jess shifted her eyes away from the camera, focusing on her lap instead. "I've been offered a new job."

"Customer services *director*, no less," Mimi chimed in, breaking into a solo round of applause. "It's simply fabulous. *And* there's a fountain in the courtyard of the building, so Jess will be working near water. Everything Myrtle predicted is coming true."

Jess's words sounded in Carla's head like the peal of church bells. Had things really been so bad that her sister wanted to leave Logical Love? She hated the frostiness between them and made a clumsy attempt to clap, too. "Brilliant, well-done, Jess," she said through gritted teeth. "That's great news."

"I haven't accepted the job yet," Jess reassured her. "I'm talking it over with someone tonight."

"Mr. Forty-Nine Percent." Mimi nodded knowingly. "We'll have to stop calling him that if things progress."

Jess puckered her mouth and exhaled.

Carla noticed that her gran had remained uncharacteristically quiet throughout the whole conversation. Lucinda's cheeks had a gray tinge rather than their usual rounded rosiness, and her upholstered curves looked like some stuffing had been removed. She plucked at the sleeves of her cardigan.

"How are you, Gran?" she asked hesitantly.

"Lucinda's been a bit peaky," Mimi chipped in.

"I don't need a spokesperson, thank you very much." Lucinda let out a huff and found a weary smile for Carla. "I'm fine, honey, just old age catching up with me a bit. Comes to us all, I suppose."

Carla thought about the letter she'd seen with the hospital logo on top. "Are you sure it's nothing more serious? Maybe you should see a doctor…"

Her gran shook her head. "I've just got a touch of the melancholies, so don't you fuss. I'll be back on my feet in no time. We want to hear about *your* travels, not about me. Where have you been so far?"

Carla gave her relatives a few details about her visits to Blanca del Mar, Barcelona and Carvoeiro, leaving out the finer details about meeting up with Adam and Pedro.

*"Passionnante."* Mimi grinned. "Where to next?"

Carla asked herself the same thing. Logistically it made sense to visit Daniel, if he was still in Majorca. "Maybe the Balearic Islands," she mused.

At the end of the call, Mimi blew her a kiss as Lucinda, Evelyn and Bertrand waved goodbye. Jess stood up, tossing her head before walking off-screen.

Carla studied her travel journal, tracing her finger across a map of Europe. She wondered if Daniel still wore his blond hair in matted dreadlocks, and chunky beads around his neck and wrists. She remembered him as a gentle soul who'd sat cross-legged on a rock to sketch the sunset.

She'd lived with him and a bunch of other travelers in a ramshackle, derelict house on a patch of wasteland, where he was their natural leader. Their commune had been a supportive tribe who ate beans from the can while sitting around a fire on the ground where the kitchen used to be. She could still feel the heat on her face and could picture orange embers floating into the night through a huge hole in the roof.

They'd washed with either a watering can or a trough in the yard, though sometimes Carla cheated by using the shower cubicles on the beach. She pulled a face, recalling the bucket in the yard they'd used as a toilet and how she'd used her skirt to gather up eggs the chickens had laid.

What had started off as a camping adventure had soon left Carla longing for a comfy mattress and pillow, not a blanket on the floor. Itchy tick bites all over her ankles had spurred her to decamp to a nearby hostel instead. Daniel had called her a *princess* and they hadn't parted on the best of terms. Even so, she remembered their time together fondly and wondered if he'd ever thought about her, too, over the years.

She looked him up on the internet and read how he'd made a fortune by setting up a solar panel business. He owned an eco-house in London and had built his own sustainable mansion in the Majorcan hills, complete with five toilets and showers that used harvested rainwater.

The profile photo on his Facebook page showed Daniel's hair had paled to gray and was now cropped short. Carla was pleased to see he still had a touch of determination in his kind green eyes, like he wanted to change the world.

His most recent post showed him holding an eco-award aloft and she glanced at the comments beneath it.

The first one said, RIP. Sleep tight, Dan.

*"What?"* Carla gasped aloud and scrolled on.

What followed was a stream of messages from Daniel's friends and family, sharing their condolences, goodbyes and memories. Carla pieced together that he'd died of a major stroke at forty-three while taking part in a climate-change protest. He'd left behind a wife and two children, aged four and eight.

Carla clamped a hand to her mouth and screwed her eyes shut, taking several minutes to try to digest this information. She imagined Daniel's children at his funeral, gripping their mother's hands, just like she and Jess had grasped Lucinda's at Suzette's funeral.

The thing she remembered most about her mum's funeral was one of her gran's sayings. *Touch a button if you ever see a hearse. It connects you to the living and stops it collecting you next.*

Even though Carla knew it couldn't be true, she'd clutched a silver button on her coat so tightly it fell off and rolled into the road. It lay there like a shiny eye looking up at the gray sky, until a car ran over it, squashing it flat. She remembered how her relatives had paced around the streets several times after the service so spirits couldn't follow them home.

It seemed a bit glib to express how sorry she was by adding words to Daniel's Facebook page, so she was glad to discover his family had set up an online memory book.

Carla took a few photos of Daniel from her travel journal and uploaded them to the site. While she thought about what to write, she bit the skin at the side of her thumbnail.

We didn't know each other long, but you left a lasting impression on me and the world. You helped me to be resourceful and resilient and I wish there were more people like you around. Thanks for some lovely memories.
Love, Carla

Despite having just eaten, she felt suddenly empty and bereft. A thought crossed her mind and she picked up her pack of tarot, plucking out the Death card. The hooded skeleton holding a staff made her shiver. Could Myrtle really have foreseen Daniel's passing?

Carla spread the cards out on her bed, examining all the pictures. The Death card undoubtedly represented Daniel, and Adam was most likely The Magician. Pedro must be The Knight of Wands, which left her with three cards unaccounted for. She ran her fingers across her chin, not sure where to go next or who she should try to meet.

Glancing at her watch, Carla saw it was 2:45 p.m. *Damn it*, she hadn't replied to Adam's message, and her decision whether to meet him or not had been taken out of her hands. She could see from his gig list that he was performing elsewhere that evening, so she wouldn't get to see him again before she left Portugal. She sent him a brief text to apologize and to explain she'd been busy.

Carla noticed she'd placed her damp towel on the bed, and water had bloomed across the corner of the family tree, making the paper translucent. She tutted at herself, gently picked it up and tried to blot it with a tissue. The paper was now so fragile that she placed it inside her travel journal for safekeeping and to allow it to dry flat. As she stroked it with her hand, she noticed some very faint lettering had appeared next to Lars's name. She couldn't be totally sure because of the sloping handwriting, but it looked like his surname was *Aakster*.

Carla promptly looked it up online, discovering it was based on the old Dutch word *ekster*, which meant "magpie."

She immediately thought about the birds strutting along Silverpool pier and she scratched the back of her neck. Could they have been some kind of omen or sign, connecting Myrtle's prediction to the family tree, or was she just being silly?

Carla usually relied on maps, flight times and logistics to in-

form her where to travel next, but she couldn't ignore a sensation deep inside her telling her to go to Holland.

Perhaps her journey to trace a mystery man from her past
was also about finding out the origins of her family curse, just
as she now sensed her own mother had been trying to do.

Without any further consideration, Carla traced one of her
exes, Ruben, to the University of Amsterdam and sent him a
quick email, asking if he'd like to become reacquainted.

# Fifteen

## Pancakes

CARLA GROWLED WHEN SHE SAW HER FLIGHT TO Amsterdam had been delayed by several hours. Her body sagged and she patrolled the shops and duty-free at the airport, spraying perfumes she wasn't interested in and browsing the extortionately priced chocolate. If this had happened while she and Tom were traveling, they'd have checked into an executive lounge where they could read posh magazines and eat freshly made guacamole and tortilla chips. It was a stark contrast to her gap year, when she'd curled up on airport floors to sleep, using her sweater as a pillow and hugging her backpack in case anyone tried to steal it.

As a middle measure, she bought coffee and a grilled cheese, and perched on the end of a hard-plastic chair until both food and drink cooled to a consumable temperature. She watched fellow disgruntled passengers huffing and milling around her.

She messaged Ruben to say she'd be late arriving in the city and he replied with a text that made her wilt further.

That is understandable. I will adjust our itinerary accordingly,
dear Carla.

A flash of copper-colored hair caught her eye and she watched
as a girl wearing hiking boots and a yellow dress strolled past
her. Something fell from her backpack, a soft toy, but she didn't
notice and carried on walking. Carla jumped to her feet, leaving her coffee and sandwich on her seat as she picked up the
limp fabric rabbit. She hurried after the girl and touched her
shoulder. "Hey, you dropped this."

The girl spun around and they faced each other. At first,
Carla thought she was looking at her own reflection. The girl
had similar hair and a Roman nose, except she was twenty years
younger. Carla could see their resemblance, but she doubted the
girl would notice it. She'd probably only see a random mature
woman who'd picked up her toy.

"Oh, cheers. I didn't hear him drop." The girl kissed the rabbit and stuffed it into her pocket. "He tries to escape from me
now and again." She smiled, turned and walked away.

Carla's eyes trailed after her, thinking about her own youth
and how easily life had since slipped from one year to another,
one decade to the next, gathering pace until it felt like a blur.
She wanted to shout after the girl, *Have fun, be adventurous and
don't get boxed in.*

Instead, she sat down on the departure lounge floor, on top
of her sweater, and ate her grilled cheese.

Carla had forgotten how pretty Amsterdam was, and her
old photos didn't do it justice. Tidbits about the city's architec-
tural history started to come back to her—most of which she'd
learned from Ruben. She recalled that the merchant's houses
built along the side of the canals were called *grachtenpand*. They
were tall and slender to avoid high taxes in Medieval times,
and their bricks were the color of cocoa, terra-cotta and white

chocolate. Their gabled roofs were shaped like bells and funnels, or stepped like staircases to historically signify warehousing and trade.

Many had been converted to houses over the years and Carla's Airbnb took up the entire second floor of a mahogany building with neat white mullioned windows stacked on top of each other. She dropped her luggage there, then set off across the city on foot to meet Ruben.

It was one of those perfect late afternoons, sunny but not too hot, people out and about but not on top of each other. There was a sound of fountains sprinkling and boats chugging along the canals.

During her gap year, Carla's main focus had been locating good-looking people in the city who knew the best bars and hostels. Now that she was older, she appreciated all the bicycles, the green spaces and tulips, even though she felt a bit motion sick after her flight.

She walked past a woman juggling bean bags and spotted a little bistro that reminded her of the place she and Tom had enjoyed their first date. After connecting through Logical Love, they'd shared texts and a couple of calls, so they already knew a lot about each other before they met.

They'd both ordered ham served with a fried egg and shared a portion of battered onion rings. They'd agreed that chunky chips tasted better than skinny fries.

Their mutual joys had included getting more than one question right on *Jeopardy*, playing Monopoly (though they both got bored if the game lasted more than one hour), cafés that served breakfast all day and feeding ducks in the park, even if the weather was drizzly. Neither of them could stomach watching horror films and preferred cheesy action movies instead. They'd agreed on the futility of superstitions and would both happily wander under a ladder, unless someone was standing at the top of it.

After they'd left the bistro together, Tom had opened the taxi door for her and placed the belt of her coat across her lap so it didn't dangle in the rain. This thoughtful act and their high match statistics had made Carla think she could possibly fall in love with him.

She hadn't witnessed the side of her fiancé that saw him jump on a plane to America at a moment's notice, or drink with strangers and an ex-girlfriend in late-night bars. If she was honest, she wasn't sure she liked it. Similarly, Tom had never encountered Carla the Adventurous Traveler, someone she herself hadn't known still existed.

And now they were in separate cities, on opposite sides of the world. Did inviting another woman to use his bathroom show that Tom was kind, naive or foolish? She was sure she could trust him, but what about Sara?

What about *herself*?

Carla watched bicycles whizzing around her and paused to read a plaque that said bikes outnumbered cars in the city by four to one. Eighty percent of Amsterdammers owned a bike, traversing the towpaths of the one hundred and sixty-five canals. During her gap year, she'd developed muscles in her legs from cycling that she hadn't known existed, and her skin had turned nutmeg brown in the sun.

She turned a corner and saw Ruben standing on a bridge waiting for her. He was as lean and angular as she remembered him, reminding her of a wooden toy soldier hanging on a Christmas tree. He now wore round wire glasses that made him look even more intellectual.

When they'd dated, he'd been studying for a master's degree in sociology, which she'd found clever and sophisticated. He was a few years older than her and had engaged Carla in highbrow discussions on gender, sustainability and diversity. They'd watched so many foreign films together that she'd started to see subtitles when they talked.

She'd loved how Ruben squinted one eye and wrinkled his nose, deep in thought, while he considered her views, making her feel like her opinions were valid and interesting. He'd dissect and analyze her discussion points, challenging her to question her own thoughts. Carla wasn't quite sure if she ever fancied him physically, but his mind had made her stomach flip.

When he spotted her approaching the bridge, Ruben raised a finger in the air, as if he was in class. "*Hoi*, Carla. It is very good to see you." His long limbs moved mechanically toward her, and he pecked her on alternate cheeks three times in a row. "You are looking super healthy. I am delivering lectures tomorrow, so we should utilize our time together prudently. Remember how we once took a bike ride around Amsterdam and I taught you the trading history of the city?"

"Um..." Carla frowned, struggling to recall this.

"You found it most fascinating, so I thought you'd appreciate an updated version." He set off walking and she had to skip a little to keep up with his stride.

"How long will it take?" she asked, now jogging to catch up with him. "Should we get a coffee together first, to catch up?"

"Perhaps two or three hours. I do not want you to miss out on anything, my dear Carla. I know you are a voracious learner."

She couldn't tell if his smile that followed was a bit patronizing or not. When Ruben slowed his pace a little, she was reintroduced to his habit of touching her elbow to steer her in the direction he wanted to go in.

"Do you remember how we spent hours in the Rijksmuseum?" Ruben asked her as they walked. "Do you remember we were asked to leave the Van Gogh Museum because we did not know the closing time? It was very amusing." His guttural use of the letter *g* sounded like he was gargling, and he said *hoor* rather than *um* to punctuate his sentences.

She was flattered he remembered their time together in such

detail. Either his memory was sharper than hers, or their relationship had meant more to him.

"Do you remember the time you rode too close to the edge
of the canal and almost fell in? You never did have a good sense
of balance. Did you have a good journey? Was the airport busy?"
Ruben listed so many more things they'd shared, and fired off
so many questions, it was like he'd written an encyclopedia
about their time together and studied it before meeting her.
Carla was left opening and shutting her mouth as she tried to
keep up with his words. It was easier to nod and pretend she
remembered everything, too.

"First of all, our bicycle ride," Ruben announced, pointing
to a line of bikes. "Let us begin."

They rode through the streets together for an hour or more,
passing many arched bridges and brightly hued houseboats.
She'd forgotten how the city had a deep, rich mud aroma from
the canals and she kept getting a whiff of the cannabis on offer
in the legalized coffee shops.

"This is wonderful, isn't it?" Ruben called to her over his
shoulder. "It is like we have never been apart."

"Yes, it is," she panted, struggling to keep up as she wiped
sweat from her brow.

He pointed out street art and hidden churches and skirted
the edge of the infamous red-light district, explaining how the
city had thrived in the seventeenth century from its trading of
fish, wood, corn, grapes and spices.

It was fascinating for sure, but Carla's stomach started to
cramp, and her leg tendons felt stretched to snapping point.

Ruben indicated they should park their bikes at the end of
a pretty, red-brick bridge and he took out his phone. He di-
rected her with precise instructions on where to stand. "A little
left, *hoor*, a little right. Is that okay? Please move back a little."

Carla smiled until her jaw ached. When he suggested they ask a passerby to take shots of them both together, she'd finally had enough. She looked around her and pointed to a cute café over his shoulder. "That place looks pretty. Shall we get that coffee?"

Ruben frowned and looked at his watch. "We are only one third of the way through our tour."

"It's easier to talk when we're not moving," Carla gently assured him. "I came here to see you, not the scenery."

Her compliment brought a smile to his lips. "Yes, of course you are right. We shall do whatever you like."

They found a table and he pulled out her chair for her, just like he always had. Carla used to find it thoughtful and attentive. Now it felt a bit odd and performative.

Ruben perused the menu. "I will have the *bruine bonensoep,* a brown bean soup. Shall I order for both of us?"

Carla tried not blow out her cheeks. Had she actually let him order her food in the past? "I'm craving something sweet, so would prefer pancakes."

"I assure you the soup will taste very delicious and is a good source of protein."

Carla tried not to feel irritated and caught a waitress's eye. "May I order pancakes and a latte, please?"

The waitress smiled and tapped out their orders on her keypad.

Ruben's left cheek twitched and he sat back in his chair. "Have you thought about me often over the years, as I have done with you? I shall tell you more about my endeavors and then I can learn more about you." He cleared his throat and spoke as if reading his CV aloud. "After we parted, I completed my master's degree and then progressed to undertake a PhD on the confines of selfhood. I am now the director of Sociology at one of the best institutes in Europe that ranks in the top one hundred globally. I was once engaged to a fellow academic. However, we found our research was more important than our relationship. I am still a bachelor," he said, holding Carla's gaze to emphasize his last point.

"That's very…impressive," Carla replied, unsure if he was boasting or just stating facts. "I personally graduated from the University of Life with a first-class honors degree."

He stared at her for a moment, her words seeming to mangle his computer of a brain. "Perhaps this is a joke?" He forced an unnatural short laugh. "Yes, I think it must be."

Carla wondered if anyone ever teased him, or if he had a sense of humor at all. "Yes, it was a joke. I didn't go back to university after my travels."

"That is a great shame. I am sorry to hear this," Ruben said solemnly, as if she'd just announced someone had died.

Carla left out a nervous chuckle. "Don't be sorry. I learned more from setting up my own business than anything I could have learned at college."

"What does your business entail?"

She sat up straight and proud. "I help cautious people find love, using a set of unique questions and algorithms."

Ruben steepled his fingers together, his eyebrows knitting as he tried to work out if this was another joke or not. "A scientific endeavor to capitalize on emotion and the need for human contact, and monetarizing it? This is most interesting. It sounds like you took influence from Maslow's hierarchy of needs." He nodded, prompting her to enter into a debate with him.

In the past, Carla would have tried to answer in a way that might impress him, welcoming a linguistic version of tennis. She'd once been in awe of this knowledgeable older man, but their age gap no longer seemed that alluring. "The idea originated from my terrible divorce," she said flatly. "I wanted to help other people find a better match than mine."

"And surely also from the 1943 'Theory of Human Motivation,' no? Humans may think they are looking for a partner, but really their needs are Maslow's third, fourth and fifth levels of love, esteem and self-actualization. Don't you think your clients need to look inward as well as outward?"

Carla considered his question. Was she herself looking outward, physically trying to find a man from her past, when she should be exploring her own intuition more? Her hunger made it a theory too deep to contemplate in a café and she was glad when the waitress set down their plates and coffees. Carla leaned over and inhaled the smell of the pancakes. "Gosh, these look fantastic. I could eat a horse," she said.

Ruben gaped at her, as if he'd suddenly found he was dining with a stranger. He adjusted the angle of his knife, fork and spoon so they were perfectly aligned, and draped a napkin across his lap. "Perhaps I have overwhelmed you with information?" he asked quietly.

"Not at all." Carla ate a piece of pancake and closed her eyes at its heavenly taste. "Your curious and searching mind might have helped to inspire my business."

Ruben's face lit up. "It did?"

She nodded. "I believe that the probability of people meeting their best match organically and by chance is very low. I calculated that introducing a range of specific questions and algorithms directly enhanced a positive outcome."

"Absolutely," Ruben agreed, his eyebrows lifting with delight at the sound of her scientific words. "I also believe that humans match through a range of other attractions other than physical attributes."

"Precisely," she said, and he beamed ever more.

"What would you like to do this evening, dear Carla? I believe the Electric Tram Museum is most interesting. Or perhaps the Body Worlds exhibition? It features bodies donated to science that have been plasticized for education and entertainment purposes. Or…" He hesitated and cleared his throat.

"We could watch a foreign language film in my apartment. I have a very good bottle of red wine and a fine selection of cheese. You would be most welcome to stay overnight, too, if you should like?"

Carla swallowed uncomfortably, realizing that he may have construed their "elevated" conversation as foreplay. In the past, she'd managed to avoid invitations to his bedroom, afraid he might pepper her with questions in there, too.

She looked around her quickly, trying to find something else to focus on, and grabbed a tourist booklet off a nearby table. "This looks interesting," she said, glad to see it was translated into several languages. She leafed through it, hoping to find something that wasn't trams, bodies or Ruben's bedroom.

Her gaze settled upon a new exhibition, Magic and the Mind—Science and Spiritualism in the Twentieth Century. The accompanying photos showed Victorian lantern slides and a ghostly figure spewing ectoplasm. "This looks cool." She turned it toward Ruben.

"Moderately." Ruben peered up in thought. "My colleague Anastacia has been involved in curating this exhibition. I believe it does not open until next week."

Carla scanned the copy. "It says here that there's a preview taking place tomorrow evening."

Ruben waved the idea away. "There are more interesting items in my itinerary." He was about to continue, but paused, watching as Carla wrinkled her nose in annoyance. "Though, of course, we shall do whatever you would like to do. I am most flexible," he added.

"I'd love to go to the exhibition," she confirmed.

He was a kind man, but there was no romantic interest from her side, which made it easier for Carla to cut their agenda short for the day. She'd be going to see Magic and the Mind tomorrow, and Ruben was welcome to join her.

They stood outside the café together and Ruben took hold

of her elbow once more. "We shall meet again tomorrow, dear Carla. But if there is anything you require that is not in your room tonight, do not hesitate to contact me." The light glinted off his spectacles, so she couldn't see his eyes.

"Thanks, Ruben," Carla said uncomfortably, extricating her arm from his grip. "I'm sure I'll get by."

# Sixteen

## Butterflies

IT WAS A RELIEF FOR CARLA TO WAKE UP THE NEXT morning, knowing she would have the daytime to herself. Her previous day of traveling, sightseeing and conversing with Ruben had drained all of her energy. All she wanted to do was have a peaceful, relaxing day, with the freedom to escape her thoughts about fortunes or men from her past for a while.

After eating breakfast alone in a local café, she took a tram to a butterfly pavilion on the outskirts of the city.

The building was from the Victorian era and had a curved roof with hundreds of panes of glass. Lush plants and tropical flowers filled the warm space with a sweet, exotic aroma, and terrapins swam in swallow pools, perching on rocks jutting out of the water. A rainbow of butterflies fluttered above her, some settling upon small wooden stands, where they feasted on melon and berries.

Carla felt her pulse slowing as she walked along the maze of narrow pathways, past all the lush emerald vegetation. Lucinda believed butterflies were a symbol of joy, change and good fortune—especially the blue ones—and Carla gasped when one with indigo and turquoise wings landed on the back of her hand. She raised her fingers to admire its delicate legs and antennae, carefully taking her phone from her pocket to take a photo. The butterfly stayed with her for a while before fluttering away, flying higher until it almost reached the ceiling.

She peered into glass cases where chrysalides hung in rows, their translucent cocoons pulsing and splitting open to reveal butterflies emerging with their wings wet and crumpled. A sign next to the cabinet informed her that they lived for only two to four weeks on average, and her heart sank. What would she do, and who would she spend her last precious moments with, if she only had such a short time to live? On the other hand, perhaps an overly long life gave people too much time to dwell on unimportant things.

She sent a photo of the butterfly sitting on her hand to Tom. My new friend, she messaged.

She promptly received a picture of a dead fly on his hotel windowsill in return.

You're beating me in the beautiful pet competition. Sorry we haven't managed to chat for a few days x

Carla could berate him for his lack of contact, but instead she sent him a shot of the butterflies breaking free from their pupas.

They're supposed to be lucky.

Is this in Portugal? he texted back. I wish I was with you ♥
Carla clicked her jaw, realizing she hadn't updated him on her latest travels. I've moved on to Amsterdam now, she replied.

Oh, cool! I've always wanted to go there. Don't they put mayon-
naise on fries, though?

She liked how he took her announcement in stride, not
questioning why she was there or who she was with. In return, she didn't ask him anything more about Sara, though she
longed to know if his ex-girlfriend was still taking showers in
his hotel bathroom. Before she could reply, Tom sent her another message.

Keep me posted on your trip. Got to shoot to a meeting now.
Love you x

Love you too x, Carla replied.

Later that evening, Carla stood with Ruben in the museum
foyer waiting to be admitted into the Magic and the Mind exhibition. A poster featured a wild-eyed man whose turban and
crystal ball reminded her of Vadim the eerie mannequin. It
said, *Alistair, Crystal-Seer. Knows all, sees all, tells all.*

Ruben looked handsomely formal in a dark blue suit, and
he'd changed his glasses to tortoiseshell-rimmed ones. Carla
wore her black linen dress with a pair of Babs's ballet flats,
and a slick of red lipstick. The other guests around her wore
an eclectic array of clothing, from jeans and T-shirts to long
floral gowns. Ruben took two glasses of red wine from a tray
and handed one to Carla without asking if she'd prefer white.

They filed inside and he greeted several people, shaking
hands and bowing his head as he received compliments about
his research and theory work. "Too kind," he said humbly, but
Carla saw the flicker of a self-congratulatory smile on his lips.

She'd have been happy to circle the room on her own, peering into the glass cabinets and paying closer attention to a glass-
topped séance table. She glimpsed a wooden Ouija board and

an ear trumpet used by mediums to supposedly listen to spirits. Might these things confirm that some of her family's beliefs and superstitions were hokum?

Her thoughts were interrupted when Ruben took her elbow and led her to the corner of the room, reminding her of the times she'd accompanied him to dinner, theater productions, lectures and galleries. He always used to lead the way, pointing things out to her as if she was his pupil.

Carla's eyes were drawn to a ceramic head with markings and words, used for phrenology. She traced her hand across her own head, feeling the bumps on her skull as she looked at the corresponding model. She was about to mention it to Ruben, but he steered her toward a group of people he'd spotted instead. "Bram was once shortlisted for the Nobel Prize," he whispered into Carla's ear. "Floris is a landscape artist who had a piece commissioned for the National Gallery in London." Each time Carla pointed out a magician's prop to him, Ruben fixated on yet another professor or dignitary he wanted to engage in conversation.

She watched as a young woman, perhaps a student, approached Ruben while twirling a finger through her hair. Ruben placed his hands behind his back and listened intently while the woman stood on her tiptoes to speak to him. He launched into an explanation about how and why Norwegian prisons had a low recidivism rate. His body loosened and his eyes shone, as if the woman's attention gave him a shot of energy.

Carla half-listened to the conversation, hearing the gush in the woman's voice. It struck her that she used to look at Ruben with the same intensity of admiration while he lapped up her attention. She noted again that they'd been more like professor and student, a symbiotic relationship rather than a romantic one.

Eventually, a man wearing a scarf so long it reached his knees interrupted the conversation, taking Ruben's elbow in the same way Ruben moved Carla along. Carla used this opportunity to excuse herself and she moved quickly across to the other side of the room. She took another glass of red wine from a waiter's tray and stood reading a framed article that told of three supposedly clairvoyant sisters who fooled their clients by using apples on strings to make banging noises.

"Congratulations," a voice said beside her. "I have seen you trying to skip Ruben's company for some time."

Carla's mouth parted in surprise and she turned to find a woman with short bobbed tangerine hair and thick black Perspex glasses perched on her nose. She could be aged anywhere between forty and sixty and was dressed from head to toe in black clothes that rustled when she moved. There was a sprinkle of small star tattoos on her right wrist.

"Oops," Carla said, feeling guilty at being found out. "Was it so obvious?"

"Not to him." The woman winked and offered her hand to Carla. Her fingers were full of silver rings with skulls, ankhs and gemstones. "I am Anastacia."

Carla recognized her name. "One of the curators?" she asked. "I haven't managed to see many of the exhibits so far, but they look fascinating."

"Several of the pieces on display come from my own personal collection, so let me show you around," Anastacia said. "I've always been interested in the unknown and the otherworldly."

They walked and stopped in front of a series of paintings that were purported to have been done by spirits, and a poster for Houdini. "Magic shows were highly popular in the 1920s," Anastacia explained. "Two of the greatest magicians of that time were Harry Houdini and Howard Thurston. Thurston believed some kind of spirit was guiding him, but Houdini was skeptical. They engaged in a friendly competition, wagering that the first one to die would haunt the other.

"I once worked as a magician's assistant to help fund my history degree," she continued. "I've been sawed in half, made to vanish and had knives thrown at me, more times than I care to remember."

"A dangerous career?" Carla was really warming to this exuberant lady.

"No lasting damage to the body is the goal." Anastacia laughed. "Audiences don't realize how much magicians' assistants are involved in the trickery. They think we're only there to hold rabbits, look pretty and to pass a top hat or two. When a magician places their assistant in a cabinet and saws through their body, followed by moving the segments around, it looks like *they're* doing all the work. But, in fact, all of the magic happens inside the box. I was a professional, a contortionist who could twist my body to fit into tiny spaces."

Anastacia headed toward a tall red-and-gold box, then opened the doors and wriggled her hand inside it, demonstrating to Carla how she could make it disappear. "I was never the prettiest girl in my youth, or the cleverest, but onstage I was both. All eyes were on me, even if the magician took most of the credit."

Carla examined the cabinet, looking all around it, not previously appreciating how much work went into magic tricks and illusions.

They visited a glass case next, populated by several crudely modeled dolls. "A popular method for a curse was to create a figure resembling the person the magic should be performed on, usually in wax or clay," Anastacia explained. "A lock of hair or piece of fabric belonging to the subject would be sought out and applied to the doll. If it was a healing ritual, the doll's leg might be bandaged, or if a living person was to be prevented from spreading gossip, the doll's mouth might be sewn up.

"Once the spell had worked, the doll would be burned or buried, therefore releasing the spell. Or, if the spell was malicious, it would remain in place."

Goose bumps rose along Carla's forearms and she drained her wine, wondering if she dared to ask Anastacia her next question. "I know it sounds silly, but a witch supposedly put a curse or spell on one of my distant relatives in the 1920s, and now allegedly all marriages and relationships in our family are supposed to fail." She shook her head in disbelief at how ridiculous this sounded. "I've always thought witches were an ancient superstition."

"One of the oldest records of witchcraft is in the Old Testament, and there are still people practicing versions of it today," Anastacia said. "There was a big spiritualist revival in the 1920s, after the First World War ended. People were having to cope with the deaths or disappearances of their loved ones, resulting in communal mourning, the building of memorials and even a desire to communicate with the dead. People with no previous belief in the paranormal turned to mediums for comfort, closure and advice. In the throes of grief, they were more open to receiving messages purported to be from *the other side*. Two of the most popular parlor games were séances and Ouija boards."

"But can curses *really* work?" Carla asked.

"If you go into an exam with the mindset you're going to fail, it possibly increases that chance. If people *believe* a curse has been put on them, perhaps that is enough to make it seem real. If your relatives go into their relationships expecting them to fail, they might subconsciously influence that outcome."

"I can see that makes sense." Carla pondered, thinking of how Mimi crossed her fingers each time she got married.

"The twenties were also when Tutankhamen's tomb had just been discovered in Egypt, so there was much talk of a 'Pharaoh's curse,'" Anastacia added. "If anyone cursed *you* today, how would it make you feel? Even if you didn't believe it?"

Carla shuddered. "Uncomfortable. But mediums can't really speak to dead people, can they?"

"Some psychics and mediums make a living from deceiving people. Others believe they have a gift—and perhaps some actually do, though I've seen more evidence of the former than the latter."

They moved on and Anastacia sat down on a wooden bench, inviting Carla to join her. "Do tell me more about your family," she prompted. "They sound most interesting."

Carla showed Anastacia photos of her gran and Jess, and an image of her family tree she'd taken on her phone. "Agatha was my great-great-grandaunt and I think her fiancé's surname was Aakster," she said. "I believe it's Dutch."

"An unusual name will give you a better chance of tracing him," Anastacia said.

Carla toyed with her pendant. "I've already googled his name and drew a blank." She surveyed a wall full of posters in front of her while she thought. "If Agatha and Lars were cursed by a witch, and then he died, is that the kind of story that might have been recorded or reported somewhere?"

Anastacia nodded. "There is a distinct possibility. Did you know there's an extensive archive of material within the University of Amsterdam library, thousands of newspapers, articles, media and materials on file of a cultural interest?"

Carla shook her head and felt a fresh wave of intrigue washing over her. If she could find out that Lars had died under *normal* circumstances, she'd know for sure that a curse didn't exist. All her family's gossip would be wiped out for good, allowing her female relatives to live and love without fear or wariness—herself included. "Is the library open to the general public?" she asked.

Anastacia shook her head. "Unfortunately not."

Carla's face fell. "Oh, well…"

Anastacia frowned, thinking for a while. "I wonder if I'll be allowed to sign someone in as my guest. Do you have any free time tomorrow?"

Carla raised her chin with hope. This sounded much more exciting than spending any further time with Ruben. "Yes. Definitely."

"Well, let's see if I can get you access, and if we can solve your mystery."

# Seventeen

Newspaper

BACK IN HER AIRBNB THAT NIGHT, CARLA SCROLLED through the photos she'd taken around Amsterdam. Although they were backlit, bright and beautiful on her phone, she missed the nostalgia and excitement of taking reels of film into photography shops with no idea how they were going to turn out. Even out-of-focus shots had a certain sense of time and place about them. She didn't keep tickets, maps or beer coasters like she used to, and her digital images might remain on her phone for years, possibly to be forgotten.

She picked up her set of tarot cards and looked at the three outstanding ones: The King of Cups, The Hierophant and The Lovers. Selecting one at random, she looked up its meaning online. The Hierophant was traditionally associated with religion, but also represented the path to knowledge and education. It encouraged you to embrace the conventional and to follow an established process. Carla decided the card must relate to Ruben, but she didn't see what importance he could have to her life *now*, unless it was by association with Anastacia.

This only left her with two cards, and Carla was certain one of them must relate to Fidele in Sardinia. She checked out the webpage for his family's diving center and completed an inquiry form, asking if he'd like to meet soon.

But was he The King of Cups or The Lovers?

The King of Cups card featured a man sitting on a throne, holding a gold goblet in front of the sea, so that card might relate to Fidele. But, then again, he *had* also been a great love in Carla's life. She held up The Lovers card next. The illustration of the naked man and woman holding hands while gazing into each other's eyes brought a flush to her cheeks.

*If I have one ex left to revisit, then why are there two cards remaining?*

Carla leafed through her journal, reconsidering every possible relationship or contact she'd made during her gap year who still lived overseas. She tried to think if she'd left anyone out but reached the end of the journal with no one in mind.

Surely, The Lovers must relate to Tom, right? Just as there'd been a glitch with the Logical Love system, Myrtle's fortune telling could be faulty, too.

If anyone could help Carla untangle her emotions, it was Tom, and her sense of longing for him suddenly felt like a heavy weight dragging in her stomach. She desperately wanted to feel his strong arms around her, his breath on her cheek and his face pressed into her hair. She pulled her pillow to her chest and hugged it tight, but it was no substitute for the real thing.

Carla picked up her phone and located Tom's number, but then she gritted her teeth. How could she possibly admit to her ongoing mission to find her old flames without hurting Tom's feelings or irrevocably ruining their relationship? It was a delicate, tricky situation and she dolefully decided against calling him. With only one week left until she returned home, she felt very much alone in her current state of affairs.

Hopefully, meeting with Anastacia at the library would confirm that Myrtle's prediction of a "significant" man from her past and her family curse were both hoaxes. Then Carla could return to the UK confident she and Tom were supposed to be together, for good. That way, she'd never have to think about the two remaining tarot cards ever again.

Carla crossed her fingers tightly.

"I hope you don't mind, I arrived early and started to conduct a little research already," Anastacia said, meeting Carla on the steps of the library. "As a historian and former magician's assistant, I am very curious."

Carla patted her travel journal in her handbag. "I really appreciate you taking time out of your day to help me. I've brought along the actual family tree in my old travel journal."

"Perfect. You'll make a fine researcher."

"I hope so."

Anastacia led the way inside, then wrote Carla's name in the guest book and handed her a pen to add her signature.

Carla had expected the library to be a little fusty, shelves upon shelves of leather-bound books and wooden ladders the height of two-story buildings, but the interior was modern and spacious, full of glass and space-age-style staircases under a white domed ceiling.

"I have good news and bad news," Anastacia said, turning to look at her. "A lot of records have been digitally transferred, which should make our search a little easier. Unfortunately, they won't all necessarily have keywords or people's names assigned to them."

"I've got all day," Carla quickly replied, in no rush to see Ruben again.

"Hopefully it won't take as long as *that*." Anastacia laughed. She took a seat and invited Carla to sit down next to her before tapping a few keys. "We only have access to the one device and I've already logged in. I've looked for engagements under the name of Agatha in 1923 and have found several, but none were connected to the name Lars."

Carla leaned forward, fascinated by a list of articles that had appeared on-screen. The majority of them were in Dutch, but a couple were in English. "If Lars was supposed to be in a relationship with someone else, perhaps he and Agatha avoided announcing their engagement publicly," she mused.

"Yes, good point, Sherlock. What was I thinking?" Anastacia tutted and shook her head at herself.

Carla paused for a moment. "If Lars was engaged to someone else, perhaps *that* announcement is there…"

"Yes, that sounds more likely. I think the lesson here is not to have too many fiancées," Anastacia noted. "It complicates matters."

Her words made Carla think about Tom again and she felt her eyes sting with tears. She really was feeling more emotional recently. She had an overwhelming urge to confide all her doubts and fears to Anastacia, to tell her she was getting married soon but was having terrible doubts about *everything*. To cover up her emotions, Carla looked down and fumbled for her journal, opening it up on the page of her family tree.

Anastacia typed in Lars's name and clicked the end of her pen while she waited for results to appear. "Hmm, nothing. I'll try general announcements in 1923. It will probably throw up lots of marriages, births and deaths, not necessarily in any chronological order."

The two women nodded to each other in agreement.

Anastacia scrolled down the page for some time until a pained expression fell across her face. "Oh," she said, flattening her lips and pointing to the screen. "I think I've found something."

Carla caught her breath. "What is it?"

Anastacia leaned back so Carla could get a better view.

The piece was very short, in a faded, old-fashioned font, scanned from a newspaper.

*AAKSTER-Lars. Nov. 25, 1923. In zijn 28e jaar. Begrafenis privé.*

Carla's tried to translate some of the text. "Does that mean he was twenty-eight years old?"

Anastacia nodded slightly.

"So, he did die young," Carla said, her shoulders sloping. Lars had been even younger than Jess when he'd passed away, and she took a moment to digest this sad thought. "What do the last couple of words mean?"

"*'Begrafenis privé,'*" Anastacia read. "It means an 'interment private,' a private funeral. It is not very common but not unusual, either." She placed a hand on Carla's arm. "Are you okay to continue?"

Carla nodded. This was the first time she'd learned anything concrete about Agatha and her fiancé, and she wanted to know more.

Anastacia added more keywords, clicking buttons and scrolling so adeptly that Carla found it difficult to keep up. She perused articles and listings until she emitted a long "Ah…" She met Carla's eyes with a solemn stare.

Carla's fingers tingled. "What is it?"

"I think I've found something else. There is a newspaper article in Dutch, an engagement announcement that says a man named Lars Aakster was engaged to marry Isabelle Roelof in 1922." She stopped reading and her face paled.

Carla searched her expression and felt a sense of fear rising inside her. "What is it?" she asked, grabbing hold of her necklace. "Is something wrong?"

Anastacia swallowed. "I have seen this woman's name before. Isabelle Roelof was a prolific medium in the twenties, not a witch." She frowned, as if searching the inner recesses of her mind. "I believe she wasn't averse to issuing curses or removing them, if she was paid to do so."

Carla felt like a centipede was crawling down her spine. "Like a business?"

Anastacia nodded.

Carla shivered as she tried to absorb this information. Her family history was like a rash she needed to scratch. "Is there anything to link Isabelle to what happened to Lars and Agatha?"

"I will take a look." Anastacia had just started to scroll again when a man wearing navy overalls arrived at her side. They spoke to each other in Dutch. "Sorry, Carla. I need to move my car. Apparently, I've parked in the space of a fellow academic." Anastacia tutted. "I'll only be a few minutes. Please do continue without me."

The last time Carla had been in charge of a computer was when she ran the database to search for a match for Jess, and that hadn't worked out well. Her hand shook a little when she typed in the name *Isabelle Roelof* and pressed the search key. Frustratingly, the two articles that appeared were written in Dutch and she could make out only a few words.

*What did you expect?* Carla sighed to herself. She copied the text but couldn't work out how to open Google Translate on the computer.

Sitting back in her chair, she tapped her fingertips on the table before leaning forward more determinedly, to input a wider search: *1920s, curse, medium.*

This time, a single article appeared—a torn newspaper cutting—and Carla's heart sounded like a bass drum in her ears as she began to read.

Fortunately, this article was in English.

## WEDDING DAY ENDS IN TRAGEDY

*A wedding day is supposed to be the happiest day of a woman's life, but for Agatha Vries it ended in tears on November 25, 1923, when her fiancé, Lars Aakster, suffered a fatal heart attack at*

*the altar before the couple had the chance to exchange their vows.*
*Whispers abound that a curse had been bestowed on the couple*
*by Isabelle Roelof, sometimes known as The Blonde Witch of*
*Tuinstraat Street, who had formerly been Lars's sweetheart*

Carla let out a gasp and she clamped a hand to her mouth.
Staring at the screen in disbelief, her vision blurred and her
surroundings seemed to vanish until all she could see were the
dark letters on the white page.

Her fingers felt uncoordinated as she scrolled down to find
a grainy photograph below the article. A woman with wavy
dark hair and full lips, like a silent-movie star, sat beside a man
with a deep side part, a thin moustache and a pinstripe suit.
They stood in front of a stained-glass window and gazed lovingly into each other's eyes.

*Agatha looks so young and glamorous*, Carla thought, ashamed
that she'd imagined her ancestor to look downtrodden. She noticed how the woman's oval face was a similar shape to her own.

All this time, Carla had denied her family legend, insisting
to Jess, Lucinda, Mimi and Evelyn that it was a ridiculous fairy
story, speculation to be scoffed at or ignored. Yet here it was
before her in black and white.

A curse had been bestowed—and it had *worked*.

# Eighteen

## Fire

CARLA RUSHED TO THE LIBRARY BATHROOM, WHERE she hung her head over the sink and splashed cold water on her face. Her body surged with adrenaline and she raised her head to look in the mirror. Shock was etched in her eyes and she grappled with her thoughts. A century of relationships in her family had been affected, including her own marriage to Aaron, and now her relationship with Tom. Why else would she be here, looking for other men while her fiancé was with his ex in America? Did everything originate from a curse uttered by Isabelle Roelof, one hundred years ago?

It seemed too ridiculous to contemplate. But poor Lars Aakster had died at the altar, before he'd taken his vows of marriage, while his fiancée Agatha had looked on. Carla's mouth flooded with something that tasted metallic.

When someone else entered the room, she snatched a paper towel and blotted her cheeks. Her ankles felt clumsy as she returned to the computer, where Anastacia sat waiting for her.

"Are you okay? I wondered where you'd gone to. You left your bag behind."

"Sorry, I had to dash." Carla's words sounded strangled, as if someone else had spoken them. She glanced fearfully at the screen to see the photograph and article were still on display.

Anastacia followed her eyes and scanned the piece. "Oh," she said, her lips forming a perfect circle. "I see you've found something."

Carla nodded, still in a daze.

"Can I get you a glass of water or some sweet tea?"

Carla shook her head, not sure what to do next or how to function normally in this situation.

"I can print off this information for you..." Anastacia offered.

Carla fumbled for her phone in her bag. She needed to get out of here, to breathe some fresh air and digest what she'd discovered. "I'll take a photograph," she said. "I feel queasy and should go."

Anastacia offered to continue the search and asked Carla to leave her phone number, so she could get in touch if she found anything else. Carla only half-listened to her words as she pulled on her coat. She thanked Anastacia for her help, scribbled down her own number and hurried out of the library. With no idea where she was heading, she stumbled on the first step and started to walk, her stride feeling aimless. She focused on her feet, watching the toes of her pumps as they hit against concrete, then grass, then gravel.

*A curse exists, a curse exists.*

She kept repeating it in her head, trying to make sense of something she'd denied for decades.

A road sign told her she was heading in the opposite direction to the city, and Carla turned and retraced her steps, telling herself she needed to concentrate.

She'd usually call Tom at times like this, but he'd probably think this was too bizarre, or not understand why she was so shaken. She was sure he'd say this had happened a century ago and she should just ignore it. He didn't know the full story of Myrtle's prediction, and Carla would have to explain everything to him in detail in order for him to understand the full magnitude of her discovery. She'd have to admit she was seriously questioning their suitability and upcoming marriage.

Carla also couldn't speak to members of her family about her discovery. Evelyn was in the first throes of love with Bertrand, Mimi was happily married (for now), and Carla didn't want to worry Jess while she was looking for a new relationship. Anything she told them might be amplified, questioned and passed around.

Carla found a bench overlooking a canal and sat down with a thump. She watched the water ripple and reflect the trees for so long that it was difficult to detect which was the real landscape—the image on top or its upside-down counterpart. There was only one person she could turn to given all of the circumstances. Babs.

Her throat burned as she made the call.

"Oh, hello, petal. Everything okay?" Babs asked, her voice high-pitched and almost too cheerful. "I've been thinking about you."

Carla paused, detecting something wasn't quite right. She decided to delay sharing her own news. "Yeah, I'm fine. Are *you* okay?"

Babs gave an audible swallow. "Yes, course, all's hunky-dory…"

But Carla heard the warble in her words. "Are you upset about something?"

"No… Yes." Babs fell quiet for a while, sniffling. "Fran's gone," she said eventually.

"Gone where? What's happened?"

Babs's breathing came in short bursts. "There was a small fire in the bar, some electronics onstage."

Carla's fingers crept across the bench to ground her. "Oh, gosh. Are you okay?"

"I was in bed when it happened," Babs said. "Fran mustn't have unplugged everything. He's always messing with the speakers, lights and stuff. I woke up and could smell smoke, so I pulled on my dressing gown and got out of there. Fortunately, the fire people came quickly. The bar and the stairs took the main hit. It could have been a lot worse."

"I'm so sorry to hear this." Carla gave a sympathetic sigh. "Was Fran there, too?"

"I haven't seen him since. I asked around, but nothing. Looks like he's run off. You'd think he'd at *least* check if I was okay." Babs's voice grew smaller. "I thought I meant more to him..."

Carla wished she could hold her tight. "At least you're okay. Are you at the bar now? Maybe he'll come back."

"I doubt it. I've had to move out, can't get to my bedroom to reach my stuff because the stairs are all charred. A few of my friends are on holiday, so I didn't want to bother them.

"One of Diego's mum's properties was vacant for a couple of weeks, so I'm staying here for a while. It's a bit out in the sticks, in Girona. If I look out of the window, I can see hills, fields and sky, and not much else."

Carla closed her eyes, her heartstrings tugging for her friend. "I wish I could help you. Is Diego there with you?"

"He's away for a couple of nights, so I'm here on my own. It's a bit spooky at night, too dark and quiet. His mum's given me some clothes to wear, but she's ninety and dresses like a nun." Babs forced a laugh. "Anyway, that's enough about my woes. How are you?"

Carla didn't manage to suppress a sigh. "You've got enough to deal with..."

"That bad, eh? Want to play swapsies with our misfortunes?"

Carla couldn't bottle up the discovery of her family curse inside her. It seemed to have a life of its own and refused to stay imprisoned. Keeping the detail light so she didn't overwhelm Babs at this difficult time, she told her about Ruben, how he definitely wasn't the man she was looking for, how she'd met Anastacia at an exhibition and then found out her family curse was real. "Things have ground to a halt for me here," she admitted.

"Don't you have two cards left, two men to find?"

"Supposedly, but what's the point? Fidele hasn't replied from Sardinia yet and I have no idea who The Lovers card relates to." She paused as a couple walked past her, kissing each other's lips and giggling. Carla resisted her urge to push them into the canal.

"I'm speechless, and that doesn't happen very often," Babs admitted. "From what you've told me, you and Tom are solid. You love each other, so don't let this stuff get to you. This thing happened years ago in a different time with different beliefs. The story might be tittle-tattle, like gossip magazines today. Don't read too much into it."

It was exactly what Carla needed to hear and she wanted more of it. "Sorry for telling you all this when you've got problems of your own."

"Your tribulations have made me feel less alone. If you need to wallow somewhere that's lonely, dull and very rural, feel free to join me."

Although Babs was joking around, Carla could hear the stress and longing in her voice. Maybe some place in the sticks was exactly what Carla needed right now. She felt like she had the flu, and her head was blocked, her senses numbed. She needed some time to think of her next plan of action and to recalibrate before she returned to the UK. "Does Girona have an airport?" she asked.

"You mean, you'll come?" Babs's voice brightened and she started to babble. "The airport's only thirty minutes away from here and you could jump in a taxi to where I'm staying. There's a spare room and you could bring me clothes that don't skim the floor and, oh, some underwear. I *cannot* wear Diego's mother's underwear garments, even if they're new with the labels attached. I need makeup too. My skin looks like tree bark."

Carla let out a cackle and it felt welcome. She knew there'd be more laughter to come if she spent time with Babs, and it sounded like she needed her, too.

"I can't say I'm at my best, either," Carla said, noticing a heaviness had returned to her legs. "I'll catch the next flight I can."

"You're an absolute star, petal."

Carla went to find a taxi to take her back to her Airbnb and called Ruben from the back seat. She told him she had to leave Amsterdam quickly and thanked him for their time together.

"Approximately sixty-five percent of our itinerary is still incomplete," he said scratchily. "You also ran away from *us* the last time we were together. These are not the actions of a reliable person and this does not bode well for you in your relationships, dear Carla. Not well at all. I would suggest..."

She listened and heard so much of her own personality in his words, recognizing so many of the sentiments, statements and questions she'd used when formulating Logical Love that it made her shudder. "I'm truly sorry," she said at the end of his speech. "Thanks, and goodbye, Ruben."

Carla couldn't remember much about her flight back to Spain, other than there were stairs up to the aircraft, a lady's legs squashed against her own for the entirety of the flight, and the pilot announced they were cruising at an altitude of thirty-five thousand feet.

The two hours spent in the air seemed to go by in a flash and before she knew it, the plane touched down at Girona's airport. Carla hopped into a taxi and handed the driver a piece of paper featuring the address Babs had given her.

She flopped her head back and looked out the window as

they left the airport behind, driving first along the highway, and then into the countryside. At the welcome sight of dusty roads, trails of trees, a team of cyclists wearing red vests and the endless blue sky that was darkening as the evening crept in, Carla let out a long exhale. She watched as two butterflies fluttered close to her window, circling each other as if choreographing a dance routine. The farther the taxi drove, the more Carla felt like she was leaving the curse and her troubles behind, at least for a little while.

When the car pulled up outside the property, her surroundings felt peaceful and calm compared to Barcelona, Blanca del Mar, Carvoeiro and Amsterdam. The only noise Carla heard was the chirping of crickets and the crunch of gravel beneath her feet.

The farmhouse in front of her was constructed from rough gray stone with a ridged terra-cotta roof. The doorway and windows were arched, set into the building in a higgledy-piggledy style, so Carla couldn't determine how many floors there were. The wooden door looked medieval as she took hold of the circular iron knocker and rapped it.

"Don't laugh," Babs said as a way of greeting when she opened the door. She swept a hand in front of her long, shapeless dress. "I know the words *frumpy* and *tent* come to mind."

Carla tried not to giggle. She focused on Babs's face as she entered the house, struggling not to look at her outfit. "I'm not saying a thing, other than 'hello' and 'it's *so* nice to see you.'"

The two women hugged so tightly in the hallway, it was like they'd both been swept out to sea and had found a rock to cling to.

They eventually pulled apart, and Carla began rifling through her suitcase. "I've brought the clothes you gave me, and I bought you some underwear and cosmetics at the airport."

"Thank you. I've got cash to reimburse you." Babs pressed her hands together in prayer. "Thank goodness you came. I hate Diego seeing me like this." She led the way into the kitchen and showed Carla some bread, cheese and a bottle of Tempranillo. "Make yourself at home while I try to look human again."

Carla was too tired and hungry to fully appreciate her new surroundings. She buttered a slice of bread and sat down with her elbows on the kitchen table, pushing her knuckles into her cheeks.

"You look how I feel," Babs said when she reemerged an hour later. Her platinum hair was now clean and silky, and she was dressed in a black-and-white zebra-stripe dress. Her eyelashes had their usual spider-leg quality.

"Gee, thanks."

They sat together, both quietly exhausted.

*Come on, Carla, pick yourself back up.* She looked around her, trying to focus on something positive. "This place is beautiful, so serene."

"It's bloody rustic, that's what it is. I feel like a fish out of water." Babs grimaced. "It doesn't even have wallpaper."

Carla had initially felt the same way about Babs's Place and had grown to love it. "When you and Mum stayed in Diego's other place, was it like this?"

Babs squinted, tapping into her memories. "It was an apartment above a pharmacy in Lloret de Mar, so it was an old building, but not prehistoric like this place. I didn't expect to bump into a ghost or suit of armor when I went to the bathroom at night. It had this stone window seat, and me and Suzy used to sit and look out of the window together. We made up stories about the customers going in and out of the pharmacy, trying to guess what they were buying, to amuse ourselves."

Carla dropped her hands away from her face. "What kind of stories?"

Babs laughed to herself. "I remember this old couple used to turn up most days, shuffling into the pharmacy and leaving with huge paper bags full of stuff. It was probably pills and medicine for their ailments, but Suzette insisted they were hosting undercover sex parties and had to stock up with accoutrements, so they donned gray wigs to buy stuff in secret."

Carla let out a loud laugh. It sounded exactly like a story her mum might tell.

"I remember she liked this red-haired guy who arrived once a week," Babs reflected. "His hair shone copper in the sunshine, and Suzy's cheeks got this kind of rosy flush whenever she saw him. My story was that he was really blond but dyed his hair orange to attract the ladies, like bees to a brightly colored flower. Your mum was a bit secretive when she had a crush on guys, never sharing her true feelings about them and—"

The ping of Carla's phone interrupted Babs's flow and Carla shuffled in her seat, wondering if Tom had messaged her. How was she going to tell him she was now back in Spain?

"Don't mind me," Babs said, nodding toward it. "I'll get more wine."

Carla nodded apologetically. She saw instead that Fidele had sent her a message saying he'd love to meet up and she showed the screen to Babs. "Another one of my exes responded," she said.

"Ooh, are you going to see him? Where does this one live?"

"Sardinia. I'd love to see him again one day, but I'm not sure I have the strength or inclination to do so right now." Carla sighed and stuffed the phone back into her pocket. "I'll probably stay with you for a day or two, make sure you're okay and then return home to England." An image dropped into her mind of her wedding dress, hanging in her wardrobe. She could tell she'd gained a few pounds during her travels and hoped the cream silk wouldn't strain across her stomach.

She and Babs ate olives, bread and cheese for supper, though Carla skipped the wine because it tasted a bit like vinegar to her. As night fell, she saw the sky was so clear the stars looked like diamonds tossed onto indigo velvet. She picked up a woolen blanket and wrapped it around her shoulders, relieved she was able to put some distance between herself and the chaos of her travels thus far.

Babs's phone rang and she picked up the call, walking into the hallway to hold the conversation. Carla heard her footsteps pacing up and down.

"That was Diego," Babs announced when she returned. "He's booked some time off work and is coming here tomorrow. I'll get to see him a day early. He's spoken to some local builders for me, and the damage to my bar isn't as bad as I initially thought, nothing too structural."

"It's nice to see you smiling again."

Babs blushed. "Diego has that effect on me. I just wish I could find a way to make things work. I told him you'd arrived to keep me company."

"If you want to spend some time together, I can make myself scarce," Carla offered.

"No need for that, petal. I told him you've had a bit of bad news and he offered to take us both out to cheer us up. I'm so glad you're finally going to meet each other. You can tell me what you think of him and what I need to do to sort things out between us."

"I'm not sure I can do that…" Carla started.

"Well, you can do a better job than I can," Babs said with her hands on her hips. "You're the matchmaker around here, after all."

It sounded like a challenge, but also something to take Carla's mind off her own issues for a while. "No pressure, then?" she said, with a laugh to Babs.

# Nineteen

## Olive Trees

THE MORNING DAYLIGHT IN CARLA'S ROOM WAS DIF-ferent from any she'd experienced before. It was clear, golden and bright, and she lay in bed sweeping her hand back and forth through the rays shining through her window, feeling the warmth on her skin.

She could hear the shower gushing and she raised an eyebrow to herself, surprised Babs was up so early when she usually languished in bed until noon. Carla washed in the sink in her room and got dressed.

"I got up early to put my face on," Babs said when the two women bumped into each other on the landing. "I want to look half-decent for Diego."

"I'll make breakfast for us. Does bread and cheese sound okay to you?"

"I don't have anything else. There may be an olive or two left if we're lucky." Babs laughed. "I think the nearest shop is a couple of miles away."

Carla bustled around in the kitchen, seeing what else she could find to eat. She was trying to work out how to use the oven, so she could at least attempt to make cheese on toast, when the door knocker thudded several times. Wiping her hands on a towel, she padded along the hallway in her bare feet.

The man standing before her, when she'd opened the door, had distinguished white temples in his dark curled hair, and his tanned, crinkled skin reminded her of a Medjool date. She recognized him from Babs's photographs, though he was now a lot older. "Diego?" she said.

He nodded and tilted his head. "You are Carla, yes?" He offered his hand for a shake. "It is very lovely to meet you."

"Yes, hello. You, too." She waved her arm toward the hallway. "It feels odd to invite you into your own home."

"It is my mother's place, not somewhere I have ever lived."

"I think it's wonderful, so charming. I love all the little windows and how none of the walls are straight," Carla said over her shoulder as she headed toward the kitchen. "Babs is still getting ready upstairs."

"It looks like we might have a long wait." Diego let out a playful sigh. "I do not believe this house is to Barbara's taste."

Carla hesitated, wondering who he meant. "Oh, Babs? I think she's very grateful to have somewhere to stay. I've brought her some clothes and makeup."

They sat together at the kitchen table while Babs banged around upstairs.

"Do not worry about making breakfast. If you can wait a little while, I know some nice places to eat," Diego said.

Carla liked his calm, peaceful air. "You knew my mum?" she said, a statement rather than a question.

"Yes. Suzette was Barbara's friend."

"I saw photos of you all together in Babs's Place."

"I was their tour guide for a while, showing them the *real* Spain, away from all the bars and tourists. I remember your mother had a keen interest in art. We all went to Figueres, where Salvador Dali used to live, to see his paintings of melting clocks and a lobster telephone."

Carla smiled. "He's one of my favorite artists, too. I didn't know Mum liked him."

Diego nodded. "I think she liked the culture here, but she also missed her life at home."

Babs appeared in the kitchen and performed a twirl. "Ta-da." She wore the zebra-print dress again and gold sandals. Her eye makeup was still bold and inky, but her lips were simple and nude.

Diego nodded in appreciation. "Now, where would you ladies like to go? The castle is beautiful, though perhaps a little hot today. Or there's a lovely local olive grove and vineyard close by. You can sample the olive oils and they serve simple lunches."

Babs glanced at Carla and they both grinned. "That sounds perfect," Babs said.

The wind danced in Carla's hair as Diego drove along the narrow roads. The olive grove was only a couple of miles away, and light dappled her face as she admired quaint whitewashed houses and the occasional bodega. Red poppies swayed in fields where the grass had dried to the color of sand and she glimpsed a tiny church made of peach stone.

When Diego pulled up in front of the vineyard, Carla looked around her in wonderment, already knowing this was somewhere special.

A tour of the gardens and olive groves took ninety minutes and she loved learning how the owners had bought a former bakery and the land in the seventies. They'd put an irrigation system in place and planted one thousand trees, a good distance apart to give them space to grow. They picked the olives by hand and pressed them using a traditional stone mill, then bottled the extra-virgin olive oil to use for cooking or as a food dressing. It could also be used to moisturize skin, tame flyaway hair or turn into soap. In the vineyard shop, Carla bought a bottle for her gran to use in her cooking, along with bars of soap for Jess, Mimi and Evelyn.

After shopping, Carla, Babs and Diego sat on a terrace so high that the olive trees below looked like rows of cabbages. The sun shone fiercely overhead and Carla was glad their table was shaded by a huge umbrella.

Their lunch consisted of crusty bread served with slabs of cheese and big juicy grapes. There were small pots filled with olive oils in shades of yellow, deep ocher and sage green. Carla took a few nibbles of everything, but traveling and her preoccupied mind seemed to have stolen her hunger away.

"Black olives are great as a snack with red wine. White wine goes better with green olives," Babs informed them.

Diego raised his eyebrow, impressed.

"I'm not just a pretty face." Babs patted her hair.

Diego was good company, telling them stories about interesting injuries he'd encountered at work, such as old people falling off roller skates or how one child got a plastic cowboy's head stuck up his nose. "He ran around the waiting room and it fell out before his appointment." He laughed.

"How long have you been a doctor?" Carla asked him.

Diego performed calculations in his head. "Over forty years. I have always worked at the hospital in Calella, not too far from Blanca del Mar. My mother was English and my father was Spanish. We moved to Spain when I was ten years old, so I consider myself to be a mix of cultures. My parents were doctors, too, and they also own several properties that they rent out to vacationers, including the one you are staying in. Barbara and your mother stayed in their Lloret del Mar apartment for some time."

"He collected more than the rent from me." Babs winked.

Diego smiled despite himself and shook his head slowly at her.

"Calella." Carla ran the name over her tongue. "I think I went to the hospital there once for a stupid injury." She recounted how she'd fallen from a horse during her gap year and hurt her arm. "I felt like such an idiot."

Diego let out a cough then recovered quickly. "It is unfortunately very common. There is something about the sunshine that makes people think they can ride animals. Sometimes even I think I am John Wayne."

Carla laughed. She noticed how Babs's eyes sparkled when she glanced at Diego and how, when Babs wasn't looking, Diego gazed back at her, too. They were like chalk and cheese, and Carla doubted they'd have ever matched through Logical Love, but she could sense something between them. It was like she *knew* they should be together.

She could also tell there was a barrier that was somehow keeping them apart, something other than their inability to have children. Spending time with the both of them filled her with a glow, but also a fierce determination. The truth of her own family's curse made her want to rally against this indictment against love, and she wondered if she was capable of matchmaking in an organic way rather than through questions and algorithms. "Babs has been such a caring, kind host," she told Diego, looking at Babs out of the corner of her eye. "She really knows how to make people feel at home."

An olive fell off Babs's fork and she looked at Carla quizzically. "Me?"

"From the minute I arrived, you made me feel welcome."

Babs toyed with a napkin. "Of course I did. You're Suzy's daughter."

Carla continued to gush about Babs to Diego, mentioning how she'd invited Babs to her wedding.

"It has been many years since I visited England to see my friends and family there," Diego mused. "A visit is long overdue for me, too."

"You should come," Carla urged, ignoring the look of surprise on Babs's face. Astonishingly, she found she didn't care if Babs's and Diego's presence might alter her numbers, meals and seating plans. "I bet my gran, Lucinda, would enjoy meeting you both, especially if you share stories about my mum."

Diego and Babs flicked questioning looks at each other, waiting for the other to take the lead and respond.

"Sounds smashing," Babs finally said with a nod of her head.

Carla stood up and gave a fake yawn, stretching out her arms. "I think I'll go for a little walk and give you both time to chat," she said, sending Babs a secret wink. "I'll see you both in an hour."

She strolled among the olive trees, dipping in and out of the mottled shadows cast on the ground by the branches. An elderly lady wearing a long black dress and a bright orange scarf in her hair used a small handheld rake to harvest the olives. She gave Carla a gap-toothed smile. "English?" she asked.

Carla nodded.

"This place is a farm and also a museum," the lady said in melodic Catalonian accent.

"Why is that?"

"Olive trees live between three hundred and six hundred years, but they do not produce olives for the first forty or fifty years of their life. They need time, patience and care to thrive. Like my husband." She laughed to herself and set about her work again.

Carla carried on walking, at first interpreting the woman's words as light and fun, before drawing a deeper meaning from them. She began to wonder about the women in her own family. Did they ever allow their relationships to grow and flourish, or did they look for problems and bail out early, self-fulfilling their family curse as Anastacia had suggested?

As she stopped to admire the gnarled trunks of the beautiful old olive trees, Carla realized she was not exempt from this tendency of Carter women.

She'd physically shoved Pedro away (though warranted) and had supposedly refused to meet Adam's parents. She'd left Daniel and fled to a hotel with running water, and she'd jumped on a plane to avoid Ruben's overkeenness. It made her question if *she* could be a common denominator in the end of her relationships. Was she also inadvertently pushing Tom away, too, by questioning their upcoming marriage? Especially because there *was* a curse in place?

In Carla's family, only Lucinda had fully committed to her relationship, compromising her own desires, and it was something Carla wasn't willing to do.

She wandered through the olive grove for a while longer, lost in her thoughts until it was time to return to the terrace.

She spied Babs and Diego deep in conversation. Babs and Fran had been sparky together, but Babs and Diego's harmony was mellow and mature, like the olive trees that bore the best fruit.

Carla coughed lightly to announce her presence and walked toward them, watching as Diego picked up his fedora and placed it on his head, twisting the brim to fit. His eyes were narrower and more serious, and Babs's movements were twitchy. The air held a prickle of tension.

The three of them stood and loitered over the beautiful view for a few final moments until Diego walked ahead to retrieve his car.

"How did things go?" Carla asked Babs.

She replied with a wistful sigh. "We love each other, but can't seem to move forward. Diego says some matters of the heart are complicated, and I wonder if he is seeing someone else… It would break my own heart if he was."

"I've seen the way he looks at you," Carla said. "I *know* you're supposed to be together. If you both come to England for my wedding, it will give you time to work on things."

A small smile formed on Babs's lips. "We might need a stick of dynamite to move us along, but you're the expert around here."

Carla was about to protest, but her words made something stir inside her. Pride, happiness…and a feeling she didn't expect. Relief.

Perhaps she wasn't such a fraud at matching people after all.

They walked to the car, and Carla shielded her eyes against the light. The sun was a burning ball in the sky, and translucent shapes started to float across her eyes, skewing her view. She suddenly felt floaty and light, like her body might sway on a breeze. The car seemed to be moving farther away from her, even though it was stationary.

"Are you okay, petal?" Babs asked, her voice sounding distant.

"No," Carla said hazily, falling into a swoon. "I don't think I am."

And that was when everything went black.

# Twenty

## Flamingo

"CARLA. *CARLA?*" THE WOMAN'S VOICE SOUNDED FAR away, as if in a dream.

Carla's eyes were closed and she could hear someone moving around her, a comforting noise that made her feel like she was being taken care of. She opened one eye in a squint, and the shape of a figure, a man, then a woman, came into view. Her surroundings were all white.

"Am I in heaven?" she asked, trying to sit up. The blur of her vision became clearer.

"Stay where you are. You fainted at the olive grove, next to the car," Babs said. "I've brought you a banana and some water."

"How are you feeling?" Diego's voice followed next.

Carla made a visor with her hand against the daylight flooding into the room. She saw whitewashed walls and linen curtains billowing in a breeze from the patio doors. They were open, so she could see the beautiful countryside before her.

A memory trickled back of her body growing heavier, as if

filled with potatoes. "Sorry, yes. I remember now," she said. "I suddenly felt too hot, and too light. I think I must be dehydrated."

Diego passed her a bottle of water. He had his doctor's bag at his side and reached into it. "I will take your blood pressure," he said.

"There's no need, honestly." Carla drank the water in one go.

"Let's check things out anyway," he offered. After kneeling down beside her, he slipped a band over her arm. "Do you still have any dizziness?" he asked as the band inflated. "You didn't eat very much at lunchtime."

"I'm not always hungry in the heat."

Diego observed her results. "Your blood pressure is a little low." He unfastened the band and helped Carla to sit up. "Perhaps we should run a few tests…"

She casually peeled the banana and took a bite. "What kind of tests?"

"You've been tired and dizzy, you fainted, and you said your appetite has been sporadic." Diego paused and cautiously glanced at Babs for her support. "Could you possibly be pregnant?"

Carla swallowed a chunk of banana and began to choke. She held a fist to her mouth with tears streaming down her face. "Of course not. I'm forty-two."

She and Tom were always careful. But then she thought how she *had* been out of sorts for the last couple of months, lethargic and picky about her food. She'd been making some very strange choices, like deciding to meet men from her past, and had also gained a few pounds. Her periods had been random and light for a while, which she'd presumed was due to perimenopause. (A few of her friends had early symptoms, too.) But surely, she couldn't be *pregnant*?

"I can arrange for you to go to the hospital," Diego said, his eyes full of concern.

"Better to get checked out, petal," Babs added.

Carla was about to insist she was absolutely fine, but she knew worry would take root in her brain. "Is there a supermarket or pharmacy nearby? Are store-bought pregnancy tests accurate?"

Diego nodded. "Around ninety-eight to ninety-nine percent. I can drive to buy a test now, if you wish to check."

Carla gripped her empty bottle so tightly the plastic crumpled. "Yes, please," she squeaked.

Sitting in the bathroom, half an hour later, the three minutes of waiting felt like eternity. Carla focused on the digits on her watch rather than on the white stick resting on its box on the floor. When the time was up, she drew a sharp breath and held it in her lungs. And then she looked down at the stick.

The two pink lines looked like the legs of a flamingo.

Oh god. She was definitely having a baby. Her head began to swim and she grabbed the side of the sink to steady herself.

She wanted to hold Tom in her arms to tell him the news, and the geographical distance between them seemed so wide he might as well be in outer space. They were supposed to be getting married in less than two weeks' time and she still wasn't absolutely, completely sure he was the right man to join her at the altar.

"You okay in there?" Babs called, rapping on the door. "Just making sure you've not fallen down the toilet or anything."

"I'm fine," Carla said, her voice sounding muffled, somehow different already. She got dressed and washed her hands, then opened the door.

"Well?" Babs said, her arms folded tightly. "Any news?"

Carla nodded and burst into tears.

Diego arranged for Carla to visit the hospital in Calella for a few more tests the next day, and he drove her and Babs there. It was the same hospital Carla had attended after her horse accident and she vaguely remembered how the sprawling building resembled a hotel.

A nurse took blood and urine samples and confirmed that

Carla was pregnant. Diego discussed dates with her and they worked out that the pregnancy must be around eight or nine weeks along. She'd need to book a scan when she returned to England, and he and the nurse agreed it was fine for her to continue traveling if she wanted to. She should just rest up and take things easy for a day or two.

The world felt out of focus as Carla took a seat in the hospital café, waiting for Babs. Because of her age, this might be her last chance to be a mother, and certainly wasn't one she'd planned or expected. She laced her fingers across her stomach, swirling her thumbs, and tried to let her situation sink in.

The tiny house she and Tom were supposed to move into wasn't suitable for family life and she wondered again if she'd still fit into her wedding dress. All their carefully laid-out plans were crumbling into disarray.

She caught sight of a heavily pregnant woman lining up to buy orange juice and thought back to when her mum had been pregnant with Jess. Suzette used to give Carla a running commentary on how her baby sister was developing.

"She's the size of a kidney bean right now," Suzette had said. Then "She's the size of the little rubber balls you win on the slot machines in Silverpool" and "She's grown to the size of a pomegranate" and "Now she's like a cantaloupe melon."

Carla had pressed her cheek to her mum's tummy, her hands resting gently on the taut skin. "Hello, I'm your big sister. I can't wait to meet you."

When Jess arrived, Carla hadn't been prepared for the rush of love she felt for the plum-colored alien. She loved the responsibility that came with holding her sister and helping to bathe and feed her. But she was hit by an even bigger wave of responsibility when Suzette's cancer arrived.

As Jess's life flourished, Suzette's time on earth had waned, and all her family's potions, lucky heather and prayers didn't count for a thing.

After Suzette's death, the usual mass of relatives descended upon Lucinda's bungalow, offering to care for the *baby* of the family, Jess. They covered up all the mirrors in the house, an old Victorian superstition that was supposed to stop the spirit of the dead from becoming trapped in the glass. At the age of ten, Carla was the big sister and considered the strong one, when she really felt like trembling jelly.

There had been lots of talk about bad fortune and how "the brightest stars in the sky burn and fade more quickly," but Carla knew, even then, that her mother's death was more likely the outcome of genetics and random mutation. Regardless, it was devastating and unjust that two young girls would be parentless for the majority of their lives.

This was the time when Carla most craved a fatherly presence— someone who smelled of leather and bergamot soap, who would squeeze her a little too tight, so her shoulders ached, and who'd take her for long walks in the country and assure her everything was going to be okay.

As the years progressed, Carla's grief spread like toothache through her entire body. It was always there, but sometimes the twinges were stronger than others. She rebelled against the superstitions in her family, seeing them as cruxes for her gran and aunts to lean on. Jess also hooked onto them, to help her cope.

As both sisters grew older, Carla had witnessed her sister knocking on wood, poring over her daily horoscope and placing a piece of jade under her pillow for good luck. A dreamcatcher hung and twirled above Jess's bed, and she loved a cellophane fortune-telling fish that curled on her palm. In turn, Carla became more practical and sensible, striving to give her little sister a secure, loving childhood. She had precious memories of her mum to revisit and cherish, whereas all Jess had were photographs.

Sitting here, waiting for Babs and thinking about Suzette, made every nerve in Carla's body tingle, telling her this preg-

nancy was meant to be. She knew that she absolutely, unequiv-
ocally, undoubtedly wanted this child. But would Tom feel the
same way?

He was the only man Carla could imagine having a significant role in this baby's life, so surely it meant her search for her
exes was definitely at an end? The King of Cups and The Lovers
cards *had* to be rendered obsolete.

Diego stayed behind at the hospital to work while Babs and
Carla took a taxi back to the house. They sat together on the
sofa in stunned silence for a while.

"I bet Tom will be over the moon to be a dad," Babs said
eventually.

Carla flashed her a hopeful smile and glanced at her watch.
"He should be waking up around now. I wish I could tell him
the news in person rather than down a staticky phone line."

"I'll get you a nice cold glass of water and you can take it
to your room."

A few minutes later, Carla sat perched on the edge of her
bed, jiggling her legs until it was a decent time to call Tom.
His phone rang for the longest time, until a woman's voice
said, "Hiya."

Carla stared at her phone, questioning if she'd rung the right
number. She checked her screen and returned to the call. "Is
Tom there, please?" she asked with a frown.

"Yup, who's calling?"

She cleared her throat. "It's his *fiancée*," she emphasized.

"Oh, right. Sure. Hold on a sec." There was a sound of the
phone clattering down.

Moments later, Tom picked it back up. "Carla. Hi." He
sounded out of breath, rather flustered. A hissing noise started
up on the line. "Sorry, I was putting some final touches to a presentation. Sara heard my phone ringing and picked it up for me."

Sara? *Again?* Carla winced and waited for the hiss to subside.
"Are you in your hotel room?"

"No, in a boardroom for a breakfast meeting. I just nipped out to grab a coffee. Is everything okay?"

Carla massaged the lines between her eyebrows, not wanting to tell Tom their news with his colleagues—especially Sara— hovering around. "I need to speak to you," she said.

"Sure, I've got a couple minutes before the meeting starts."

"We'll need more than that. It's important."

"Oh, right. Okay." He paused for a few seconds. "Just a moment…"

Carla heard muffled voices in the background.

"It's okay," Tom said, returning to the call. "I've told Sara to start the meeting without me. You sound serious. What's up?"

Carla took a deep breath and closed her eyes, aware that this was the most momentous news she was ever going to break to anyone. In an ideal world, there'd be a drum roll before she spoke. "I'm pregnant," she said.

A high-pitched whistling noise suddenly sounded on the line and she screwed up her face, waiting for it to end. "Tom?" She raised her voice and shook her phone. "Are you still there?"

"Yeah, I'm here and…" His words dissolved as crackling took over the line. "When did this happen? *How* did it happen?"

"I don't know exactly when. I only found out yesterday. I fainted and did a pregnancy test." A blush rose to her cheeks. "I think we both know *how* it happened."

"We've always been careful. You said you were being careful," Tom said, stumbling over his words. "I didn't expect this… I mean, we're in our forties."

"That's not ancient." Carla's face pinkened, this time with annoyance. "It's something we're *both* responsible for. Having children at our age isn't uncommon."

"I can't believe this has happened."

"It was a shock for me, too. Now that I've come to terms with it, I feel kind of…excited."

"You do?" he exclaimed, an edge to his voice. "You've changed your mind?"

"Changed my mind from what?"

"When I joined Logical Love, I answered all the questions and stated I didn't want children. I've never wanted them and presumed I'd match with someone who didn't want them, either."

The tips of Carla's ears began to burn. With regard to children, she'd ticked the "open to discussion" box. That meant she and Tom should have never matched. The glitch in the database must have altered their outcome.

"Didn't you put the same thing?" he prompted.

"I've never ruled out having kids. It's something we've never really discussed."

"We didn't need to. That's why people join your agency, because it gets these kinds of conversations out of the way, up front, so couples can be sure their priorities and life decisions coordinate *before* they meet. Or else, why would they use the service? Why would you and I have used it?"

Carla felt like she was sinking down to the bottom of a deep lake with weights around her ankles. The database problem now looked more critical than ever. Tom had reminded her she'd personally created a system with the potential to turn marriages into ticking time bombs.

She and Tom had selected each other based on a series of questions and algorithms that were skewed. Perhaps they *had* leapfrogged a huge chunk of their relationship, relying on checkboxes and multiple-choice answers instead. Had they missed out on getting to know each other more intimately through late-night chats fueled by wine because everything between them had already been determined, listed, checked and approved?

Carla took a deep breath before responding. "There were several glitches in the system around the time we matched, and

Jess has been investigating them. We're still the perfect team," she tried to reassure him, but her insistence sounded hollow.

She heard Tom speak briefly to someone else. "Look, sorry, Carla, I have to go," he said. "The others have arrived, and my head is reeling. I'll have to call you back later, okay?"

"When?"

"I'm not sure. We're heading off, straight after this meeting, for a few days to visit a factory that produces board games. I don't know what my schedule will be and when I can next get back in touch. I need time to think about everything. You're telling me that technically we shouldn't be together—"

"We're going to be *parents*," Carla interrupted, her heart racing. "That surpasses everything. We *know* how we feel about each other…" She let her words peter out, knowing her efforts were futile, at least for now. In time, she hoped Tom would be as delighted and excited as she was, because his current response made it feel like a pebble was lodged in her throat. If he didn't want the baby—and if he didn't want *her*—it would prove Myrtle had been right all along. The family curse would win. Again.

But there was nothing she could do or say right now. Tom had to make up his own mind, and she had to let fate take its own path, for once.

Carla said goodbye to him, hung up and then defiantly tied her hair into a ponytail.

Looking down at the gentle dome of her belly, she spoke to it, just as she'd done with Jess. "Hello, you," she whispered. "I know things are a bit messy right now, but don't worry, because we'll figure everything out. You've already traveled with me to Spain, Portugal and Amsterdam, so I think you're a tough little thing. Though I must warn you, our family isn't exactly 'normal.' They'll probably shower you with four-leaf clovers and hope you're born under a full moon, but they'll also love you more than anything, just like I will. Just like your father will, too." She closed her eyes, hoping, praying. "Whatever happens, *we'll* be fine. I promise."

As she left her bedroom to go find Babs again, Carla realized she'd crossed her fingers so tightly her knuckles had turned white.

# Twenty-One

## Window

CARLA SAT AT THE KITCHEN TABLE WITH BABS THE next day, resting her chin glumly on her fist. Everything she knew and loved seemed to be breaking apart and floating around her, out of her reach. Her midriff felt taut, and her emotions were tidal. One moment, she felt so full of energy she could run a marathon, and the next, she had the motivation of a dishcloth. It was difficult to tell if her lethargy was due to the heat in Spain, hormonal changes or from Tom's lackluster reaction to her pregnancy news. She felt like her family curse was hitting home, and questions about their suitability only continued to abound. Her voice shook when she asked Babs, "What if Tom doesn't want to get married any longer?"

Babs sat painting her nails lilac. "You can't force that decision and you've thrown the guy a curveball. He'll need time to let things sink in," she said.

"Tom told me he's never wanted children and he sounded so resolute about it, like there was no way he'll change his mind."

"He might adapt. I've always wanted kids, but I had to accept it wasn't going to happen. It sounds like Tom's experiencing my circumstances in reverse."

Babs's reasoning didn't do much to stop Carla's upset from morphing into anger throughout the day. She stomped around the farmhouse, drinking water to prevent another fainting spell, and ate the fresh food Diego had stocked in the fridge.

Babs spent a couple of hours on her phone before reporting back to Carla that she was going to return to Blanca del Mar, where she could keep an eye on the renovation work starting on her bar. A friend had returned from holiday and Babs was going to stay with her for a while. "It's too remote for me here, but I'll stay as long as you want to," she added. "Have you decided where you're going to next?"

Carla shook her head. She didn't want to keep checking her phone for calls or messages from Tom, but the screen was like a magnet to her.

"Do you want me to hide it from you?" Babs reached out her hand to take it.

Carla clutched the device to her chest and shook her head, feeling like a toddler about to have her favorite toy removed.

"You need to relax and forget about Tom for a while. Do something to keep busy."

It was easier said than done, and Carla jumped to attention when her phone vibrated in her hands. She caught her breath and prepared herself to see her fiancé's name on the screen, but it was Jess's instead. Her spirits plunged and she carried the phone to her room, positioning it on the dressing table while she sat on the bed.

"Gran thinks we should both grow up and make amends," her sister said gruffly on Facetime. Her lips were thin and tight, as if she had no choice in the matter.

"She's probably right," Carla admitted. "Where is she?"

"In bed, nursing a cold."

"Is she okay?"

"Just a bit tired."

"Are Mimi and Evelyn okay?"

"Yes, fine."

Their conversation was so stilted that Carla let out a sigh. "Look, Jess," she started. "I know we had words about the database, but I don't want to fall out with you over it. How did your interview go?"

Jess fidgeted with her collar. "Really well. They offered me the job."

Carla felt her stomach plummet even more. "Oh, Jess..." She took a moment to think. "I really don't want you to leave."

"It's a bit late for that now. We've not been getting along. You don't trust me at work, and this new company seems great—"

"Of course I trust you," Carla interrupted, her face full of hurt.

"No, you don't, not fully. Myrtle's reading was a wakeup call that I'm thirty-four and need to move on with my life." Jess looked away. "Anyway, I've been calling all the couples who matched during the twelve-month problem period, just like you asked me to. There's been several separations but the overall success rate is pretty high and..." She trailed off. "Myrtle said I'd be working near water soon, and I saw the fountain in the courtyard. Omens do exist."

Carla thought about magpies and tarot cards and the curse, and she nodded in agreement. "I'm starting to think they might, too."

Jess closed one eye. "Did you really just say that?"

"I've had an eventful few days."

Carla could tell Jess about the men she'd met and the places she'd visited, but that wouldn't bring them close together again. It felt like she and her sister were on opposite ends of a swing bridge as it opened, and she had to find a way to jump over the gap, even if it meant revealing something that could severely impact Jess and her relationships, too. "I found out that Mum carried out some research into our family tree during her travels."

Jess shrugged a shoulder. "And?"

Carla persevered. "I found out that Agatha, our ancestor, was engaged to a man called Lars."

Jess's face remained unimpressed.

"He *did* die at the altar before they married, because I read about it in an old newspaper article," Carla said, hesitating before adding her big reveal. "It also stated a curse really *was* cast on our family."

This time Jess wriggled herself upright. "Are you making this up?"

"No. I'm the realist, remember? The one who doesn't believe in fairy tales. But I saw this with my own eyes." Carla located the photo and article on her phone and sent them to her sister.

Jess waited for the image to load. "Wow, Lars and Agatha look so young and gorgeous," she said.

"That's what I thought, too."

"I guess I always believed in the *story* of a curse without thinking how it really played out," Jess pondered aloud. "It seems kind of awful that Lars was only twenty-eight. That Isabelle Roelof woman was a witch in all senses of the word."

"It makes me wonder what happened to Agatha, if she ever found love again," Carla mused. "I don't suppose there's any way we can find out."

The two sisters both swept their hair back off their forehead at the same time. Then they noticed and twitched a smile at each other.

"I've missed you," Carla said softly.

Jess worked her lips, not finding a response. "I've got something to tell you, too. Bertrand has asked for Mimi and Gran's blessing for him to propose to Evelyn. Of course, they said yes.

He's going to wait until after your wedding day to pop the question, so he doesn't steal your thunder. He's such a cutie."

"That's fantastic, great news. Yes, he does seem very sweet." The words *wedding day* made something catch in Carla's throat, and tears welled in her eyes.

"What's up?" Jess frowned. "I thought you'd be pleased."

"I am." Carla looked down, resting a hand on her belly.

"Oh." Her sister paused and her eyes widened. "Wait, you're not *preggers*, are you?"

Carla pursed her lips, ruing her sister's sixth sense. Jess had also predicted Mimi was going to marry again before their aunt even announced it. "Please don't tell anyone, including Gran, Mimi and Evelyn," she pleaded. "It's very early days and I've only just found out. I think Tom is in shock from the news."

Jess chewed her bottom lip. "Now that the database has been fixed, I ran yours and Tom's details through the system to check if it's working properly again. I saw that he doesn't want kids..."

Carla briskly rearranged her dress. "I don't want to talk about it. I'm beginning to think Logical Love isn't the best way for people to meet."

Jess gave her a hard blink. "Don't be silly. It works brilliantly for lots of people. It's just a bit, well, regimented."

"Maybe," Carla said stiffly.

The two sisters fell quiet for a while, until Jess jerked her head. "Hold on a sec."

"What?"

"The photo you sent me. There's a stained-glass window behind Agatha and Lars."

Carla shrugged. "So?"

"If I upload the image to Google Lens, I can find similar ones online. We might be able to source where the photo was taken."

"I presume the church is in Holland."

"I'll get back to you in a sec." Jess hung up.

When Jess called Carla back a few minutes later, her eyes were wide and wild. "You are not going to believe this," she started. "I found the window and it *is* in a church…in Preston."

"In Amsterdam?"

"No, silly, in the North West of England."

Carla's brain rattled. "What's it doing there? Lars and Agatha were Dutch and so was the newspaper article. Do you think they had a prewedding photo taken in England?"

"It's the only explanation I can think of, unless there's a window exactly the same in Holland, which seems highly unlikely. And there's something else, too. In the picture I found, I can see the full window."

Carla's phone pinged as Jess sent the image to her.

"Can you see it?" her sister asked.

Carla leaned closer to her phone and saw exactly what Jess meant. In the bottom right-hand corner of the window, among the leaded panels and painted in broad brushstrokes, was a magpie. "Aakster, ekster, magpie," she said. "Lars's surname."

"I know, *right*. There's something very strange about this whole scenario."

Carla leaned back on her bed, at the very least glad the frostiness between her and Jess was thawing. "I'd look into it further, but I'm back in Spain with Babs."

Jess toyed with her hair as she thought. "I could go to Preston, which is much less glamorous. When are you coming home?"

Carla pursed her lips and considered the question. "I don't know. My search here has pretty much ended and I'm waiting for Tom to call me about the baby. He said he needs time to think about everything. I had considered going to Sardinia next, but…" She shook her head.

Jess gave an indignant huff. "So, you're going to sit on your backside waiting for your fiancé to call when you could be checking out a gorgeous Italian island? Well, I know what I'd do."

"Hmm." Carla paused, thinking her sister might be right.

After their call ended, she again checked to see if Tom had messaged her back yet and folded her arms firmly when he hadn't.

Jess had made a good point. Why should she sit around here, in the middle of nowhere, waiting for Tom to make his move? If Carla returned to England, he'd probably remain in America for several more days, and he was also with his ex. Babs was moving back into the civilization of Blanca del Mar, and from what Carla understood, it was fine to travel while pregnant. Plus, a flight to Sardinia should take less than a couple of hours.

Carla also realized she was no longer only looking for a man of great importance to her. He'd have to be highly significant to her unborn child, too.

Out of all the men she'd dated during her gap year, Fidele was the one she'd loved the most, the one she'd regretted leaving behind.

She now knew her family curse did exist, so could that mean she and Tom had been doomed from the start?

Carla paced around her room, considering all her options before deciding she couldn't keep thinking *What if?* She had less than two weeks before she walked down the aisle with Tom, if they *were* still going to get married, and she wanted to know for sure.

Without further ado, Carla messaged Fidele back to say she'd love to see him again and that she'd arrive in Sardinia the following day.

Her search was firmly back on.

# Twenty-Two

Ring

BEING PREGNANT FELT LIKE A GOOD REASON TO BOOK a room in a boutique hotel in the seaside town of Castelsardo, on the northwest coast of Sardinia. During her gap year, Carla had slept on a lumpy mattress in a small room above Fidele's diving center, and this fresh, pretty hotel room felt like some kind of delayed compensation. Her bed came with the fluffiest pillows, and the spacious balcony gave her a beautiful view of the emerald waters of the Gulf of Asinara.

If she stood outside and turned to the right, she could see a mosaic of brightly colored houses in shades of cornflower blue, lilac, sunflower yellow and pistachio tightly packed together on a rocky outcrop that was topped with fortified walls and a citadel.

The hotel was only a couple of hundred meters away from Fidele's place, and Carla watched as a group of people wearing ill-fitting wetsuits headed along the beach to board a small boat. The sight of them brought back memories of the time she'd once spent here.

She and Fidele used to tour hotels throughout the area, giving short diving demonstrations in the swimming pools, so tourists could "try dive" before signing up for lessons. Carla had helped with transporting the scuba tanks and other equipment down to the beach, offering reassurance to anyone who was nervous about going underwater.

Many shipwrecks lay strewn on the island's seabed, and Fidele sometimes took the more experienced divers out to visit them. The decaying carcasses of the ghost ships offered up a whole underwater city bustling with activity—soft and hard corals, giant moray eels, sea slugs and starfish.

By the time Carla and Fidele rinsed the wet suits after the day's diving, the sunset made the sky look alight with fire.

One night, Carla had found him sitting on a rock looking out to sea. Fidele had handed her a spare bottle of beer and they'd both opened them on the rocks. After clinking them together, they'd pocketed the caps and talked for hours about their families. Fidele wore a blue glass eye on a leather thong around his neck, a little like her own.

At the time, Carla had been acutely aware that a closeness was blossoming between them. There'd been something magnetic and positive about him, and when they'd kissed for the first time, his lips fit hers perfectly and tasted of beer and salt. From that moment on, they were rarely apart, working together by day and sinking into each other's arms at night, the sound of laughter and music in the restaurants beneath them.

*All good things come to an end*, Carla had told herself, and as the summer season fizzled away, tourists dwindled, too. Time sped up and she also thought it was time to move on.

Fidele had taken her hand by sunset and asked her to stay with him in Sardinia. It was something Carla had wanted, too, so easy to picture a life for them together. But, by now, she hadn't seen Jess and Gran for almost a year, and she was missing how the leaves turned to orange and scarlet on the trees in

England. She felt she should be wearing a wooly hat, scarf and boots, instead of a beach dress and sandals.

She'd expressed all of this to Fidele while knowing she couldn't ask him to leave behind the island and business he loved so much.

When they'd parted ways, Carla had sobbed, knowing this man she loved and the beautiful island they'd temporarily shared would hold a place in her heart forever.

Fidele had lingered in her thoughts for a long time afterward, and she could still almost feel his warm fingers wrapped around hers and see the moonlight reflected in his eyes. After all this time, she sometimes wondered what might have happened if she'd stayed.

She'd expected to feel nervous and apprehensive about seeing him again, but instead she felt calm, almost as if their reunion was supposed to happen.

Carla strolled along the promenade toward the diving center, and Fidele grinned as soon as he saw her. His black curls had been shorn and he now sported a beard. Carla had forgotten just how strong his nose was in profile, a high hook on the bridge, and his eyes were still the deepest chocolate brown. Fidele set down the scuba tank he was carrying and let out a whoop. He sped toward her, scooping her into his arms.

He smelled of the sea, a salty tang that brought back even more of her feelings for him, some of which put a flush in Carla's cheeks.

They finally pulled apart and looked at each other.

"I didn't think you were going to reply to me," Carla remarked.

"One of my sons is supposed to look after the website inquiry form. He is seventeen, so his brain is not always alert." Fidele laughed. "I'm so glad you're here."

"I'm happy, too."

*"Hey,"* a woman shouted and waved at Fidele from the beach. She held up her ring finger to him.

"Ten minutes," he called in reply and fixed his attention back on Carla. "The lady dropped her wedding ring in the sea," he explained. "Fortunately, we were practicing in the shallow water. I'm going to see if I can find it before the sun starts to set. Care to join me?"

Carla thought about squeezing into a wetsuit and shook her head. "I think I'll pass."

"The water is warm and refreshing." He smiled persuasively. "You will only need your face mask, snorkel and fins."

Carla tilted her head, a memory just in reach. "I remember there was an octopus who lived on a rocky shelf close to shore. I think you called it Knusa?"

Fidele beamed, delighted she'd remembered. "Yes. It is a Norwegian name meaning 'to tear something to pieces.' The little guy is still there."

Carla frowned. "It can't be. They only live for a few years."

"He must have told his relatives about the place and they moved in. Good news travels fast." Fidele laughed and he nodded toward the dive gear on the beach. "Tempted?"

Carla looked out to sea, and it looked so peaceful and inviting, the perfect remedy to wash away her worries about Tom, and she changed her mind. "I'll see you back here in ten minutes," she said.

"Good! I will tell the lady to wait for a little while."

Carla returned to her room and changed quickly, wondering if Fidele would notice her body was curvier than it used to be. *How could Tom not want this baby?* she thought, glancing in the mirror. She put on her swimsuit and draped a scarf around her waist as a sarong. After placing her travel journal in her bag to show Fidele, she returned to the beach.

While she was selecting a face mask and snorkel in the diving center, a couple of women loitered on the promenade.

"I can't believe I dropped my damn ring in the sea," one of them groaned.

"Lucky for you that gorgeous instructor is going to look for it. He's totally fit in that tight black wetsuit."

"We're looking for my ring, remember? Not the local wild-life."

They both laughed.

Carla joined Fidele on the beach. They walked to the end of the jetty and slipped into the sea from the end. Fidele's yellow fins disappeared below the surface, and Carla pushed her face under, treading water as she watched him.

Her face mask made everything look clear beneath the waves. Fish flitted all around her, their silver, gold, striped and orange bodies flashing in the rays of sun that cut into the water. Down deeper, she admired an eagle ray gliding over gnarled bands of coral and the spiral shell of an enormous conch.

Fidele's movements were as languid as the morning tide that kissed the shore. He glided effortlessly throughout water, whereas Carla had never been a natural swimmer, her arms and legs clumsy and unable to find a pleasing rhythm. As a child, she'd once owned a windup toy shark that swam in circles in the bath, and she imagined she'd also move that way in a con-fined space.

All she could hear was the sound of her own breathing and her limbs moving through the water. Her thoughts about Tom, Logical Love and other men fell away, replaced with a feeling of tranquility.

Fidele connected his thumb and index finger to make an okay sign, and when Carla returned the gesture, it was like they'd both slipped back in time. It was easy to imagine that, after their time in the water, they'd return to his little room above the diving center to strip off their clothes and climb under the covers, their skin still damp and salty.

Carla watched as Fidele searched among the corals, skeptical he'd ever find the ring and feeling preemptive sympathy for the woman waiting on the beach. But she'd forgotten how well he knew the reef. After a while, Fidele attracted her attention and made a thumbs-up signal to indicate he was going to resurface, and she caught a glimpse of something shiny in his hand.

Carla raised her head above the water, and they bobbed on the waves together.

"I found it," Fidele shouted to her.

"*Really?* Well done." Her mood soared even more.

They swam back to the shore, where the woman hugged Fidele for a few seconds too long, followed by her friend, who did the same thing. They hung around while he peeled off his wetsuit. "Ladies, you are most welcome," he said with a bow, throwing a towel around his neck. They scuttled away whispering to each other and giggling.

Fidele turned to Carla. "You can leave your mask, snorkel and fins here. My team will put all the equipment away. I think we've earned ourselves a drink before dinner."

*Dinner sounds lovely*, Carla thought. After dealing with Tom's disappointing reaction to her pregnancy news, she looked forward to sitting at a tiny table on the promenade, eating cheese pastries or *fregola*, a unique variety of Sardinian pasta, just like old times.

After they'd showered and got dressed again, Fidele took the top off a cooler and helped himself to a beer. Carla selected a bottle of lemonade and they walked barefoot across the road to sit down on the sand. It only took minutes for the sun to turn copper, sinking down toward the sea.

Carla took a swig of her drink and smiled at him. "Tell me more about your life. What have you been doing for the last twenty years?"

"Wow, has it really been so long?" Fidele shook his head. "I have been very lucky. I have a wife and four sons. Plus, three octopuses." He laughed.

*Wife?* Carla froze with her bottle pressed to her lips. She'd managed to persuade herself he might be single and waiting for her, as per the man of Myrtle's prediction. A wave of regret washed over her, both sweet and sour, and she drank more lemonade to disguise it. "A dad of seven, wow. Congratulations. I'm so happy for you," she said, straining a smile and trying not to feel jealous.

"And you? Are you happy?" he asked.

"Oh…yes, of course." Carla didn't want to open up *that* can of worms. "I'm about to get married for the second time, the week after next. I don't have any children—or sea creatures. How old are your boys?"

Fidele counted on his fingers. "They are nineteen, seventeen, twelve and ten. Like a football team," he added, his eyes shining. "They are cooking dinner for us tonight. Please expect something simple, rather than a sophisticated meal."

"It sounds wonderful." She smiled a little ruefully, her dream of a romantic candlelit meal for two sliding away.

"They are going to call to us when it is ready."

A delicious cooking aroma soon filled the air, and Fidele stood up when he heard someone shout his name. He offered his hand to help Carla to her feet, and they carried their empty bottles back across the road. The diving center was now closed for the day, and he opened a small gate, leading to a narrow passageway that she didn't recall.

At the back of the building was a small courtyard, strung with fairy lights in the trees. A long table was set with a white tablecloth, plates and cutlery. The air was warm without a breeze and Carla could still hear the distant shush of the waves. "It's beautiful," she said, understanding clearly why Fidele had never wanted to leave, and why she'd been so tempted to stay.

"Thank you. It is my small paradise." Fidele turned and waved to someone, a woman with a flock of graying curls who'd entered the yard. "Do you remember Eve?"

Carla glanced at the woman. Her arrival was unexpected, and Carla frowned, racking her brain. *Eve?*

As the woman drew closer, Carla recognized more of the woman's features. And that was when it hit her. She'd once known a fellow traveler named Eve and had been friends with her throughout her time in Sardinia. There was a photograph of them both in her travel journal, holding a fish that they'd let slip back into the water, and she could now see they were one and the same person.

"Oh…yes," Carla said, hoping Fidele wouldn't hear the mix of surprise, disappointment and regret in her voice. "Of course, I remember Eve."

She gazed all around her at the lights in the trees swaying in a warm breeze, and the tablecloth fluttering, and the warm smile lighting up Fidele's face as he looked at his wife. She returned Eve's grin even though she felt a lump growing in her throat and she tried to look pleased to see her, struggling to cover up the envy that was rippling inside her. Because Eve had stayed in Sardinia to carve out a life and family for herself with Fidele.

And Carla hadn't.

# Twenty-Three

## Photos

EVE'S SMILE WAS WIDE AND WELCOMING, CRINKLES radiating from her eyes. Her curls were tamed with a green bandanna, and her limbs were bronzed in her white shorts and Guns N' Roses T-shirt. "Oh, my days, Carla," she exclaimed, moving in for a hug. "I can't believe you're here. I was so excited when Fidele said you'd been in touch. It's so great to see you. The boys and I have been out buying food at the market this afternoon and our meal is almost ready. Do you remember how you showed me how to dive, all those years ago? You were so lovely and kind, beautiful inside and out. You haven't changed one bit."

Although Carla was motionless, her body felt like she was moving, as if she was standing on a boat. An alternative life flashed before her eyes, one where she'd stayed in Sardinia with Fidele.

After leaving the island and her gap year behind, Carla had felt aimless when she'd arrived back in England, eventually entering a marriage that had hit the rocks. After her and Aaron's divorce, she'd been so focused on setting up her business, on maintaining her composure and on ensuring *other* people found the right partner, she had quite forgotten that romantic, adventurous Carla ever existed.

In their Mediterranean paradise, Fidele and Eve had embraced a beautiful, simple life together, and it seemed to have worked out wonderfully.

"It's so great to see you, too," Carla said, her lips wobbling a little. She patted her hands to her sides. "So, you guys got together and married, then?"

Eve flung an arm around Fidele's neck and planted a kiss on his cheek. "Yup. We took a leap of faith, and just look at us now."

Fidele beamed back at her.

"That's great." Carla forced a smile, though her sense of loss was sharp. She mentally struck The King of Cups from the tarot deck, before the night had even started. Fidele seemed unlikely to be the significant man supposed to be waiting for her.

The three of them sat down and continued chatting until Fidele and Eve's sons appeared in a line. They each said hello and introduced themselves.

"What have you cooked for us, boys?" Eve asked. She added under her breath to Carla, "I am teaching them to look after themselves, so I don't have to do *everything* around here. I said they didn't have to eat with us tonight, to give us adults a chance to talk."

The boys served *zuppa Gallurese,* a cross between a lasagna and a casserole, made with layers of rustic bread, cheese, herbs and meat broth. This was followed by *seadas,* crisp, deep-fried pastries filled with lemony fresh cheese and soaked in warm honey.

Eve and Carla swapped stories about their gap years, comparing which countries they'd loved the most and discussing some of their favorite sights. "Do you feel you ever missed out by staying in one place?" Eve asked her husband.

"Never." Fidele shook his head. "If you are happy at home, why look anywhere else? Real happiness comes from here." He made a heart shape with his hands against his chest.

"You have obviously never lived in rainy old England, where the view is of the terraced house opposite and the dogs in the yard." Eve laughed, her eyes encouraging Carla to join in. "Sometimes, when you are younger, you don't know who you are yet, or where you belong in the world, and you have to travel to find yourself. If I hadn't traveled to Sardinia, you and I wouldn't have met."

Eve and Fidele looked into each other's eyes, and candlelight danced on their faces.

Carla curled her fingers, feeling like she was intruding. "How did you two get together?" she asked, curious how long it had taken Fidele to find love again after she'd left.

"It happened a few months after you went home," Eve answered tactfully. "I dated a couple of other guys while I was here, but things didn't work out."

Fidele nodded in agreement.

"I went on one date with this drunken guy who was hassling me to go back to his place when Fidele showed up and rescued me, like a fairy-tale prince or something."

Carla's smile felt tight, and she wondered if her hosts would be lovey-dovey all night.

When she'd first started dating again after her divorce, it hadn't been a positive experience. One of her dates had accidentally left his wallet at home so she had to pay for his meal, drinks and taxi, and another asked if he could sleep on Carla's sofa because his wife had kicked him out. One brought his mother along because she liked to vet his potential girlfriends.

Carla had attended a speed-dating session where the selection of potential suitors had been far too old, too young, too brash, too timid or preened like pedigreed cats. She'd met one of them afterward for a proper date and he'd taken her to an Argentinian-style steak restaurant, even though she'd been vegetarian at the time. In comparison, her subsequent dates with Tom had almost been perfect.

All this talk about Eve and Fidele's big love affair made her mouth feel dry. "I've brought some photographs with me," she said to change the subject. "I kept a travel journal during my travels and thought you might like to see them."

"Wicked." Eve's eyebrows lifted. "Yes, please."

Carla opened the book, realizing there were more photos of her and Fidele than she'd originally thought.

Eve didn't seem to mind. "Hah, look at your amazing hair," she said to her husband. "It was so luscious."

He swept a hand across his head. "I might grow it back."

Eve reached out to stroke it, too. "I don't think that's gonna work, babe." They leaned across the table and kissed.

Carla's jaw began to ache.

She pointed to a photo of a group standing outside Fidele's diving center. Eve stood to the far left of the shot wearing a red bandanna and not looking very different at all.

"A real trip down memory lane." Eve sighed contentedly after browsing through them all. "I've been sorting out some old photos, too. When Fidele mentioned you'd been in touch, I dug them out. I think we should design a page for our website showing the history of the diving center and use some of the shots."

"I love this idea," Fidele said.

"Mwah." Eve blew him a kiss and disappeared inside to fetch the pictures.

"I thought meeting Eve again would be a nice surprise for you." Fidele grinned, topping up Carla's glass with water. "I knew you would enjoy catching up together."

Carla smiled and nodded. The truth was, she remembered

Eve used to have a reputation for being a party girl, known for hopping in and out of bars and beds. Not that it mattered now. Eve had gotten her man, and she and Fidele seemed extremely happy. And besides, Carla wasn't jealous about their relationship at all. Not one little bit.

Eve returned and placed three paper envelopes on the table with dates written on the front. "Remember when it took days to develop photos?" She laughed, opening the first pack and then leafing through them. "Happy days. I'm looking for any of you, Carla. I think I may have several of our diving adventures." She turned the shots this way and that, passing the images across to Carla to take a look.

It was strange seeing shots of herself she hadn't seen before, laughing and drinking beer on board a boat. Carla remembered she'd joined a group of others on a sailing day trip. "Where was this taken?" she asked. "Where did we go to?"

Eve peered across the table. "We sailed across to Corsica for the day and stopped for a picnic and a swim. Do you remember we went to the caves of Bonifacio and were supposed to visit the castle? Instead, we all found a cute terrace bar overlooking the harbor and stayed there drinking all afternoon."

"Oh, yes." Carla only semirecalled this. She recognized some of her fellow travelers but not others. She looked at her own sun-kissed cheeks and her unlined skin and she wanted to say to herself, *Don't go home, Carla. Not just yet. Stay and see where things lead with Fidele.*

"Here's one of you and me. Just look at us, we're so young," Eve gushed, sliding across another photo.

It had been taken as a portrait format shot, with Carla and Eve occupying the bottom half of the image. They pressed their cheeks together and laughed as they clinked beer bottles. Above them, photobombing the shot, was a young blond guy who wore a T-shirt with the name of the bar on the front. He

wore a napkin over one shoulder and held up two fingers behind Carla's head, to make bunny ears.

Carla's smile froze. It then fell away from her lips completely,
and her blood cooled in her veins. She *knew* this man but hadn't
realized she must have randomly encountered him while day
tripping in Corsica twenty-one years ago. Her fingers stiffened
as she gripped the photo and she tried to avert her gaze, but she
couldn't stop looking at *him*.

Then, out of the blue, an unwanted thought hit her like a
freak wave.

Oh god, he couldn't possibly be the man represented by The
Lovers card, could he? She felt the blood drain from her face.

"Are you okay?" Eve asked. "You look like you've seen a
ghost."

Carla swallowed and tapped on the shot. "Do you remember this guy?"

Eve's curls shook. "No. He looks like he worked in the bar…"

"Did we *meet* him?"

Eve shrugged. "If we bought drinks at the bar, or if he served
us, we must have."

Carla scratched her arm without realizing it.

"Are you cold?" Eve said. "I can bring a blanket, and the
boys can make coffee for us."

Carla started to stand up, wanting to distance herself from
the photo. She dropped it back onto the table face down. "I
should go," she said hurriedly. "It's been so lovely to see you
again, but it's been a long day."

"Oh, sure…" Eve said with a surprised shrug. "Are you sure
you don't fancy another drink?"

Carla shook her head and gave an involuntary shiver.

Eve stood up, too. "We should meet up tomorrow, if you're
free," she offered. "I can take you up to the citadel. Do you
remember the amazing views out to sea?"

"Yes, sounds lovely," Carla said. She hugged Fidele and Eve

good night and set off back to her hotel, feeling like she'd borrowed someone else's legs.

Carla swiped her room card and entered her bedroom, then
switched on her bedside lamp. She yanked the doors open
to her balcony and stood leaning with her arms outstretched
against the railing. A breeze had picked up and she looked at
the expanse of inky-black sky above her and the sea below.
She googled The King of Cups on her phone and again saw a
distinguished man clasping a gold goblet in front of the waves.
The card represented a stable relationship and told her not to
suppress her impulses. It was connected to the water, and she
just knew it had to be Fidele.

Which only left The Lovers.

Carla felt shaky again and she gripped the railing, taking
several gulps to try to catch her breath.

Could the man in Eve's photo really be the same person
Myrtle had seen in her reading?

"*Please* don't let it be him," she said aloud. But her voice was
swallowed up by the sound of the waves and the hot night air.

# Twenty-Four

Insect

SLEEP EVADED CARLA THAT NIGHT. SHE DRANK WATER from a bottle, pulled her covers up to her chin and wrestled them off again. She went to the bathroom a couple of times and reopened the patio doors to let some fresh air into her room. Back in bed, her legs wouldn't stay still, jerking as if they wanted to dance without her. She refused to look at her phone, in case she had an urge to search for the man in the photo, to find out where he was now and if he was single. She prayed he was happily married, the same as Fidele, so he couldn't possibly be the only contender left for The Lovers card.

Carla tried to distract herself by thinking about all the other pressing issues in her life. It had now been several days since she'd spoken to Tom, and part of her wondered if he'd been in an accident, or if he was just taking time to let the pregnancy news sink in. Was he still dead set against having children?

She stared at the ceiling, drifting off and waking intermittently. Something buzzed close to her ear and she batted a hand to swat the insect away. She pulled the pillow over her head as a barrier and eventually drifted off into a light sleep, only to be woken by her phone pinging at five o'clock in the morning.

She groaned when she saw her sister had messaged her.

I've got news. It's not urgent, I can't sleep. Club Insomnia, Jess texted.

Carla groggily propped herself up in bed. I'm there too x, she texted back.

Sorry, did I wake you?

I'm not sure if I was awake or asleep.

A few seconds later, Carla's phone vibrated and she pressed it to her ear. "Hi," she said with a yawn.

"Hi," Jess said, equally sleepily. "Do you remember when we used to wake up early in our bedroom and whisper to each other, thinking no one could hear us?"

"Then Gran used to knock on the wall and shout for us to go back to sleep," Carla added.

"And we'd both be exhausted in school, later on? This feels a bit like that."

Carla smiled to herself. "What's your news?"

"I paid a visit to that church in Preston," Jess said. "It's only fifty miles away, and the stained-glass window was there, just as it looks in the photo, complete with the magpie."

"You didn't shoot up in flames for heresy?"

"Don't worry, I left my runes and sage at home, and I dressed smartly, too. The vicar looked ancient, like he'd been there forever, and a church didn't seem the right place to tell him our family was cursed. I talked to him about the window, though, and he told me some interesting things…"

Carla plumped up her pillow and got comfortable. "Tell me more."

"When I mentioned Lars and Agatha, he started to talk as if he'd known them personally, a long time ago. He mentioned they were a quiet couple who both lived into their eighties."

Carla's brow crinkled. "Was he talking about the same people?"

"I reckon so. He mentioned the couple were Dutch."

Carla's mouth parted with confusion, and she felt the need to recap what she knew. "So, we know a curse was cast, and it was announced in a newspaper that Lars died because of it, but then we find out that he and Agatha both lived in England until a ripe old age?"

"Yes," Jess said. "That's it. The vicar also told me they had a son named Willem. He died several years ago."

"So, we can't ask him anything..." Carla mused aloud.

"What's there to ask?"

"I don't know." She just felt, *knew*, that there had to be more to this story. "So, Lars and Agatha somehow managed to outwit the curse?"

"It looks that way. But that's not all. The plot thickens," Jess said, her breath quickening. "The vicar said Agatha was a glass artist and she designed the window in the church. That could be why the design features the magpie. He still had some records on file, so could tell me the window was installed in December 1923."

Carla batted the buzzing insect away from her face again. "But Lars died in November 1923, in Amsterdam. The newspaper article says so. How did he and Agatha manage to have their photo taken in front of the window in December, in England?"

"I have no idea. My head hurts thinking about it."

Carla's logical side kicked in. "There's obviously some mistake. The church records must be wrong or something. We need to look at the positives here. Even if a curse was bestowed on Lars and Agatha, they somehow managed to escape it. It looks like it didn't work."

"But how?" Jess asked.

"Maybe curses aren't true after all," Carla reasoned. However, Anastacia's talk of spirituality and Pharaohs' curses in the early twentieth century left her feeling not *quite* certain.

Both sisters took a moment to try to make sense of everything but failed.

"Where are you up to with your search?" Jess asked.

Carla glanced toward her bedside drawer. "There's only one card left now."

"Which one?"

Carla grimaced, not wanting to think about *his* face, about *his* name. "The Lovers," she muttered.

"Ooh," Jess said. "Who's that supposed to represent?"

"I'm not sure."

Jess tutted. "You always mumble when you're lying. You're going to marry Tom in ten days' time, so you need to find this last guy quickly."

"Um…how are things going between you and Mr. Forty-Nine Percent?" Carla asked.

"Switching the subject, I see," Jess said with a small laugh. "Last night he made me spaghetti carbonara and it was so gorgeous I've renamed him Mr. Fifty-Eight Percent."

"I'm glad you're giving him a chance."

"Me, too," Jess said. "I've also been speaking to more couples who matched during the problem year at work, and the majority report to be happy, even if their percentage matches are lower."

Carla gritted her teeth. "You didn't tell them that?"

"God, no. Ignorance is bliss. I even told some of them you're getting married, to prove the system works."

"Perhaps believing they're well matched makes couples act that way, just like our family automatically thinks their relationships *won't* work out," Carla said. She ran her fingers over her bedsheets, mulling over a question. "Do you think women in our family drive people away, so they can't get close to us? Is it something *I* do?"

Jess clicked her tongue. "I suppose we're a force to be reckoned with, and you need to be a strong character to deal with that. After your divorce, you hardly gave anyone else a chance, and Mum obviously thought we'd be okay without our dads in our lives. Do you think they even know we exist?"

It was something Carla had asked herself many times. Had she and Jess been born out of loving relationships that had failed, or were they the results of one-night stands? Had Suzette ever given their fathers a chance to be part of their lives?

She could remember a few of the men who had dipped in and out of Suzette's life. She'd seen some of them only once, whereas others had lasted longer. They'd suddenly appear and present Carla with lollipops, dolls, hair bobbles and skipping ropes, saying "Surely this is your little sister, not your daughter" to Suzette. Carla would give them her best death stare while her mother dissolved into giggles.

When Suzette fixed her green-blue eyes on you, it could make you feel like the most important person in her world. But this attention only lasted briefly before shifting somewhere else. She hadn't been a neglectful mum, just an erratic one.

"I don't know if our dads know about us or not," Carla finally replied. "Perhaps they weren't that interested in us."

"Doesn't that *hurt* you?" Jess's voice sounded smaller. "To know that someone so important was missing from our lives? I never even tried to win races on school sports day, because there was no one to ruffle my hair and say *well done* afterward. My dad didn't know me, or he chose not to be there…"

"Gran and Granddad were always there for us."

"That was lovely, but not the same."

Carla understood. She'd also longed for someone to kick a football with, who'd teach her how to skip stones on a lake. Sometimes she'd lain in bed at night and pretended her dad was downstairs in the kitchen, cutting the crusts off her cheese sandwiches and rubbing an apple on his shirt to make it shine.

"I hardly have any memories of Mum," Jess added. "I remember falling asleep on the bus once, wedged between you both. My head rested on Mum's shoulder and she was humming to me. The sun was shining through her window and I felt all warm and safe, like I never wanted to leave your sides."

Carla couldn't recall this moment. Her memories of her mother were more random and sporadic, like how Suzette once made her a blue nylon jumpsuit to wear to the school disco party when she was nine years old. Her mum proclaimed it was "Coolio" and "Everyone will want one."

The jumpsuit attracted whispers and smirks because the other kids were wearing all the latest fashions, like Nirvana T-shirts or blouses with puffed sleeves. When Carla had arrived home from the disco, she'd ripped her outfit off and stuffed it under her bed.

Suzette had surveyed her with her hands on her hips. "People laughed at David Bowie and he did okay. You should try to stand out, not fit in."

But Carla had just wanted to be like the other kids, especially when Suzette got cancer and her copper hair came out in clumps from her treatments.

She remembered her mum pushing Jess briskly in her stroller, the sun bouncing off her bald patches on her head. Suzette had tried to disguise the glassy sadness in her eyes with oversize sunglasses. "Nothing to see here. I don't need your sympathy," she'd snapped if anyone looked at her. "If your lives were more interesting, you wouldn't have to gossip about mine."

"I still feel guilty about leaving you to go traveling," Carla admitted to Jess.

"Don't be. I thought it was cool. I thought *you* were cool. But I was jealous of you for a long time."

Her subsequent pause told Carla it might still be the case.

"I have to go," Jess said eventually. "I promised to go out for breakfast with Evelyn, Gran and Bertrand this morning. Bertrand's found a knitting café where all the teapots wear little woolen sweaters. Let's catch up again soon."

"Yes, let's do that," Carla said, her thoughts now in even more of a spin. She lowered her phone and clasped it in both hands, wondering if the curse was a make-believe thing after all. Or was it real, and Lars and Agatha had outsmarted it?

If anyone had told her a few weeks ago that she'd be lying in bed in Sardinia, contemplating her impending marriage and the possibility that her family's curse was *real*, all while preparing to meet an old flame and his wife for a day out, she wouldn't have believed them. It was just all too bizarre.

Carla took a long shower and went down for breakfast in the hotel restaurant. Finding herself surrounded by couples and families, she forced herself to eat some bread and fruit.

She meandered along the seafront, admiring the turquoise waves and watching locals chat over espressos and fresh pastries. Café owners opened up striped umbrellas, and the sound of brush bristles scraping against paving stones filled the air.

She had never really been a people watcher but found it fascinating to look more closely at everyone around her, assessing who might have chemistry together and who didn't.

Two men with tattooed calves brushed hands as they walked their dogs, their gaze fixed on their Chihuahuas before shifting over to each other. An elderly couple, both wearing matching khaki shorts with too many pockets, sat on a bench and broke a sandwich in half to share. It was not lost on Carla that the man gave his wife the bigger piece. A young man laughed uncontrollably as his girlfriend picked him up for a piggyback ride, his legs jiggling as she broke into a run.

Carla noticed all their wistful smiles, flicks of hair and blatant stares of desire, and it made her feel warmer inside.

Fidele stood waiting for her outside the diving center with

his two youngest sons draped around his waist. "Sorry, but Eve is feeling a little poorly," he explained. "Maybe we shouldn't have asked our sons to make the food last night. Are *you* feeling okay?"

"Yes, I'm fine, the food was lovely. That's a shame about Eve. I hope she'll be okay."

"It may take a day or two for her to recover and I have to look after the diving center, so I'm afraid I can't accompany you today." He pursed his lips with a regretful smile.

"That's fine, honestly." Carla told herself she was feeling very tired anyway. "Please give my love to Eve."

Fidele nodded and reached into his pocket to take out an envelope of photographs. "She asked me to give you these duplicate photos." He handed them to Carla, his fingers lingering close to hers when she took them. "You and your husband must come to visit us again soon, after your wedding."

They both knew it was unlikely to happen, something that made her heart feel heavy. "I'd love that," Carla said anyway. "I'm so glad you found happiness with Eve."

"I was happy before her, too," Fidele said, and they looked into each other's eyes with a sense of understanding and also helplessness.

Carla could tell Fidele wanted to embrace her, and she wanted to hold him, too, but there were two young boys hanging around his waist, tugging on his T-shirt and wanting to go to the beach. The reality of the situation was unavoidable. "Bye, Fidele," Carla said softly, hoping they weren't the last words she'd ever say to him.

"Bye, Carla," Fidele replied. "And thank you."

"Thank you, too."

Carla turned and walked away from him with the corners of her mouth curving down. Tears swelled in her eyes and she headed into a beach shop as a brief respite from the glare of the sun. A bright red backpack sat on a table, and Carla remembered how she'd once traveled so lightly during her gap year, without tugging her cumbersome baggage around. She hastily bought it, hugging it to her chest for comfort as she hurried back along the promenade toward her hotel.

Once she was inside her room, Carla closed the door and leaned her back against it, sliding down to the floor. Her cheeks were hot and wet from tears, and she used her fingers to wipe them away. Everything suddenly felt too much to bear. Her problems with Tom, the reality of the curse, saying a final goodbye to Fidele, and The Lovers card seemingly guiding her toward a past relationship she'd tried to forget. Her pulse quickened whenever she thought about *that man*, and not in a good way.

Carla decided to stay in Sardinia for the night, ready to move on again in the morning. Her hotel room was expensive, and she was feeling homesick, really missing her gran.

She tried to compose herself by sifting through all her clothes, removing the plainer ones and leaving them in a pile on top of her suitcase. Hopefully the hotel owners could use them or donate them to charity. She stuffed the tarot cards into the side pocket of her new backpack.

Eve's photos were the last thing she packed, and her fingers twitched as she opened the envelope. She slid out the photograph of the man sticking his fingers up behind her hair and thought that it was the kind of silly thing he always used to do.

She'd tried to ignore all the signs around her pointing toward this man's existence. Carla had seen him grinning from the *Find Your Happy Place* billboard that Fran had sped past on the highway in Spain, and on the TV property show when Babs had applied her makeup. Carla had torn her eyes away from him both times, trying her absolute best to force him out of her thoughts.

And then she'd spotted him again in Eve's photograph. A third sign.

The number three was considered lucky in many cultures, the first odd prime number, the Holy Trinity, three acts of a story, good things coming in threes. Carla realized the only way she could complete her search for her exes—and to assure herself that The Lovers card did, or didn't, mean anything—was to reach out to the man in the photo.

She took a snap of it on her phone before pushing the envelope of photos into her backpack.

Just thinking about *him* again made Carla's heart feel exposed, red and beating for everyone to see. She could still recall every digit of his phone number, even if she hadn't used it for years, and her hand shook as she dialed it.

It wasn't a surprise to reach his answer machine, his lack of availability always a sore point between them.

The voice on the other end sounded familiar and warm, like he was still part of her life and had never left it.

Carla waited until the voice recording ended, and she left her own in return.

"Hi, Aaron, it's Carla. Your ex-wife. Ring me back when you get this message."

# Twenty-Five

## Watch

NOT LONG AFTER SHE'D LEFT THE MESSAGE ON AARon's answering machine, his assistant got back in touch with her to put a meeting in his calendar. He would be working in his Paris office for the next few days if she was available to come then. Or would she prefer to wait until he was back in the UK?

Carla wanted to get their meeting over with quickly. He was the last man she was looking for, the one she had to discount if she still wanted to walk down the aisle with Tom. He'd been in her life for the longest, and she was glad he was treating their catch-up as a business appointment rather than a rendezvous.

She had no recollection of meeting Aaron in Corsica during her gap year but the evidence was there in the photograph. She really should be traveling back home to England to prepare for her wedding, but instead Carla was going to fly to France. She left her hotel in Sardinia early the next morning in a hurry and arrived in Paris by early afternoon.

The French capital was the supermodel of all others and

wasn't shy about owning its grandeur and beauty. It was Carla's second time here, and any sugary photos posted on social media didn't do it justice. It was like the color saturation settings had been turned up on the city, with avenues of tall emerald trees, and the Seine shining teal blue. The dome of the Sacré-Coeur reminded Carla of an intricate meringue, and the scarlet canopies on restaurants shaded diners who chatted over croissants and milky coffee.

As she walked along the Parisian rues, avenues and boulevards with her backpack, each building she passed seemed to have shuttered windows and curled wrought-iron balconies. The romantic swirls of the art nouveau metro signs and streetlamps contrasted with the stark glass pyramid of the Louvre art museum.

Carla loved overhearing arguments on street corners and admired how French people were so straightforward, knowing what they wanted and where they were going, all while looking so chic.

She still couldn't believe she was doing *this*. That she was actually here. The more she thought about her situation, the worse it seemed. Was she a bad person for going to see her ex-husband just before she got married again? *If* she got married again. Tom still hadn't called her back and she had no idea how he was feeling.

She pictured him wandering around game factories in America, the noise of the machinery drowning out his worries. Maybe he'd be schmoozing in meetings while his thoughts were with her and the baby.

If Tom really loved her, after learning about their mismatch and her pregnancy, hopefully he'd still accept her as she was. And then she'd *know* he was the right person for her and that they were still perfect for each other.

But Carla had to put matters from her past to rest, to face, unpick and resolve things she'd run away from. It had never been her intention to keep secrets from Tom, and she wanted to be the best version of herself in the future. Unfortunately, that also meant meeting with Aaron.

As she walked, Carla sensed love in the air all around her. She spotted fingers trailing over the smalls of backs, and lips waiting to be kissed. A man with an abundance of chestnut hair stood talking in the street to a woman with a platinum crop. Their body language was a little awkward, their bodies angled away from each other, but Carla detected something stirring between them, new and delicious, that they had yet to discover for themselves. She bought two red roses from a street vendor and handed them over with a smile. At first the man and woman stared at her, frowning as if she was strange, but then they glanced at each other and laughed, their barriers breaking down. *"Merci beaucoup,"* the man said with a bow.

An elderly lady wearing a purple pillbox hat with a veil was looking around for somewhere to sit, so Carla offered the crook of her arm and suggested that she settle next to a gentleman in a tweed suit who was alone on a wooden bench. The two nodded cordially to each other and the man offered his bag of peaches for her to take one.

Focusing on these couples made Carla think about Aaron even more, bringing her thoughts back to the first time they'd met.

There had been a brief period of time when her gran had talked about downsizing from her bungalow, and Carla had helped to set up a series of appointments to view various other properties. A newly built block of apartments was fresh to the market and she arranged to meet the property developer at the premises so he could show them both around. Carla and Lucinda had stood outside in the rain for ten minutes waiting for him to arrive.

When he had eventually pulled up in a shiny gray Mercedes, Carla's eyes had hardened. He wore a finely tailored suit and a gold Rolex that was too large for his wrist. He'd introduced himself as Aaron Frame and apologized profusely for his lateness. He'd let them in and showed them the glossy kitchen with built-in appliances and the bedroom with the Juliet balcony. He'd reeled off his spiel about financial plans, deposits, service charges, low-cost energy and maintenance fees, making Carla feel increasingly inadequate. It had been three years since she'd returned from traveling and she'd struggled to slip back into her routine at home. Life on campus and the structure of lessons had felt too stifling after her travels and she'd dropped out of university. Afterward, she'd taken on several admin roles, with any kind of proper career alluding her. Living with Jess, who had now turned seventeen, had also taken its toll.

While Lucinda had examined the wardrobe space in the bedroom and considered where she might display her ornaments, Aaron had rolled up his sleeve and looked at his watch.

"Sorry, are we holding you up?" Carla had snapped. Her socks were soggy from waiting outside in the rain.

"No, apologies. It's my mum's birthday today and I promised to take her out for afternoon tea. The traffic's been appalling all day and my appointments have stacked up. I'm running late and I hate to keep clients waiting, or rush them during their viewings. I'm hoping I'll still get to Mum on time." He'd looked around him and knocked on the windowsill.

Carla had stared at him. "Why did you do that?"

"Habit, I suppose. Isn't knocking on wood something to do with spirits and protection? My mum's interested in things like that."

"My family, too."

"Mum carries this horrible old rabbit's foot around with her." Aaron wrinkled his nose.

Carla had smiled wryly, feeling a little warmer toward him. "I can totally relate."

Lucinda had appeared in the doorway of the living room. "The apartment's lovely but not the right fit for me," she'd said. "The feng shui is all wrong."

Aaron and Carla had shared a knowing glance and he'd handed her his business card. "My mission is to find the right place for the right person," he'd told her. "Let's find something with better vibes for your gran."

"So, you're a matchmaker?" Carla had asked, pocketing his card.

He'd laughed and his blue eyes crinkled. "Yeah, I suppose you can call it that. Now I'd better go to see my mum."

Lucinda had decided to stay in her bungalow after all, because new properties had less space for all her clothes and trinkets, but Aaron and Carla started to see each other anyway. He'd showed her around new developments with solar panels and penthouse views, though Carla struggled to imagine living somewhere so swanky. They'd visited Edinburgh, Cardiff and London to view properties, and taken airplanes at a moment's notice to visit his overseas clients.

When Carla had first dined in fine restaurants with Aaron, she hadn't been sure which cutlery to use when presented with a plethora of knives and forks. She'd been uncomfortable at first, too conscious of her lack of qualifications when they'd dined with CEOs, business proprietors and other property developers. But she did have a good knowledge and experience of several European countries, and possessed a natural air compared to Aaron's more corporate presence. Over a short time, Carla had become surer of herself, dressing smarter and feeling more at ease with his clients. Aaron was also attentive and encouraging, which made her feel interesting.

Any disagreements between them usually started off small, like whether tomatoes should be sliced or quartered (Carla thought they should be sliced because they sat in a sandwich better), or if it was rude to eat in the street (Carla said it was, whereas Aaron claimed it wasn't). They were very different people, so friction seemed inevitable.

Aaron was a shouter and a slammer of doors, whereas Carla was a sulker, using silence to show she was upset.

After their arguments, they would passionately make up.

"Marry me," Aaron had said, propping himself up on one

elbow in bed, following a disagreement about whether grapes should be kept in the fridge or not (Carla thought they were better served cold). And although she knew it was foolhardy and that she was acting without thinking, she'd said yes.

They'd flown to Paris for their honeymoon, where they'd made love before breakfast, after dinner, anytime really. For the rest of their time, they'd explored the city together, visiting so many beautiful parks and art galleries that the sights had become a blur, though Carla had particularly loved the soft watercolors of Monet's waterlilies and the *Mona Lisa*'s steely gaze. After their showy wedding, their anonymity in the city had felt intimate and intense. She and Aaron held hands everywhere and even skipped together. Their hunger for each other soaked into Carla's skin, her entire body, because she loved him so much.

She'd really *loved* him.

Aaron always said his ambition was to have an office in Paris with a view of the Eiffel Tower and he'd asked about hers. Carla's gap-year travels were still bright in her mind—not just the places she'd visited and the sights she'd seen, but also the people. She was in her midtwenties and didn't feel like a fully formed person yet. "I don't really have any," she'd admitted.

"Don't worry," Aaron had said. "One day you'll find your inspiration somewhere."

Carla just hadn't expected it to come from their devastating divorce.

And now she stood outside her ex-husband's Parisian office, staring at his name on a brass plaque next to the smoked-glass revolving doors.

A bout of dizziness made her feel lightheaded and she held a hand to her chest. If Tom hadn't told her he wasn't interested in children, would she have come here at all?

She took a deep breath, held it in her lungs and pushed the glass door.

Inside the building, the lobby had a cool glamour, all white marble, fresh flowers and impossibly attractive people sweeping around. The men looked like they should appear in aftershave commercials, and the women all sported vermilion lipstick. The lady behind the reception desk had shiny hair pulled into a ponytail and she stared haughtily at Carla's curly copper mop.

After introducing herself and confirming she definitely *did* have a meeting with Aaron Frame, Carla sat down and positioned her backpack between her feet. Her palms were sweaty and she felt more like the young traveler she'd once been, not the divorced, pregnant fortysomething woman she now was.

She waited for what seemed like ages but was actually only ten minutes. Each time she heard footsteps, she sat up straighter, preparing to greet her ex-husband.

Carla's ears pricked up when she heard chatter coming from the top of a staircase and watched as a pair of brown handmade shoes descended, followed by a body and face that she knew all too well. She was aware of a vein pulsing in her neck and the sound of her own breath growing sharper.

And then there he was in front of her, with his tousled blond hair and matching stubble, wearing the smile that had always made her melt.

Aaron.

Carla stood up, her arms hanging by her sides, lost in a mist of memories and emotions that made her brain whirl.

"Carla," Aaron said, sweeping forward and taking her into his arms, as if they were still married and had been apart for twelve weeks rather than twelve years. "You look absolutely stunning. I'm *so* glad you're here."

He insisted on giving Carla a tour of the building and, at first, she thought he was showing off how well he'd done for himself since their divorce. She soon realized he was actually seeking her approval. Each time he pointed out his desk, or a world map marking his other offices, or a shelf full of awards, Aaron glanced at her to examine her expression before he carried on.

Carla was deeply impressed by her ex's achievements, though

didn't want to show it. "I can't see the Eiffel Tower from any of the windows," she remarked.

Aaron stopped still in the middle of an office. "You remembered my dream," he said, and for a moment his eyes appeared glassy. He held out an arm and ushered her toward a tiny corner window. "There." He pointed. "If you stand on your tiptoes, or on a box, you can see the top of the tower. We might have to climb onto the roof for a better view."

She'd forgotten about his ability to laugh at himself and how this made him even more attractive. "Oh yes, I can just about see it now. Impressive."

"I like to think so."

Carla's stomach rumbled, perhaps from hunger. Or maybe it was the baby warning her not to get wrapped up in her ex-husband again.

"You sound hungry," Aaron observed, glancing at his Rolex. "Would you like to go grab something to eat? There's a coffee shop next door. I'm afraid I have another meeting lined up, or else I'd join you."

She pointed at her backpack. "I should check into my hotel first. I picked up a sandwich at the airport."

"Where are you staying?"

She showed him on her phone.

Aaron sucked through his teeth. "That's not a great area. I've got access to several empty properties. I'm sure I can find you somewhere much nicer..."

Carla waved his offer away, determined not to accept his help. "I bet I've stayed in worse places. It will be fine." She was certain Aaron would protest and insist that he knew better, just like he used to do. But instead he pressed his lips together.

"In that case, let me take you to dinner this evening," he said.

# Twenty-Six

## Kiss

UNFORTUNATELY, AARON HAD BEEN RIGHT ABOUT Carla's hotel. Her room reeked of cigarette smoke, and the carpet was threadbare with some unpleasant-looking stains. She flung open her window, convincing herself the room would suffice for a night or two, and she stuffed her backpack under the bed for a semblance of safekeeping.

She couldn't wait to leave again, and she took herself for a walk before she went to meet Aaron.

Carla loved how Paris took on a different atmosphere at dusk. There was an underlying sexiness that wasn't so apparent during the day, like how the original cancan dancers of the Moulin Rouge reputedly didn't wear underwear beneath their flouncy skirts. Mopeds zipped through narrow streets and peals of laughter rang out from bars and cafés. An air of anticipation hung in the squares as people waited for the Eiffel Tower to light up when it went dark.

She crossed the Seine over a bridge where lovers had fastened thousands of padlocks to the railings. Couples gathered and posed for photographs, attaching locks marked with their initials and messages of love. Carla took out her phone and snapped a few shots of them before walking to the place she'd arranged to meet her ex-husband. She almost tripped over her own feet when she saw Aaron was already waiting outside the bistro they used to frequent on their honeymoon. She recognized its bluey-grey exterior and rose-gold signage immediately.

He greeted her with a kiss on the cheek and pressed his hand to the small of her back as they went inside. The gentle warmth of his fingers radiated through Carla's body and she tried not to quiver at his touch.

The bistro's interior looked exactly the same, too, and Carla thought she even recognized a waiter or two. As she and Aaron sat down together, it was easy to forget they were no longer married.

"Merlot?" Aaron asked, looking up at her from the wine list.

Even though she'd love a big glass of red, Carla shook her head. "Just sparkling water for me, please."

If Aaron was surprised, he didn't show it. He leaned in toward her and asked about her business. Whenever he focused his attention on someone, he could make them feel like the only person in the room. Her mother and Aaron had that in common.

"The agency is called Logical Love," Carla told him, careful not to reveal that he'd been the inspiration behind it.

"It's a very clever idea. There are lots of cautious people out there, scared of falling in love and getting hurt. It's a lot easier to be reckless when you're younger." He smiled tightly to himself. "How's your family? Jess, Lucinda and all your aunties?"

Carla was surprised he remembered their names but, then again, why wouldn't he? He'd once been part of her family, for the four years they'd been married. He'd even allowed Mimi to read his tea leaves and didn't run a mile when she'd regaled him with stories about the family curse.

She gave Aaron a brief overview of the years they'd been apart, including how she usually sat in her office surrounded by paperwork and flowers when she wasn't attending other people's weddings.

They both ordered boeuf bourguignon followed by tarte Tatin, and when Aaron picked up his glass of wine, she noticed he wasn't wearing a wedding ring.

"Do you have any children?" he asked.

Carla had anticipated this question and ordered herself not to look at her belly. "No. You?"

"Nope." Aaron's eyes swept away briefly, as if recalling something sad from the past. "I see you're wearing an engagement ring, though. Are you here because you're getting married again?"

She jutted her chin and held his gaze. "Why would I come here because of that?"

"Because when people are about to embark on something big and new in their life, it makes them look backward in time. They get this overwhelming urge to revisit their history."

Carla felt her cheeks flush and she set down her fork. "I don't remember you being this perceptive before."

"Perhaps divorce made me a better person." Aaron smiled to himself. He sprinkled salt on his food and threw a few stray grains over his left shoulder. He moved his leg, and his knee accidentally brushed against hers.

A hot ripple spread through Carla's body and she inched away from his touch.

"Tell me about your husband-to-be," Aaron said. "Are we alike?"

She shook her head. "You couldn't be more different. He's calm, studious, kind and—"

Aaron gave her a look of amusement. "Are you saying that I'm not?"

Carla raised a firm eyebrow at him. "And he doesn't interrupt me when I speak," she added. "Tom listens and he's so creative.

We met through my agency and have a fantastic compatibility score."

"That's great," Aaron said, pressing a napkin to his lips. "It really is."

Carla toyed with a strand of her hair, wondering how much to tell him about the past few weeks. "Of course, my family dragged me to a fortune teller, just to make sure. She read my tarot cards and claimed to see someone in my past who'll be important to my future. She highlighted six cards, and each is supposed to correspond with a man I met during my gap year. Apparently, my happiness hinges upon one of them." She gave a disbelieving headshake.

Aaron nodded. "I remember how your family was superstitious. And yes, my mum still carries that horrible rabbit's foot everywhere with her." He stroked the knot in his tie for a moment. "I thought there had to be a good reason for you to fly to France to see me. Unless it was for my good looks and charm?"

Carla sighed, laughing despite herself. "Nope, sorry."

"And yet, here you are…" His words were light yet loaded.

"The tarot-card thing is ridiculous," Carla blurted out. "I wasn't even aware we'd met during my gap year. You did work as a bartender in Corsica? I saw a photograph of you there."

Aaron frowned at her. "Are you sure it was me?"

Carla took out her phone to show him the photo.

Aaron let out a surprised, sharp laugh. "Yep, that's me all right. I was only there for a few weeks."

"I don't recall you ever mentioning it."

Aaron took some time to answer. "I was a bit ashamed, to be honest."

"About working behind a bar?" she asked incredulously. "What's wrong with that?"

"Nothing. I just did something very stupid."

"Why, what happened?"

Aaron sipped his wine. "A friend of mine was in trouble. She owed some rent money to her landlord, and he'd demanded she pay it that evening, threatening to throw her out on the street if she didn't. But then someone stole her purse. The banks were closed and there were no cash machines around, so she begged me to help her out. I didn't have that kind of money, either, so I borrowed some from the till of the bar I worked in, right at the end of the night. I swear I was going to pay it back first thing the next morning so no one would notice. It was a pretty dumb thing to do, but the owner didn't really like me, so I couldn't ask him for a favor. Anyway, he saw me taking the cash and called the police. I spent the night in custody and lost my job. It was all pretty horrendous. After that, I kind of erased Corsica from my memory. When you and I talked about our travels, I didn't mention it to you. I don't recall you going there, either."

"I only went there for a day trip," she said.

They both looked at the photograph again.

"I bet you thought I looked hot in that T-shirt." Aaron found a grin. "Even I think I look great."

Carla tutted at him. "I didn't even notice you."

Aaron set his wineglass down. "Are the tarot cards really so silly if they brought you here? Which card am I supposed to be?"

The roots of Carla's hair prickled and she struggled to utter her next words. "Perhaps The Lovers," she murmured.

Aaron leaned forward again, so closely Carla could feel his breath on her neck. "I suppose we could find out if the prediction is true," he whispered.

Carla immediately shot back as if scalded. Her head told her to run away, but she had too many things to discuss with him, and too many things she needed answers to. She speared a piece of beef and struggled to swallow it, even though it was tender. "Never."

"Fair enough. I'm sorry things didn't work out between

us," Aaron said. "I was always in a rush—to do things, to go places, to be someone. If I'd have taken more time, listened to you more, things could have been so different. We might even still be together."

Underneath his confident swagger, he'd never been so sensitive or vulnerable with her before, and his blue eyes displayed a new sincerity and maturity. Carla swigged a glass of water to ease a flare of regret.

"We were young," Aaron continued. "You'd lost your mum and helped to raise Jess. You were surrounded by all those superstitions, and your gap year overseas gave you a taste of the real you. And then I came along and proposed to you."

"It was something I wanted, too..."

"I should have allowed you time to grow. If I could turn back time, I'd do things differently."

Carla felt the memories rush back to her, along with the pain of their marriage ending. "You just wanted everything straightaway, a wife, travel, a business, a home...a child..." She let her words fall away, her cheeks burning when she remembered some of their volcanic arguments. "The portfolio of things didn't mix."

"I shouldn't have taken that damn job." Aaron shook his head.

They both picked up their glasses and took a long swig.

Carla and Aaron had been married for over two years when he'd been offered a job in Toronto and had asked Carla to join him. She'd hugged him tightly, full of happiness for him, while also scared of moving away from her family. She was still in a post-wedding haze of homemaking, hosting barbecues and thinking of starting a family, *not* moving somewhere a thirteen-hour flight away.

Aaron had gushed about advancing his career, all the snow and beautiful green spaces, low crime rates and maple syrup. "After a couple of years living in Canada, I'd love to move to Paris. I want an office with a view of the Eiffel Tower..." he'd said.

He always approached everything with zeal and it had been easy for Carla to get caught up with his big plans and ideas. In bed at night, Aaron drew his visions in the air with his hands while Carla wanted to sleep. He was like a tornado spinning around her and she wanted to step out of the eye of the storm sometimes, especially when she'd found out she was pregnant.

When she'd presented the white stick with the two lines to her husband, they'd held hands and danced around their living room together until they were so exhausted they'd collapsed in a heap on the sofa.

"Oh gosh, we're going to be parents." Aaron had beamed and they'd looked at each other with eyes full of astonishment and wonder.

The next few weeks had been a rush of buying pregnancy books, making doctor appointments, throwing away cream cheese from the fridge and buying underwear in a bigger size. They'd agreed not to tell their families until after Carla's twelve-week scan, their secret making things feel even more precious.

Although it had been early days, they'd discussed names for their baby. Carla liked the classics: Lucy or Emily for a girl, perhaps Oliver for a boy. Unusual ones appealed to Aaron more, like Zorro or Bowie. Carla drew a line at them, and they'd agreed that when their child arrived, they'd look at him or her and just *know* the right name.

*This changes everything*, Carla had thought to herself. *Now we'll stay in England.*

Except her pregnancy had added an extra layer of complication to their plans. Aaron started to talk about Canadian education systems, plowing ahead with their move, and the speedometer on their lives revved up a notch. Carla felt like she was on the median strip of a highway, watching cars whoosh past her as she waited for a gap to cross.

They'd held hands tightly when they'd gone for the first scan, looking forward to telling their loved ones about the pregnancy. Carla could still remember the deafening silence of the sonographer as she'd examined the ultrasound image on-screen. Carla had lain there feeling vulnerable with her stomach exposed and shiny with gel, until another nurse had entered the room. The two medical professionals exchanged a few whispered words together.

"I'm very sorry, we can't detect a heartbeat," the sonographer finally said, handing Carla a wad of blue tissue to wipe her belly.

Carla looked at Aaron, and they both numbly faced the screen. "But I can see the shape of the baby. Maybe it hasn't had time to develop properly yet." She'd grasped at thin air as a tear trickled down her cheek.

The sonographer's tone had been kind but firm. "Ultrasound can detect a fetal heartbeat in pregnancies beyond eight weeks but there's no cardiac activity here. I'll arrange for a doctor to talk through the options available to you."

"Options?" Carla had asked in a daze.

"We can let things happen naturally or make another hospital appointment for you."

In the small dim room, Carla and Aaron gripped each other's hands so tightly it hurt.

She'd opted to return to the hospital, where she'd had an anesthetic administered. When she next woke up, she felt totally empty, as if all her internal organs had been removed, too.

Carla and Aaron had dealt with the miscarriage in different ways. She stayed at home, taking comfort in routine and being close to her friends and family, whereas Aaron went full steam ahead with the plans to move overseas. As they pulled in opposite directions, the invisible threads that held them together strained to the point of snapping.

She remembered that they'd attended a glitzy property industry party a few weeks later, even though Carla said she didn't want to go. Aaron had kissed her on the cheek and promised they'd only stay for an hour or so.

She'd worn a red satin dress she wasn't comfortable in and had watched as her husband charmed other people like he didn't have a care in the world.

After a couple of hours, Carla had tapped on her watch to point out the time, and Aaron responded to her gesture by leaving her at the buffet table while he complimented his boss's wife on her earrings. Carla had stared at the food and felt as small and shriveled as the sausages on sticks.

She'd raised it with him when they got home. "Did you really have to talk to *everyone*?" She'd sat down heavily on the bed. "There was no point in me joining you."

"Just being friendly." Aaron laughed while hanging up his suit in the wardrobe.

The way he'd dismissed her concern had lit something in Carla's chest. "You left me standing on my own."

"You're a grown woman. You can make conversation, too."

"It was your event. I didn't want to go in the first place."

"I do things for you, too." Aaron huffed to himself, tipsy after the champagne he'd consumed.

Carla was fully sober at this point and folded her arms tightly. "I'm *not* going to Canada if you're acting this way."

He'd tutted and banged his wardrobe doors shut. "Of course you are."

"I *said* I'm not. Perhaps it's time to choose between me and your job." She didn't really mean it but wasn't able to stop herself blasting the words at him.

"Okay, then," Aaron had said dismissively before climbing into bed. He'd started snoring within minutes, so Carla had to endure a night of broken sleep.

When he'd tried to hold her the next morning, she'd shoved his hands away. Her body had been stiff as she'd waited for an apology that never came. She'd wanted Aaron to say they weren't going to Canada any longer, but he'd gotten out of bed and showered without a backward glance at her.

Carla had refused to kiss him when he'd left for work. "If you go to Canada, we're over," she'd told him.

"Okay, then," Aaron had replied, and it became his stock answer for anything to do with their situation. Whenever he repeated *Okay, then*, blood thumped in Carla's ears.

They'd soon reached a deadlock, with Aaron gathering his belongings together as if they were both still leaving, and Carla hoping her spiky silences and disinterested conversation told him otherwise. She'd willed him to change his mind, but refused to beg him to stay.

Things continued like this for a couple of months until, one day, she'd returned home from work and found Aaron's keys and a letter waiting for her on the doormat. He had locked the door and posted them through the letter box.

Since that day, Carla and Aaron had never talked through the buildup to their divorce, and they'd never got closure from each other. His calls to her from Canada had been awkward and so were her replies. She couldn't even remember which one of them instigated the divorce, and for a relationship full of fire, their split had been remarkably quiet and dull.

Aaron gestured to a waiter in the bistro and ordered two coffees. "I regret taking the job in Canada," he repeated, his mouth twisting.

Carla began to doubt her actions, as well. Had she been right or wrong not to join her ex-husband overseas? Had she overreacted about the party? Sometimes she even found herself quartering tomatoes rather than slicing them. "I shouldn't have given you an ultimatum," she said. "I needed more time to process our loss."

"I let you go too easily. I was immature and didn't believe in compromise."

"I pushed you away."

"We pushed each other." Aaron toyed with his knife for a

while. "Do you really want to play board games for the rest of your life?" he asked.

A shiver ran down Carla's back. "How *on earth* do you know what Tom does?"

"I'm a curious person." Aaron raised his palms. "I may have looked you up from time to time…"

Carla set her jaw. "I need someone stable and secure in my life. Not someone who packs a suitcase and races off overseas at a moment's notice."

"Like *you're* doing now?"

Carla slapped a palm on the table, making her cutlery jump. Aaron was the only person in the world who could send her emotions into a tailspin so quickly. She raised her hand and gestured for the check, then took out her purse to pay it.

The waiter brought it over, presenting it on a silver plate.

Aaron whipped the bill off the plate before Carla could reach for it, something he used to do all the time. Another of his bad habits was answering her phone before she could get to it, which also made her fume.

"I said I'd take you out for dinner, and I don't think you should stay in that hotel tonight," Aaron said.

"I don't care what you think."

"Oh, I think you do. Or else you wouldn't be here."

They both folded their arms and shared fiery stares.

"Look," Aaron said eventually, his voice softening. "I have access to a new penthouse in the city. It's been freshly renovated and is ready to go on the market. Why not stay there tonight instead?" He took a plastic key card from his pocket and showed it to her.

Carla shook her head. "Absolutely not."

"Please," he said. "I want to know that you're safe. At least let me walk you back to your hotel, so we can check out the area together."

Carla looked into the eyes of the man who'd once been her

husband, the man who'd made her toes tingle when she'd kissed him, who could make her laugh and cry at the same time, and the last person in her search who could still possibly mean something to her.

And she ended up saying *yes*.

# Twenty-Seven

## Croissants

THERE WAS SOMETHING DECADENT ABOUT WAKING up in a strange room, especially a luxurious one with a chandelier and a king-size bed. The Egyptian cotton sheets were fine and soft beneath Carla's fingertips, and she noticed one of the silk cushions on the bed still had its price tag attached. She could hear traffic and birdsong outside and glimpsed dozens of rooftops through the intricate iron railings of the balcony.

With some reluctance, she eased herself out of bed and padded across the polished wooden floors toward her en suite bathroom. It was the size of her living room at home and featured a pink rolltop bath with gold feet. Luxury toiletries sat on every surface and Carla poured a generous glug of rose-scented *bain moussant* into the water while she ran a bath.

She exhaled as she stepped into the bubbles and shaved her legs for the first time in ages. *This is the life*, she thought to herself, relishing soaking in the warm water.

Afterward, she wrapped herself in a fluffy robe and towel

dried her hair. She put on one of Babs's summer dresses and sat down at an art nouveau dressing table to apply some makeup.

*Thank goodness I listened to Aaron and didn't stay in that awful hotel last night*, she thought.

After their dinner at the bistro, Aaron had escorted Carla back to her hotel, as promised. "This isn't a good area," he'd repeated as they passed groups of people hanging around in doorways. "Please believe me."

Carla had glanced around at the pink neon lights in bars she hadn't noticed during the daytime and at the litter scattered around her feet. A man lay in a doorway clutching a bottle of brandy, shouting something to her in French. Reluctantly, she'd finally agreed to Aaron's offer to stay in the penthouse apartment.

After she'd retrieved her backpack, they'd strolled along the banks of the Seine together. Lights from all the barges and houseboats cast turquoise and silver ripples on the water, interspersed with reflections of the stars, and the Eiffel Tower was like a gold arrow pointing to the sky.

Never in a million years had Carla ever imagined she'd be back in Paris with her ex-husband. Although she knew she wasn't being unfaithful, spending time with him—in such a romantic setting—felt illicit.

Aaron had swiped a card to let them into the building and they'd taken an elevator up to the eighth floor. Carla could smell plaster and fresh paint, and the silence of their surroundings had felt like a secret.

"We're the only ones here," Aaron had said in a hushed voice that added to the intrigue. "Viewings don't start until next week." He'd opened the door to the apartment and motioned for Carla to enter first.

Her mouth had fallen open at the sight before her.

The apartment was vast, all stripped floorboards and a smoked-glass dining table set for six people using the finest tableware. The cream linen sofa and chairs had chic chrome legs, and vintage copies of *Vogue* were arranged artfully on the bookshelves. Touches of luxury were everywhere, including designer rugs and expensive scented candles, which made the place look fit for royalty.

Aaron had slid open the full-length glass doors and stepped out onto the balcony. "Join me. The view is magnificent."

Carla had stood at his side and they'd both looked out across the city.

"Sometimes, I visit these places and turn around to tell you something, to look at something, and of course you aren't there. There's nothing lonelier than visiting beautiful places and not having anyone to share them with," Aaron had confessed.

"Surely you show them to your clients? You must have dated other women after me."

He'd smiled tightly in response. "More than I choose to remember, though somehow, my thoughts always come back to you." As he'd turned to face her, the lights of Paris sparkled in his eyes. "It would be nice to spend some more time together. Here. Tonight."

Carla had closed her eyes, her lashes brushing her cheeks. It was easy to remember how warm and soft his lips were, how their bodies fitted together so well, but she shook her head.

"I can sleep on the sofa," Aaron had added. "We can just talk."

Carla could picture wrapping herself in a blanket and talking to Aaron by candlelight until the early hours of the morning. It was too easy to imagine a soft rap on her bedroom door in the middle of the night and his silhouette moving toward her.

"Aaron…" she'd started.

"Yes?" He'd tilted his head, moving a little closer to her.

Carla had breathed in the warm air and knew she had to sear the moment and stop everything in its tracks, before anything went any further, even if it meant revealing something to him that she hadn't yet told her family. "I'm *pregnant*."

"Oh. Right." Aaron's fingers had snapped into his palms, and his voice took on a more businesslike quality. "Congratulations. When are you due?"

"I don't know the exact date."

He'd nodded, and a mistiness in his eyes told Carla he was recalling the string of events that had ended their marriage. "Then I'm glad you're here and not staying in that scruffy hotel," he'd said softly.

He'd put his arm around her shoulder, and nothing about it had felt romantically charged. It was closure, an apology and a wish-you-well gesture all rolled into one. She'd let him hold her for a while, her head finding a place in the hollow of his neck.

"You'll make a brilliant mum. I've always thought that. I wish I'd had the chance to experience it for myself, if things had worked out between us," Aaron had whispered into her hair. "If things ever change in your life, don't work out with Tom, you know where to find me. I've never stopped loving you."

Carla had closed her eyes, knowing his words had come too late. She'd needed to hear them over a decade ago as they'd limped toward their divorce. *Thank you*, she'd mouthed.

They'd talked a bit more on the balcony and Aaron had left the apartment in the early hours. As they'd stood facing each other on the threshold of the building, the hug they'd shared had been tinged with regret.

After he'd left, Carla had settled down to sleep with her curtains open so she could look out at the city skyline. She'd thought about the men she'd revisited and realized each one had been important to her, in their own way.

She'd learned about culture and the power of curiosity from Ruben, and to be aware of her own boundaries from Pedro. Adam had given her confidence and a touch of glamour, and Daniel had taught her to be resourceful. Fidele was kind, patient and had immersed her in nature, showing her what a steady, stable life—and love—could look like. And Aaron? She could see now, in hindsight, that he'd offered her an interesting yet familiar comfort, a buzz of excitement *and* intensity. Their whirlwind, tumultuous love had existed in extremes, just like the erratic relationship she'd shared with her mum.

They'd *all* influenced Carla. So where did that leave Myrtle's prediction? Which one of these men could possibly help her to crush her family curse, once and for all?

Her attention had finally turned to Tom, and she now felt ready to tell him *everything*. Even though they hadn't met during her gap year, she was sure he had to be *the one*, especially now that they were going to be parents. It no longer mattered to her if any predictions or curses said otherwise.

Carla shook her head, dragging her thoughts away from last night, and hummed as she applied more makeup. She jumped when a knock sounded on her bedroom door, and her mascara slipped from her fingers.

A paper bag and cardboard cups appeared on a silver tray, followed by Aaron's smiling face. "I thought you might like breakfast in bed," he said. "I've brought warm croissants and some fresh coffee. Are you decent?"

"Yes," she said, reaching down to pick up the mascara. "Fortunately for you, I am."

He perched on the edge of her bed and they ate together, carefully pressing their fingers to their lips so they wouldn't get flakes on the sheets. It reminded Carla of their honeymoon when they were younger, less jaded, less wise. It wasn't so much a last supper, but a last breakfast together before they resumed their usual lives.

"I can show you around Paris today," Aaron suggested hopefully. "Perhaps we could…"

Carla pressed a finger to her lips. "Shhh. Let's just enjoy our food."

He nodded. "I've bought some freshly squeezed orange juice,

too, vitamin C for the baby. I'll go get it," he said, then stood and headed into the living room.

Carla covered her knees with her robe and ate another croissant, breathing in the serenity of the apartment and gathering some strength for her journey home, and for seeing Tom again.

She'd left her phone charging in the living room overnight and it took her a while for her to realize it was ringing. The noise echoed around the voluminous space. Carla placed the breakfast tray to one side and got off the bed, hurrying into the other room to answer the call.

Things seemed to fall into slow motion as she saw Aaron reaching for her phone. Carla rushed forward, holding out a hand to stop him, but her fingers swept helplessly through thin air.

She could only watch as he pressed her phone to his ear and said, "Hello, Aaron Frame speaking."

Carla's eyes widened with fear, and she hoped and prayed that her ex-husband hadn't just picked up a call from her fiancé.

Aaron listened, pulled a face, shrugged and lowered the phone. "Not sure who that was," he said. "They hung up."

Carla grabbed the phone from him and frantically examined her call list. Her entire body stiffened when she saw Tom's name. "You should have let me get that," she said with a deep groan. "Tom and I haven't spoken since I told him I was pregnant. I've been waiting for him to get in touch."

"Sorry. I go on autopilot when I hear a phone ringing."

Carla sank down onto the sofa and grabbed a cushion for comfort. She combed her fingers through her hair, her mind racing.

"Is there anything I can do?" Aaron asked.

"Maybe disappear for a while."

"Fair enough." He wandered back into the bedroom and closed the door behind him.

Carla nibbled her thumbnail as she called her fiancé back.

"I see you're with your ex-husband," Tom said coldly when he picked up. "Where are you now? Still in Amsterdam? Or is it Portugal, or perhaps Spain?"

"Ah, um, Paris," she murmured. To her, it made perfect sense how she'd come to be here, the various paths she'd taken. To Tom, it must come as a surprise, and an unnatural one at that. She heard him take a sharp breath.

"Care to explain what's going on, Carla?"

She dug her fingers into the cushion. "It's not how it might seem..."

"Really?" He barked a laugh. "I don't think you're looking at things from my perspective. I encouraged you to take a break in Spain and didn't say anything when you moved on to Portugal or Amsterdam without telling me first. Now I find out you're in Paris with your ex-husband. Isn't that where you went on honeymoon together?"

Carla swallowed away a lump in her throat. "Yes."

The silence that followed was packed full of disbelief.

"I've been stuck in the back of beyond, viewing paper recycling factories with strangers and watching the machines rumbling," Tom said. "I couldn't take in a word anyone said to me because all I could think of was you and our baby."

"I've been thinking about that, too," Carla jumped in. "But it's been days since we last spoke and you told me you've never wanted children... You made *us* sound like a mistake."

"I've never seen kids as being part of my life, and the news came out of the blue. To be honest, I was stunned, shocked. Then images began to emerge in my head, and I started to picture us pushing a stroller together, and building sandcastles on the beach, and eating fries from the paper in a bus shelter in the rain. They're all the things I loved doing as a child with my parents and I wanted to tell you all this, without being hampered by time zones and schedules and problematic phone lines."

"And your ex-girlfriend?" Carla couldn't help adding.

"Well, yes. I didn't want Sara around when we spoke. I can't understand why you're with Aaron after everything you told me about your relationship. Why Paris?"

Everything he said was true. She hadn't been very complimentary about her ex-husband and had blamed him for many things. Carla hugged the cushion with her free hand, picking at a stray thread as she tried to think of what to tell Tom. "You know how I went to see the fortune teller? Well, Myrtle told me someone was waiting for me overseas, a man I'd met two decades ago, and I've been trying to find him…"

"Is that why you met Adam? And now Aaron? You've been catching up with your exes?" Tom's voice sounded strangled.

Carla screwed her eyes shut. "Yes, though it sounds more deceitful than it actually is. A relationship curse *does* exist in my family, and I've seen actual proof."

Tom fell quiet for a long time. "Are you kidding me?" he said eventually.

"No. I think I believe in it." Carla's cheeks turned red. "This hasn't been a romantic trip, even if it sounds that way."

Tom's breathing was hoarse and he took a long time to reply to her. "Despite everything, I want to believe you…"

"I still want us to get married," Carla said, afraid what his response might be. She gripped the cushion even tighter.

Tom swallowed and cleared his throat. "I think I still want that, too," he said quietly.

The words lay delicately between them, as if they might break if either of them said anything else.

"I'm going to fly home in a few days. What about you?" Tom asked.

"I'm ready to come home now."

"Okay. Well, let's talk properly when I get back, so we can try to sort everything out. But, Carla…" he added.

The firmness of his voice caused her to gulp. "Yes?"

"We need to look forward and focus," Tom said. "Nothing

else can go wrong or come between us. I don't think we can survive any more drama or issues before we get married. Agreed?"

"Agreed," she said, and meant it.

Tom hung up without saying goodbye or that he loved her.

Carla's whole body wilted as she surveyed her overpolished surroundings. As she peered out of the window, the skies over Paris looked lemony and faded.

Aaron sidled into the room. "Well, that seemed to go well," he said, performing an exaggerated shrug.

Carla threw the cushion at his head.

"Hey. I was just saying."

"I need to leave for England. I want to go home," she said.

"Okay. Sure." He paused. "I actually have some urgent business there…"

"Aaron," she warned. "I need to be with my family, be with Tom. I want to get married without any more problems."

"You're also pregnant and we're going to the same place, so doesn't it make sense to travel together?" When she didn't answer, Aaron tried again. "Come on, Carla. Can't we agree on one little thing, just this once? Will it really hurt us so badly?"

Despite fighting against it, Carla found a small smile. She was tired and didn't want to face wandering around Charles de Gaulle Airport on her own. "Okay, then, I agree," she said. "Let's go back home."

# Twenty-Eight

## Crows

DESPITE ALL OF CARLA'S EFFORTS, AND THE PHYSICAL and mental exhaustion from the past couple of weeks, she could not fall asleep on the plane back to England. She was glad Aaron was seated at the front of the aircraft, so they didn't have to converse.

Questions whirled nonstop in her head. What was going to happen when she saw Tom? When exactly would he arrive home? Their wedding was only eight days away and Carla wanted to make sure everything was going to be perfect from now on. She would get her nails done, source blankets, perhaps even make her own sugared almonds as a gift for guests to take away from the reception. She would catch up with friends and visit the house she and Tom were going to move into. The more she could involve her fiancé in her plans, the closer they could become again. They could put all this behind them.

The flight from Paris to Manchester took only ninety minutes, and in that short space of time, the golden light of France fell away to the misty gray of the English skies.

She met up with Aaron again after they'd disembarked. He claimed Lucinda's bungalow was on the way to his office, so they took a taxi together away from the airport.

In the back seat of the cab, Carla clamped her knees around her backpack as they sped along the highway. Her thoughts zoned out as Aaron remarked on the drizzly weather, how it was cold for late May and about some of the properties he was developing in England. He eventually realized her attention was elsewhere and they sat together staring ahead, watching as the road signs counted down the miles until they reached Lucinda's place.

The taxi turned a corner and Carla leaned forward when she saw a small group of people gathered on the pavement outside the bungalow. When she recognized several of her relatives in dark clothing, her heart started to race. "What's going on?" she said, feeling something acidic rising in her throat.

"It doesn't look like a garden party," Aaron commented, straining his neck for a better look. "I'll get out with you, to see."

He paid the driver, and Carla exited the car, her bones stiffening as she drew closer to the members of her family. They nodded slightly when they saw her, their faces somber and their eyes filled with sadness.

A wave of alarm hit Carla. *"Gran?"* she said, thinking how Lucinda had tried to hide her hospital letter. She shouted it even louder. "Gran?" Her knees threatened to give way as she looked frantically around her. Aaron took her arm to help prop her up.

Carla struggled to focus on individual faces, wanting only to see Lucinda's gray hair and olive eyes. When she spotted an extravagant plume of black feathers heading in her direction, she sidestepped her way around a group of her cousins. "What's happened?" she asked Mimi, panic continuing to bubble up inside her. "Where's Gran?"

Mimi dabbed a tear from her eye with a gray lace handkerchief. She was dressed in a black satin Victorian-style dress that reached the floor. "Oh, darling. Lucinda went to the hospital and…and…" She stumbled over her words and hung her head.

Carla gripped Aaron's shoulder to steady herself. "Oh god, *no.*"

He was solid beside her. "I'm so sorry," he said under his breath.

Someone took hold of Mimi's arm and tugged her away before Carla could ask her anything else.

She screwed her eyes shut, praying this wasn't really happening. People all around her were murmuring about hexes, bad luck and omens, their low whispers sounding like chants. Carla wanted to yell at them to shut up. She should never have left her gran, shouldn't have gone chasing around overseas, should never have doubted her and Tom. Her tears came thick and fast, streaming down her face and wetting the ends of her hair.

Her relatives swarmed around the lawn until Carla saw the crowd part, letting someone through. Carla stared at the ground, overwhelmed by sorrow. But then she saw a small flash of color. A pair of shoes grew closer, and she could make out that they were embroidered moccasins. Carla's gaze crept tentatively up the person's body, taking in their generous curves and a paisley headscarf. She almost crumpled to her hands and knees when she saw her gran standing before her.

Carla let out a gasp of relief and her tears fell even harder. "*Gran.*"

"Thank goodness you're here, honey," Lucinda said, circling her arms around Carla's back and holding her tightly. "I've just got back from the hospital."

Carla held her tightly, too, burying her face into her shoulder. "Are you okay? I thought that you'd…gone."

She stopped when she saw Mimi heading back toward them. "Sorry I was whisked away, darling," she said. "I was going to tell you that Lucinda has been at the hospital with Jess and Evelyn." She swallowed and pressed a hand to her neck.

Carla looked all around her again, this time trying to locate her sister. There was still a sense of dread in the pit of her stomach. "Why? What's happened? Why is everyone wearing black?"

"It's all so absolutely dreadful," Mimi said. "Bertrand and Evelyn were at the library yesterday afternoon, choosing books together. They were discussing their next knitting project when he complained about feeling dizzy. Evelyn made sure he sat down and went to get him a glass of water. It only took a couple of minutes, but she returned to find him slumped forward at the table. Evelyn yelled for help, but it was too late. Bertrand had already passed. Evelyn is beside herself, absolutely devastated. We all are. Our family curse has claimed yet another—"

Carla raised a palm to stop Mimi's next words. "Please don't say that," she said firmly.

Mimi pressed her scarlet lips together and nodded. "Jess is with Evelyn at the funeral home right now, talking about *arrangements.*"

"Evelyn insisted on doing it straightaway," Lucinda told Carla. "Bertrand didn't have any other family she's aware of and Evelyn wants to keep busy. Our extended family has turned up to help." She paused and glanced over at Aaron, who was talking to one of Carla's cousins. "What's *he* doing here?"

"Don't worry, he's with me," Carla said. "We traveled back from Paris together and were pulling up in a taxi when we saw a crowd."

Lucinda raised a questioning eyebrow. "Paris?"

"It's okay, Gran. Everything's fine. Aaron's actually been really helpful. I'll tell you more about it later."

Carla walked with her gran into the living room, followed by Aaron, who accompanied Mimi. More of her family members had gathered, and she saw many aunts and cousins, some relatives she didn't recognize, some she did recognize but couldn't quite remember their names. Their black clothes and hunched shoulders reminded her of a murder of crows.

Her eyes narrowed when she spotted Myrtle sitting in the corner of the room. The fortune teller wore her black velour tracksuit, silver running shoes and winged eyeliner, and her violet eyes swept across the room, as if taking in every detail.

Carla's first instinct was to stride over and demand that Myrtle explain the tarot cards and the prediction she'd made that had almost destroyed her impending marriage. Instead, she spun around and forced herself to go into the kitchen, knowing it wasn't the right time or place for any kind of showdown. She helped her gran and Mimi make cups of tea and took out her anger by hacking crusts off ham sandwiches.

Although the bungalow was full of sorrowful women, Aaron said he'd stay. He helped to press hot beverages and plates of sandwiches into shaky hands, and Carla overheard him commiserating and uttering soothing words.

As the sky grew darker outside and the rooms in the bungalow became dimmer, the front door opened and Evelyn staggered in, propped up by Jess. Evelyn's cheeks were hollow and her eyes circled with mauve. When she saw everyone waiting for her, her body started to cave in on itself.

She was instantly surrounded and embraced by her family. Carla watched as this marvelous array of ladies acted like foot soldiers, coming together to do battle. Fingers caressed Evelyn's arms and hair, and the number of women saying *sorry* together sounded like a song. They led Evelyn to the sofa, where a pile of cushions and blankets awaited, urging her to drink, eat and rest. Mimi sat down beside her sister, their foreheads pressed together as they shared the grief.

It was then that Carla spotted Jess standing in the corner of the living room, seeming so small, with her bottom lip trembling. She looked exactly the same as she did when their mother had died. Overcome with a sense of empathy and responsibility,

Carla attempted to weave her way across the room to comfort her sister. However, in the few seconds it took, Jess was gone. Carla searched room after room for her sister but couldn't find her anywhere.

She felt a hand on her shoulder and turned to find Aaron wearing a caring smile. "I overheard Jess saying she needed some time alone," he said. "Evelyn's gone to lie down, too."

Carla nodded at him, grateful for his update and presence.

Later on that evening, Mimi wore a pair of black rubber gloves to wash the pots. "Oh, darling, it's all so terribly tragic," she said, her elaborate paste earrings swinging as Carla joined her at the sink. "I spoke to Evelyn earlier and it transpires that Bertrand had an existing medical condition, a small hole in his heart that he'd only just told her about. She says he was such a kind person, he didn't want to worry her with it. Evelyn had waited her whole life to find her soulmate and then he was gone in the blink of an eye."

Carla thought about Evelyn's glow when she'd spoken about carving initials into a candle. It was one of the few times she'd seen her aunt truly happy. Lars and Agatha might have found a way to outrun the family curse, but poor Evelyn and Bertrand hadn't managed to, and now the legend would become even more ingrained in the family history. The dark rain cloud hanging over her and Tom's wedding day had turned into a downpour, and her heart sank when she thought about telling him her aunt's bad news.

"Carla, darling. I need to speak to you about something very delicate," Mimi said, dropping her voice to a hush and removing her gloves. She placed them on the side of the sink and let her hand rest on top of them. "Evelyn told me about the funeral arrangements and apparently the next available date is the first of June, in the afternoon."

Carla nodded, not really taking this in. Then the words appeared to shift, collide and boom in her head. Her mouth fell open and she let a cup clatter into the sink. She didn't notice as the china cracked and broke in two. "But that's my wedding day," she said in disbelief.

Mimi pursed her lips. "Evelyn was in such a state, she agreed to the date without realizing it. Jess was waiting for her outside the room, so didn't pick up on it. I phoned the funeral folk and asked for an alternative date, but the next one available is a whole week later. I can ask Evelyn if she's willing to wait, but she's been *destroyed* by all this…" She let out a mournful sigh.

Carla wiped her hands on a towel, rubbing between each of her fingers. *All* the omens were stacking up against her wedding and it was easy to believe it really was jinxed. If she and Tom went ahead with their ceremony, it couldn't be a joyous occasion with Bertrand's funeral taking place on the same day. Even if they postponed his funeral until after her wedding, there would be a sense of foreboding hanging over her big day. She couldn't possibly ask Evelyn to move Bertrand's funeral date on her own behalf. Carla pressed a hand to her stomach and leaned on the kitchen countertop.

"Are you okay, darling?" Mimi asked. "Sorry to press you, but is the funeral date okay?"

Carla felt like the universe was spinning around her and she started to feel queasy. Her trip overseas had set a string of events in motion that would never have happened if she'd stayed in England. How could she refuse her aunt the funeral date she'd already agreed to? "Yes," she managed to whisper. "It's okay."

"Thank you, darling." Mimi said, wrapping an arm around her. "I truly am sorry."

Carla heard a familiar voice cackling in the living room and glanced through a gap in the door. She saw Myrtle holding up a cup to read someone's tea leaves. *"Myrtle,"* Carla seethed aloud, her eyes becoming slits. Everything had started with *her.*

The fortune teller somehow seemed to know she was being observed and threw a stare back in Carla's direction.

Mimi looked at the two women in turn. "Um, is everything okay between you and Myrtle, darling?" she asked hesitantly.

"No," Carla said. "Did Myrtle tell Evelyn anything about her future during her tarot reading? Did she predict something bad might happen?"

Mimi gulped. "I'm not sure. I know I like to tell everyone the story of a curse, but we can't be absolutely sure it claimed poor Bertrand. Myrtle might be the only custodian of the truth."

Carla's phone suddenly pinged with a text that rang through the air. Several heads instantly pivoted in her direction. "Sorry," she mumbled and took it from her pocket, quickly changing the settings to silent. The message was from Anastacia in Amsterdam.

I've explored the library archive extensively and haven't found anything else with regard to Lars and Agatha. I found evidence that Isabelle had a daughter, Eva, who died a decade ago.

Carla sent her a quick thank-you for the information, planning to call Anastacia back at a more convenient time. She felt a hand gently squeeze her shoulder and turned to see Aaron standing beside her. "I should go find a hotel for the night," he said.

She'd quite forgotten he was still here and tore her thoughts away from Anastacia and Myrtle. "Thanks for staying around and supporting me. You've been brilliant."

"Anytime," he said with a tired smile. "I hope Evelyn's okay and that things go well with Tom." He opened his mouth to add something else, then thought better of it. "I'll say goodbye to your gran on my way out. Take care." He gave her a hug and kissed her on the cheek.

Carla nodded numbly. She watched Aaron's back as he left the room, dealing out embraces and kisses as he went, and she couldn't help thinking that after all this time, he still felt like part of the family.

# Twenty-Nine

## Flowers

CARLA RETURNED TO HER OWN FLAT AND SHIVERED in the chilly hallway as she lugged her backpack through the front door. Compared to the heat and color of the last couple of weeks, the space felt cramped, subdued and uninspiring, as if she'd left a brighter version of herself behind overseas. There were boxes of her things all around, packed and ready to go, waiting for her and Tom to begin their new life together in a new home.

Her phone buzzed and she saw a message from Aaron saying that he'd booked a hotel in Manchester for several days. She felt grateful he was sticking around for a while.

Taking a deep breath, Carla dialed Tom's number. When it went to voicemail, she left him a message, informing him of Evelyn's loss. She omitted any mention of the funeral date, deciding it was best to tell him in person. His words echoed in her head yet again. *No further drama or complications.* How on earth could she tell him their wedding day couldn't take place unless they shared it with Bertrand's funeral? All her relatives would think her marriage was jinxed, and she could see why.

I'm so sorry to hear about your aunt. Are you okay? Tom replied in a text. I'll call you back when I can get a better signal. I'll see if I can get home any sooner x.

Carla felt too weak and sad to summon a response. It felt like the wrong time to ask how he was feeling about their baby, so she placed her phone back down.

Tears pricked her eyes as she unpacked her backpack and stuffed the clothes into her washing machine. The leopard-skin print, tassels and bright garments Barbara had given her looked too frivolous to wear in England. But at the same time, the white blouses and black trousers hanging in her wardrobe no longer appealed to her. She stood in her underwear in the kitchen for a while, goose bumps covering her whole body, unsure of what to do next. Her limbs felt heavy and she moved only when a neighbor walked past her window.

In her bedroom, Carla pulled on her dressing gown and shoved her travel journal into a drawer in her wardrobe, out of sight. She didn't think about the tarot cards remaining in her handbag.

Before she closed her wardrobe door, she caught sight of rhinestones glinting on her wedding dress. A cluster of subtle ones formed a rose to the left of the bodice and she choked back a sob as she unhooked the gown from the rail. The ivory silk stuck to her skin with static as she held it up to her chin.

She remembered spotting it in the vintage boutique's window while shopping with her gran. "Do you *really* want to wear a secondhand dress?" Lucinda had asked. "What if the person who wore it before you had bad luck?"

But Carla had stared through the glass and somehow *knew* she'd found the right one. The silk column dress was simply and elegantly cut, so different from the fluorescent white dresses she'd tried on in wedding boutiques, with their flouncy skirts and fussy lace. It looked to be the right size and she'd gone into the shop to try it on.

As soon as she'd emerged from the dressing room, her gran had gasped. "It's gorgeous, honey. You look like an angel. The color really suits your hair and complexion."

Carla had stared at herself in the mirror and run a hand over the dress. It had felt right and looked right. She'd swallowed away a lump in her throat, knowing her mum should be sitting next to Lucinda, sighing with pride.

Lucinda had sensed her emotions and taken her hand. "This is going to be the happiest day of your life," she'd promised. "I think Tom will love the dress, too."

In her bedroom, Carla clutched the dress. Perhaps buying a secondhand one had meant bad fortune after all.

She hung it back in her wardrobe and slammed the door shut.

After taking a shower to try to warm her shivering body, she put on a shapeless navy dress and went back downstairs. Leafing through all her mail, she found the leasing agency had send a card prematurely. *We Hope You'll Be Happy in Your New Home.*

She sighed and slapped it face down on a shelf, wanting to be somewhere else—anywhere else but here—as she waited for Tom to arrive back in England.

There was still going to be a flock of relatives at her gran's place, and Carla didn't have the strength to face them. In the weeks to come, when they all eventually found out about her pregnancy, she'd no doubt be under siege with familial advice, like *wrap a red thread around the baby's wrist for good luck* or *drink lots of milk so the baby will have a clear complexion.*

Carla looked around her, taking in all the boxes and the rest of her unopened mail. She felt the urgent need to be surrounded by love and color again. To be among some happier stories. So, she took a taxi to the Logical Love office.

On arrival, she looked up and noticed that one of the hearts in the Logical Love logo was missing. It was hard to believe it had only been three weeks since she and Jess had discovered the glitch in the system, contributing to the confused mess of Carla's once-steady life.

She found her office was bursting with blooms, reminding her of a park conservatory with all the roses and tulips on display. Some still had thank-you tags attached to them, sent from successful Logical Love matches.

She carefully tended to each flower individually, pulling away soggy leaves and browning petals. She poured away yellow water and gave the bouquets a fresh drink.

Jess's silver pixie ornament sat on the desk, giving Carla a wicked grin.

Her sister's report about the couples who'd matched during the twelve-month problem period was also waiting in front of Carla's computer. She made herself a coffee and sat down to read it.

Her sister had done a great job, running all the couples' data through the system again to ascertain their true match percentages. Jess had contacted and talked to the clients, framing her call as a new "aftercare policy" to see if they had any concerns or questions about their matches. She'd made notes next to each name, and Carla was impressed by her attention to detail. At the end of the report, Jess had written a short summary.

*Although the majority of clients matched during the problem year scored statistically lower in their revised percentages, and therefore shouldn't have technically been placed together by our database, 74% of the couples reported they were satisfied or very satisfied with their current relationship.*

Carla let out a sigh of relief, her body deflating. Seventy-four percent was good, not much higher or lower than usual. But a wave of confusion also threatened to consume her. What was the point of the Logical Love system she'd created, and her entire business ethos in general, if the algorithms hadn't really affected people's compatibility with each other? She'd tried to protect people by finding their ideal matches, but it looked like they didn't need her help at all.

She chewed her lip and spotted a few gift bags sitting on one of her shelves, a regifted red heart-shaped casserole dish among them. Tags said *Happy Wedding Day, Just Married* and *To the Happy Couple*, and sadness hit Carla like a wrecking ball.

She spun away from them and felt her elbow nudge against a vase on her desk. It wobbled and she could only watch as it toppled over, crashing onto the silver pixie ornament. The glass shattered and water soaked Jess's report. It dripped off the edge of her desk and pooled onto the carpet.

"Damn it!" she yelled, then grabbed a handful of tissues and threw them onto the puddle.

She swiped the pixie off her desk and it hit the wall, its head snapping off and landing on the floor, laughing at her.

Fatigue suddenly came crashing down upon her, so heavy it was like being buried under a pile of rocks. Carla sat in her chair and cradled her head in her hands, her fingers kneading the roots of her hair. Her tears were a hot torrent down her face and she absentmindedly reached for her eye pendant, clenching it in her fist. She felt the chain snap and fall loose around her neck. The one thing that reminded her of her mother the most, and now that was broken, too.

Everything around her was cursed.

She and Tom were cursed.

And it was all down to Myrtle.

Consumed by self-pity and a sizable chunk of self-loathing, Carla let out a series of anguished sobs. She reached for tissues but they all sat in a sodden heap.

Her whole body shook and she only raised her head when a series of rhythmic creaks sounded on the staircase. Not wanting Jess to see her in this state, Carla quickly sat up and wiped her face with her hands. She looked in a mirror on her desk and cringed at the red rings surrounding her eyes, which made her look like she'd removed a pair of swimming goggles.

Her door opened, there was a flash of white fabric and Carla attempted a watery smile to greet her sister.

But it wasn't Jess who stood before her.

It was Diego.

# Thirty

## Onion

DIEGO'S FEDORA LOOKED ULTRAWHITE UNDER THE office lights and his tanned skin rather sallow. "I rang the doorbell but it didn't work." He gestured toward the stairs. "The front door was ajar."

"Oh." Carla tried to recover her surprise. She smoothed a hand over her hair several times to gain some composure. The skin on her cheeks felt tight from her tears. "It's, um, lovely to see you. Is Babs here, too?" She threw the clump of sodden tissues into her wastepaper basket and hoped Diego hadn't noticed her sunken eyes.

"We called to see your grandmother first, on our way to the hotel, and she told us the sad news about your aunt's fiancé. I am so very sorry for your loss. Babs and Lucinda have a lot to talk about and I offered to check into our hotel."

"But you've ended up here?" Carla asked, confused.

Diego cleared his throat. "I needed some fresh air, after the flight. I overheard Lucinda mention you might be here. She says you can be a workaholic."

Carla nodded, still not sure why he'd come to see her. "Did Gran tell you about the date for the funeral?"

"Yes, on your wedding day. Again, I am so sorry. Have you and your fiancé decided what you are going to do?"

"I'm still waiting for Tom to arrive back from America so I can tell him face-to-face." Carla's lips wobbled and she found it difficult to speak. She looked down and tried to use her hair as a shield to cover her distressed face. When her tears threatened to escape again, she overzealously rearranged a bouquet. "I'll make us both coffee," she said, avoiding eye contact as she headed for the door.

In the kitchen, she made their drinks and tried not to spill the cups when she carried them back into her office.

She found Diego standing in front of her framed business ethos. "This is interesting and very noble," he said as he read it.

Carla sighed and plonked herself down in her chair. "After my divorce, I thought I'd engineered a solution to prevent people from getting hurt. I've since realized it's going to happen anyway."

"This is life," Diego agreed. He surveyed her many cards. "Bad things happen and you deal with them the best way you can at the time. Your clients appear to love what you've done for them."

His kindness brought a lump to Carla's throat, and the emotion she'd been holding back suddenly overflowed. A desperate and feral-sounding noise burst out of her, and tears cascaded down her cheeks.

"Oh dear." Diego fumbled for a cotton handkerchief in his pocket and pressed it into her hand. "I did not mean to upset you."

"Thanks," Carla said, between gulps of air. "It's not you, honestly. It's all *me*."

"It is okay. Please take your time. You have nothing to apologize for." He picked up her cup and handed it to her gently. "Take a sip of this."

His calmness and the warmth of her coffee helped Carla's pulse to gradually slow. "You can tell you're a doctor." She softly laughed through her tears.

Diego circled the room to give her a bit of space, intermittently glancing back over his shoulder to check on her. He stopped when his eyes settled upon a photo of Carla, Jess and Suzette. Jess was tiny and Carla had both arms wrapped around their mum's neck.

Carla dabbed her eyes with Diego's handkerchief. "I think Mum would be horrified that I've been trying to rationalize love. She was a free spirit."

"I remember…" Diego smiled and she could tell his thoughts took him elsewhere. "You do look like her," he said. "You have the same hair and eyes. It was tragic that she died so young."

Carla felt a familiar stab in her rib cage and wanted to rub it away. "It was thirty-two years ago and I still miss her every day."

Diego nodded. "She was very proud of you and Jess."

Carla hesitated and frowned. One by one, the hairs on the back of her neck stood to attention and she tried to assemble some time frames in her head. Her senses became more alert and something was telling her to question Diego. "My mother left Spain before I was born. When did she mention Jess to you? My sister is eight years younger than me…"

Diego's Adam's apple bobbed and he took a quick gulp of his coffee. His eyes shifted as he thought of his reply. "No doubt Suzette wrote to Barbara and told her of such things."

Carla shook her head, knowing this was unlikely. Her mum had been diagnosed when Jess was one year old. In the midst of such devastating news, all while caring for a baby and a young child, would Suzette really have written to an old friend in

Spain? One she hadn't seen for years and that Carla hadn't even known existed? Was *proud* a word Suzette would have used to describe her baby? A mist swirled in Carla's mind, not allowing her to see clearly yet. "How well did you actually know my mum?"

A look of longing in Diego's eyes was fleeting, but Carla spotted it. The feeling in her belly intensified. "Were you once *together*?" she asked him.

Diego froze then nodded slightly.

Carla feverishly calculated more dates in her head. She noticed the aquiline shape of Diego's nose and his curly hair. Ever since she'd met him, he'd felt somehow familiar, like there was more she should know about him. She'd seen him in photographs with Babs and Suzette, a friendship that had resulted in him and Babs falling in love in Spain. Had there been more to the trio's story than that?

Carla was overcome by a realization so strong she almost didn't dare to ask her next question. It seemed too big, too monumental, but deep down inside, she knew it was right. "Are you...my father?"

Diego screwed his eyes shut, his features stationary as he took in this moment. A lone tear escaped and wound down his face. "Yes," he whispered. "I believe that I am."

The earth suddenly stopped spinning for Carla.

Her breath faltered as she tried to begin to process this unexpected news. She wanted to skip, sing and cry at the same time. She tried not to look at Diego because she didn't think she'd be able to stop. Did he have a kink in the left-hand side of his hair that wouldn't lay flat? Did he love cherries but hate strawberries? Did he eat omelets but didn't like eggs on their own?

But she also felt a surge of abandonment. Why had Diego lived in Spain for so many years without reaching out to her? He'd known about her all this time, but she didn't know about him. He hadn't been there to put Band-Aids on her knee, or

to comfort her after her mum's death. She had so many questions and didn't know where to begin.

She stole another look at him.

*He's my* dad?

Diego upturned his palms. "I have been wondering how to
tell you, *if* I should tell you..."

Carla reached out for her desk to anchor herself. "What happened between you and Mum? Why didn't I know anything
about this, about you, until now?" Her emotions veered from
joy to anger, then back again.

"I should sit down," Diego suggested. "So I can tell you the
full story."

Carla couldn't feel her limbs as they faced each other across
her desk.

"As you know, my parents rented an apartment in Lloret to
Barbara and Suzette, many years ago," Diego began. "I remember they were fun girls, both so adventurous. They were always
diving, or dancing, and laughing together, though I noticed
Suzette had a quieter, more studious side that wasn't so apparent to others. There seemed to be a weight on her shoulders
that she carried around.

"I used to call at the apartment each week to collect their rent
money and to also make sure they weren't having any parties.
One of my parents' former tenants set fire to the kitchen in the
property, so they were wary about young people staying there.

"Suzette was sometimes alone when I called, and we talked
about the best places to visit in Barcelona. I liked how she was
hungry for knowledge and she quizzed me all about my family, telling me that hers was very superstitious. She showed me
her eye pendant—the one you've been wearing—and claimed
it protected her. Your mother informed me she and Barbara had
attracted some unwanted attention on their travels and wanted
to learn a Spanish phrase or two to respond."

"What did you teach her?" Carla asked, touching the broken chain that lay on her desk.

"It is a long time ago, but I still remember. *Eres tan feo que hiciste llorar a una cebolla.* It means 'you're so ugly you made an onion cry.'"

Carla let out a laugh she didn't expect. "I thought it might be something far worse."

He smiled. "I may have taught her those things, too. Your mother was easy to talk to and I liked her company very much. We talked and laughed over glasses of wine, and things slowly developed between us. It made me very happy." Diego's eyes then clouded. "Suzette told me not to tell Barbara about our special friendship."

His beleaguered look told Carla that Babs *still* didn't know about Diego's relationship with Suzette. "Why not?" she asked hesitantly.

"Your mother said she wasn't looking for a relationship. Whenever I asked to take her out for a meal, or for a day trip, she refused. I felt like I was her little secret, something I did not care for."

"She pushed you away?" Carla let out a knowing sigh.

Diego nodded. "Suzette told me about a curse that meant relationships in her family ended in disaster. There are many superstitions in Spain, so I tried to understand. But then she announced she was returning to England and things were over between us before they had the chance to flourish.

"Barbara wasn't ready to return home just yet, so she stayed in Spain, and my parents were happy to retain a reliable tenant. I was studying to be a doctor and still collected the rent money in person each week, just to be sure." He rolled his eyes a little.

"Barbara missed Suzette and invited me to join her at the cinema and to watch bands perform. She asked me to show her around Barcelona, telling me she would make me less serious." He shrugged. "I was happy to let her try, especially because I was missing Suzette, too. Though, of course, I could not tell Barbara this."

He paused for a moment, seeking out Carla's eyes. "You might think that having a relationship with both Suzette and Barbara sounds questionable, but it never felt that way to me. It took several months for me to fall in love with Barbara, and Suzette didn't keep in touch when she returned home."

"Did Mum tell you she was pregnant?" Carla asked.

Diego shook his head. "No, not for some time. When Barbara and I found out the news, we both presumed Suzette had met someone in England and had his child." He looked down and twisted his hands together. "I only found out you were mine when you were nine years old…"

Carla's jaw hung open. "*Nine?* Mum kept it from you until then?" She also wanted to yell at him that she was now forty-two. Why had it taken him so long to admit he was her father?

He nodded slightly. "Suzette only ever wrote to me once, after receiving her cancer diagnosis. Her time was ticking away and she wanted me to know I was your father. She sent me a photograph of you, the first I'd ever seen, and I faced a terrible dilemma about whether I should tell Barbara about you or not.

"She knew about Suzette's cancer, and my family was also pressing us to have children, so it was a tough time for her. Barbara and I were undergoing fertility treatment, so how could I tell her that I already had a child with Suzette? It might have broken her heart.

"I also felt surplus to your life and to Suzette's, though there were many times I thought about getting in touch with you…"

Carla's vision blurred. She'd never known whether she'd been conceived from a one-night stand, a loving relationship or if her mum even knew the identity of her father. Except for sharing the news with Diego, Suzette had taken the identity of Carla's father to her grave. She dug her nails into her palm.

"I can't believe it's taken me forty-two years to know about you, for us to meet."

Diego's face was also full of emotion. "We did meet once before," he admitted. "Many years ago, in the hospital."

Carla wrinkled her brow, trying to think back in time. "My fall from the horse?" she asked, recalling the only time she'd been injured in Spain.

"Yes. I was working there and remembered seeing you in the waiting room. Your hair and eyes were so much like Suzette's it was like seeing her double. It had been twelve years since she'd sent me the photograph of you and I checked your name and address on a hospital form you completed. Carla Carter. My daughter and only child. I could not believe you were here! I was the doctor who drove you back to your hotel after your accident. You were in a lot of pain and it wasn't the right time for me to tell you I was your father…"

Carla nodded numbly. "Twenty-one years ago."

"I kept telling myself to reach out to you afterward. One day passed and then another and still I did nothing." Diego hung his head. "Barbara and I kept trying for a family until we were well into our forties, but it did not happen for us. I'm not proud about keeping these things from her."

He looked so lost and ashamed that Carla reached out and took his hand. A warmth slowly and surely washed over her, as if she was bathing in a sunny lagoon. She was with her *father*. Her baby was going to have a granddad. It was awful he hadn't been part of her life for so long, but his explanations made sense. She understood why he'd hung on to a secret.

Diego's shoulders relaxed a little. "As soon as I found out you were pregnant, I was overcome with pride," he said, his voice lifting. "I have missed out on seeing my daughter grow up and I do not want the same with my grandchild."

"That won't happen," Carla promised fiercely.

"Things will not be easy," he warned. "I will need to tell Barbara..."

Carla thought about Babs's fragile side that she didn't allow many others to see. "Please be gentle with her. She's noticed you've seemed happier and thinks you might have met someone else."

"I looked that way because I'd seen *you*."

They both grinned cautiously at each other.

"I *had* to come back to England to see you," Diego continued. "I wanted to be here for you and the baby, and to see you walk down the aisle."

Carla scratched her neck. "I don't think my wedding is going to happen. Everything is stacked against it."

Diego took time to think of his response. "The thing I have learned over the years from my patients, especially ones nearing the end of their lives, is to never give up hope. Listen to what your heart tells you, because if you ignore it, it can cause you great pain."

Carla sniffed and nodded. "I'll try."

Hesitantly, Diego stood up and slightly raised his arms. Carla stood and stepped forward, too, and her surroundings fell away as she leaned into his embrace. She inhaled and Diego smelled of leather and lemon soap, just as she'd always imagined a father would. His hug gave her a shot of strength, making her feel like she could do anything, face anything. Even Tom.

Diego pressed his cheek against the top of her head. "Please don't say anything to Babs about anything just yet. I need to work out how to tell her..."

"I'll leave it to you."

Neither of them heard or saw the door opening behind them, until a gasp told them they had company. Carla raised her head and saw Jess and Babs standing there. Her sister's arms hung limply at the sides of her cotton dress, and Babs's mouth hung open with horror.

Carla and Diego quickly pulled away from each other.

"I'm sorry. Are we interrupting *something*?" Babs asked, her eyes piercing into them.

"Babs and I met at Gran's house," Jess said. "What the hell's going on?"

Babs curled her lips. "*What* exactly are you hiding from me?"

Diego moved and tried to take her arm. "I'm sorry, I need to tell you…" He floundered, struggling to find the right words.

He and Carla shared an anguished look and they knew there was no way out. They had to tell the truth.

Carla also didn't want to lie to her sister, and without space and time to think of a more delicate response, she blurted out to Jess and Babs, "Diego is my father."

# Thirty-One

## Tickets

THE ROOM SEEMED TO TURN INTO A SCENE FROM A stop-motion film. Jess jerked back and her eyes widened with shock. Babs bared her teeth and lunged at Diego. "You—" she shrieked.

"I can explain," he said, trying to stop her from grabbing him. "Please."

Carla stood in the middle, not knowing where to turn first. It was like she'd thrown a grenade and was witnessing the aftermath.

She watched Diego take hold of Babs's arm, then lead her to the corner of the room, trying to calm her down. Babs clenched her fists and yelled at him, jabbing her finger in the air.

Jess turned on her heel and ran out of the office.

Carla sped after her, managing to catch her in the corridor.

"Sorry to interrupt your little family reunion," Jess seethed as the two sisters stood outside the kitchen. "I'll leave you guys to it."

Carla upturned her palms. "Please don't be like this, Jess…"

"Like what? Like the poor baby who lost her mother? Who's been looking after your business *and* Gran *and* our bereaved aunt, while you've been having a great time sleeping your way across Europe? It's a good thing your wedding is canceled."

Carla's mouth dropped at her sister's words. In the heat of the moment, she could see why Jess might be overawed by everything. But this was too much. "You *know* that's not true."

Jess tossed her hair. "Don't patronize me. You're the one with the baby on the way, with the fiancé, and your business, and the memories of our mother. And now you've got a dad, too. Congratulations."

"It's not like that at all. You're my sister and—"

Jess shot Carla a disdainful stare and pushed past her.

Carla stumbled backward and could only watch as Jess fled down the stairs.

"*Half* sister," Jess shouted back at her.

Carla didn't know whether to chase after her or to see if Babs was okay. She sped back into her office to find Babs sobbing in Diego's arms. He raised his head to look at Carla and his eyes swam with pain.

She took another step forward, but he shook his head and mouthed, *No, not now.*

Carla crept backward out of the room. She hurried down the stairs and opened the door, trying to phone her sister when she couldn't see her anywhere. Outside, the sky was murky, heavy rain starting to pelt down. *Jess is only wearing a dress,* Carla thought as her call rung out. Her sister didn't pick up.

She didn't want to lock the door with Babs and Diego still inside, but she needed to get to her sister. Her mind whirred as she tried to think where Jess might go. Maybe back to her apartment?

She left her keys inside the door, grabbed a coat from a hook in the hallway and booked an Uber to take her to Jess's place.

Carla circled around outside her sister's ground-floor apartment and knocked on the front door several times. All the rooms were dark except for a small light switched on in the kitchen. She cupped her hands to the window and peered inside.

Tarot cards were spread out on the kitchen table and there was a pile of runes, things Jess turned to when she needed guidance. There was a ripped photo of a man Carla assumed was Mr. Forty-Nine Percent, and her heart tugged for her sister.

The rain fell harder and a drop snaked down Carla's back. She doubted Jess would return to their gran's place, to be among all the family mourners. Narrowing her eyes, Carla spotted another photo pinned to Jess's kitchen wall. Carla, Jess, Lucinda and Ted posed beside Vadim, waving their fortune tickets in the air. It was a happier time with their family, at the place Jess loved the most.

"Silverpool," Carla said out loud. "It has to be."

It was too far for her sister to walk there, so she'd probably taken a taxi.

Carla booked another Uber, smarting at the cost of using so many cabs. When the car arrived, she ran toward it to escape the rain and spent the next half hour watching droplets shimmer on the car's windows as it headed toward the seaside town.

She knew they had arrived when she smelled the familiar aroma of doughnuts. Carla zipped her coat farther up to her chin when she got out of the car. The rain fired down even more heavily, and her hair stuck to her forehead as she stared at the amusement arcade on the opposite side of the road.

Children squealing, electronic music and flashing lights lured her toward them. The arcade was closing down, and she watched as vendors collected the day's takings, switched off the machines and wheeled them back inside.

Vadim's chamber still took pride of place on the pavement. The genie appeared to be staring at her, his hand hovering above his illuminated crystal ball. A green light shone upward, making his features even more eerie than she remembered.

Carla watched as Jess emerged from inside the arcade. Her dress was wet, and a coin shone in her hand. Carla breathed a sigh of relief and started to cross the road.

Jess fed her coin into the machine's slot, and the mannequin came to life. "This is Vadim speaking. I can read your future…" he boomed, casting his hand from side to side.

Jess stooped down to pick up her fortune ticket.

Carla shouted her sister's name but a truck rumbled past, drowning out her voice. When she eventually reached Jess, she placed a hand on her shoulder.

Her sister jumped around. "What the hell are you doing here?" she gasped.

"I'm worried about you."

"Well, don't be. I left you alone to play happy families with Diego."

Carla shook her head. "I only found out he was my father minutes before you arrived."

"Well, go home to Tom, then. Leave me alone. I don't need your sympathy."

Carla blew into her cheeks in exasperation. "He's not back from America yet and it's unlikely we'll get married." She absentmindedly took a coin from her pocket and fed it into the slot. Vadim did his thing and she plucked out a ticket, clutching it in her hand.

"Because of the funeral date?" Jess said. "I suppose you think that's my fault?"

"I'm not blaming you for anything, Jess." A drop of rain trickled down Carla's forehead. "We won't be getting married because I don't think Tom will still love me after he discovers the full story behind my travels. I'm not the perfect person *you* seem to think I am. I've made a mess of everything." She shrugged and looked down at her soggy ticket.

A man appeared wearing a yellow high-visibility jacket. "Come on, ladies, we're closing now." He pulled the plug on Vadim, tipped the box and wheeled it inside. Vadim's head wobbled, as if mocking them.

"Please, let's get out of the rain." Carla looked down at her stomach. "I'm getting cold."

Jess looked at it, too, and her harsh expression slipped a little. "Yes, let's go somewhere else," she agreed.

Carla took off her coat and held it over their heads as the two sisters scurried along the street looking for shelter. Shops and cafés were closed for the day and a group of men stood outside a pub, smoking and laughing. Carla shook her head, not wanting to push her way inside. "The pier," she suggested. "There's seats and shelter there."

She and Jess headed toward the Victorian wooden structure that stretched out to sea. The waves churned hypnotically, and their red hair weaved and tangled as they walked toward a café with its shutters down. Some of the tables and chairs were under cover, and the wind dropped as they turned a corner. Carla sat down while Jess remained standing.

"So, you have a father?" Jess asked, looking at Carla then quickly away. "I'm guessing he's not mine, too?"

"Sorry, I don't think so." Carla shook her head. "Diego and Mum met while she was traveling. She kept me a secret from him for a long time."

"So, we *are* only half sisters," Jess confirmed, staring ahead at the waves.

"We're full sisters," Carla countered firmly. "We share the same mum and we grew up together. It's been me and you together for our entire lives. We even picked yellow wallpaper with peach birds when Gran wanted us to have something pink and floral. Do you remember we used to talk about them before we went to sleep?"

Jess swallowed, remembering. "I used to say there was a king and a queen bird…"

"And princes and princesses. And lots of aunts and cousins."

"Just like our own family."

"I used to plait your hair and tell you bedtime stories." Carla gave a small smile.

"You said that Cinderella couldn't possibly wear glass slippers, because they'd break."

"Maybe I was wrong. I was certainly wrong about other stories, like our family curse."

Jess sat down beside her, hugging her own arms to keep warm. "Why did mum keep you a secret from Diego?"

Carla wrapped her coat around her sister's shoulders. "She told him about our family curse and that she didn't want a relationship. Diego didn't know Mum was pregnant and she only told him about me when she found out she was dying. By then I was nine years old," she explained. "Babs can't have children, so Diego didn't disclose that he'd had a child with Mum."

Jess twisted her mouth. "So many secrets and lies."

"Secrets, yes. Though I think they're stories rather than lies." Carla reached out to touch her sister's arm and was relieved when Jess didn't pull away. They sat together for a while, listening to the sound of the sea swirling. "What happened with Mr. Forty-Nine Percent?" she asked softly. "I went to your apartment and saw you'd ripped up his photograph."

"You mean Mr. Zero Percent? He dumped me last night."

"Oh, Jess. I'm sorry."

"What chance does love have in our family?" Jess tutted and looked down. "Sorry about earlier. I didn't mean everything I said to you."

"It's okay," Carla soothed, feeling apologetic, too.

"I've been thinking about everything Myrtle told me," Jess said. "She said I'd meet someone and I did, but we split up, so I won't be getting engaged. She said she could see me holding a baby, but it's probably yours. I've been offered a new job, but I'm not going to take it, so I won't be working near water anytime soon. I've interpreted all the things she said in the wrong way. So maybe you have, too…"

"It's possible." Carla stared along the pier to where Myrtle's hut sat in the distance. "Why don't you want the new job?"

Jess shrugged a shoulder. "I love working at Logical Love, but I also want to do my own thing. I've lived in your shadow since the day I was born."

"That's not true," Carla said. "You got all the love and attention, while I was the big, brave sister having to fend for myself."

Jess glanced at her. "I never thought of it like that."

"I didn't mean for you to feel overshadowed at work," Carla said. "I need to make lots of changes."

"Like what? Did you see the report I left in your office? Most couples I investigated are happy."

"Traveling and meeting people has made me see things differently." Carla took hold of her sister's damp hand. "Please stay at Logical Love to help me fix this business. It could be a joint project, not just you working for me."

Hope glimmered in Jess's eyes. "You really mean it?"

"Yes." Carla realized she was still holding Vadim's ticket and held hers up. "Perhaps we should read our fortunes before they disintegrate."

Jess opened her ticket and read her fortune aloud. "'You are creative and thrive on ideas. Pay close attention to details and you will fly, finding the answers you seek.'" She stared at it for a long time. "Were they always this vague?"

"Probably." Carla smiled as something caught her eye, a flicker of light inside Myrtle's hut. She pointed toward it. "Perhaps we should visit Myrtle and have our fortunes told properly. It looks like she's there now. We can get out of the cold."

Jess shivered and she blew a droplet of rain off her nose. "I think I'm going to go home and get warm. I've had enough of fortunes for some time." She removed the coat from her shoulders and passed it back to Carla.

"Let me call you a taxi," Carla offered.

Jess stood and began to walk backward in the rain. "I'm a grown woman now," she said defiantly. "I can do these things for myself."

"Okay," Carla called after her, knowing she was fighting a losing battle. "Do whatever you want but stay safe."

"You, too."

Carla watched until Jess hailed a taxi and got inside it. She waved to her sister as the car pulled away and found she was still holding her own ticket. Carla peeled apart the soggy paper and read her fortune.

*Your magpie nature allows you to gather a variety of people and objects. Now you need to gather the truth. You're nobody's fool, so don't let others take advantage of you. Seek the truth and prosper.*

The words made perfect sense and for the first time Carla wasn't creeped out by Vadim. She slipped the ticket into her pocket and started to march toward Myrtle's hut.

# Thirty-Two

## Shadows

CARLA STOOD IN FRONT OF MYRTLE'S HUT, AND THE rain did little to cool her burning desire to get some answers. Had the curse caused Bertrand's death, and which man from her travels was supposed to be *the one?* Could it really be Aaron? The sea churned, and the granite-gray sky tried to swallow the hazy sliver of moon.

No one else was around and the amusements on the pier were closed, so it was unlikely the fortune teller was still open for business, but Carla sensed Myrtle was inside the small wooden building. She tried to peer through the tiny windows into the darkness.

"Myrtle. Open up. I know you're in there." She rapped on the door and waited. When there was no response, Carla banged her flattened palms against the wood, refusing to leave until the door creaked open by a few inches.

Carla inserted her foot in the gap, pushing the door open farther to barge her way in. There was a flash of silver from

Myrtle's running shoes as she moved through the waiting area and disappeared back into her room.

Carla locked the front door behind her and followed Myrtle into her lair.

The flames from a multitude of candles reflected golden in the crystal ball, and shadows writhed across the walls. Myrtle sat there looking remarkably calm with her fingers laced in front of her. "I knew you'd come," she said.

Carla slammed her hands on the table and leaned forward. "You owe me some answers."

"I don't owe you anything."

"I can't believe you had the nerve to turn up at Lucinda's house after Bertrand's death, to tell our relatives' fortunes. Do you enjoy making a living out of peddling suspicion and misinformation?" Carla snapped. "You told me Tom wasn't the right man for me, and then, because of your interference, I went overseas searching for men from my past. My relationship is now hanging together by a thread."

"Nobody made you do it," Myrtle said with a sniff.

The two women locked eyes with a ferocity that made Carla's cheek twitch.

She yanked out a chair and sat down opposite the fortune teller. "I need to know something right now. Are Tom and I supposed to be together or not?" she demanded. Rummaging in her pocket, she took out her purse and thrust two twenty-pound notes in Myrtle's direction.

"I usually charge more than that." The fortune teller made a show of holding the notes up to the light, checking to see if they were real. She placed them neatly under her crystal ball. "As a family member, I'll give you a discount."

Carla glared at her. "I was happy with Tom, until you told me he wasn't the man for me…now everything's ruined."

"You can't lay all the blame at my door. I'm a medium, not a mind reader." Myrtle folded her arms tightly. "Do you still have the recording you made of my reading?"

Spotting the defiance in her eyes, Carla huffed and took out her phone. She hadn't listened to the recording since playing it to her gran and she reluctantly pressed the play button.

Myrtle leaned forward and listened to it, nodding through-out. "Everything I told you is true," she said afterward, with a triumphant air.

"I traced and met several men from my past and *none* of them are going to be part of my future." Carla took the box of tarot from her bag and thrust them in Myrtle's direction. "I want to know if The Lovers card relates to my ex-husband."

The fortune teller opened the box, located the card and turned it over in her fingers. She looked at the picture and then into her crystal ball. "I can see you and a man who has dark curly hair."

Carla frowned, ruling out Aaron. "Does he have a beard?" she asked, wondering if she could also jettison Fidele from the running.

Myrtle shook her head and looked again. "He is dressed all in white, and I can see he's with a woman who has red hair." She pointed at Carla. "It's *you*."

Carla blinked several times, instantly picturing Diego's white fedora hat, and a thought began to glimmer in her mind, grow-ing bigger and brighter. Did the six tarot cards Myrtle gave her only relate to her exes? Could one of them, The Lovers, possi-bly indicate a different man from her past instead? Carla tapped into her intuition and what it was telling her.

And everything suddenly became crystal clear.

"You didn't see *me* in this card at all," Carla said, fixing her eyes on Myrtle. "You saw my mother. I met my father recently and didn't know we'd met during my gap year. Suzette and Diego were The Lovers. Not me and anyone else."

Myrtle bristled. "I never said Tom wasn't the right man for you. I *said* I saw someone overseas waiting for you, someone you met twenty-one years ago while traveling, of great importance to you, who you'll love forever. Isn't all that true? Does it not relate to your father?"

Carla was about to retaliate, but she considered Myrtle's words. "You said the man I met would help to end my family curse," she said, feeling suddenly weary. "I discovered my ancestor Agatha was happily married to her husband, Lars, for many years, so she managed to escape it."

Myrtle raised an eyebrow. "Haven't Evelyn and Bertrand recently succumbed to it?"

"Is that really true? Or it was just bad fortune, due to Bertrand's medical condition? What do you know about the curse?" she demanded.

Myrtle toyed with her earlobe while looking upward, taking time to consider Carla's question. "I sit here month after month, year after year, listening to our many relatives and their variations on the story of the curse when I'm actually the only one who knows what really happened," she said smugly. "Lars Aakster was indeed betrothed to Isabelle Roelof when he met and fell in love with Agatha Vries."

*Myrtle knows all their surnames*, Carla thought. She sank back in her chair to listen. "What else do you know?"

Myrtle continued her explanation. "Isabelle was so incensed when she discovered her fiancé's affections lay elsewhere that she tugged out a lock of her own hair and issued a curse upon Lars and Agatha, calling for their union to crash and burn. Not only that, she also cursed every generation of their families, so that all relationships would fail from then on—"

"It didn't work," Carla interjected. "Lars and Agatha got married and—"

"Do let me finish." Myrtle drummed her fingers. "After Isabelle cast the curse, Lars and Agatha pleaded with her to revoke it. They *begged* her. Isabelle only agreed on one condition, that Lars pay her a sizable sum of money, something he didn't have. He hadn't disclosed to either Isabelle or Agatha that he had a secret gambling habit that had left him in great debt. One of his creditors had even broken into Lars's home and threatened him with an axe if he didn't repay what he owed.

"Agatha was a practical woman from a decent family who found herself caught up in the middle of these threats, curses and lies," Myrtle continued. "She loved Lars and thought he was a good man, despite his weaknesses. Agatha had previously researched mediums and psychics because both her parents had been killed during the First World War and she'd contemplated trying to contact them on the other side. She'd found it difficult to discern who might be genuine or not and had qualms about delving into the paranormal. She'd noticed these purveyors of the mystical were far more enigmatic and charismatic than Isabelle, and she put forward an idea that could prove beneficial to herself, Lars *and* Isabelle."

"What was it?" Carla shifted in her chair, immersed in the story. "How do you know all this?"

Myrtle ignored her last question. "If the news got out that Lars and Agatha had married, his creditors could possibly target them both. So, in a bid to throw them off his trail, Agatha suggested they concoct a story claiming Lars died *before* he had the chance to exchange his vows. This would allow them to escape to England, marry in secret and start over. People would assume Agatha had moved away after her devastating loss."

"But how would Isabelle benefit?" Carla asked.

"A timely newspaper article or two proclaiming Isabelle's skill at casting curses would raise her profile dramatically and bring clients flocking to her."

"Wouldn't they fear her?"

"There was a lot of money to be made from issuing curses *and* lifting them. If Isabelle loved anything more than Lars, it was money and notoriety."

Carla frowned. "But how could Lars and Agatha just disappear? What about his death certificate? There wouldn't have been a body."

"The three of them were clever enough to cover all bases. Isabelle had several unscrupulous clients she could call on for favors, whether they were enamored by her or scared stiff. As a glass designer, Agatha had connections to the church and its records. If we *knew* exactly how they did it, others might have been able to uncover their secret and track them down."

"Point taken." Carla paused, still needing more clarity. "So, that means the curse existed for a short time until Isabelle retracted it, and it *is* just a myth that's been passed along the generations?"

Myrtle suddenly shot out a hand, taking hold of Carla's fingers and squeezing them tightly. "Do you really think that a curse is gossip that can be discarded so easily? I haven't finished the story yet," she said. "Though I should warn you it will change the way you think of our family, change the way you think of *yourself*, forever…"

By now, Carla was getting used to Myrtle's stagy ways, even though the fortune teller's fierce glare still made her shiver. "I'm listening," she said with a gulp. "What happened next for Lars and Agatha?"

"After their marriage in England, Lars and Agatha changed their surname to Smith. Lars swore off gambling and he and Agatha started afresh. They had a son, Willem, together and lived a quiet, content life. Agatha continued with her glasswork and Lars took up accountancy.

"Meanwhile, in Amsterdam, Isabelle sent an anonymous tip to a newspaper advising of Lars's death and her own part in it. She asked Lars and Agatha for a photograph to feature alongside the story and they agreed to send one. Anyone Lars was indebted to would think he was dead."

*So, that's why the article didn't appear until one month after Lars's death,* Carla thought. *He died in November but the stained-glass window he and Agatha were photographed in front of wasn't installed until December.*

Myrtle continued, "Through the article and other carefully placed rumors about Isabelle's skills, she became revered and in high demand. The majority of her income came from seances and the lifting of curses.

"Sometime later, she had a daughter, Eva, who attempted to follow in her mother's footsteps. Disappointingly, she didn't have her gift."

Carla nodded. There was still something swirling inside her, telling her there was more to learn. A curse had been cast and then retracted, so why had it then influenced generations of women in her family? "I *know* there's more," she said, staring Myrtle down.

Myrtle briefly glanced upward again and nodded. "You're right, there is. When Willem reached adulthood, he became interested in his family origins in Holland. He uncovered a newspaper article that Lars had kept, about the curse and his supposed death.

"Intrigued by this, Willem traced Isabelle, who refused all contact with him. He persevered and eventually reached out to Eva instead. They met and fell in love, trying to keep their relationship a secret from their parents, until Eva discovered she was pregnant…"

Again, Carla wondered how Myrtle could possibly know so much about the past, and in such great detail, too. Rumors and whispers had abounded throughout her family for decades, yet the fortune teller had been the custodian of many secrets, never mentioning her deep knowledge about the curse until now.

Carla's eyes were drawn to the photos of other fortune tellers on Myrtle's wall and to the tiny, colored glass windows that appeared dark without light to shine through them, immediately reminding her of Agatha and her stained glasswork. And she thought about all the elements of the story and felt something shift inside her, like when the rays of the sun emerge from behind a cloud.

It was then she *knew.*

"Lars and Agatha were your grandparents on one side of the family, and Isabelle was your grandmother on the other side," she said, finally piecing things together. "Willem and Eva were your parents."

Myrtle paused, her violet eyes growing even more vivid. She nodded enigmatically, as if about to reveal something for the first time ever. "There was a lot of hatred between my grandparents, and they refused to acknowledge the other even existed. As a young girl who loved all three of them, it was difficult for me to understand and deal with. I grew up with goodness and love on one side of my family, and superstitions and mysticism on the other. Willem's side of the family feared my gift, while Eva's side nurtured and encouraged it."

Carla thought about this for a while. "If Isabelle issued the curse and then lifted it, why has the story endured?"

"My parents befell a series of mishaps in their lives—a car accident, illness and bad luck—and my father became suspicious that Isabelle hadn't lifted the curse after all. Each time something went wrong, he became more obsessed, and it curdled his relationship with my mother. I overheard you once saying that a real curse is people's belief in it, and that was the case for Willem and Eva." Myrtle clawed a hand down her neck. "It tore my parents apart."

Carla could empathize with Myrtle's parents, recalling how wretched she'd felt after her split with Aaron. "So, you've known the real story all along, and didn't try to stop it from spreading?"

"Lars, Agatha and Isabelle had siblings. The story became like a tree growing and getting stronger. I'm only one branch of that tree."

"And you also had a steady stream of superstitious family

members paying you to tell their fortunes," Carla accused. "You make money from keeping the curse going…"

Myrtle's lips twisted into a small smile. "I need to make a living, and my hut needs renovations. *You* charge clients for services that aren't essential, and so do I. We both like to intervene and encourage."

"Don't compare us. We're nothing alike," Carla scoffed, while finding it difficult to argue with Myrtle's logic. The fortune teller had answered her questions about their family history, but not her one about Tom. Was he the right person for her or not? Could she even trust anything this woman said?

Myrtle looked at her watch and took the money from under her crystal ball. "I have to go home to cook dinner. I assume you'll want to talk to your fiancé…"

"If he still *is* my fiancé," Carla corrected.

"That's for you to decide. I am only the messenger." Myrtle stood up and picked up her keys, hesitating before her next words. "I'm in my sixties now, not a young woman any longer. One day, I'd like to pass my business on to someone else who has *the gift*. I think it still runs in our family…"

Carla barked a small laugh. "Not me," she said.

"I told Jess I could see her working near water soon. Maybe she's been looking into the wrong job." Myrtle raised an eyebrow and put on her jacket.

Carla thought about her little sister and how her sixth sense appeared from time to time. *Hmm, perhaps*, she thought to herself. But she didn't say anything to Myrtle.

Carla left the hut first and stepped onto the pier. The sky was now black, and she pulled up her collar against the rain. As she started to walk away, she thought she overheard Myrtle talking to someone else inside her hut. "Oh, be quiet, grandmother," she swore she heard the fortune teller say. "I've told Carla what she needed to know. You're always meddling in something or other…"

Carla stopped dead for a moment, listening to see if anyone replied, but heard nothing.

She walked away, shaking her head, then suddenly realized there was one more question she hadn't asked Myrtle. Did Lucinda, Suzette, Carla and Jess descend from Agatha's side of the family? Or from Isabelle's?

Carla watched silver clouds drifting across the moon, before she threw back her head and roared with laughter. She suspected she already knew the answer.

# Thirty-Three

## Tea

FOLLOWING THE TURMOIL AND THE ENLIGHTENMENT of her encounter with Myrtle, Carla wanted to focus on something more positive instead, and she arranged to see a midwife at her local doctor's office.

"Your first scan is usually performed when you're around twelve weeks pregnant," the midwife explained. "From the dates you've given me, I'll make an appointment for you in two weeks' time."

Carla was glad the scan would take place *after* Bertrand's funeral, rather than before it. It didn't seem quite right to look at a potential new life on-screen before saying goodbye to a life that had ended.

All six of the tarot cards Myrtle had given her had now been accounted for. Diego had been the important man waiting for her overseas, though connecting with her exes meant Carla had learned more about herself than she'd ever thought possible. She only hoped Babs had managed to understand and accept Diego's explanation about his relationship with Suzette.

If there was such a thing as the calm before a storm, Carla was experiencing it now. She felt strangely at ease as she walked away from the doctor's, mentally readying herself and gathering strength to face Tom when he finally arrived home.

As if he knew she was thinking about him, Carla received a text message.

Hi. Just to let you know, I've landed back in the UK. As you can imagine I'm exhausted after traveling for hours. My parents are arriving tomorrow (they decided to fly here early) so I'm going to meet with them. I'll get back in touch with you when things have settled down a bit.

Carla stared at the message for ages. Did Tom sound cold toward her, or was he just tired? Had he omitted a kiss at the end of his text on purpose? Didn't he want to ask if she and the baby were okay? Was he still upset about her Paris trip to see Aaron?

She ordered herself to be patient, to allow him space to settle back into his normal life, to address his jet lag and spend time with his parents.

Time was something she had to grant to Jess, too. Since they'd talked on the pier, her sister had retreated to the confines of her apartment, reporting to Lucinda that she was more upset about Mr. Forty-Nine Percent and Bertrand's death than she'd originally thought. She didn't want to try to be positive and face her family yet. And she was going to give thought to Carla's business proposal.

Carla wondered if Jess was also taking time to accept Diego's arrival. She contacted a local florist and arranged for a bouquet of flowers and a card to be delivered to her sister.

Mimi took over sorting out the funeral arrangements with Evelyn, whether she liked it or not, and agreed to keep things simple. Evelyn didn't want to return to her own apartment until after the funeral was over, so she remained at Lucinda's house, where she was looked after by a rotation of relatives.

Carla decided not to return to work for a while and she hung around her gran's bungalow, too, making numerous cups of tea for her family. She went to the supermarket and bought vegetables, which she made into hot soup. The number of her relatives dwindled as time went on, but some were stalwarts who insisted staying day and night to support Evelyn.

Aaron rang Carla a couple of times, to check in and ask if there was anything he could do to help. She was grateful for his support, recognizing that she'd been guilty of focusing on all the arguments within their marriage and disregarding all of his good attributes.

For a long time, Carla had believed she'd made a big mistake by marrying the wrong person, but she could now see that she and Aaron had been two young people who'd still been learning about each other. They'd been under a great deal of stress after the miscarriage, and they'd both handled it differently. Carla no longer felt regretful about their time together, only how things had ended between them.

Despite the somber circumstances, Lucinda embraced the company in her home. She bustled around her sitting room, offering cakes and moving her acorns and ornaments around to create more space. "Poor Bertrand made me realize that you only get one life and I have to make the most of it," she told Carla over a cup of tea in her kitchen. "I love you and Jess to bits, and I like working at the agency, but getting older has made me feel all plain and invisible again. I need something else to sink my teeth into, something just for me."

"You're the most amazing person I know and I'm glad you're feeling more like yourself." Carla smiled softly. "I know something that might help you to keep busy in the future..."

Lucinda perked up. "You do? What is it?"

Carla tried not to think back to her previous pregnancy. When she looked into her gran's eyes, she didn't need to speak.

"Oh, honey," Lucinda exclaimed, jigging on the spot. "Are you...?"

Carla nodded. "Jess guessed and I wanted you to know, too. Though we should keep it to ourselves for the time being."

Lucinda mimed zipping her lips. "I'm absolutely over the moon for you."

"Jess and I have been worried about you," Carla admitted. "I saw you hiding a hospital appointment under a place mat. What was it for?"

"I don't want to keep a secret from you, either," Lucinda said. "I've been feeling very low recently, out of sorts, like I had no place in the world. So, I made an appointment to speak to someone. I lost your mum, and I lost Ted, and I know it was years ago, but I still feel the weight of their loss and it sometimes drags me down. I wanted to talk to a professional, someone who'd listen to me and help, so I can claw my way out of this dark space."

Carla beamed at her proudly. "You've done the right thing, Gran. Jess and I are always here for you, too, if ever you want to talk. We all have so many things to look forward to."

"I know and I'm ever so grateful for you girls. In fact, I decided to follow in your footsteps... I went on Facebook to see if I could find Juan again."

"You did?" Carla's jaw dropped. "Is he still...around?"

"You mean, is he alive?" Lucinda laughed. "Yes, he's in his early eighties and runs the family restaurant with his two daughters and their families. He was certainly surprised to hear from me after all this time. He said he's thought of me often over the years, and we're already making plans to meet."

"Oh, Gran. I'm so pleased."

"I don't know what he'll be expecting." Lucinda ran a hand over her belly. "I'm not the slender young thing he used to know."

Carla shook her head. "No, you're even more beautiful now, like how mature olive trees bear the best fruit."

Lucinda grinned. "I'll have to remember that when I chat to him. In the meantime, I need to make ten more cups of tea for our family."

"It's a good thing I bought more tea bags," Carla said.

She and her gran stood next to each other in the kitchen as they poured hot water into cups and allowed two minutes for the tea to brew before using the back of a spoon to press the tea bags against the inside of the cups. Carla poured the milk, her gran stirred, and they worked in tandem to deliver the drinks and retrieve empty cups.

Afterward, they reconvened at the kitchen table.

"You and Tom will work things out, won't you?" Lucinda nursed her teacup with both hands. "Especially with the baby?"

Carla ran her tongue over her teeth and missed having her eye pendant to hold on to. "I just don't know. I've made a mess of everything, so I don't know how he'll respond when we meet."

"It was a big surprise to see Aaron with you, especially after everything you went through with him."

"Myrtle's tarot cards indirectly led me to meet him in Paris, so I had to go."

"I thought you didn't believe in that stuff," Lucinda said with a wink.

Carla recalled her recent talk with Myrtle. She was no longer *exactly* sure what she believed. But now she was more open-minded.

"After all your marriage troubles with Aaron, I was really worried about you," Lucinda admitted. "You were so down for months afterward."

"I know, and Aaron and I have talked and cleared the air." Carla sighed to herself. Her feelings still rippled with confusion about her ex-husband, and also about Tom. The Lovers card hadn't related to either of them. She looked at her gran and knew she could trust her, knew she'd faced similar romantic dilemmas in her life. "Do you think Tom is the right fit for me, Gran? Or do you think it could be Aaron?"

Lucinda laced her hands together and thought for some time. "I think only you can answer that, honey," she said. "You don't need my opinion or validation. It will come down to your own feeling of just *knowing*."

The thing was Carla *didn't* know. Not for certain. And that was the problem.

"Don't be too hard on yourself about Tom." Lucinda patted her knee. "The whole 'quest to find ex-lovers' was mostly mine and Myrtle's fault, and I'm happy to tell Tom that." She looked up in thought before adding, "Mimi is convinced that our family curse is to blame for poor Bertrand, and also for ruining your wedding day. She's ever so upset."

"Mimi mustn't think like that. I went to see Myrtle last night and I *know* that a curse didn't attack anyone."

"How can you be so sure?"

Carla told her gran the real story of Lars and Agatha, how a curse was cast and lifted by Isabelle, and that Myrtle was their granddaughter.

Lucinda sat with her mouth agape. "Well, I never," she said. "That story has been kicking around our family for a century, and it took you to get to the bottom of things."

"Mum started the investigation, Jess and I picked it up, and Myrtle helped to end it."

"So, she isn't all bad." Lucinda raised an eyebrow. "I told you that."

"No, maybe just *half*-bad," Carla said, pausing to sip her tea. "In time, I want everyone to know the real story behind our family curse."

Lucinda thought for a while. "Telling Mimi would help it spread like wildfire," she suggested.

"That means there's a chance people will also mishear it or invent their own version. Let's think how best to pass it on, after the funeral."

"If it's okay with you, I'll tell Evelyn now," Lucinda said. "It might bring her a little comfort to know that nothing sinister or superstitious is behind her loss."

Carla agreed that was fine. She finished her tea and washed her cup in the sink, holding it under the running water for longer than was necessary. Lucinda noticed, headed over and turned off the tap. "What else is on your mind? Besides Tom and the baby?"

"You can tell?" Carla turned around to face her. "There *is* something else," she eventually admitted. "Something big."

"I'm all ears, honey. You can tell me anything, and I won't persuade you to go overseas this time."

"That would be helpful." Carla rested her hands gently on Lucinda's shoulders. "I've found my father."

Lucinda's mouth fell open. "You have?"

"You've already met him, too. He came here with Babs to see you." Carla confirmed to her gran that Diego was her father.

Lucinda opened and shut her mouth again. "You certainly have been busy. Babs stayed to chat to me about Suzette while Diego went to check into their hotel. Neither of them said a word to me about *this*…"

"Babs didn't know at the time. It came as a big shock to her, just as it did to me. Jess found out about it before I had a chance to tell you. She was upset at first, but we've worked things out."

"Well, I never," Lucinda said, stunned by all this news. "Suzette didn't utter one word to me about your dad's identity. I suppose I can understand why she kept her pregnancy a secret from Babs."

"Diego's going to explain everything to her." Carla's jaw muscles tensed, hoping that Babs was going to be okay. "Did

Mum ever tell you who Jess's dad might be? I think she'd also love to find him one day."

Lucinda ran a hand across her chin, her thoughts taking her back in time. "I'll give it some thought, honey. There was one of Suzette's boyfriends I liked, someone she met while traveling who had red hair, though I don't know how you might trace him."

Carla thought back to the photos in Babs's sitting room and wondered if a mission overseas, to find their mum's exes, awaited Jess. "If anyone can find him, I think Jess can," she said.

# Thirty-Four

## Home

TOM MESSAGED CARLA, ASKING IF SHE'D LIKE TO MEET him at the house they were supposed to be moving into. She wondered if he'd chosen it as a neutral space to tell her their relationship was over, or if he wanted to check if the place was suitable for a family of three. She replied to say that she would.

Her bones felt like concrete when she arrived early and let herself inside. She and Tom both had a set of keys.

She took off her shoes and meandered around downstairs in her socked feet. The living room and kitchen looked much pokier than she remembered, and the furniture included in the rental package was all the same insipid shade of gray.

As hard as she tried, Carla couldn't picture herself sitting on the tiny sofa, bouncing a baby on her knee while Tom made brunch in the cramped kitchen. She couldn't *hear* the clatter of saucepans and a ring of laughter. She looked all around her and knew there wasn't enough space to store all of Tom's board games. Through the back door, she saw the narrow strip of paving stones that could never be described as a "patio garden." The house was located at the side of a busy road, not a good place for a child to play outside. Perhaps they'd been too giddy about moving in together when they'd agreed to the rental terms. They'd both thought the house was cute and cozy rather than tiny.

Carla went upstairs, where images chosen by the leasing agent lined the walls, artful black-and-white shots of palm trees and sunsets. In the main bedroom, she didn't feel any glimmer of attraction to the pristine carpet and the bed's leather headboard. She couldn't imagine her and Tom snuggling under the covers as man and wife.

She knew this was no longer the right home for her, or a baby, so where did that leave her and Tom? She'd sold her own apartment, and the new buyers would move in soon. There was hardly enough space in Tom's compact house for two people to live there, never mind with a baby.

Sitting down heavily on the bed, Carla wrung her hands together. Her insides churned as she waited for Tom to arrive. If he told her they were over, confirmed they weren't compatible, she felt like she might crumble into a pile of dust. She had so much explaining to do it made her head spin, and she still hadn't told him the date of Bertrand's funeral yet.

When she heard his keys rattle in the front door, she sat up with her back straight and stiff, listening for his footsteps on the stairs. Each creak made her heart pound faster.

Carla held her breath as the bedroom door opened, and then there he was, her fiancé, her friend and the father of her child. "Tom."

He looked both familiar and like a stranger, with a hint of a tan, stubble on his chin and purple semicircles under his eyes. His arms hung by his sides, and a small black gift bag hung from one finger. "I stopped at your gran's place first, to drop off a sympathy card for Evelyn. It's so awful about her fiancé.

I'm so very sorry," he said. "It's nice your family have gathered around to look after her. This gift had arrived for you, and I said I'd bring it here."

"It doesn't look like a wedding present," Carla observed.

"That's what I thought, too." Tom set it down next to her on the bed.

She hoped that he'd join her, really needing a hug from him. Instead, he retreated and leaned a shoulder against the door frame.

"How was your journey home?" she asked him.

"It took a long time, eighteen hours from door to door." Tom turned his head, so he wasn't looking at her. His mouth was set hard and he rubbed his nose as if summoning up the courage to tell her something. "I've been thinking it doesn't feel right to go ahead with our wedding after your aunt's loss," he said, getting straight to the point. "It feels like yet another thing telling us not to go ahead."

Although Carla knew he was right, she still felt like she had a rock lodged in her throat. It hurt when she tried to swallow, and she didn't even have the strength to nod her head. "Did gran mention the funeral date to you?"

"No," he said with suspicion in his voice. "Why?"

Carla sighed. "Evelyn arranged it to take place on our wedding day. She was in such shock she didn't realize the date at the time. Mimi tried to change it, but..." There was no point telling Tom about the option of postponing it for a week when the decision had already been made.

"Well, that's the final nail in the coffin for our wedding day," he said. Then his grim expression turned to one of horror. "Sorry, I didn't intend that terrible pun."

"It's okay."

"So, it's definitely off?" He hung his head.

"Yes. Sorry."

"Me, too."

For a while the only sound in the room was their breathing.

Eventually, Tom lifted his chin. "Perhaps Evelyn can use our wedding reception as a wake for Bertrand. We've ordered and paid for all that lovely food and it'd be a shame for it to go to waste."

Carla's belly plunged even further. In the back of her mind, she'd hoped there'd be another way forward for her and Tom, even if she didn't know what it might be. "That's a thoughtful idea. Thank you. If Evelyn's fine with that, I'll get in touch with the caterers to see if they can offer a buffet rather than a sit-down meal. I'll need to cancel the silver balloons, too." She tried to think of other things she needed to do but her brain felt like it was filled with soup.

Tom looked up at the light fixture, a simple glass dome, and Carla noticed a cobweb drifting from it, long and fragile.

"Everything's stacked against us," he said. "Our match on Logical Love was wrong, you've been running around after your exes, and now this." He slid down the wall and sat on the carpet with his legs stretched out in front of him. "My parents are arriving later today. I'm going to pick them up from the airport."

Carla looked up. "Oh, I could—" She started to offer to join him, but Tom shook his head.

"It's fine. I'll get them. I've not seen them for a few months and it will be nice to catch up…"

*Without you.* She could tell he'd left those words off the end of his sentence, and they were noticeable in their absence.

"I'm not looking forward to telling them about all this," he added.

"Have you told them about the baby?"

His eyes lifted for the briefest moment. "Not yet. I wanted to talk to you about things first. It's probably best to tell them our wedding is off first and let that sink in. I'll let everything settle for a while."

*Settle*, Carla thought, picturing how pith floated in home-made lemonade. It never vanished. It only sank. "I've made an appointment for a scan," she said. "The week after the funeral."

Tom's eyebrows knitted. "I've really hated the thought of you being alone and pregnant, overseas."

"Mum's friend Babs and her partner, Diego, were with me some of the time. It wasn't the same as being with you, though. I've missed you a lot."

She waited for him to say the same thing back, but he only nodded. *Don't push him too much*, she told herself. Carla started to chatter, her words running away to fill their silence, about Babs and Diego and how they'd flown here for the wedding. She took a deep breath before telling Tom the story of how she'd discovered Diego was her father.

"Gosh, I'm so pleased for you," he said, visibly surprised. He moved a little, as if he was going to cross the room, but then he stayed put.

"It's great, but we've missed out on being part of each other's lives for four decades. We have lots of catching up to do, and Babs looked very upset by the revelation. I hope they can work things out. There's so much love between them." Carla hoped he'd get her hint and she worked her jaw until it cracked. She had to at least try to explain her whole overseas quest to Tom. "I told you about Myrtle's prediction, about how someone important I met during my gap year was waiting for me overseas?"

He sighed and nodded.

"I thought it might be an ex, but it was Diego."

Tom glanced at her with cool eyes that she couldn't read. "Carla, I'm really too tired to dissect all this. Marriage is based on trust, and I didn't expect your ex-husband to answer your phone, in Paris."

His words stung her. "Sara answered yours..."

"It's really not the same."

"Isn't it? I saw the photos of you both in the bar. She showered in your room and you two had breakfast together. When

I called to tell you I was pregnant, she picked up your phone. How do you think that made me feel?"

Tom scratched his collarbone. "Yeah, I can see how that might have looked. But I met her by chance, didn't plan it. Unlike you, with the people you traced and revisited."

"You invited her to your room. I'd call that a plan," Carla fired back. "I was swept along by a prediction, a failure in my business, pregnancy hormones and a shocking revelation from my gran. I felt wounded you found time for work that you couldn't devote to our honeymoon. I didn't mean to do anything to hurt you."

Carla could explain how the superstitious culture of her family had been set in stone, and that fortunes and omens were a way of life she'd tried to eschew, but it felt like she was swimming against a strong tide. She could tell Tom that she'd needed to put ghosts to rest in her previous marriage, and that she really wanted to eat brunch with him again and play Connect Four, as if none of this had ever happened. But Carla was suddenly overcome by a tiredness that made her whole body feel shrink-wrapped.

"What hurts most is that you didn't tell me the truth about your trip," Tom said.

"I did try to. Several times. If I've learned one thing, it's that life and love are messy and I can't control either of them. They're not something I can navigate with questions and checkboxes. It's about listening to my instinct and taking chances, even if they don't work out." She rested a hand on her stomach.

Tom's eyes followed it, and his expression softened. "Is everything okay with the baby? How are you feeling? I was totally unprepared for the news."

"Me, too."

"At least we have that one thing in common," he said wryly.

She crumpled the bedsheet beneath her fingertips. "Will you come with me for the scan?"

He blinked at her, his eyebrows raised in the middle. "Yes, of course. I want to be there." He stood up and moved across the room toward her. "I've thought of nothing else since you told me about the baby. I wanted to run out of that factory and jump on the next plane home. It's been torture, not being able to hold you."

*You could do it now*, she thought. *Please do it.*

Tom looked to the side of her, trying to find something else to focus on. "Perhaps you should open the gift."

Carla flipped over the tag and scowled when she read the message.

*I saw this and thought of you. I wish you a sparkling future.*
*From, Myrtle.*

Carla wasn't sure if it was mischievous or kind. "It's from the fortune teller," she told Tom.

"Oh. Great." He sat down beside her.

The bag wasn't fastened and Carla plucked away a piece of black tissue paper that covered the gift. She took it out, not expecting to find a rhinestone-encrusted Magic 8 Ball. Carla remembered her friends at school gathering around one in the playground, asking questions and shaking the ball so it "magically" gave them an answer. *It Is Certain, Most Likely, My Reply Is No, Outlook Not So Good...*

"I haven't seen one of those things for ages," Tom said.

"Me neither." She passed it to him.

"Shall we give it a go?" he asked.

Carla raised an eyebrow at him. "You really want to do that?"

He nodded slightly. "I feel like we need *something*."

Carla wanted to tell him she loved him, trusted him, valued him, wanted to be with him and that she wanted to raise their child together, but instead she asked the ball a question. "Will things be okay between me and Tom?" she asked aloud.

Tom shook the ball and they both waited for an answer to appear.

In gray words the window said *Cannot Predict Now.*

Carla and Tom both found a small laugh.

"It could be worse," he said.

Carla thought so, too.

Tom stood up and she followed suit. They were only a couple of feet apart and a moment passed between them, an opportunity for them to fall into each other's arms and to whisper that everything was going be okay.

But they both stepped back, and the chance passed in the blink of an eye.

"I'll see you at the funeral," Tom said, and he turned to leave.

"Yes, see you there," Carla whispered after him.

# Thirty-Five

Story

CARLA WASN'T SURE HOW SHE WAS GOING TO MAKE it through Bertrand's funeral service. Her special day had been wiped out, a day full of love and happiness obliterated and replaced with one full of loss and sadness. Hordes of her relatives, even more than had gathered at Lucinda's house, had all showed up to support Evelyn instead of celebrating her and Tom's wedding.

Carla needed to stuff her head with random thoughts so she didn't break down and cry. As she stood in the church where her wedding should have taken place, she looked around at the tiny details, like how the roof joists joined together like fingers reaching in a point, and the number of pews (she counted sixty the first time, then sixty-two the next). She tried to remember the names of all her relatives and thought Mimi looked like a jackdaw in her black feathered coat. She focused on her feet, the chilliness of the room, how white the hymn sheets looked lying around and the contrast of Jess's copper hair against her

black dress. She heard the doors at the back of the room swing
open and turned to see Aaron walking in. He took a seat on
the far left of the back row, followed minutes later by Tom,
who ushered his parents to the far right.

Evelyn was seated in the front row and had knitted herself
a black sweater for the occasion, with the large initials *B & E*
stitched onto the chest. Bertrand hadn't officially been family yet, but he'd been on the verge of being indoctrinated. It
turned out that he did have a few distant family members, and
a couple of his male cousins stood at the front of the church,
seemingly overwhelmed by the mass of women in front of them.

The funeral officiant said a few words and invited one of
Bertrand's cousins up to address the room. He sported a similar
semicircle of black hair to Bertrand's, and used a microphone
to tell everyone how his cousin hadn't done anything particularly exciting, adventurous or noteworthy, but he'd been a
gentle, caring man who was deeply in love with Evelyn. He'd
been excited about becoming part of something bigger and had
recently discovered a passion for knitting and candle making.

When he finished, Evelyn stood up shakily.

"I can do it. I'm used to an audience," Mimi offered.

Evelyn shook her head. "He was my soulmate, not yours,"
she said firmly and took her place at the front. She looked
around the room timidly, but her voice came out surprisingly
strong.

"The thing about being part of a family is..." she started,
touching the lettering on her sweater. "Their happiness is your
happiness, and their pain is your pain. They're there to celebrate
with you when things go right, and to lift you up when they
go wrong. I know that Bertrand wouldn't want my sadness to
be contagious because, although our time together was short,
it was also very happy."

Evelyn paused to gather more strength. "This day should
have been a happy occasion for Tom and Carla, and I thank

them for the beautiful space they've given me to say goodbye to the love of my life."

Carla turned and briefly met Tom's eyes. He gave her a half smile then looked down at his hands. She caught sight of Aaron watching them both.

Evelyn continued, "I think Bertrand would like us all to eat and drink together, to talk about the weather, and wool, and our favorite books. He'd like this to be a goodbye but also a hello, to friends and family we haven't seen for a while, or who we haven't yet met." She smiled at Bertrand's cousins.

Her voice faltered and she wiped away a tear, stepping to the side as if to sit down. But then she changed her mind and looked out at the gathering, her voice growing louder. "There's something else that it's very important for you to know and I'd like to invite Carla up here to share it with you."

Carla froze at the sound of her name and she pressed her hand to her chest. *Me?* she mouthed.

Evelyn nodded. "For decades, there's been conjecture about a curse running through our family," she explained. "I'm sure there's talk of it here today, and it's time we all listened to the true story."

Carla stood up and her legs felt spongy as she made her way to the front. She felt like invisible dry ice was puffing around her, reminding her of the first time she'd met Adam, and it made her want to choke.

Evelyn bent her head to whisper in Carla's ear. "Lucinda told me all about Agatha and Lars. I don't want to become a sad footnote in our family history, like Agatha, and I don't want anyone else to be afraid. Our family is gathered here and it's a chance for them all to listen and learn."

Evelyn sat back down and Mimi proudly squeezed her hand.

When Carla faced all her relatives, the inside of her mouth dried. "I'm here to tell you that there *is* proof that a curse existed in our family..." she said into the microphone.

A crescendo of whispers and mutters immediately rose from the mourners.

Carla lifted a hand to quell them. "The story I'm about to tell you isn't rumor or gossip. It's the truth, and it's important we change our narrative, to give us and the ones we care about a better chance of accepting each other."

She proceeded to share the account Myrtle had given her, about how two young people had fallen in love one hundred years ago and battled against the odds to be together. A young woman called Agatha Vries had outsmarted a curse and lived a long and happy life with the man she loved. And wasn't that something to celebrate and inspire, rather than to fear?

Carla hoped the story would spread like ripples from a pebble thrown into a lake. She looked toward Aaron, who wore a proud expression, and she noted that Tom's face was still with understanding.

"Oh," Carla added before she sat down. "Tom and I will be donating any wedding gifts you've given us to Bertrand's favorite charity, for rehoming neglected cats. We thank you for your generosity."

The funeral officiant's eyes were wide with bemusement when he took over from Carla on the microphone. He read a few scripted words about Bertrand, and everyone joined in a prayer and sang one of his favorite songs, "Yellow Submarine."

After the service, everyone filed outside to head across the road to the community hall that Carla and Tom had booked for their reception. She noticed some of her relatives walking briskly around the surrounding streets, no doubt to shake off any spirits that might try to follow them.

She stood in front of the hall for a moment, taking deep breaths and thinking that she should now be Mrs. Carla Taylor, and how this should have been the happiest day of her life. Instead, she felt blank and detached. It was windy and she watched as the trees swayed, casting off pale pink blossoms so they danced in the air like confetti. People around her wore black instead of bright colors and pastels. Perhaps it was fate that this would happen, all along. Her travels and search for the mystery man couldn't have influenced this situation. All her thoughts were foggy and she was too tired to pick them apart right now.

"Carla." She heard a man's voice from behind her.

She turned around to see Aaron approaching. "Oh, hi," she said.

"I hope you don't mind me coming along. I know I'm not part of your family any longer, but I kind of got attached to them again at your gran's place and one of your cousins invited me. Your speech was really emotional, got me here," he said, thumping his chest.

She smiled at his generosity. "I'm glad you came."

"I should go, won't outstay my welcome by sticking around for food…"

"You're more than welcome. Honestly." Carla looked over his shoulder and saw Diego and Babs approaching. Her heart skipped a beat and she raised her hand in a tentative wave.

Aaron followed her gaze and stepped to one side.

It was odd to see Diego wearing a formal dark suit rather than the light clothes he wore in Spain. Carla longed to embrace her dad but, out of respect for Babs, she hung back.

Babs's shoulders were arched in her shiny black coat, her eyes swollen and pink. Diego stood beside her, his back stiff and face weatherworn.

Carla felt like pinching herself. This man was her *dad*. There were so many things she needed to know about him, and so many things for him to learn about her. But right now, she was concerned about Babs and the fallout of the bombshell revelation. She had no idea what to say, not knowing the outcome of Babs and Diego's conversations on the subject. The fact they were here together today looked positive. "Um, hi," she said, still hanging back. "Thanks for coming."

"We're sorry about your aunt's friend, and about your wedding," Diego said softly.

Babs wouldn't meet Carla's eyes. Her movements were twitchy and she touched her bag and her coat lapels. She unfastened a button and fastened it again. "It's a windy day for a wedding anyway." She tutted. "Might have blown your tiara off."

"I wouldn't want anyone to be hit by a flying headpiece," Carla agreed.

"It brings to mind that baddie in the James Bond films, with the deadly bowler hat. What was his name?" Babs turned to Diego, who looked baffled by this turn of conversation.

"Oddjob," Aaron chipped in.

Babs flapped a hand. "Yes. That's him." Her lips then pinched and she fixed her eyes back on Carla. "I'll just be straight with you, petal, it's better that way. I don't blame you for any of this pickle. It's Suzy I'm furious at."

Diego opened his mouth. "Barbara, I have tried to—"

She silenced him by holding up her palm. "We were best friends. We talked about everything, but she kept all *this* from me." She looked him straight in the eye. "Suzy didn't tell me about you, or Carla. One moment we were having a great time on holiday, then she left and I barely heard from her until she had cancer…" Babs exhaled and shook her head.

Carla waited until she'd run out of steam. "I can't speak on Mum's behalf, but I'm sure she did what she thought was best at the time. The decisions she made must have been difficult for her. I think she loved you very much."

Diego started to speak again but Babs cut him off.

This time, Diego didn't take no for an answer. He turned and stood face-to-face with Babs. "My relationship with Suzette was lovely but fleeting. With you, *everything* is different. We've loved each other for more than forty years and when we are together, I feel like I am home. Even though things haven't always been smooth between us, and you may have found other friends, I still think of you as my life partner. We can choose to be angry with Suzette for not telling us these things, or we can try to understand and forgive her. Is it not punishment enough that I have not had Carla in my life, in *our* lives, for four decades?"

Babs's eyes filled with tears and she gave him the slightest nod.

"I made my decisions to protect you," Diego said firmly.

The four of them stood together, the wind making their clothing flap. Carla wanted to wrap her arms around Diego and Babs and hold them tightly, but everything felt too soon, too sensitive right now.

Diego took hold of Babs's hand. "I would still love for us to be married one day." He looked deeply into her eyes. "It is what I have always wanted."

Carla's ears pricked up at what sounded like a proposal and she glanced at Aaron, who was wearing an excited grin.

Babs lowered her eyes, thinking for a few moments before she fixed Diego with an expression that was regretful but resolute. "I'm sorry, but I can't marry you."

Diego took a step backward, treading on Aaron's toe. "Oh."

"Ouch," Aaron said.

"I do love you, you silly thing." Babs reached out to squeeze Diego's bicep. "I just think love is a private affair and I don't want to give it an audience. I don't need a piece of paper to seal our relationship, but I would like to live with you again."

Diego stared at her for a while. "I think that is the most sensible thing you have ever said."

"I've got more wise nuggets where that came from. Do you think you can give me a chance?"

After a little consideration, Diego said, "I do."

"I do, too," Babs replied.

Aaron performed an exaggerated shrug. "You guys almost did it just then."

Carla wondered if this was really a fitting conversation for a funeral, but then she thought Bertrand would be pleased by this outcome. "It means you won't officially become my stepmother, but you'll be like a step-grandmother to my baby," she told Babs.

Babs's eyes misted over. "Oh, petal. I'd never thought of it like that." She winked at Diego. "Perhaps I could be persuaded to make a trip down the aisle, especially if it meant a new outfit…"

He laughed and circled his arm around her waist, pulling her close.

"What's going to happen between you and Tom?" Babs asked Carla.

She placed a protective hand on her stomach. "I may have to go it alone, like Mum did."

"Well, Suzy did a great job with you. I always said I wanted to be part of a big family. I just didn't expect it to be like this."

They heard someone approaching, and Jess appeared at their sides with a small *hi,* then she turned toward Diego. "Our lot can be pretty overwhelming but you get used to them after a while. If Carla is your daughter, it must mean we're related in some way, too, or else I'm totally up for being adopted. There aren't many men in our family, so others may try to grab for you, too. Be warned."

Babs dissolved into laughter at the fear in Diego's eyes.

Lucinda arrived in the doorway and waved her arms to get everyone's attention. "Time to come inside, people." She took hold of Carla's arm as they made their way into the room that was supposed to have hosted her wedding reception.

All of Carla's mismatched family was there together again—her ex-husband, her fiancé (if he still *was* her fiancé), Tom's parents (who should have become her in-laws that morning), her newly discovered father, her potential stepmother, her aunts, sister, her beloved gran, plus lots of others. She thought she even saw Myrtle tucked away in a corner.

She'd contacted the catering company who'd changed the table decorations and napkins from floral to a pale gray. There were flowers instead of balloons, and a buffet instead of a three-course meal. Gentle music played instead of a disco, and there was lots of chatting and reminiscing among her relatives. She heard Agatha's name passed around, followed by adjectives like *inspirational* and *brave*.

Carla looked across the room at Tom, who stood talking to his parents in the corner. She didn't know if it was the appropriate time to introduce herself or not and felt relieved when she saw the three of them heading her way.

Tom's father shook her hand warmly. "It's lovely to meet you, Carla. I'm sorry for your loss—and about today."

Tom's mother wore a kind but guarded smile. "We thought we'd just pop in to pass on our regards. We're not staying to eat."

"Of course, that's fine. Thank you for coming."

Tom's parents both looked at Tom for guidance on what they should do now.

"I'm going to take Mum and Dad for a drive," he told Carla. "If that's okay?"

"Yes, of course. Hopefully I'll see you all soon," she said.

"That would be lovely," Tom's mum said.

"Take care, love," his dad added.

Tom gave Carla a brief peck on her cheek and left her alone.

Her heart felt like it might snap in two as she watched him through the window, walking down a gray path outside instead of down their wedding aisle. Her shoulders rounded as she took a seat. The tables had been arranged in a U shape around the outside edge of the room.

Carla noticed Aaron chatting with her relatives and she watched as he flattered and flirted and charmed, just like old times. He poured glasses of wine for them and pulled out their chairs. He went to the buffet table, where he took a tomato, cut it into quarters and popped the pieces into his mouth, one after another.

Carla sat by herself, unable to eat a thing.

After a while, Aaron came over to speak to her. "Sorry, I have to go," he said, looking at his Rolex. "It's been great catching up with your family."

"They seem to enjoy your company."

"Well, they're only human," he teased. He kissed her on the cheek and placed his hand on the small of her back just a couple inches too low. "If things don't work out with you and Tom, you know where I am."

"France? England? Canada?" she asked him, subtly wriggling away from his touch.

Aaron smiled. "Mainly England, with a few trips to Paris. Not too far away at all. I know some lovely properties if ever you're looking to move. Diego's been telling me his elderly parents own a few properties in Spain they might want to sell."

Carla stared at him. "You just can't help yourself, can you?"

"Absolutely not." He laughed. "I'll say a quick goodbye to Jess before I go."

Carla watched as he dipped back into the room and bowed to kiss Jess on the back of her hand.

*Some things never change*, she thought with a shake of her head.

# Thirty-Six

Lucky

IT WAS THE DATE OF CARLA'S FIRST SCAN, AND SHE tried not to lose herself in a flashback, recalling the hush of the dark room, the image frozen on-screen and the whispers of the medical professionals as they discussed her upsetting situation. She tried not to picture her ex-husband's eyes glistening with tears and how his lips had quivered when they'd received the bad news.

Carla turned the radio up and toured the hospital grounds looking for somewhere to park her car. All the spaces were full, adding to her heightened stress levels, and she thought she might have to drive somewhere else instead. The clock on her dashboard told her she had twenty minutes until her appointment. If she had to park somewhere off-site and then walk back to the hospital, she'd be cutting it close. She circled the parking lot once more and gripped her steering wheel, when she saw someone pulling out of a space.

*A stroke of good luck*, she told herself.

She deftly parked before anyone else spotted it. As she pulled on the hand brake, Carla noticed that "Lucky, Lucky Me" by Marvyn Gaye was playing on the radio.

*Two. That's two good omens so far.*

"Good parking," Diego, who was sitting beside her in the passenger seat, observed. He'd offered to accompany Carla to the hospital, and they'd left Babs, Lucinda and Jess in the bungalow bonding over fresh concepts for Logical Love. "Are you feeling okay? Would you like me to come inside with you?"

Carla tried not to hyperventilate and drank water from a bottle. The hospital had given her instructions to drink four cups before the ultrasound, to give a clearer view of the baby. "I said I'd meet Tom in the reception area. Are you sure you don't mind waiting for me?"

"This is what fathers are for. I hope everything goes well." Diego leaned over and gave her a hug.

It was something that still felt unusual, but also made her warm inside. "Thanks...Dad," Carla said, trying the word on for size.

Diego closed his eyes and beamed.

Carla took a deep breath and got out of the car. She waved to Diego and headed toward the hospital. Her stomach was bloated with water and she was desperate for the washroom.

Tom was already waiting for her inside the building.

He still looked tired and drawn, but his stubble was now gone. His hair was longer than he usually wore it and color had returned to his cheeks.

Carla wanted to hold him, like she used to, but his shoulders and jaw were stiff. It was like there was a sheet of glass between them that neither of them knew how to break.

As they both sat down, she tried to make a joke about their lack of physical contact. "I've drunk so much water, it's a good thing you didn't squeeze me just then." She jiggled a leg, trying to keep her thoughts off her bladder. "There could have been an accident."

"Thanks for the warning. I'm wearing new shoes," Tom said with the slightest smile.

Carla looked down. "They're very nice shoes."

"Thanks. I wore them to the funeral."

"Oh. Sorry, I didn't notice."

"We both had a lot on our minds."

"Yes, yes, we did."

Carla was glad they were conversing, even if it was awkward.

They didn't speak for a while and her eyes swept over the posters on the wall—tips for breastfeeding, weaning and how to put on a diaper. Information for when everything went right, not for when it went wrong.

Tom broke their silence. "I arrived early and sat in the car listening to the radio for a while. 'Lucky Man' by The Verve came on. It's one of my favorite songs."

"I didn't know you liked that one. I like it, too."

*A third good omen?* she thought.

"I hope the title refers to me," Tom added.

Carla pricked up her ears. "I didn't think you believed in things like that."

"I'm trying to be more open-minded."

"When I pulled into the parking lot, 'Lucky, Lucky Me' by Marvyn Gaye was playing," she said.

"Good track." Tom nodded. "I haven't heard that one for ages."

A nurse appeared and called them into a dim room where a sonographer sat waiting. She introduced herself as Sonia and told them more about the scan.

Carla lay on her back with her top rolled up. The gel tickled when it squirted onto her stomach.

"Sorry, it's a bit cold." Sonia pressed the transducer against Carla's belly and moved it around.

Carla stared up at the ceiling, trying to avoid looking at the screen. Her thoughts were free-falling, her mind replaying the dreaded words that had stayed with her and Aaron for years. *There's no heartbeat.*

She looked at the corners of the room, at the unlit lighting strip, at the signs on the wall showing how to wash your hands properly. Time seemed to take forever and Sonia kept pressing and moving. Carla was aware of Tom's shallow breathing and her fingers curled into her palms, needing to touch something, feel something, because she didn't have his hand to hold.

Eventually Sonia spoke again. "The baby is growing well and has a nice strong heartbeat."

Carla heard a whoosh of breath and realized it came from her. Tension evaporated from her body and she felt like she was floating.

"Would you like to look at the screen?" Sonia asked.

Carla saw Tom was already facing the computer, his handsome features lit by a silver light. She saw wonderment in his eyes.

She slowly turned her head, too, focusing on the gray shapes on the screen. She could see a head and arms and legs, and something seedlike and dark pulsing away.

"That's the baby's heart," Sonia said, pointing at it.

Carla felt her lips start to tremble, and tears suddenly burst from her eyes, flooding down her cheeks. She felt Tom's hand seek out her own and he squeezed her fingers tightly. His thumb soothed the back of her hand.

"You're seventeen to eighteen weeks pregnant," Sonia said.

"Oh gosh. I had no idea I was that far along. Almost halfway there."

"Would you both like to know the sex of the baby?"

Carla's and Tom's eyes met and they nodded excitedly to each other. "Yes, please," they chorused.

"You're having a boy. Congratulations." Sonia printed out an image of the baby and passed it to Carla. "We'll get you booked in for your twenty-week development scan and I'll leave you here to get dressed and to use the washroom."

"I *thought* I was getting bigger," Carla said to herself. She wiped her stomach with tissue and repositioned her top. When she stood up, her urge to pee returned and she noticed Tom staring at her.

"Your face is glowing," he said. "I've been longing to tell you, but a funeral didn't seem the right place to do so."

"Thanks," Carla replied. She threw the tissue into a bin.

"Carla, I want to—" he started.

But Carla really, desperately needed the toilet. She performed a jig on the spot and couldn't wait any longer. "Sorry, Tom. I've got to use the bathroom." She pressed the photo into his hand and ran for the door.

"Carla…" he called after her.

They met ten minutes later at the front of the building. Impending parenthood felt exciting and scary and now very *real*. Knowing her pregnancy was going well so far meant Carla could start to plan and tell the rest of her relatives. No doubt word would soon get around like the beat of jungle drums, especially because she was carrying a boy.

"I'm so relieved everything's looking okay. Would you like to go for a walk?" Tom asked her.

"Oh, sorry." Carla gestured over her shoulder. "Diego's waiting for me in the car. I should get back to him."

"Oh, okay." He worked his lips. "Perhaps another time."

She patted her hands to her sides. "We'll need to meet up to discuss the baby."

"Yes. A little boy. Wow."

"It's highly unusual for my family."

"I'd have been happy either way," he said softly.

"Me, too."

They idled awhile longer.

"I'll walk you to your car," Tom offered.

"It's okay. It's not far."

"I'm in no rush," he said, passing her the photo of the scan.

"I'll get you a copy of it."

"Thanks. My parents would love to see it."

"Are they well?"

"Yes. They're loving England, but not the weather. They said to say hi."

She smiled. "That's nice. Please say hi back from me."

They walked toward the parking lot, their footsteps sounding louder than usual. When Tom's shoulder accidentally brushed against hers, a tingle of electricity ran through her. From the look on Tom's face, she thought he might have felt it, too.

"Sorry," he said.

"Sorry," she said back.

"Not sure what that was. Maybe some static."

Carla nodded. "Yes, probably."

They both stopped walking and turned to look at each other. *What if?* Carla thought. What if Tom hadn't gone to America? What if she hadn't gone to see a fortune teller with her family? What if she hadn't retraced her exes?

But she had to accept these things had happened and she couldn't change them. She and Tom had to deal with the future, however it might look. And Carla didn't want to face it by using fortunes *or* statistics. She was happy to live her life with her family around her and was ready to give fate a chance.

She no longer wanted to ask *what if?* She was going to ask *what next?*

"Sorry things haven't worked out between us," Tom said, emotion catching in his voice. "We'll work hard to be the best parents that we can be."

"Yes, and I'm sorry, too." Carla choked back a sob, hoping he didn't hear or see it.

Tom leaned forward and kissed her on the cheek and Carla

felt the strange sensation again. A tingle. A zap. Like the touch of an electric eel.

"Bye, Carla," he said, turning to walk away.

Carla lowered her head, blinking back the tears blooming in her eyes. "Bye, Tom," she whispered under her breath.

Back in the car, she crumpled into her dad's arms.

# Thirty-Seven

## Match

*Three months later*

ALTHOUGH CARLA WAS A MATCHMAKER, SHE'D NEVER been sure of the best way to wait for a date to arrive. Did you look at your phone and feign surprise when you sensed their presence, or did you vanish into the bathroom and twiddle your thumbs to kill time? Did you gaze out of the window to wait for them to arrive, so you could stand up to greet them?

She arrived at the bar twenty minutes early and looked around for a seat. Should she sit in the corner, so she could see the whole area? Or take a seat in the center of the room?

Each time she heard the door opening, her stomach jittered, causing the baby to give a little wriggle. She was now over seven months pregnant, and her bump was glorious and obvious in her blue jersey dress.

Carla decided she wasn't going to play it cool and took a seat in the window so she could look through the glass *and* also see the door. She left her phone in her pocket so she wasn't tempted to play with it.

When her date arrived, he was two minutes early and greeted her with a small smile and a wave. He'd bought her a small bouquet of pink roses and white tulips, the kind where the stems sit in a bulb of water so they don't dry out.

*Practical and thoughtful*, she noted to herself. *A good start.* "Thanks, they're beautiful," she said, bowing her head to smell them.

"Sorry if I'm a bit late," he said.

"You were on time and I was early," she replied with a smile.

"I'll get us some drinks. What would you like?"

Carla looked over his shoulder at the selection behind the bar. "Maybe a pint of nonalcoholic cider."

He looked a little surprised. "Good choice."

Carla surveyed him as he waited at the bar. He had a strong back and shoulders, and he dressed smartly. She liked that. There was a flash of a gold watch on his wrist, which neither attracted her nor put her off.

"Cheers," he said, when he sat back down, clinking his glass of red wine against her cider. "So, do you come here often?"

His cheesy comment broke the ice and they both laughed.

"Not as often as I'd like to, these days." She stroked her bump.

It didn't seem to faze him. "So," he said. "Tell me something about yourself."

Carla sipped her drink, peering at him over the top of her glass. He was good-looking but not overly confident about it. His collar was askew and she found she wanted to adjust it, so she could touch his neck—a good sign. "What would you like to know?"

"Let's start at the very beginning. What's your favorite color?"

She was surprised he hadn't asked about her job or where she lived, first. "Probably yellow," she said. "It reminds me of sunshine and daffodils, but I'm fond of orange, too."

"Cool," he said. "I also like those colors."

Since her wedding day that never was, Carla had thrown herself back into her job, as well as interior decorating, to prepare for the baby's arrival. Aaron had unexpectedly found a two-bedroom apartment in a new development for the over-sixty crowd, with beautiful communal gardens and plenty of space for her gran's ornaments. It had been love at first sight for Lucinda.

"I know I'm supposed to live here," she'd said as she'd looked out of the south-facing bay window. A ladybird had scuttled across the sill, and Lucinda, Carla and Aaron had shared a glance, knowing it meant good fortune.

Lucinda suggested that Carla buy her bungalow. "I'll give you a great deal," she'd said with a wink. "There's plenty of room to park a stroller in the hallway, and the baby could have a playroom."

Her gran had insisted on saying goodbye and thank you to each of the rooms she'd be leaving behind. "There are some lovely memories here, of me and Ted, of Suzette, and you and Jess. It will be nice to keep it in the family."

Carla was sure she'd love living here, too. "Do you mind if I keep the gold maneki-neko cat for good luck?" she'd asked her gran. "I think the baby will love it."

"I think your granddad would love that, too. He bought it for me, many moons ago."

Lucinda settled into her new place well and had already started to bake for the other residents. She and Juan chatted online together most evenings and were going to meet up in Spain soon. Mimi had already put on a one-woman theatre show in the communal sitting area and Evelyn had taken to knitting on a bench in the gardens, gradually opening up to anyone who asked about the sheep sweaters she was making to raise money for Bertrand's favorite cat charity.

Carla sipped her nonalcoholic cider and looked up at her date again. "So, what's *your* favorite color?" she asked him in return.

He thought for a moment. "Probably bright green, as in the grass at Wimbledon or those parrots you sometimes see flying around parks in London. It reminds me of when tiny shoots push through the soil in spring."

*A lovely answer. I really like this man*, Carla thought.

"I thought you might choose gray," she said. "Men seem to like that color."

"I'm never sure if gray is a color or a neutral," he mused. "My apartment used to be all gray, which was practical, but dull. I once had this girlfriend—well, fiancée—who used to leave these little things around my place, a pink plastic photo frame or a yellow ceramic vase. They didn't really match but I liked them. I kind of miss them..."

Carla leaned forward. "You miss her, or the things she left behind?"

"Both." He let out a sigh. "I *really* miss them both."

Carla smiled ruefully to herself. "And I miss leaving them around for *you* to find."

She watched as Tom's eyes lit up.

"You do?" He touched the back of her hand and she felt a zap inside her again. Carla could now distinguish it from the kick of her baby, who seemed to have taken up playing football in her stomach.

After their first baby scan, she and Tom had gone their separate ways for a while. He was busy following up on all the contacts he'd made in America and had received several offers for collaboration on his board games. *Unique, innovative* and *practical* were the words used to describe them. His parents stayed in the UK for a few more weeks and were planning to come back soon, so they'd be here when the baby arrived.

Carla had packed up the rest of her belongings and moved into her gran's bungalow. She printed out the photographs she'd taken during her time in Spain, Portugal, Sardinia, Holland and France and pasted them into the back of her travel journal, alongside any tickets, beer coasters, maps and timetables she'd collected on her journey, until there wasn't a blank page left.

She, her gran and Jess were going to spend more time on the family tree, to bring it up to date with all their relatives (though they were unsure how they could fit them all on one page).

Jess had continued to work on developing a new angle for Logical Love, offering matches in a more organic way, and the sisters planned to manage the updated business together. Arnie had left Data Daze and was helping them to set up a new system. Carla could sense an obvious attraction between him and her sister that didn't need her input or percentage statistics. Perhaps Jess might be engaged within the year, after all.

Carla had felt like there was a golf ball lodged in her throat when she'd discovered Tom had renewed his membership at the agency, and she had defiantly updated her own data, too. She ran their match through the system again and it had increased to seventy-two percent, a high score if not the shiny eighty-four percent she thought they'd once had together.

*Does everything really have to be perfect?* she'd asked herself.

Carla and Tom had met in the interim for a couple more scans. Those times together in a darkened room had been magical as they'd watched the grainy shape of their baby grow, from the size of a pomegranate to a honeydew melon. She'd lain there longing for him to hold her hand again, or to offer to take her for a coffee afterward, but Tom had been friendly and distant, and Carla had accepted she'd hurt him deeply.

One day, after he had continued to occupy all of her thoughts, she'd decided to just phone him and invite him on a date. Because they had to start somewhere. When he'd picked up, she'd skipped the pleasantries. "We should get to know each other again from the beginning, like we've only just met."

"*Carla...*" he'd protested at first.

"We missed a whole part of our relationship because of Logical Love and we're having a child together," she said. "I never even knew what your favorite color or season was. Did you ever know mine?"

"Blue?" he said. "Autumn?"

"No."

"Pink and summer?"

"See what I mean?"

It had taken him a while to consider her invitation, but he'd eventually said yes.

And now they were sitting here together in a bar, starting right at the beginning again.

Tom bought them another round of drinks. "How is Jess doing?" he asked.

"She's working on the new arm of the business, but we're struggling to think of a name. All the ones we've thought of sound shady." Carla laughed. "Flexible Love, Open Love, Adaptable Love, Organic Love…"

"I can see what you mean." Tom laughed, too.

"For now, we've given it the working title of Lucky in Love. I'm not sure it's quite right."

"I like it." Tom nodded, giving the name some more thought. "What about Destination Love?"

Carla rolled it around on her tongue, noting it related to his board game that was hopefully going to be a breakout hit. Destination Next was already in the preproduction stages in America. "I like it," she said. "I was also thinking of Illogical Love, because that's what love often is. Sometimes you shouldn't fit with someone, but you do. There might be barriers and reasons keeping you apart—"

"But you want to break them down," Tom added, his eyes flitting to hers.

Carla blushed. "We've been working on a first draft of a new business ethos." She took a piece of paper from her bag and handed it to him.

*No one's perfect and neither are we. We're the sister agency to Logical Love, helping you to find your partner in a way that suits*

Phaedra Patrick

*you best. Whether you're a pragmatist, a realist, a romantic or a dreamer, we'll help you to find your match. There's no absolute guarantee you'll find your soulmate, but you'll have fun, meet interesting people and broaden your horizons along the way. And if you do feel ready to take a leap of faith, to follow your head or your heart, you're in safe hands.*

"I love it," Tom said. "It's more realistic, more human."

"Jess has also got a part-time Sunday job, in Silverpool. Myrtle wants to pay for renovations to her hut and she needed some extra help." If she was being cynical, Carla might say the fortune teller's prediction that her sister would be working near water soon was more like a strategy. "She's also talking about traveling, to see if she can trace her father."

"I'm glad she's pursuing things that she loves," Tom said.

Carla decided against giving Tom an update about Aaron, wanting this date to be just for them, and *not* about any of her exes. Her former husband had recently joined Logical Love and had already found an eighty-five percent match with someone, the highest score ever for the agency and one they'd never have achieved together.

Tom leaned down and picked up a gift bag she hadn't noticed him carrying alongside the bouquet. "I got you something," he said, passing it to her.

"Thanks." Carla dipped her head to open it. She peeled off the tissue paper and cradled the box on her lap. The board game was called New Beginnings and she eased off the lid.

"It's a prototype," Tom quickly added. "It needs a lot of work, but the basics are all there."

Carla opened the board and watched in wonderment as paper figures and objects sprung to life—a stroller, tree, house, family and even a dog. The more she looked, the more she saw finer details, such as a journal open on a kitchen table and even a tiny pack of tarot cards. There was a Magic 8 Ball sitting on the bed.

"Each player has to travel around the board, discovering family stories along the way and undertaking tasks to win the game."

"And what's the prize at the end?" She raised her eyes to his.

"I've not decided that yet. What do you think it should be? What should the person be looking for?"

Carla stared at the board, deep in thought. "Perhaps family is enough."

Tom sat back in his chair, a smile spreading across his face. "I think so, too," he said.

And in that one moment, if Carla had still harbored any doubts that she'd chosen the right person to be with, they flew away. She didn't need any statistics and percentages to confirm that Tom was *the one*. Her own gut instinct was more than enough.

Her family curse was gone, replaced by hope. And it might take time to extinguish all the worries, expectations and superstitions completely, but a drink together in a bar with the man she loved was a good place to start. Carla still thought that you *could* actually choose your family, and she'd chosen Tom.

She placed her hand on her stomach, feeling another kick from the little boy growing inside her, as if he was agreeing with all their sentiments. She reached out for Tom's hand and held it against her belly, so he could feel the movement, too.

"It looks like he can't wait to play New Beginnings with us, too." Carla smiled.

★ ★ ★ ★ ★

# Acknowledgments

A great deal of time and effort goes into publishing a book, and writing is only part of the process. I'd like to give a big thank-you to my brilliant agent, Clare Wallace, for her advice, hard work, perceptiveness and encouragement. Also, the wonderful support of the entire team at my literary agency, including Darley Anderson himself, Mary Darby, Tanera Simons, Georgia Fuller, Salma Zarugh, Francesca Edwards, Chloe Davis, Rosanna Bellingham and Sheila David.

Thanks to my fantastic editors, Erika Imranyi and Nicole Luongo, at Park Row Books/HarperCollins in the USA, who make writing my books such a positive and collaborative experience. I appreciate the work and dedication of the entire Park Row team, including Leah Morse and Emer Flounders in PR and publicity, and the editing, design, marketing, sales and distribution teams.

A special mention and thanks go to my friend Janine Mc-Kown for her medical advice relating to the book, and also to my college friend Philip Spencer Absalom-Gough and his wife, Tess Absalom-Gough, for their diving expertise. Any mistakes I've made in the telling of this story are entirely my own.

Writing a book can be a solitary process, so I'm grateful to my wider support group of other writers. It's great to know so many kind and talented people are just the click of a button, or a coffee, away. Thank you especially to B.A. Paris, Roz Watkins and Jacqueline Ward.

I'd like to thank booksellers, librarians, bloggers, reviewers and readers everywhere for their amazing support and for helping to spread the word about my writing. My books couldn't happen without you.

Finally, a huge shout-out to all my family and friends. Writing for a living is a dream come true but can also be a very strange, emotional and sometimes stressful career, and I appreciate all your love and support.

# Questions for Discussion

1. Women in Carla's family are very superstitions. Are there any particular superstitions you believe in or always carry out?

2. Who was your favorite character in the book and why?

3. Do you ever look back at your past jobs, relationships or decisions and wonder what might have been? Or do you put the past to rest?

4. Do you believe in mediums and fortune-telling? Why or why not? Have you ever had your tarot cards read? Did any predictions come true? Did meeting Anastacia and Myrtle in the book change any of your perceptions?

5. Which scene in the book resonated with you the most? Did any of them surprise you?

6. Carla lost her mother when she was ten years old. How might this have affected her decisions and behavior in life? Did Suzette's passing affect Jess any differently?

7. Dating agencies can be a useful way to meet potential romantic partners. Do you think romance should be left to chance, or does love sometimes benefit from a helping hand?

8. How would you describe the book to someone else? Is it a romance? Uplifting fiction? A coming-of-age story? Or something else?

9. Carla has many female relations who support each other in times of need. How do you and your family (or friends) help each other?

10. What was your favorite location that Carla visited in the book and why?

11. Do you think Babs and Diego will ever get married? What might their wedding day look like?

12. Did you find the ending of the book satisfying, or would you have preferred a different outcome for Carla?

13. Did *The Year of What If* remind you of any other books? How did the title relate to the story?